IGNITE
BENEATH THE BLAZE

LUNA MASON

Cover Design: Coffin Print Designs

Formatting: Peachy Keen Author Services

Author's Note

IGNITE is a stand-alone, DARK Irish Mafia Romance with a primal game of survival. It does contain content and situations that may be triggering to some readers.

This book is explicit, intended for readers 18+.

Please enter Decadence at your own risk. For a full list of triggers please see my website:

www.lunamasonauthor.com

Please keep in mind, the first third of this book, may give the illusion that it is *lighter* dark mafia romance, as it gives rom-com vibes, the main characters are hilarious. Do not let that fool you. **You will be slapped in the face with a brick of dark romance by the halfway point. Enjoy x**

To keep up with Luna's chaos, find her on social media:

Instagram: @authorlunamason
Her FB Reader Group- Luna Masons Mafia Queens
Sign-up to her newsletter here: https://bit.ly/3SShFuW

And if you want signed books, store exclusives and all the *naughty art,* you can purchase directly from my store: www.lunamasonbookstore.com

Yes, you can have a primal kink and still have zero interest in actually running.
So, grab something to drink, relax, and let Conan Quinn chase you down, claim you, and savagely ruin you.
*And the best part? You get to **keep cozy and stay spicy**.*
Just keep flicking those pages…

Look at you.
Being such a good fuckin' girl for Conan.
Now, **RUN.**
He's got his mask on, and he's ready for you…

PLAYLIST

Listen here on Spotify: OFFICIAL IGNITE PLAYLIST

- Levitate, Sleep Token
- Sports car, Tate Mcrae
- Monster, Skillet
- Dirty Little Animals, BONES UK, Arcane, League of Legends
- Hated, Beartooth
- Take on the World, You Me At Six
- Drown, Bring Me The Horizon
- Last November, mgk
- Another Life, Motionless In White
- DiE4u, Bring Me the Horizon
- Voices, Motionless In White
- Nowhere To Go, Bad Omens
- There's Fear In Letting Go, I Prevail
- High Enough- RAC Remix, K.Flay, RAC
- I Feel Like I'm Drowning, Two Feet
- DIRTBAG, WesGhost
- Pale Moonlight, Dayseeker

- Southbound, Artemas
- I Like You Best, Ella Red
- Kool-Aid, Bring Me The Horizon
- Fighter, The Score
- Sleepwalking, Bring Me The Horizon
- Coming Undone, Korn
- She Keeps Me Up, Nickleback
- SMUT, Jutes
- Choke Me, Breaker
- Sleepyhead, Jutes
- The First Time, Damiano David
- Supermassive Black Hole, Muse
- Limerence, Jutes
- Make up sex, MGK, Blackbear
- Happiest Year, Jaymes Young
- The Night We Met, Nath Brooks
- Man or a Monster, Sam Tinnesz, Zayde Wølf
- Hold On, Chord Overstreet
- Memories, Dean Lewis
- Dancing On My Own, Calum Scott
- Provider, Sleep Token
- Dangerous, Sleep Token
- Soaked, Shy Smith.

PROLOGUE

HALLIE

2 years ago…

Song – Levitate, Sleep Token

The doors to the operating room explode open, and my heart shoots into my throat. One look into Finn's pale gray eyes and I already know, the second he opens his mouth, the ground will split beneath me.

He doesn't need to speak. Just a subtle shake of his head. Eyes full of pity.

The sob rips out of me before I can stop it, sharp and strangled. I suck in a breath that goes nowhere, my chest collapsing inward as if something vital's been torn from it.

I drop to my knees. The floor meets me hard, but I barely feel it. Everything around me blurs as my sobs unravel into wild, choking cries.

"I'm so sorry, Hallie. They tried everything," Finn whispers beside me.

I swat the words away like they burn. I don't want them. Don't need them. This can't be real.

I bury my face in my hands and let the grief break me open, wide and raw. I see flashes behind my eyelids—me as a little girl in the garage, fingers greasy from helping him with his cars, his laughter echoing around us.

All the times he held my hand when life felt too big, too brutal.

His voice right before surgery, still strong, still him.

"If this is the last time, I need you to know I'm so proud of you, Hallie. I love you so much. Always remember that. You've got a bright future ahead of you, I promise."

My dad's final words to me.

I'd kissed his cheek and told him to stop being so dramatic and that I'd be right here when he woke up.

I was wrong.

He's not waking up. He's not coming back. And now, I'm alone.

I don't know how long I stay there, folded in on myself like I'm broken. Finn sits beside me in the silence, his hand rubbing soft circles into my back like he can hold me together.

"Come on, let me get you home, Hallie."

He has to lift me off the floor—my body too heavy, too hollow—and carry me to his Mercedes. The drive home is wrapped in silence. I can't even see through the tears.

When he pulls up outside the house, I force in a shaky breath.

"Is there someone I can call to be with you? I know how tough this is. But I promise, it will get easier."

I shake my head. No. I don't want anyone. Not now. Not even my best friend, Lily. I just want the dark. I want my bed and my dog, Bertie. I want to curl up and cry until nothing's left.

"I'll be fine," I croak.

The second I open the car door, Finn's there beside me.

"Let's have a coffee. I can't leave you like this."

I nod, just once, it's all I can manage. He follows me inside.

My father is everywhere. His face on the walls. His scent in the air. His soul in every corner.

"Go sit down, I'll make the drinks."

I move through the space like a ghost. My legs barely hold me. I collapse into the sofa and tuck my knees in, facing away from the photos. Just one glance at his smile and I feel like vomiting.

Finn returns and hands me the coffee, taking a seat on the opposite sofa. Quiet. Always so quiet. That's how he is at work, disciplined and controlled. I've watched him over the last year. Learned from him.

He's the youngest heart surgeon the hospital has ever had, and he's still the best in his field. Respected by everyone, even when he's covered from neck to toe in tattoos.

"You don't have to stay, Dr. Quinn."

He raises a brow.

"I lost both my parents not so long ago. Although it feels like yesterday. My brother, Conan, struggled with my mother's death. And the pain I just felt from you, is the same I did with him. So, I want to make sure you're okay."

For the first time since I walked out of that hospital, something cuts through the numbness.

"You have brothers?"

He nods.

"Two. Declan and Conan." His Irish accent is warm and low, a strange kind of comfort.

"Oh, cool. I always wished I had siblings."

My voice cracks around the confession. My mom and dad split when I was six. I moved here with Dad and never looked back. I didn't need a relationship with my mom when I had him.

"Trust me, it can be awfully testing at times. Especially the youngest one. Conan is always trying to wind me into a frenzy with his antics."

He sighs, but there's affection buried in it.

I like the sound of this Conan.

"But, I love them to fucking death."

A laugh slips out of me. Finn smiles.

"What made you want to become a nurse?" he asks, settling in with his coffee, his foot resting on one knee.

"My dad got sick for the first time when I was a teenager. We were in and out of hospitals, and I don't know, it just felt like my calling. I wasn't sure I was cut out for… what you do. So I decided to be a nurse. I wanted to help people, I guess."

I'm too chaotic to be a surgeon.

He leans forward, places his cup on the table.

"It's going to be okay. You know that, right? You are more than capable of doing anything you want."

The words are sharp but kind, stern enough to make me sit up straighter.

"That's what Dad used to tell me." The tears rush back. I can barely keep them in.

"Look, take some time off work, as long as you need; I'll cover it. You need to heal and find the thing that makes you happy in life. You need a break."

I twist the rings on my fingers, eyes locked on my lap.

"You've nearly worked yourself to death recently,

Hallie. You might think I don't notice, but I do. You deserve a break."

I can't look at him. He's still my boss. Dr. Quinn. Cold, calculated, and terrifying. But tonight, there's something softer about him, something human.

"Is that what your brother did?"

He shakes his head slowly.

"No. He went into self-destruction, Hallie. That's why I want you to do the opposite."

The lump in my throat threatens to suffocate me.

"Okay. I think I know what I'll do."

He straightens his tie, lips curving.

"Let yourself grieve and then find happiness."

I sink back into the cushions, a little lighter somehow.

"You're not a bad boss, you know that, right?" I say, then pause. "And friend."

He chuckles, running his hand through his dark brown hair, slicking it back.

"Don't you dare tell anyone that. I reserve being nice for family and friends. No one else."

I believe him.

"Your secrets are safe with me. Now, would you like a wine? I need something stronger than coffee."

Yes. God, yes. I want to forget today ever happened. And Finn is right. I don't want to be alone.

After a glass of Dad's finest red, Finn leaves. I find myself in his bed, cocooned in the blankets that still smell like my dad. I press my face into the pillow and cry like I'm drowning.

Tears fall until I've got nothing left. Until my skull aches and my throat's raw.

This house, it was never just a house. It was our home. Because he was here.

He was my constant. My compass. My everything.

And now it's just walls and silence.

All I have left are the memories. And a garage with the cars we spent our lives fixing together.

Maybe that's where I'll find him again.

Maybe that's where I'll start to heal.

Maybe that's where I'll find a little piece of happy.

For both of us.

CHAPTER 1
CONAN

2 years later…

Jesus fucking fuck.

I've been punched in the head more times than I can count. Stabbed, too. But this shard of glass in my thigh? It burns like hell, worse than any knife I've taken.

If it weren't embedded in my flesh, I'd already be chasing down the assholes who ran me off the road, grinding their skulls into the tarmac until the rage bleeding through my veins finally quieted.

Smoke pours from the Bugatti's hood, the thick stench of it clawing at my throat. My jaw ticks.

"You hanging in there, Con?" Finn's voice cuts through the speaker—tight, clipped.

"Hanging in? Are you worried about me, big bro?" I throw back, forcing a smirk I don't feel. Pain rips up my leg.

Having a surgeon for a brother is useful, especially when your hobbies include bare-knuckle fights and underground cages. I've always craved the chaos—still do. It's the only place I feel alive.

Mom hated it. But she's not here anymore to tell me I'm throwing my life away.

"This is nothing," I mutter, watching blood soak into the fabric of my ruined suit.

Finn exhales. "Hallie will patch you up. How much blood have you lost?"

The question lands like a warning. I glance down again, watching crimson pool beneath me.

"I don't know, Finn. I didn't bring a measuring jug."

My thigh is soaked. The glass is buried deep. I'm not sure which hurts more—the wreckage of my Bugatti or the pain in my damn leg.

"Can you wiggle your toes?"

I grit my teeth and flex. Relief. They move. Although, I am starting to panic now that he's mentioned the blood loss thing.

"Yeah. Toes are good. How long until she gets here?"

"Ten minutes. She's already on her way. Please, don't be an asshole to her. She's…" He trails off.

My brows lift. That hesitation? That's not nothing.

"She's what?"

"She's been through a lot, and she's finally coming out the other side. I'm mentoring her. Just… don't be your usual ass self. Be nice."

I scoff. "When am I not a delight to be around?"

Laughter crackles in the background, Reggie or Rowan, one of the Murphy twins.

"Really, Conan? Your main daily purpose is to rile someone up."

Fair point.

"Fine. I'll play nice with Nurse Hallie."

"Good. This is what you get for leaving mid-wedding. Karma is a bitch."

"Mid-wedding? No. I did all that. I left mid-party. There's a difference, Finn. I was only going to bring Veronica back to the cabin. She's at a club."

"You have an entire selection of women inside Inferno. All of them obsessed with you, for some fucking reason. And yet, you're running into town for—?"

"For someone I want to chase through the woods tonight," I interrupt, scratching at my jaw. "Not someone to tie up in a damn sex club."

Inferno's fun. The pain, the power, the punishments—it scratches an itch. But what I like? It's deeper than that. Rawer. Primal.

And not every woman can handle it.

When I find one who can, I don't let her slip through my fingers. Even if it means ditching my brother's wedding reception to go collect her myself.

"Don't come at me for my kinks. I don't even know what twisted shit you're into, Doctor."

Finn clears his throat. "Because it's none of your damn business. You stay in the woods, I'll stay in Inferno. How's the pain now?"

"Fine." It's not. But thinking about her—barefoot, breathless, running from me—makes the pain ebb.

"Good."

"My car is fucked though."

I'd just had it wrapped matte black, too.

"Wait till I get my hands on the dickheads that did this. I'll beat their heads through the hood of their own car."

"I'll get Rowan to tow it to your garage later. You're fine, that's all that matters."

"Aww. Big brother's getting soft in his old age."

They worry. I know they do. I make reckless choices—it's what I do. Make a mess, then fix it. Or let them fix it for me.

That's family. That's how we were raised.

"Shut the fuck up, or I'll tell Hallie to make sure it hurts."

I chuckle, already planning my next move.

"Yeah, yeah. I'll win her over with my charm, brother. Don't you worry."

CHAPTER 2
HALLIE

"Come give Momma a cuddle," I coo to Bertie, my golden retriever.

His head flicks up, and he bounds toward me on the couch, launching his fluffy and extremely heavy body onto my lap.

"Awww. Can't resist, can you?" I scratch behind his ears as he snuggles against me.

Since Dad died, Bertie and I have been inseparable. He was his best friend, and now he's mine.

"Hal. What time are you going to work today?" Ben calls out from upstairs.

"Shift starts in two hours," I shout back, rolling my eyes. He already asked me this over breakfast.

It's starting to piss me off—his constant need to know my whereabouts.

I'm either at home, at work, or at the gym. I'm hardly interesting enough to keep tabs on.

His heavy footsteps echo down the stairs, and as I turn to look at him, he's finishing styling his black hair in the mirror.

I mean, he's hot. He's got a decent job running the finances for his cousins.

And the accent. That's what won me over on our first date. Deep and British. Delicious.

He spins to face me with a smile and walks over.

"Get that lump of a dog off you and give me a hug."

I frown and keep stroking Bertie.

"Don't be mean to my dog," I snap back.

"I'm only playing. I just want to snuggle with my girl before I go to work."

I chew on the inside of my mouth.

"It's 6 p.m.? Seems late to start working?" I tap Bertie, and he jumps off me so I can stand.

Ben's arms hook around my waist and pull me close.

"Business dinner. Anyway, you know it's our six-month anniversary this weekend," he whispers, brushing his lips along my cheek.

Interesting deflection there. That's just one of many lately.

Late-night dinners, work calls, emergency appointments. I'm surprised he even stayed over last night.

"I do," I lie. I had no clue. Who celebrates six-month anniversaries?

"Dinner? Hotel? How does that sound?"

I should have butterflies. Shouldn't I?

"Perfect."

He presses his lips against mine, and I close my eyes. Nothing. I feel nothing.

Maybe it's because the anniversary of my dad's death is coming up. I've felt pretty numb since I lost him.

Maybe once I get my spark back, I'll feel something more for Ben.

He pulls away and assesses me with his blue eyes.

"You don't seem excited. In fact, nothing I do excites you. When's the last time I even had my dick in you?"

I cringe at his words and take a step back.

The only time I feel any kind of life is when I'm behind the wheel of my Shelby.

My best friend, Lily, keeps telling me it's not me, it's just that I don't like Ben. Maybe she's right.

"I just have a lot going on." I tap my head, and his face softens.

"Always so busy in that head."

I nod. He has no idea what it's like to live inside my brain. It's like a squirrel on crack lives in there—every hour of every day—frantically running from one idea to another. It's exhausting.

"So, dinner Saturday?" I ask, switching the conversation.

"My treat."

There's an awkward silence as he adjusts his tie.

"Good. Well, I need to get going. Shall I come here after and wait for you to get back? What time would it be?"

I nod and offer him a smile.

Something isn't right between us, and the longer it goes on, the more I'm starting to think it isn't me. But I suppose he's making an effort to see me more.

"Sounds nice. Probably about two am. Take my spare key by the front door and let yourself in."

I wrap my arms around his neck and go up on my tiptoes, pressing my lips to his, trying to quiet my racing thoughts.

Nope.

Nada.

Maybe I'm broken. I haven't had an orgasm in what feels like years now.

"Mmm, I'll be ready and waiting in bed for you, beautiful."

Great. Just what I need after a shift.

"Have fun at your meeting," I whisper.

As he gives me one more kiss before leaving, a wave of relief washes over me when the front door closes behind him.

Peace.

Slumping back onto the couch, Bertie joins me again and I rest my head on top of his.

"What do you think? Does he need to go?" I whisper to him and laugh. He's not going to respond to me.

"How about a ride in the car and walkies?"

Now that gets his attention. Bertie yelps in excitement and pounces to the floor, his tail wagging wildly.

And just like that, my stress melts away at the sight of his happy little face.

I'd be happy just with my dog. My baby and my cars are all I need. Oh—and my job.

Just as I slip the harness on Bertie, my phone vibrates on the couch with the one name I'd never ignore.

Dr. Finn Quinn.

I pout, picking it up. It's his brother Declan's wedding today. What could he want?

"Dr. Quinn. Everything okay?" I ask as Bertie whines by the front door.

"Yes. Well. No, actually. Conan's been in a car accident and looks like he'll need some glass removed from his thigh. I'd go, but I've had too much to drink to be anywhere near a needle."

I cringe. Ouch.

"Okay. You want me to do it? I can get to the hospital in fifteen."

There's a moment's pause.

"Could you pick him up? I'd rather not have this put on his medical records. For his fighting career and such."

I swallow.

"Uh. Sure. I don't have anything here, though."

Finn blows out a breath. I keep telling him I need my own office, but the hospital finance director won't give me one yet.

"Use my office and lock the door behind you."

My heart races, but this means he trusts me. Which, as his mentee, means everything.

He's the top of his field, and I want to be the top of mine.

"Text me the location and his number. I'll leave now."

"Appreciate this, Hallie. Thank you. If Conan is a pain in the ass, just don't numb it."

I chuckle. I've heard lots about Declan and Conan. They seem like a close family.

"Will do."

I cut the call and crouch down to Bertie.

"I promise, I'll take you out as soon as I'm home. Or maybe Lily can come over and walk you." I kiss his head and take off his harness. He grunts and takes himself back into the living room.

"Love you," I call out.

Before I leave, I lock up and turn on the new camera so I can keep an eye on him.

As I climb into the driver's seat, I take a deep breath. My beast.

My dad left me some inheritance, so I took Finn's advice.

I fixed up his car and bought myself my dream car. Well,

then I supercharged it, renewed all the pipes, and made it as loud and as fast as I could.

It's given me the freedom to smile again.

The engine roars to life, and a warm fuzz erupts in my veins.

Conan has always intrigued me. I guess now's finally the time I get to meet him.

CHAPTER 3
CONAN

"I think she's here," I tell Finn as headlights roll up behind me, cutting through the darkness. The car stops, but the low, deep purr of the engine—the kind you feel in your ribs—sends a ripple of suspicion down my spine.

That's not a regular car. That's muscle. A Shelby, if I had to guess.

My grip tightens around my pistol.

"Finn. What fucking car does she have?"

He chuckles. The smug bastard.

"Oh yeah. She loves her cars, Con. Have fun. Behave and listen to her."

The line goes dead.

I grunt as I push open the door, trying to haul my ass out while half-slumped in pain. My hand hooks onto the frame, and I drag myself up.

"Fuck me," I hiss as a sharp jolt tears through my thigh.

A hand, small and warm, lands on my waist.

And I swear to God, I see stars.

Shit. Heart attack? Or something worse?

"Put your weight on your good leg and let me help you," she says, soft but firm. Sweet as fucking sugar, and just as addictive.

I glance left. Her caramel hair catches the light, those soft curls gleaming like a goddamn halo.

She's tiny. Barely comes up to my chest. But confident as hell.

"I don't want to fall and crush you, darlin'."

"You won't. We need to get you to a hospital, so chop, chop, Conan."

She slips her arm around me, guiding me toward her car like she's done this a thousand times. But then I see it.

Low grumble. Matte deep blue wrap.

Holy fuck.

"Is that the Shelby GT500 Heritage Edition?" I ask, even though I already know.

"Yes. Supercharged. Remapped. The works. Now, get in. Please."

She flicks her gaze to my leg, blood soaking through my pants.

The interior hits me with the smell of cherries as I collapse into the passenger seat, dragging my leg in with a grunt. As she slides behind the wheel, I finally get a full look.

And damn. I'm fucked.

If I wasn't bleeding out, my dick would be harder than steel.

She catches me staring.

"What? Never seen a woman drive a powerful car before?" she snaps, eyes on the road.

Feisty.

"No, darlin'. I'm not judging. I'm admiring."

The way she handles this beast—smooth, precise, fearless—it's almost erotic. She weaves through traffic like it's child's play.

"Yeah?" She flicks her eyes to me, and my heart pounds.

She's beautiful. Sharp jaw. Soft lips. Hazel eyes that could pin a man in place. Her curls frame her face like she walked off a dream and into a car ad. Then her eyes snap back to the road, and I exhale.

I run my hand over the carbon fiber dash.

"She's a beautiful beast."

"She's my baby." She taps the wheel, smiling like she means it. Wind lifts her hair, and I forget all about the pain in my leg.

"Where'd you learn to drive like this?"

"My dad. We used to fix up his cars and he'd take me on track days. I've tried to keep up the legacy, I guess."

There's a hitch in her voice. A flicker of pain she tries to bury.

"Sorry," I say. "Bet he would be proud of you, though."

She shrugs and tucks a curl behind her ear.

"I guess."

I swallow hard. I know that kind of pain. I live with it. Mom's face in that hospital bed used to haunt me. Still does.

"What's the fastest you've gone in this beast?" I ask, needing the shift.

She side-eyes me at the red light.

"You aren't a cop, are you?"

A chuckle bursts out of me. If only she knew.

I press a finger to my lips. "Your darkest secrets are safe with me."

She nods. The light turns green—and fuck me, I'm pinned to the seat as she punches it. The engine roars, the speedometer climbs, and my adrenaline spikes right alongside it.

Jesus.

"She drives like she owns the goddamn world. I would love to race you in this," I murmur.

"I'd leave you in the dust on the track," she smirks.

I laugh, my stomach flipping. This woman is trouble.

"Oh, Hallie. You don't know who you're playing with here."

"What, you think you'd win in a smashed Bugatti?" she counters.

Ouch. Low blow.

"I'll fix it up in no time, trouble."

She chews her lip as we approach the hospital, eyes scanning for a spot. She drives through quite a few.

"I fucking hate reversing in a space, okay?"

I raise both hands. "No judgment. We won't race backwards."

"Good. Also, we'd have to make it fair. Two Shelbys or two Bugattis. To see who's actually got skills."

Fair enough. I could find a Shelby. If I weren't about to get stitched up in a place I'd rather set on fire than walk into.

Hospitals fuck me up. The last memory I have of Mom was in a place just like this. Cold walls. Machines beeping. Her pale face. Gone.

It's the memory that flashes when I lose it in the cage. When James didn't get back up. When my hands wouldn't stop.

Hallie cuts the engine, dragging me back.

"That was way more fun than an ambulance trip," I tell her, leaving off the beautiful owner bit.

"Glad it distracted you," she says, brushing her fingers across the wheel. That glimmer in her eye? Fuck me—it does things.

"You think you can walk, or should I grab you a wheelchair?"

I scoff. "I'll limp. It's just glass."

She pouts and then nods. "To be honest, if it hit something important, you'd have bled to death by now."

Jesus Christ.

My throat tightens. Definitely not funny.

But she laughs, like it's just nurse banter. Finn does that too, makes jokes about me dying while holding a scalpel.

Her hand rests on my good thigh. My pulse goes off the rails.

"I was joking. A few stitches and you'll be good to fight."

I raise a brow. "How much do you know about me exactly?"

And why the fuck don't I know anything about her? Finn's kept her hidden like a goddamn secret.

"I know you're funny, hot-headed, and an incredibly skilled cage fighter."

I nod. "Carry on. I'm enjoying the praise."

She giggles. I grin.

"Maybe sit through the needle first, then I'll tell you the rest."

Once I'm in Finn's office, she returns, and I nearly fall off the damn chair.

White coat. Black-rimmed glasses. Hair in a messy bun.

Holy hell.

I shift uncomfortably, sucking in a breath. All I can imagine is her on her knees, looking up at me. Professional Hallie is a problem.

She rolls over a cart of supplies, snapping on gloves.

"I'm going to get the glass out first. Then I'll need you

to take your pants off so I can clean it up and see how many stitches you'll need. Sound good?"

I nod. "There are much better ways to get me to strip."

She smiles, not missing a beat.

"I don't want germs from your clothes getting into the wound."

"Right. Not a time for jokes."

She's focused. Steady. Sexy as hell.

"Deep breath. This might hurt."

I brace. The metal tool glints under the light, and then searing, white-hot pain rockets through my thigh.

I grit my teeth, fighting the urge to wreck the room.

I can't scare her.

The glass clinks into the metal bowl. She presses a cloth to the wound.

"Pants off, please."

I fumble with my belt, stripping them off and tossing them aside. Boxers. Thank God.

She clears her throat as I lean back, one arm behind my head.

"Relax for me."

Her voice is soothing, yet commanding, it gets me to exhale. She dabs the wound with antiseptic and…

"Good boy."

My eyes snap open. Blood rushes south.

"Am I?" I smirk. "Do I get a reward, Nurse Hallie?"

Her cheeks flush.

"I might have some stickers somewhere."

"Hmmm." I nod, pretending to consider it.

"You'll need a few stitches. Are you good with needles?"

Her eyes lock on my heavily tatted forearm and hand. I think she's just realized her answer.

"No. Petrified. Can you hold my hand?"

She giggles, tapping my thigh.

"I need two hands to stitch you up. I can call in another nurse?"

I run my tongue along my teeth. "No. I'll be brave for you."

She heads to the shelf for supplies. I let myself breathe.

This woman. Cool as hell. Sharp. Sassy. A fuckin' dream in a white coat.

"Wow," I mutter under my breath.

She glances back. "Wow?"

Shit.

I didn't know I had a nurse fantasy. But I'm sure I do now. I'm now not sure if I missed the part where she drugged me with something.

Why the hell did 'wow' just leave my mouth?

"Umm…" I chew my lip, scrambling. Finn told me to behave. She works for him. She's holding a needle.

She rolls back to me, stitches prepped.

I grin, cocky again.

"Do I get another good boy when you're done?"

I hope she says yes.

CHAPTER 4

HALLIE

Dear God. This man. I'm burning up.

I'm not sure how I'm supposed to concentrate when he's this distracting. Not just to look at. But he's funny as hell.

And for some reason, my damn brain-to-mouth filter is not working around him.

This is my job. I need to be professional.

"Maybe. If you stay still."

I offer him a sweet smile and get to work, stitching the wound back up.

I'm acutely aware of his stare in the side of my head.

Doing my best to keep this as neat as possible, by the time I get to the final stitch, I blow out a breath.

"You'll need to rest for a few days. Keep it clean. The stitches will dissolve over time. Although, if it starts bleeding or looks infected, just pop back in. Or speak to Finn."

As he goes to sit up, I hold up my finger and his eyes widen.

"I'm not quite done. I need to cover it."

"Okay, Nurse Hallie." He salutes me and lays back down.

I hold back my laughter. I can't believe I called him a good boy.

Nor can I believe he was kinda into it. A man of many secrets, I bet, just like Finn.

I finish up bandaging the wound and bite back a grin as I look into his deep green eyes.

"Good boy. You're all done."

I swear he growls under his breath, and I squeeze my thighs.

He's so handsome. The tattoos give him a scary edge, but there's a spark in his eyes that gives him away.

A lightness. I bet many people fear him, but to me, he relaxes me yet has me burning up inside.

Grabbing his pants from the floor, I hold them out to him, and he smiles as he takes them out of my hand.

"I'll. Um." I clear my throat. "I'll go wait outside for you." I point to the door and awkwardly step back.

"Why? I'm not taking my boxers off. You've just stared at it for the last hour. I don't need privacy at this point."

I stay rooted in the spot as he slides on his pants and yanks them up. As he does, his shirt rises, and I get a view of his six-pack. And of course, more ink.

I wonder if every inch of him is tattooed.

He even has a star under his eye.

Maybe each one is a story.

"You okay there, Hallie?" he asks.

My eyes meet his, and my mouth falls open.

"Yeah, just looking at your ink. You've got a ton of it."

"I must like pain." He flashed me a cheeky grin.

"Physical is sometimes better than mental."

A somber look flashes across his face before he replaces it with a smile.

"Yeah, you can say that again. Fighting, tattoos, fucking, and cars. They're my distraction."

I chew on my lip as he takes a hobbled step towards me.

Jesus, he towers over me, looking down at me.

"Sounds like a good combination there," I tell him.

"Do you need a lift home?" I ask, checking the time on my watch.

"To my garage, please. You got time?"

He scratches at his stubble; it's slightly darker than his dirty brown hair.

"Shift doesn't start for another hour. I came in early for you."

He stares into my soul for what feels like a lifetime. I'm holding my breath until he clears his throat.

"Thank you for patching me up. Can I have your phone?"

I blink at him. "Why?"

He flashes me a menacing grin.

"I wanna add my number to your contacts. If you ever need anything, I owe you one favor. You call me, I'll do whatever you need."

I frown and shake my head.

"Being a nurse is literally my job, Conan. I don't need favors, honestly."

His face becomes stern. This darkness flashes across it that makes me shiver as he opens his palm and holds it out.

"This is how I work, trouble. You scratch my back, I'll one day scratch yours. You never know when you'll need me to fix something for ya."

Letting out a huff, I slide my phone out of my white coat pocket, unlock it, and place it in his ginormous palm.

Did he just call me trouble?

He's busy tapping away and I just stare around the room, waiting.

"Done. I'm saved as Beast."

I laugh, looking at his name on my screen and hit edit, then type 'ie' at the end.

"Beastie sounds better."

Grabbing my keys from the side, Conan opens the door for me. As I walk through, his hand grazes along my lower back as he guides me back to my car.

"Need any pain meds?" I ask as we get to the reception area.

"Nah. A whiskey will sort it later."

CHAPTER 5

CONAN

Hallie chats away about how her friend has an art gallery show tomorrow night and how her calves are killing her from Pilates.

I haven't spoken back much, because quite honestly, just hearing her yap her heart away is soothing.

She's happy to chat, I'm good with keeping my mouth shut and listening. Although her phone keeps buzzing in the cup holder, but no calls are coming through her system. It's irritating.

"You wanna see what it is?" I ask.

She keeps glancing at it and frowning.

"You wanna just look for me? I can't be bothered to pull over. My passcode is 141069."

"Sure."

I type it in and swipe at the notifications. Some sort of security camera app telling her someone is in her house.

"Hallie. Do you live with anyone?"

"Me and my dog. Why?"

"Well, it's saying someone is in your house, darlin'."

I scratch at my head.

"It says I can live view, want me to?"

I don't wanna overstep a boundary, but I want her to be safe. Fuck it. I left my gun in my Bugatti.

"Er. Yeah. It'll probably be Bertie up to mischief."

I click the button and the sound blares through the system. My mouth drops open as I'm watching some random pale-assed guy rail a blonde model-type woman.

"Conan. What the fuck is that?"

Her face pales.

"Pull over."

I don't wanna die in a Shelby. At least not one I'm not driving.

She does as I say, her hands shaking as I hand her the phone. Her hand covers her mouth as she gasps.

"That motherfucker," she spits out.

"Who is he?" I ask.

I know the answer, but I want to hear it.

"This bastard was my boyfriend. One I was probably going to dump, but, not the point. The fuck does he think he's doing in my goddamn house?!"

Her fingers squeeze her phone so tight they go white. So I peel it out of her grip.

"What a fucking idiot he is," I mutter.

"He's the idiot? More like I am. How embarrassing."

A tear rolls down her cheek, and I instinctively lean over to wipe it away.

"Don't cry over this ass. Looks like he's a shit lay anyway. You can do better."

I pause as she sucks in a shaky breath and looks into my eyes.

And there it is, I'm lost in them.

"I have an idea that might make you feel better."

Finn may kill me for this, but this is my kinda therapy… the revenge type. And I feel Hallie may enjoy it too.

And I'm a guy. I know hurting our ego is the best way to get us.

"I'm listening."

I stroke a stray strand of her silky hair behind her ear.

"We go and teach him a lesson. He's not expecting you back, I assume?"

She shakes her head.

"Okay. Picture this. We crash through the door, your legs wrapped around my waist. We're tearing each other's clothes off. I'm kissing the life out of you. You're moaning in my mouth. We ignore him and his pathetic performance. We give them something to watch that's far more exciting. Show him you do it better."

Her pretty eyes go wide and I chuckle, pushing down my erection that's growing.

That sounds fucking perfect.

A naughty smirk tugs at her lips. I can't tear my eyes from them.

"I… like that plan."

"You in? We fuck with him. He doesn't deserve your tears, trouble. Let's make him pay. Then we kick his sorry ass out of your house."

Her beaming grin only excites me.

"You sure you wanna get involved in this? What if it turns nasty? He boxes, he might punch you or something."

A deep chuckle vibrates through my chest.

"Hallie. You think this skinny-ass man has a chance? I'd knock him out even if that glass was still sticking out of my leg. Don't you worry about me."

She blows out a breath.

"And the whole kissing part, that doesn't bother you?"

I rub my hand over my face.

How is she this unsure of herself? She's a knockout. Funny and pretty damn cool.

"Hallie. I'm damn sure any man that walks this earth would never, ever turn down a kiss from you."

Her cheeks heat and she goes to turn away, but instead I grip her chin to keep her eyes on me.

"It's your turn to be a good girl and show this scumbag that he ain't shit. Fuck him for disrespecting you."

Her bottom lip trembles, and I run my thumb along it.

This is not how I anticipated my night going, but I'm fucking glad it did turn out like this.

"Now, we're going to park this loud-ass car a block or so away from your house. We gotta keep the element of surprise. Then, we initiate phase two… getting it on." I give her a wink.

She giggles and my chest swells, making me rub against my skin.

"Okay, bossy."

I tut.

"Trouble, you have no idea. Now drive."

I lean back in my seat, adjusting my cock to try and hide how turned on I am.

It only gets worse as she races us back to her house.

The whole time I'm picturing bending her over the hood and spanking her tight ass.

Fuck.

This guy truly is the dumbest man on the planet. How could he let her slip through his fingers like this?

CHAPTER 6

HALLIE

Conan helps me out of the driver's seat, towering over me beneath a streetlamp.

"You good?" he asks.

What the hell are we doing? But adrenaline's already in my bloodstream, hot and alive. I love Conan's plan. Mine would've been dumping Ben over text and sending him his own live sex tape.

But this? This makes me feel powerful.

Conan's right. Fuck Ben. For humiliating me. For playing me. For screwing some cheap ho on my couch. That's my home. My sanctuary.

And with a guy like Conan? Ben's going to wish he never met me.

"I'm good."

Goosebumps scatter across my skin as Conan presses his palm against my lower back and guides me down the street.

"Left or right?" he asks as we approach the end of the road.

"Second on the right."

I inhale deeply as we reach the stairs. Are they still fucking?

I glance back at Conan. He holds a finger to his lips and follows me silently up the steps. I slip the key in and turn it without a sound. As soon as the door clicks open, his hands grip my hips, spinning me around to face him.

I gasp, our noses brushing. I can't fucking breathe. All I hear is the blood pounding in my ears, everything else fading—even the stars.

All I can see are those green eyes.

"Kiss me, trouble."

I loop my arms around his neck and drag him down. My mouth crashes against his.

His tongue slips in, brushing mine, slow and deliberate. Holy shit. I feel everything I've been missing.

Pure, raw electricity. His hand slides up my side, wrapping around my throat as he deepens the kiss.

I moan into his mouth and jerk back. No. This isn't real.

Except... it is. No kiss has ever felt like this. Not even close.

My lips are swollen. My face flushed. That didn't feel fake. Not even a little.

"What happened to our 'performance'? He can't see us here," I whisper.

Conan's hands frame my face, warm and wide. "That, darlin', was our practice kiss. Just for us."

I'm supposed to hate the male species. But Conan? He's doing a damn good job redeeming the entire population. He's sweet. Dangerous. And so fucking hot I can't think straight.

"Let's do this?"

A slow smile creeps across my lips. Despite everything

—being humiliated and fucked over—what I feel right now is power. And… yeah. I'm turned the hell on.

"Careful with your leg. But come on, beastie. Let's go."

A growl rumbles in his chest as he scoops me into his arms. "Revenge is beautiful," he whispers against my lips.

As planned, I wrap my legs around his waist, arms tight around his neck, and he kisses me. Ferociously. Like he needs me to survive.

We move down the hallway, fumbling with the living room door. Our mouths never part.

"Fuck, Hallie. I need to be inside you." His deep Irish accent drenches my panties.

My eyes fly open—he winks, bites my bottom lip, then crashes his mouth back to mine.

I moan. Loud. Grinding against him, completely lost.

And it's not fake. Not even close.

My fingers tangle in his hair, pulling him deeper just as he pins me to the wall.

"You taste so sweet, baby."

"Hallie! What the fuck?!"

Ben's voice rips through the air.

Conan grins against my lips. "Showtime, trouble."

My pulse spikes. Rage simmers beneath my skin.

"Don't let go of me."

He holds tight. Steady. And over his shoulder, I come face-to-face with Ben, flushed, naked, holding my fucking cushion over his limp dick.

"Get the fuck out of my house," I seethe.

Ben shakes his head, hand dragging through his black hair.

Bertie barrels in from the kitchen, barking, teeth bared.

"It's okay, boy," I say softly, and he plants himself at my side, solid and loyal.

"You're cheating on me?" Ben's voice cracks.

I choke on a laugh.

"Are you fucking serious? You just pulled your cock out of her ten seconds ago." I point to the blonde, who's now cupping her tits like it'll save her from the shame of being caught.

"Get out. Both of you. And I'll send you an invoice for a new couch, you sick bastard."

Conan squeezes my ass. I jolt in his arms.

"Can I?" he murmurs.

I have no clue what he means, but I nod.

He sets me down, steps forward, and scoops up the pile of clothes draped over the couch.

Ben's face drains of color.

"Fuck off," Conan growls, pointing to the door.

Ben steps toward us, puffed up like he might actually try something.

Conan laughs menacingly.

"Buddy, I've seen enough of your little dick and pale ass to last me a lifetime. Either run for the door, or I'll throw you through the window. Your choice."

The girl bolts, grabbing her dress from the floor, nearly faceplanting into the table on her way out.

What a shitshow.

"Are you having a hard time hearing?" Conan starts moving toward him.

Ben glares at me, eyes wild. "You brought this fucking brute to beat me up?"

I shrug, face blank. "I brought him back to finally get an orgasm, Ben. It's been years."

Ben's nostril flares. Conan chuckles darkly behind me.

"Leave," I say, voice cold. "I don't want to touch you. I don't want to look at you. We are over."

Fuck. That felt so good. Like a weight has been lifted. That's all Ben is to me, a dead weight.

"Hallie. I can explain."

Oh, this will be good.

I stomp over to Conan, who slips a thick arm around my waist.

"Please, Ben. Explain yourself. Tell me how you accidentally brought a girl into my dead father's house and, poof, you both ended up naked and your dick ended up inside her."

Ben shakes his head.

"I didn't fuck her, Hallie."

"Still lying." I drag a hand down my face.

"Look behind you, dumbass, and wave to the camera." I point to it, mounted beside the flatscreen.

His mouth drops open. His face drains of all color.

"I never want to see you again. We're so fucking done. Get the fuck out of my house!"

"Hallie. Baby. We can work through this. I just needed a fuck; that's all it was. You won't put out, and a man has needs—"

Conan scoffs.

"Use your fucking hand, then," I snap.

"I'll make this right. One more chance—"

I shake my head, disgust curling in my gut.

"No. I didn't want to fuck you before, and I sure as hell never want to again. Now, for the last time. Out. I've got needs of my own to take care of."

I look up at Conan and bat my lashes. He turns, eyes dark.

"You naughty, naughty girl," he whispers.

He's playing the part like a pro.

Ben scuttles past us but pauses at the door. I roll my eyes.

"I wouldn't waste your time with her," he mutters, voice bitter. "Boring as hell in bed. All she does is work and nap. Or cry about her dead dad."

Conan stiffens. His hand drops from me.

And just like that, he shifts. The air cracks.

The fury in his eyes? It's like nothing I've ever seen before. His beast is unleashed.

CHAPTER 7
CONAN

I've got my hand around his throat, and he's slamming into the wall before my brain even catches up.

"You just don't know when to shut the fuck up, do you?"

The asshole grins.

"What are you gonna do about it, you Irish prick?"

I laugh. Low. Dark.

"You're only across the pond from me. You know what my kind are capable of. I'd pick your next words wisely. Or you'll end up in the same state the last Brit that fought me did."

I lean in, close enough to taste the fear bleeding out of him.

"I caved his face in, and he left in a body bag, just in case you're wondering," I whisper so only he can hear.

His face goes the same pale shade as the drywall. My fingers clamp tighter around his windpipe.

"Is that how you speak to women? Huh? Have some fucking respect."

Then I feel her. Hallie. Behind me. Her presence doesn't just calm me, it reins me in.

I don't cave his jaw like I want to. Instead, I yank him by the shirt and drag his sorry ass to the front door, flinging him out onto the pavement like trash.

"Come near her again, I'll fucking kill you."

He scuttles back on his ass, the coward in him finally showing.

"She's going to regret this. Mark my words. She needs me to protect her."

Slowly, I blink at him.

"Protect her from what, exactly?"

If there's anyone around here who needs protecting from, it's me and my brothers.

But then he grins. That same grin men like him always hide behind. Something in his eyes flickers, too alive.

"You'll see."

Hallie's hand brushes my back.

We watch Ben disappear into the dark. I don't like the way it swallows him whole.

"Who exactly is Ben?" I ask, turning to lock the door.

"Umm. No one, really. Works for his cousin's business. Finance crap, I think. He's from London."

I nod, the threat still circling in my brain like a shark scenting blood.

The recognition in his eyes—that was no accident.

"Last name?"

"Edwards."

That's going to Declan tonight. I want every damn thing there is to know about this Ben Edwards.

I glance at her. She's twirling her thumbs. But her eyes —there's a glimmer in them that wasn't there before.

"Do you need a lift home now?" she asks.

Her hand is trembling. Just slightly.

"Are you meant to be going back to work?" I take a step closer.

Her dog's panting, chest heaving in time with the tension thick in the air. She strokes his head.

I crouch, holding out a hand. He sniffs it, nose wet against my skin.

"That'a boy." I scratch behind his ear, and his tail goes wild.

When I stand, I'm towering over her again.

"Sorry. I love dogs," I tell her. She smiles like it's the first safe thing she's done all day.

"Yeah. Me too. He was my dad's."

She exhales, and it cracks something in me. The kind of sorrow you feel in your bones. I pull her into me and hold her. Tight.

There's no way she's leaving. No way I'm letting her out of my sight. Not until I figure out what the fuck that threat meant.

"Okay. How about, and you can tell me to fuck off, you let me call Finn and explain. Get you the night off work. We sit and watch movies, drink coffee, or whatever sickly sweet stuff you like. And then I'll stay on the couch until Finn collects me in the morning. We can also go get your car too."

She looks up, confused. Frowning.

"Why?"

"Why what, trouble?"

She pouts. And fuck, it does something to me. Something I shouldn't let it do.

This is comfort. That's all. She's a family friend. This is what I should be doing.

"Why are you helping me? You don't know me. You

could've just run out the door after Ben and left me to it."

I bite my tongue. She's not wrong. I don't know why I care this much. Why is it sticking to my ribs?

"Because I'm not an asshole. And I think you're really fucking cool."

She smiles, soft and bright. Her eyes go glassy. I brush a knuckle down her cheek.

"Thank you, Conan."

"You're welcome. And see, I told you I owed you one."

She giggles. It's a sound that doesn't belong in this moment. But I let it live. I let her have it.

Friends. That's the line. And rule number one? You don't fuck your friends.

My hand rubs over the wound on my thigh, pain pulsing under the pants. She notices.

"I told you to be careful."

Her voice is clipped. Stern. It makes my cock twitch.

"I'm a naughty boy, Hallie. I can't help it."

She tuts and rolls her eyes. Christ. I like it too much.

"Does it hurt? Want me to check it, make sure you haven't broken a stitch?"

I shake my head. "No. But I'd love a drink. That'll cure me."

"Dr. Quinn is going to be pissed at me." Her gaze drops to the floor.

"Trouble, I've had twenty-nine years of winding my brother up. I'll take the rap for this one. He won't think anything of it, I promise. Trust me, it's a skill of mine."

I grin and she softens.

"Where's your keys? I'll go get your car now instead so it's done, and I'll call him while I'm doing it, and by the time I get back, we'll be sweet to just relax."

"I could use a glass of wine. Or bottle."

CHAPTER 8

HALLIE

"Lily. You are not going to believe this," I whisper-hiss down the phone.

Lily is my lifelong best friend. The woman who's seen me at rock bottom and dragged me back from it, bloody knuckles and all.

"What? You finally came?"

"Ha-ha. No. Look, I don't have long, but I caught Ben cheating while I was patching up Dr. Quinn's hot brother. And now he's in my house and wants to stay the night to look after me."

The line falls silent.

"Damn, Hallie. I don't see you for three days, and this happens. How hot is hot?"

I tap my nails on the counter, trying to keep my voice steady.

"Way over six feet tall, covered in tattoos, rugged… you know, like scary but gorgeous."

Oh my god. I sound like a horny teenager.

"The kind that will fuck you up against a wall and choke you good?"

57

"Lily!" I gasp.

The deep rumble of my Shelby echoes down the street.

"He's back with my car now. Come over tomorrow night."

"Oh, I will be there. Don't do anything I wouldn't do."

"So that's essentially do anything I want."

"Love you," she whispers, giggling.

"Love you too."

I end the call as Conan strides into my house, the air shifting with him. My stomach flips when he kicks off his shoes and lifts his gaze to me.

The way he stares—it's like I'm his prey. Like he's already decided how I'll fall.

"How did you find her to drive?" I ask.

"Ugh," he groans.

"She's fucking gorgeous, Hallie. That fucking roar of the engine makes me hard just thinking about it."

I swallow hard and reach for my wine.

"Here." I slide him one of my dad's favorite whiskeys. He used to get them imported from Ireland. I figure Conan would approve.

"A whiskey girl?" He tilts his head, settling on the stool across from me.

"Sometimes. I like this one anyway."

He takes a slow sip, licking his lips. There's a glint in his eye, something dark and amused.

"I'd know that flavor anywhere. You got the bottle?"

I nod and duck to grab it from the cabinet. He takes it, studies the label, and smiles—soft, sad.

"This one was my dad's pride and joy. He spent years perfecting this recipe."

My mouth falls open.

"Your dad made this? Oh my god. My dad would be kissing your feet if he were still alive. He lived for this."

He nods, a flicker of something reverent passing through his eyes.

"I've not seen it here in the States. Only the ones I flew over."

"My dad used to get them shipped every six months. He once took a trip to Ireland, fell in love with it, and never let it go."

"Well, you know what they say…"

He leans across the counter, and my breath stutters. He's close. Too close.

"W-what do they say?" I whisper.

"Once you get a taste of the Irish, ya never go back."

A giggle bubbles up, and I try to hide it behind the rim of my glass.

"I thought it was about the luck of the Irish?"

"That too. I mean, I've been your lucky charm tonight, haven't I? Your ex is racing around the street butt naked right now."

I glance past him to the couch and narrow my eyes.

"Wanna help me burn it?"

He knocks back his whiskey.

"Now?"

I laugh, smacking the counter.

"No. I don't think my neighbors would appreciate that. I'll have a removal company get it tomorrow. You're really down for anything, aren't you?"

He grins, pouring himself another glass.

"Yes, darlin'. I'm the fun Quinn. I'll get you into trouble and back out of it all in one night."

I believe him. He's lightning in a bottle, wild and untouchable, but if you cross him, it's game over.

We settle into a quiet rhythm, the radio humming softly in the background.

"Don't listen to what that asswipe said earlier. You aren't boring. You're quite the opposite, actually." Conan's voice cuts through the silence, sharp and sincere.

"I don't care if he thinks I am. And I guess… sometimes I am. But there's a whole side of me he never met. I know I'm cool. Just for the right people."

He raises his glass, and I clink mine against his.

"Cheers to that, trouble."

We knock them back.

"And you're a damn good kisser. You know, if Small Dick didn't interrupt us, I was about to take you upstairs. I lost my brain there for a bit."

My eyes widen. My skin burns.

I have no idea what this is, whatever's building between us, but it makes me feel something I haven't felt in years.

Sexy. Seen. Real.

Since my dad died, I haven't done anything for myself. I've just existed. Drowning quietly in grief while pretending I'm fine.

But tonight? The voices in my head, the ones that whisper I'm too much or not enough, they've gone quiet.

Tonight, I'm just me. The girl who laughs too loud. Who chases adrenaline. The girl who serves revenge cold with a smile on her lips.

I watch Conan swirl the liquid in his glass. Does he regret telling me that?

I take a breath. Screw it.

Maybe I deserve someone who knows how to fuck. Someone who won't make me feel like a placeholder.

And I'd bet every cent I have that this man does. Then I can go back to my toys.

"I wouldn't have stopped you." I say it steadily. Confidentially.

His head snaps up.

And I swear, my lungs stop working.

Feral. That's the only word for the way he looks at me.

Whatever leash he had on himself? Gone.

He stands abruptly and rounds the counter. I stay still, look up at him through my lashes, heart pounding like war drums.

"What do you want from me, Hallie?" he asks, voice lowered to something dangerous and divine.

I squeeze my thighs together.

He's way out of my league.

I could never give him what he needs. I'm boring. Plain ol' boring Hal. Just like Ben said. Stupid, stupid Hallie.

CHAPTER 9
CONAN

Sleep Token – Even In Arcadia

I can see her spiraling inside her head.

Like I can hear every single doubt rattling through her mind like shrapnel. It's chaos behind those eyes, and I want to silence every piece of it. Just for a moment. Just enough to remind her who the fuck she is.

I cradle her face, one hand on each side. My thumbs stroke along her temples, slow. Gentle. She doesn't flinch. That's a win. This girl is sending me fucking crazy in the best way, and she needs to know what she does to me.

Fuck whoever broke her confidence. I'll hunt them all down and grind their faces into the dirt. If it's Ben, then I'll gladly end him.

But right now? I need her to remember the version of herself who let me slam her against a wall with my tongue down her throat just to piss off her loser boyfriend. *Ex-boyfriend.*

"Come back to me, trouble. Fuck what Ben said. Fuck anyone who has ever made you doubt yourself. They ain't worth it. You are so much more than they could ever be. You, Hallie, are a badass. You're funny. You have impeccable taste in cars. You're kind and caring. You are drop-dead fucking gorgeous. You made me hard while sticking a needle in my leg. You made me hard when you giggled. Do you need me to continue the list? Or can I just fuckin' kiss you now, for real this time?"

She sucks in a shaky breath. I roll my tongue along my teeth to stop myself from doing what I'm burning to do.

There's something she said earlier, something I can't get out of my head.

Something that damn near brought me to my knees.

And maybe that's where I want to be.

"Or do you want me to be a good boy and get down on my knees and beg for you?"

Her eyes go wide. She licks her lips slowly, and the switch flips in her. I feel it. Like an electric charge between us as her nails drag over my shirt. That touch hits like a spark. Fuck, it burns like it too.

I'm holding back. Every muscle in my body is begging to snap. But I won't. She needs this—control. Power. I want to be the one to give it back to her.

"I don't ever do this, Conan. This isn't who I am normally. I don't bring men back and have sex with them."

I press a finger to her lips. Her words crash against her teeth, stopped by my touch.

"There is nothing wrong with a woman feeding into her desires, trouble. Women having sex does not make them disgusting, or a whore, or anything else. We're all human, we all have urges; men and women are no fucking different. So while it makes me hard as hell knowing you don't do this often, I wouldn't have given a shit either way. I just want you."

And I mean it.

This world has fucked up everything for women. Taught them shame. Like they're not allowed to want things. Need things. Like pleasure should only ever be a reward, never a right.

Bullshit.

For the small amount of time we actually walk on this planet, why can't we just fuck who we want, when we want, and exactly how we need it?

Everyone would be a lot happier running through the woods and fucking against trees like the feral fuckin' animals we all are born to be.

Her mouth opens. Closes. I wait.

"Just one night? And we tell no one."

She means my brother. Yeah. I get it. It's not worth the fallout. Not tonight.

"Secret is safe with me, darlin'."

She shifts on her feet. That pout is pure sin. Every second that ticks by just turns the fire up.

"Get on those knees then, beastie."

Fuck.

My heart damn near breaks through my ribs.

I hold the counter for support, my thigh screaming, but I don't care. Not one bit. This injury won't ruin tonight. I'll tear it back open before I give this up.

She grabs my whiskey and tilts her head back, letting the liquid sit in her mouth. When her fingers run through my hair, my breath catches. But when she yanks my head back and spits that whiskey into my mouth—

Holy. Fucking. Shit.

The burn of the whiskey hits, but it's nothing compared to her.

"Kiss. Me. Please," I beg.

She steps back, smirking, and undoes each button of her black shirt like she's teasing the gods. The red lace underneath makes my cock throb. She tosses the shirt aside, and I can't look away.

"I wanna run my tongue along them," I tell her, looking at her perfect breasts.

So many things I want to do to her. And not enough hours in the night.

"Maybe I'll let you."

"Stand up and take your clothes off," she orders.

I don't hesitate.

I'm on my feet, tearing off my loafers, shirt, and pants— gone. My cock presses tight against my boxers, already begging for her.

She stares, voice low.

"All of it."

I kick them off, and my dick springs free. Hard. Throbbing all for her.

"You going to return the favor, trouble?"

"Holy fuck," she breathes out, her eyes fixed on my cock.

I stroke myself. Slow. Just enough to keep the edge simmering.

"I'll take that as a compliment."

"Strip for me, darlin'. I've shown you mine, you show me yours."

She steps out of her jeans, leaving only red lace and a jaw-dropping view.

"Stunning. Be a good girl for me and turn around. Let me see."

She spins. And I almost lose it.

"Bend over the counter." I switch some control back.

She obeys. Legs apart. Back arched. Fucking heaven.

"I've not touched you yet, and you're panting. How wet are you for me, Hallie?"

"Soaked, Conan. I think you need a taste, don't you?"

Her words shred what little control I had left.

I drop to my knees. Again. And I'd stay here forever for her.

Sliding her panties down slowly, I tear them clean off and kiss up her thigh, savoring the heat radiating from her.

"I bet you taste sweet."

I spread her with my fingers and lick her once. Long. Deep.

She moans; it's shaky and beautiful.

I go again. This time, my tongue plunges inside while my finger circles her clit. My other hand anchors her hips, grounding her to me.

"Conan."

Her hips roll, chasing my mouth like she needs it to breathe.

I want her screaming.

I pull my hand back and spank her, hard.

"Fuck!"

Her cry echoes through the room as I feast on her like a man starved. Her taste is everything. I need more.

"Come for me, trouble."

My cock aches, but I don't stop. I won't stop. Not until I feel her fall apart beneath my hands.

And still—it's not enough.

I want to see her.

I want to watch her break.

CHAPTER 10
HALLIE

I scream as he lifts me by the waist, spinning me to face him and placing my ass on the counter.

"I wanna see your pretty face when you come, baby."

He brushes my hair from my face, lips hot and greedy over mine.

I clamp my thighs around his hips, breathless.

"Fuck, I'm struggling not to ruin you, Hallie."

I blow out a shaky breath, and his hand flies up, wrapping tight around my throat.

His other hand dips between my thighs, circles my clit, and then drives two fingers into me.

My mouth drops open. A helpless sound escapes.

"Am I being a good boy for you? Huh? Making you come?"

I try to nod, but his grip's firm around my neck.

"Y-yes."

I lift one leg, my foot landing on the counter, spreading wider for him.

"Oh, you want me deeper, do you? My filthy girl."

He growls the words against my lips and pushes a third finger in.

I cry out, stretching around him, my body trembling.

"Is this what you need?"

His fingers move faster, harder, making my head spin.

"Such a good fucking girl, baby. I can't wait to have my dick in this tight pussy."

I bite my tongue, trying to swallow the scream clawing its way up.

He eases his grip on my throat, and I gasp.

"I'm so close," I whisper, my voice wrecked.

"I know. I can feel it."

He crushes his mouth to mine, just as the violent climax hits. My moans are swallowed by his kiss while he finger-fucks me through it.

"So beautiful when you come for me," he murmurs against my lips.

My chest heaves. He pulls his fingers from me and presses them to my mouth.

"Now it's time for you to taste what I do to you."

He pushes them past my lips. My eyes go wide as I suck them clean.

"Dirty girl."

He bites his lip, eyes locked on my mouth as he slowly draws his fingers out.

"Feel better now?"

I wrap my arms around his neck, tugging him closer, feeling the solid press of his cock against my sensitive, swollen pussy.

It's massive. Like, jaw-droppingly, medically concerningly huge.

And I've never been with a man this size.

He is a beast. And for the first time tonight, I'm scared.

I close my eyes. I may have bitten off more than I can chew.

Because if that's what his fingers can do—what the hell happens when he fucks me?

Is death by orgasm a thing? Shit.

I'm a nurse. I should know these things.

"Hallie. Stop panicking. My dick isn't going to break you."

He's amused. "I mean, you might be sore when I'm done. But you'll survive, I promise."

My eyes snap open. "How did you know?"

He chuckles, and I ease a little.

"I saw the way you looked at him."

He brushes his lips along my jaw. "And I can read minds."

I press a finger to his chest, raising a brow.

"If you can read minds, what exactly am I thinking right now?"

His hands glide along my thighs, his rough palms squeezing.

I'm thinking about dropping to my knees and sucking him off until he forgets his name.

"You want to get on your knees and let me fuck your face. Am I close?"

I gasp. He laughs.

"Close enough. I was also thinking about how I want to hear you moan for me."

His eyes go wide. My cheeks flush.

"Oh, I'm sure that mouth of yours will get you exactly what you need. I have one rule, though."

He lifts me from the counter, carrying me into the living room, stopping by the same wall we made out at earlier.

"What's your rule?"

He sets me down, my back to the wall.

"You get yourself off while you suck my dick. I want to hear you too. That'll be enough to make me come so hard down your throat."

I swallow hard as he puts pressure on my shoulder. I drop to my knees.

"And Hallie," he growls, "I'm going to fuck your face. Roughly. Brutally. Primal style. I want your tears and cries. You good with that?"

I lick my lips and spread my legs, fingers slipping between them.

"Yes, beastie."

"Hmm, mmm."

He slides a hand through my hair, grips at the roots, holding me steady.

"If it's too much, you tap my leg. Need me to stop quickly, slap my cut."

"I won't need to stop," I say, voice full of fire.

I want to impress him. I need to hear him moan.

"Good girl. Let's test that theory, shall we? Too much talking. Not enough sucking."

I open my mouth and he slides in slowly. Almost like he's trying to feel out if I can actually take him.

I look up. He's glaring down at me, fire in his eyes. Hunger.

I circle my clit. He groans, pulling out.

Then thrusts in harder, deeper. I gag around him. That earns me a moan.

"That was halfway, trouble. Good job."

Halfway? Shit.

His grip tightens in my hair. It stings. I keep fingering myself.

He moves faster. Rough. Needy.

"Oh. Fuck. Hallie."

Tears roll down my cheeks. I moan around him, sliding two fingers inside myself.

He grunts, breath ragged.

"Hallie. Shit. You're so wet for me."

I moan. He clenches. His dick keeps hitting the back of my throat, over and over.

Everything blurs. My throat relaxes.

I'm close. So fucking close.

"Be a good little slut and come sucking my cock, trouble."

His deep voice sends shockwaves through me.

"Good. Fucking. Girl."

His moans grow louder. Mine do too.

He roars my name and I crash over the edge.

I come hard, seeing stars as he spills down my throat.

When he pulls out, I go to stand, but my legs buckle. He catches me and carries me to the couch.

"You good, baby?"

He strokes my cheek.

"Yeah. Really good," I croak.

"That was mind-blowing, trouble. So fucking good. The way I could feel you moaning around my cock? Spectacular."

I glow at his praise.

"Thank you. I tried."

He smiles, cheeky.

"I needed that." I tell him.

"An orgasm?"

He lifts my chin and I nod.

"It's been a long, long, very long time."

I pause.

"Well, I can give them to myself easily. But a man? Years. You broke my brokenness."

His brows knit. He grabs my face.

"Don't ever say you're broken again. You, trouble, were never the problem. You felt how hard I just came down your throat, right?"

I giggle.

"Yes. I felt a lot in my throat, Conan."

"Say it for me. I am not broken, I just have poor choices in men who don't know how to pleasure a woman. I was never the problem. I'm hot as fuck."

"I really have to say the last bit?"

He nods.

"Yeah. Say the whole thing, and I'll give you another orgasm. I'll make you come so hard you pass out. Now say it."

I swallow and meet his eyes.

"I am not broken, I just have poor choices in men who don't know how to pleasure a woman. I was never the problem. I'm hot as fuck."

"Such a good girl."

He kisses me, and my heart races.

"Do I get my prize now?"

A buzzing sound cuts through the air.

Then again.

"Let me get that first," I whisper.

I dart to my clothes and dig out my phone.

Dr. Quinn.

"It's your brother."

Conan shifts on the couch. "Answer it. I'll keep quiet."

I pick up.

"Dr. Quinn, everything okay?"

"Could you make it in for a shift? Four hours max. I'll

meet you there to oversee. I wouldn't ask if it wasn't an emergency. We've had staff off sick. We need all hands. I'll pay you double."

Sadness creeps in. I glance at Conan, casually lounging, bare and breathtaking.

But I need the cash.

I almost fell behind last month. Lily had to bail me out.

"Yeah. Give me twenty minutes."

He must hear the disappointment in my voice.

"Is Conan with you?"

I hesitate. "Yes."

"I'll send someone to collect him. Ten minutes. I'll see you in my office in thirty."

"Okay."

"Thanks, Hallie."

Click.

I toss the phone on the counter.

Conan's already on his feet.

"Fun's over. I gotta work."

He growls.

"My brother ruining our night?"

I nod. "Not his fault. Emergencies. Understaffed. Nature of the job."

Conan grabs my hips and backs me into the counter.

"You have someone picking you up in ten minutes."

"Ten minutes is plenty. I want another taste to keep me going until next time."

My eyes fly up.

"Next time?"

"You promised me a whole night..."

"A one-night stand means one night, wherever it gets cut off, beastie."

I tap his chest. He grabs my hands.

"I don't follow rules, trouble."

He leans in and runs his tongue along my neck.

"Now, you owe me. No take backs."

He kisses my jaw. Then devours my mouth.

Deep. Hard. Intoxicating.

I moan against him, melting. At least I got to experience this once. It's like I'm alive again.

"I'll see you soon, beautiful."

He backs away.

I'm clinging to the counter, breathless.

"Maybe," I mutter.

It's complicated. I work too much. This was a moment. A wild, beautiful night. But maybe that's all it should be.

He grabs his clothes and yanks them on.

"Quickly put something on your neck, baby. I've left a mark. Something to remember me by."

I press my fingers to my throat, watching him go.

At the door, he looks back.

"Look after yourself, trouble. You know how to reach me."

CHAPTER 11
CONAN

Two whole days and nothing from Hallie.

I'm pining for her, and I'm pissed off at myself. Probably because I didn't fuck her.

That's what I tell myself. But the truth? She's funny as hell. A firecracker with a soft heart and a stubborn streak that makes me want to bite.

I check my phone again. Still no reply from Declan. Oh, maybe my cell is broken?

I shake my head. Declan isn't replying because he's on his honeymoon with Charlotte this week. Drago's watching their daughter, Isabella. But tonight, I'm on duty for Uncle Conan's bedtime story hour.

My phone pings with a text and I nearly drop it from excitement. Which soon leaves me when I see Declan's name, not Hallie.

DECLAN

I've sent the info to Enzo, and I'll forward any reply. Who is he? Why are we looking into him?

Another text comes in.

DECLAN

Actually, don't answer. My wife might stab
me if I do any work this week. I'll see you
Monday.

One less thing to worry about. We're looking into that
slick bastard, Ben. I don't trust him, and I sure as hell didn't
like the slimy threat he slid Hallie's way.

Even if she never wants to see me again, she looked after
me. She doesn't deserve his bullshit.

I need to stop thinking about her.

After a quick cardio burn with the ropes, I head for my
therapy—beating the shit out of the punch bag. Every jab
helps bleed off the rage bottled in my chest. Keeps me
sane.

My trainer quit on me last week. Said I wasn't taking the
title seriously. Then I may have accidentally punched him
too hard in the nose.

He's wrong. I've bled for this.

I've worked my ass off since we moved to the States.
Yeah, I fucked up. I killed James Bowen in the underground
cage. But that was then. Now, I'm clean. Undefeated.
Ranked in the UFC top ten.

Win this next fight, and I've got a shot at the championship belt.

I pound the bag again, fists slamming harder. Kicks
follow. Sweat slicks down my spine. My lungs burn. My
mind still won't shut up.

Caramel hair. Big eyes. That sweet fucking mouth.

It was supposed to be one night. We didn't even finish
the damn night.

I have to get her out of my system.

I throw one more punch. It rattles up my arm, white-hot pain flashing through my shoulder.

"Fuck!"

"I thought you were told not to train. You're supposed to be healing that wound."

I steady the bag and glance over. Finn.

Grey eyes, unreadable. Hair perfect. Suit pristine, like he stepped out of a mafia funeral and not my gym.

"It's healed," I lie.

"Bullshit," he says flatly. "Also, did something happen with Hallie? She's been skittish around me. I'm blaming you."

He walks closer, adjusting his cuff like he's about to interrogate me.

"No. Nothing."

Finn narrows his eyes.

"Don't lie to me, brother." He points a finger like Dad used to and my jaw tics.

"Nothing happened. I helped her with something. She got called into work. Rowan picked me up. That's it."

"Then why is she asking me to check your stitches instead of doing it herself?"

That fucking stings. She doesn't want to see me?

"I don't know," I admit, voice tight. But I want to.

"Declan's back from his honeymoon this weekend. We'll finalize the details for the Decadence Chase. I assume you've confirmed all your contestants?"

Shit.

"I haven't checked."

Finn gives me a look like I'm already on thin ice.

"Finish up and shower. I'll meet you at your cabin to redress the wound. You good?"

I nod. But my thoughts are stuck on her.

Why is she avoiding me? I liked her. I thought she liked me too.

I don't want her avoiding me. I don't want her career fucked up because of me, either.

As Finn reaches the door, I clear my throat.

"Finn?"

He pauses.

"If you, uh... wanted to see a girl more than once, would you text her?"

He blinks.

"Me?" He presses a tattooed hand to his chest. "You're asking me that?"

"Yes," I mutter.

"You talking about the girl you were meeting the night of the crash?"

"Yeah," I say quickly, hoping he doesn't catch the truth.

He always does.

"What's there to lose?" He shrugs. "Text her. Worst case, she ignores you. Then you find your next victim for the woods."

I clench my fist. Asshole.

"Or... you chase her directly into the woods?" His grin sharpens.

"Got it."

Hallie liked it rougher. Wonder how she'd handle my kind of chase. I bet she'd run. I bet I'd catch her.

The door clicks shut behind him.

My palms are sweating as I dig through my gym bag for my phone.

I texted myself from her phone in the hospital. I find the message and hover my thumb over the screen.

This feels more dangerous than stepping into a ring.

I type fast before I lose my nerve.

ME

Hi, trouble. You okay?

It sends. Too late to take it back.

I stare at the screen. Has she read it?

Fuck.

I shouldn't have sent it. She's ghosting me. She doesn't want to see me. She didn't even come to check my stitches.

I pace the mat, phone clutched in my fist. I feel crazy.

Shit. Shit. Shit.

I should've just let her go.

But I swear I felt something. That spark my mom used to talk about. The one that tells you she's it. *The one.* I wasn't even looking.

Two minutes pass. Still no reply. No read receipt.

I consider throwing the phone into a wall. Or off a cliff.

No. What if she replies?

I laugh through my obsessive psycho moment, tossing the phone onto the mat. I rake a hand through my sweaty hair.

I need to get a grip. I've got a fight in a couple of weeks and no damn trainer. Time to focus on that.

CHAPTER 12

HALLIE

"**D**oes he not have any social media at all?" Lily whines, reaching for the wine bottle.

I've opted for whiskey instead.

"Nope. Nada. Just trust me—he's sculpted like a Greek god. Hung like one too. Ink on every inch of his skin. And the mouth on him? I'm pretty sure he could get me off with his words alone."

"You're blushing!" she squeals, her blue eyes lighting up.

I bite back a grin.

"A girl can fantasize. It was one time. That'll be enough to keep me going."

She rolls her eyes and flicks her long blonde hair over her shoulder.

"Does it have to be only one time? I mean, you didn't even get to the good part, right? You're not working tonight... text him."

I shake my head.

"No. I can't. It's too complicated. His brother is my

boss. And who's to say he even wants me again? He doesn't strike me as the type to go back for seconds."

Lily frowns and taps her rings against the rim of her glass.

"Give me your phone." She holds out her hand.

"No!"

"You're not telling me something. You can't sit still, and you're twirling your thumbs. Spit it out."

I let out a huff. The only downside to having a best friend is she can read me like a goddamn book.

"He texted me earlier today."

She grins like it's Christmas.

"Saying?"

"Hi, trouble. You okay?"

I chew the inside of my cheek. I don't know what I expected. More? Less? Nothing?

Resting my chin on my palm, I wait for her verdict.

"And you replied what?" she asks.

"Nothing." I scrunch my face up. "I messed up, didn't I?"

She nods, eyebrows raised.

"Yeah. You did. Reply to him."

I don't want to admit I got scared. That I assumed he'd be done. I bailed on him. He didn't even get inside me. I figured he'd lose interest.

And now I feel shitty for assuming that. I guess I haven't had many experiences that proved otherwise.

Men usually want one thing.

Except Conan is asking if I'm okay.

"He called you trouble. That's cute. Does he know what else you get up to?"

My eyes go wide.

"No."

"I bet he'd find it hot. He loved your car, right?"

I nod.

He did. And he made me laugh. Made me feel safe.

Dammit. Why didn't I text him back?

"It's not too late to reply. Tell him you were working. You seem giddy about him—don't ignore your gut."

I sigh and unlock my phone, staring at the message.

"What do I even say?"

She shrugs and lifts her glass of red.

"Just be you. Sounds like he's into that."

Chewing my lip, I type.

ME

Hi, beastie. Sorry, got caught up at work. I'm good, thank you. How are you? And are you looking after your stitches?

I hit send and down the rest of my whiskey, heat rushing to my cheeks as a vivid image flashes back—me spitting whiskey into his mouth. Right here. On this damn kitchen floor.

"Ew. You guys did it here, didn't you?"

A sly smile pulls at my lips.

"Maybe. Maybe it was right on that chair." I point at her.

"Ugh. Don't. I need to get laid, Hallie."

I laugh and turn my phone screen face down, already itching to flip it back over.

"Ben is single now," I joke.

"Ew. Absolutely not. I wish Conan had thrown him through the window. Asshole deserved it."

"Yeah, but it was funny enough without me having to pay for a new window."

A pit curls low in my stomach.

"I have extra money this month from my extra shifts, I can pay you back."

Lily places her hand over mine.

"Hallie. Don't worry about me. I'm good. Just take care of what you have to and pay me back when you can. I'd rather you didn't nearly kill yourself in that car."

A shadow flickers across her face.

"I haven't raced in weeks."

She sighs and squeezes my hand just as my phone vibrates on the table. She hates that I street race. Even though I'm pretty damn good at it, it scares her. That's why she gave me the money, she's scared I'll enter again.

"Yeah, but all it takes is a split second. I need you, Hallie. Now read that text before I explode with excitement. I have to get back to the gallery soon. I can't live with the suspense."

I chuckle and pick it up, a smile spreading across my face when I see his name flash on the screen.

BEASTIE

I would have preferred it if you checked my stitches rather than my brother. He didn't call me a good boy. It's just not the same.

I giggle just as another message comes in.

BEASTIE

I'm good, though. You did a good job on it.
Thank you.

My heart flutters.

"What did he say?" Lily asks.

I read them out, and she grins.

"Cute."

I nod. He kinda is.

ME

You're welcome. And good boy for being
brave having Dr. Quinn check them.

I watch the screen. He's typing.
My stomach flips.

BEASTIE

You really are trouble, aren't you?

ME

Maybe…

"You want a ride to work? I fancy going for a drive," I ask Lily.

As soon as the words leave my mouth, Bertie bounds into the kitchen and plops at my feet.

"I think he wants to come."

His tail wags like crazy and Lily jumps up, ruffling his head.

"Sounds good. Why don't you swing by and see lover boy?" She wiggles her eyebrows.

"No! We're friends. That's it."

And I have no clue where he actually lives.

She rolls her eyes and grabs my glass—thankfully I've only had a few mouthfuls.

"Flirty friends. Who've had each other's genitals in their mouth. Yeah. That's what friends do."

"Lily!"

"What? It's true!" She laughs, arms snaking around my shoulders from behind.

"I don't want anything else. Ben's put me off that for a long time. Conan is just… a friend."

"Whatever you have to tell yourself, Hallie."

I get up and grab my coat, but not before glancing at my phone again. A familiar ache pinches my chest when I don't see his name.

Maybe it is for the best.

Or maybe…

ME

I'm going for a drive… want to join me?

I stare at the message. Then delete it before I hit send. The phone vibrates in my hand.

BEASTIE

Have a good night, darlin.

Oh.

I guess that conversation's over.

CHAPTER 13
CONAN

"For the love of God, Conan. Let one of us text her!" Rowan lunges for my phone, fingers just missing as I yank it back.

Reggie doesn't move. Just sits there with his arms crossed, unimpressed. Typical. He's the quieter twin, but his expressions cut deeper than most people's words.

"I said, 'Have a good night, darlin'," I grunt, lifting my beer to my lips.

Even Reggie's slit eyebrow goes up at that.

"What?" I ask him, jaw tight.

I trust his judgment. The twins might be a couple years younger, but they've seen shit. Lived through worse. That's why we dragged them with us from Ireland when everything went sideways.

"That was one way to kill the conversation," he mutters, grabbing his beer and sipping like he's already bored of this.

"Well, all she said was maybe. What the hell was I meant to say?"

The twins glance at each other. A shared look. One that says you're a dumbass without needing the words.

Declan slides into the booth beside me like he owns the place. Of course he found us here. Inferno is our second home.

Decadence is our chocolate factory, the means to hide our other business activities. But, actually, it does pretty well across the globe. The perfect front. Behind the gates, though, that's where the darker shit happens. Mainly in Inferno.

The sex club of the elite mafia. A gateway to Enzo and all the top mafia families across the world. The Quinn brothers? We own it and maintain order through our various Decadence Games. Mine is The Chase, which is up next. Declan's shit show game already happened, and it ended with him landing a wife.

"What'd I miss? And how did I know I'd find you three here?" Declan flags down the waitress with a lift of his chin.

"I'm here for the booze," I say, jerking my thumb at Rowan and Reggie. "And these two are here for the pussy."

Declan narrows his eyes at me.

"And you're not? You sick or something?"

That earns a round of deep, belly-shaking laughs from the whole table.

"No. Conan's got a crush and doesn't know how to text like a normal human," Rowan says between gulps of beer.

Declan stares at me like I've grown a second head.

"A crush? Christ. Are we teenagers again? You haven't had a crush since ninth grade, Con. Should I be calling Finn?"

I grip the neck of my bottle until it creaks under the pressure.

"It's not a crush. It's nothing."

Rowan leans back, smug.

"Whatever you say, big man."

Declan waves for a round of whiskeys and stretches out, comfortable as hell.

"Where's Charlotte?" I ask, changing the subject. "She's nicer to me than you."

"Writing. Probably napping. I kept her busy last week."

"Yeah, yeah. Spare me."

Declan leans in closer, voice low.

"I got that information you asked for. But it's not clean. Ben doesn't really exist—not on paper, anyway. But I've got an address for a strip club he's linked to. All of it's in your email."

My stomach twists. I knew something was off about that fucker. Works in finance for his cousins, yeah right. Clearly that was a lie he spun to Hallie.

"I'll check him out."

I need to check on Hallie, too.

Declan's gaze sharpens.

"This about her?"

"Yeah." I nod once. "She's just a friend. You know I don't do more than that."

He lifts a brow but lets it go and checks the time on his Rolex.

"Then go check on her," he says, smirking. "Like a good friend would."

He slides out of the booth, and I follow, grabbing my jacket.

"I'm off, shitheads. Things to do. Gym tomorrow? I need some victims." I glance at the twins.

I need to hit the cabin. Grab some stuff. Make sure she's okay.

That's all it is.

Just me being a friend.

CHAPTER 14
HALLIE

I see dim headlights parked outside my house. Checking the time—it's eleven p.m.

Who the hell—?

A weird feeling settles in my gut.

I pull into the garage and hit the remote to shut the doors. My hand slips into the glove box for my gun. The cold weight grounds me.

I grab my phone, finger hovering over Conan's contact. Then—

Bang, bang, bang.

A loud knock sends a jolt through me. I nearly drop the phone.

"Hallie! It's me. Ben."

A groan slips out. The hundred missed calls didn't send a clear enough message?

I slam the car door and storm through the garage entrance, swinging open the front door.

"What?"

He flinches, just slightly, then his eyes rake over me. I grip the door tighter.

"I want to talk, Hallie. Please?"

There it is. The puppy dog eyes. The ones that used to work.

"No. Fuck off."

"It's important. If you hear me out, I can stop it. If you take me back, you'll be safe. You need me."

I grit my teeth so hard it hurts.

"No. No, I don't, Ben. I don't need a cheating, lying asshole of a boyfriend. I don't need anyone. Now get off my property before I call the cops."

His eyes flicker. Something darker. Scary.

He lunges.

The door flies open, knocking me off balance as he shoves his way inside.

"Listen to me!" he shouts, voice wild.

Bertie barks like mad, growling, hackles up beside me.

"Shut that fucking mutt up and stop being a stupid bitch. I'm giving you a way out!"

His voice cracks. He's manic.

"A way out of what?" I ask, my voice steady, masking the fear rising in my throat.

I've never seen him like this. Ben's always maintained control.

Now? He's unhinged.

"It's all a game," he mutters, yanking at his hair. "A sick and twisted game."

"Are you high? Or drunk?" I ask.

His head snaps up. Red eyes. Wild stare. I'd say he's high.

"No," he snaps.

"Right. So what game are we playing? The one where I'm a stupid bitch who takes her cheating ex back? Because I'm not playing."

I slip my phone out of my back pocket, careful not to let him see.

"We're playing the one where his whore ex takes him back so she doesn't die."

My breath catches.

"I'm calling the cops, Ben."

He lunges again.

His hand clamps around my wrist, and the phone goes flying. We crash to the floor.

Pain explodes across my forehead as I hit the side table. A scream tears from my throat.

"Get off me!"

I kick, hard, landing a shot to his stomach. He rolls off with a grunt, and I scramble away.

I grab the lamp from the floor, gripping it like a bat.

"I'm trying to save you! Hallie, I fucked up. I did something bad—and now I'm trying to stop it."

I don't care. He's not going to scare me into taking him back.

I crawl to my phone, snatch it, and type 9-1-1. I hold it up, thumb poised over the call button.

"Get out or I'll press dial. Your choice."

I feel the blood trailing down my face, warm and sticky. My hands tremble.

His face twists with rage.

"You'll fucking regret this. Good luck, Hallie."

He storms out.

The door slams so hard the walls shake. Tires screech, and he's gone.

I don't move.

I just stand there, heart pounding against my ribs, breath ragged.

Then I sink to the ground. My knees give out. Tears

stream down my face. My whole body trembles. I clutch my legs to my chest and try to breathe.

I've never feared for my life before. But that was terrifying. I don't want to be here.

Bertie whines and nudges his nose against my shoulder. I bury my face in his fur. This is the one thing that grounds me. The only connection I have left to Dad.

After I clean up the blood and throw some clothes into an overnight bag, I grab Bertie and leave.

I shoot a quick text to Lily:

ME

Crashing at yours tonight. Don't ask. I'm okay. I'll explain when I get there.

Part of me wants to call Conan. He'd show up. No hesitation.

He'd make me feel safe. But I don't make the call.

I'm not his burden.

CHAPTER 15
CONAN

"You look like shit, Con," Finn says.

I toss my phone on the counter and stifle a yawn, slumping onto the barstool while he messes with the coffee machine.

"Nice to see you too, brother. And why the hell are you in my cabin?"

He pours the coffee into a chipped mug and turns to face me.

"Did you sleep? You've got your big fight coming up."

I roll my eyes and grab the mug.

"I'm well aware. I don't need babysitting."

He chuckles, pulling a packet of cigarettes from his back pocket.

"No. But you're my little brother, and I know this week's always rough. Normally I hear the axe throwing before dawn. Today? Silence. Figured I'd check in."

I sigh and light a smoke. Axe throwing does sound fun, actually.

"Why doesn't it get easier, Finn?"

I rub the pressure building in my chest.

"Because we loved Mom to fucking death, that's why. You probably more than all of us. It'll always hurt. You just… learn to live around it."

I nod, my throat thick.

She'd know what to do about Hallie. She'd see right through me, too. I drove to her house last night. I wanted to just see her. But she wasn't in.

Finn's stare sharpens.

"Why did you turn up at my hospital last night?"

"I—uh…"

Shit. Nothing good's coming to mind fast enough.

"Well?"

"I was looking for Hallie. My wound hurts."

He arches a brow. Then frowns.

"It… hurts?"

"Yeah. A lot."

He glares like Dad used to when he knew I was full of shit.

"Don't lie to me. You know better than that."

I run a hand over my jaw.

What do I even say? That her psycho ex is using a fake name and runs a strip club? That Declan's got me the dirt, and now I've got a death wish with Ben's name on it?

Wait.

"Look. That night she patched me up, she caught her ex cheating. We went back to her place to get rid of the prick."

Finn pinches the bridge of his nose.

"Tell me you didn't fuck her."

I blink, stunned. Fury floods my veins. I stand up.

"No. I didn't. But her ex threatened her. I didn't like that, so Declan did some digging."

I pull up the email and slide my phone across the counter.

"Read it. I'm worried."

He reads in silence, jaw tightening.

"So who is he?"

"No clue. But I'm gonna find out. I went to her house last night too, and she wasn't home."

Finn taps his ringed fingers against the marble.

"I'll send Reg and Rowan to check out that club. If it's legit, we'll know. Keep an eye on her. I'll track what I can from the hospital side. No need to pull Enzo in. Yet."

I scratch my stubble.

"You'll never trust him, will you?"

He glares.

"You don't let the devil in the door, Con."

I like Enzo. Guy's useful. And fast. There's nothing he can't hack. But Finn's not wrong—everything in our world comes with a price.

Right now, we're paying ours by running the Decadence games.

Last week, the idea of chasing girls through the woods would've gotten me hard.

Now? I couldn't care less.

Hallie's in my fucking head.

"You have Hallie's number?" Finn asks.

"Yeah. I do."

"Good. Don't scare her off. Keep it light. From a distance. If it turns bad, I'll clean it up."

His grey eyes flash. That gleam—cold, clinical—means only one thing.

Finn's version of "cleaning up" is the kind that ends lives and erases the mess without a trace.

Me? I'm the brutal kind. Smash the skull, leave the body. Let people remember.

Like James Bowen. Front row execution.

"You coming to my fight?" I ask.

"Wouldn't miss it. In case you need backup."

"I'm getting better. This is pro fighting, not underground anymore. I can't lose my head. Don't wanna rot in jail."

He chuckles.

"Right. Staying on the right side of the law. How many people have you killed since James? Outside of the cage?"

I smirk.

"Still less than you, psycho."

"That's not a brag, Conan."

I pause.

"Is Hallie working today?"

He checks his watch.

"Yeah. For another hour, I think."

I push up from the stool. I know where I'm going before I hit the gym.

JOGGING THROUGH THE HOSPITAL CORRIDOR, I glance at the clock.

Twenty minutes left on her shift.

The nurse behind the front desk watches me like I'm a walking, talking fantasy.

"Hey. I'm here to see Hallie. Dr. Quinn sent me."

Name drop my brother. Instant access.

She taps her keyboard, clicking her pen.

"Sorry, sir. You just missed her. Finished ten minutes ago."

"Fuck," I mutter, clenching my fists.

Guess I'm heading to her house next.

"Was it medical or personal?" she asks.

"Personal. It's important."

She leans across the desk, lips brushing my ear like we're in some kind of fucking movie.

"She probably went to her exercise class. Up the road. Elites. She's there every Friday."

I pull back, eyebrow raised.

"Cool. Thanks."

I head back to the McLaren and hit the dial on Finn's number. He answers instantly.

"Security. Tighten it. A redheaded nurse just told me where Hallie is. Didn't even push her."

"I'll have a word," he says, voice clipped.

"Cool. Speak later."

Reg and Rowan are headed to Starlight, Ben's sleazy little kingdom. I'll probably join them.

I pull into the parking lot and spot her Shelby.

My cock twitches.

Not sure if it's her or the damn car—or the image of her behind the wheel, legs spread, eyes wild.

Inside, the place smells like roses and estrogen. The women behind the desk stop talking and stare.

"Are you lost, sir?" the blonde asks.

"Don't think so." I grin. "I'm here for..." I scan the posters on the wall. "Pilates?"

They look at each other, barely holding in their laughter.

The blonde pouts, clearly amused.

"Sir, have you done a Pilates class before?"

I frown. Not once. I only recognize the name because I remember Hallie talking about it the first night we met.

"Nope. First time for everything, right?"

She laughs and shakes her head.

"Take it easy in there, big man."

"I work out every day. I'm a cage fighter, I'll survive."

I slide her a twenty.

They giggle like I've just walked into a lion's den naked.

"What?" I ask, narrowing my eyes.

"Nothing. Have fun. First door on the right. Grab a mat from the hallway."

I shake my head and smirk.

I'm not here for Pilates.

I'm here to see her.

To make sure she's safe.

And if I get to watch her ass wiggle in those tight workout leggings?

Well, that's just a bonus.

CHAPTER 16
HALLIE

Song- Soaked, Shy Smith.

I stretch out my hips in the frog position on the mat. Back row. As always, my usual spot.

The door creaks open behind me. Every head turns to see who dared interrupt mid-warm-up. And then—Holy. Hell.

The air shifts. Audible gasps emerge. One girl straight-up squeals. But me? I can't move. Can't blink. Conan Quinn. Conan fucking Quinn just walked into my Pilates class.

Black joggers slung low, a tight white tee stretched over every flexed inch of his tattooed torso, and, God help me, a bright pink mat under one arm. His green eyes find mine across the room. He grins like the devil. And walks toward me like he owns the floor.

"Do you know him?" Emma, the girl next to me, whispers. I nod, not tearing my eyes from his. He stops in front of me and looks down. That smile still lingering.

"Hi, trouble."

My breath catches. Words die in my throat. I push my curls forward to hide the cut on my temple, even though I layered on the concealer. I'm not ready to talk about that.

"H-hi." I give him a small wave, and he drops his mat next to mine like it was always meant to be there.

"Well, ladies, we have a new member today," our instructor announces.

Conan turns to her. The whole class openly ogles him like a Greek god just wandered into Pilates. He clears his throat. "Um. Hi. I'm Conan. I'm training for my next fight, and I've been told this class will help."

My brow arches. Coincidence? He sits down and tries, bless him, to copy my pose.

The way he's already grunting doesn't bode well. Flexibility and Conan Quinn were never destined to be best friends.

"Right. Let's start with our double leg stretch. We'll work on the floor first today," the instructor says, clapping as calm music fills the room.

I lie back, legs pulled to my chest. Conan copies, sort of. "Now, deep breath in, release the legs on the breath out. We'll do ten."

By number three, my core burns. I sneak a glance. Conan's face is already flushed. His legs aren't even close to straight.

By number six, he's flat on the floor, arms stretched above his head.

"Fuck me," he whispers.

I shoot him a look, biting back laughter. This is going to be so entertaining.

Fifteen minutes in, Conan's dripping sweat, bright red, and trembling on all fours.

"Hallie. What the hell is this?" he huffs. "Why are my

muscles burning? My legs are fucking wobbly, and I don't know if I can stand up."

His face is a picture. Absolutely horrified.

I burst into laughter. "You'll be fine, beastie. Only another half an hour to go."

His jaw drops. "I'm not even halfway?"

I shake my head, still trying not to laugh. He's trying so hard. It's almost endearing.

"We've not really started yet. You can squat, right?"

He drags himself upright, wiping sweat from his fore-head, arms and legs shaking.

The instructor struts over. He groans under his breath.

"Help. Me," he mouths.

"You're on your own," I whisper back.

"What kind of fighting do you do?" she purrs, placing a hand on her hip and pushing her chest forward.

Conan clears his throat. "MMA."

"Wow. That explains why you're so…" She drags her eyes down his body. "Fit."

My hands clench into fists at my sides. Heat flushes up my neck. I have no claim on him, but this? This burns.

Conan chuckles. "I thought I was, until I came here."

She steps closer, laying her hand on his bicep. "We can work on your flexibility. You'll be a pro in no time."

I want to claw her eyes out.

Next thing I know, I step beside him and my hand is on his ass.

He licks his lips, smirking at me.

I freeze. Did I just claim him in front of a room full of women by full-on ass-grabbing my not-even-boyfriend?

Yes. Yes, I fucking did. Maybe I should try therapy instead of group fitness next time.

"He's good. I've got him covered. Thanks." I flash her a

smile, fake as hell, and give his ass a little squeeze for good measure.

Pity. I quite liked her. Now I want to claw her eyes out.

"Oh." Her face drops. She recovers quickly, plastering on her professional smile. "Okay. Warrior pose next," she chirps and backs away.

Conan turns to me, amusement practically radiating off him. "I thought bossy Hallie was my favorite. But jealous Hallie, claiming me in front of a group of women? That takes the prize."

I jump back like he's just scalded me. He laughs softly.

"I was helping you," I whisper.

"Yeah. Helping me not get laid? Gee. What a good friend you are."

I pout. "Who said we were friends?"

"Oh, is that how you're playing this?"

"Maybe."

His jaw does that adorable twitch of his. "I suddenly don't like that word anymore," he mutters.

We return to the workout, but now his grunts and groans are even more distracting.

"Now it's time for the cat stretch," the instructor announces.

I sneak a glance as the girls in front of us get into position. All asses in the air. Is he watching them?

No. He's watching me. Eyes locked.

"You waiting for me so you can get a look?" he whispers, wiggling his eyebrows suggestively.

I ignore him and drop to all fours.

"No. But you are, aren't you?" I ask, looking over my shoulder at him.

I sit back into the stretch with a moan. "That feels so good."

I make sure he hears every syllable.

"Hallie," he groans, adjusting himself.

"Come on, beastie. One last stretch. Be a good boy."

He squeezes his eyes shut and exhales hard. "You're making this really fucking hard for me, trouble."

"I'm making quite a few things hard."

I wiggle my ass in the air.

"Stop. It. Or I can't be held accountable for my actions in here. Is exhibitionism your thing?"

My body burns.

"What's the blush for, darlin'? Worked out too hard, or you turned on?"

I sit back on my knees and huff. "You're distracting, Conan."

His teeth flash in a grin. "Ditto."

When the class finally ends, I roll up my mat, heart still pounding. I glance over. Conan's already watching me, his expression unreadable.

"You've got a one-on-one session now, haven't you?" I nod toward the instructor still hovering nearby.

"Still jealous?"

The class empties, whispers following us like shadows. But I'm locked in his gaze, my pulse screaming.

"Class is over, Conan."

We're the last two in the room. He steps closer, brushing my hair gently away from my face. His eyes darken.

"Hallie. What happened to your head? That looks like it hurt." His voice softens, that Irish lilt wrapping around me like smoke.

"I—I tripped. Caught it on the table."

He exhales sharply. His jaw tightens. His eyes drop to my side. My hands shake.

"Try again. The truth this time. I want full name,

address, occupation, and fuck, blood type even. They aren't getting away with this."

My stomach knots. His fury is palpable, barely contained at this point.

"It was Ben," I whisper.

"That fucker."

He steps in, cupping my face. "When? Where? What did he do?"

Tears burn behind my eyes. "Last night. He barged into my house, saying I had to get back with him. Said he couldn't protect me unless I did. He was ranting, completely paranoid. I think he was high." My breath catches. "He scared me. I hate admitting that, but… he came into my house. I was alone."

Conan pulls me into his arms. I collapse against his chest, letting the tears fall.

"You should've called me, baby. I would've sorted him."

I shake my head, voice muffled against him. "I didn't want to bother you. I'm not your problem."

He pulls back, cupping my cheeks. His face is softer now, but no less intense.

"You're my friend. I don't have many outside my family. Let me look after you? It's what I'm good at."

I nod slowly, eyes searching his. I trust him. I do. "Should I be worried he's going to come back? I can't keep staying at Lily's."

He brushes his thumb over my lip, gaze locked on mine. "I'll fix this. I'll make it safe for you to go home."

"Thank you," I breathe.

"You're welcome. I want to take you somewhere. My safe haven. A place you can go if you ever need to."

Something about the way he says that… "Follow me there?"

"Yeah."

He releases me, and my chest tightens with the loss of his warmth. But then he laces our fingers together and leads me outside.

To his brand-new McLaren parked next to my Beast.

"Holy shit. That is what you got to replace the Bugatti?"

I run a hand over the fresh black paint. Ugh. It even has black alloys.

"Replace? Not so much. You'll see soon enough."

"She's beautiful. Like… makes me horny, beautiful. Is that a thing?"

He folds his arms across his chest, grinning. "Yeah. It's a thing. Wanna drive her?"

He tosses me the keys. I just about catch them.

"What? You'd let me?"

He nods. "You saw what happened to the Bugatti. You probably won't smash this one worse than that."

I rummage through my bag and hand him my keys. "You take mine?"

"Oh, fuck yeah. Now that'll get me hard—listening to her purr for me."

I laugh, and he squeezes my shoulder.

"Friends?"

His tone is light, but his eyes are searching.

I nod. Heart pounding. "Yeah. I think we can say that now."

"I'll race you there?"

He tips my chin up, nudging his nose against mine. Not a single one of my past 'friends' ever did that. But I'm not pulling away.

"Maybe another day. To make it fair, I'll get us two of the same cars and we'll go to a track. Today, you gotta follow me so you know where I hide."

"Hide what? Bodies?"

He shifts his weight, gaze flickering away.

"You don't wanna know the skeletons I have hiding."

CHAPTER 17
CONAN

As we pull onto the highway, I keep an eye on her in my rearview.

She's handling my baby like she was born in the driver's seat. I expected no less. If she can manage this beast, she's safe in any of my cars.

The fact that she chases the thrill with speed?

Makes me harder than I should admit.

I push down on the accelerator, engine roaring beneath me. Fuck, I need to get myself a Shelby. Just so I can race her.

I hit dial on Rowan's contact and bring the phone to my ear.

"You managed to send a text yet, shithead?" he answers, already mocking.

"You want my fist through your head later?" I snap.

"Nah, I gotta keep my face pretty for my date later."

"Date… you mean a brawl in a strip club?"

I slow for a red light, Hallie pulling up beside me with that goddamn smile that knocks the air out of my lungs.

"I might meet a woman while I'm there."

I roll my eyes. "Yeah, yeah. To take your virginity?"

"Fuck off. I'm not a virgin. Ask Reggie!"

I scoff. "And why would he know?"

He clears his throat. "We—uh. Share sometimes. Chicks dig twin action."

I scrunch my nose. Sharing? Let alone with one of my brothers? That's a bloodbath waiting to happen.

"Interesting overshare. Anyway, change of plans. I'll meet you two there. Make sure you've got enough guns."

There's a beat of silence.

"Should we tell Declan and Finn?"

"No. Finn told me to look out for Hallie. I'm just doing my damn job." Lying's starting to come easy when it comes to her. But I'm not lying about the intel. I just need his address. I'd rather end him with no witnesses.

"Fine with me. Just don't fucking kill him if he is there. I can't contain your rage. And the dead can't speak."

I chuckle. He's not wrong. I gotta keep my MMA license clean and hear what the bastard has to say before I break his jaw.

"You make me sound psychotic." I pause, then slam my foot on the pedal to see if Hallie keeps up. "Also, you're wrong. The dead can speak. We just have to blackmail a medium or whatever."

"Fair point. And no, you're not psychotic. That's Finn. You're more of a… short fuse. You wear your emotions on your sleeve. On the plus side, that means you've got them."

"Right. Thanks for that. Did you train to become a shrink recently, Rowan?"

"Nah. I just know psychos. You kinda have to when your fucking twin is one."

It's always the quiet ones. Finn and Reggie prove that. Silent. Deadly. Monsters, but ours.

"Well, we wouldn't change our brothers, so we live with it. I'll meet you at the club at seven."

"You got it, Con."

I cut the call and signal left, heading down the gravel road to my solace.

As I roll into the unit, Hallie pulls up beside me. From the outside, it's nothing, just another industrial shell. But behind that steel door?

It's my kingdom.

I get out, stride to her door, and pull it open.

"M'lady." I offer her my best mock curtsy as she slides out.

Fuck. She looks good behind the wheel of my car.

"So. What's this place, then?"

I tap my nose. "Come on."

I unlock the metal door and shove it open.

My busted Bugatti stands on the lift in center stage, a monument to obsession. Ever since I got behind the wheel of one in Russia, saving Charlotte from her douche ex-husband, the first thing I did on my return was buy this.

"You fix them up yourself?"

I nod, hand on the small of her back as I guide her in.

"This is awesome."

She turns left and gasps.

My collection. My pride.

"Is that—?" She rushes to the one-of-a-kind gold-plated Aston Martin.

"Yeah, that's her."

She spins to face me, eyes wide. Mouth parted.

"Okay. Which is your favorite?"

I move to the only car under a cover and yank it off.

"Shut up. The Ford GT40? What is it, like 1960s? It's immaculate, Conan. Oh my god."

That pitch in her voice, like pure delight, it swells something in my chest I don't want to name.

"She was my dad's. Had her shipped over after he died. Did a few fixes. She runs like a dream."

"That's incredible," she breathes. "A proper car. You have taste, sir."

"That I do." I bite the inside of my cheek.

"So. Mechanic by day, fighter by night? What else don't I know about you?"

Everything. That I'm born into a mafia family. That I've killed for sport and family. That I ran an underground ring before I was legal. That I live in a repurposed chocolate factory with a secret sex club hidden inside. That I want to bend her over the hood and make her scream my name.

Or maybe… I want her to run. So I can chase.

I shake my head. "Not much more to tell."

She steps closer, air crackling between us.

"Lies. There's way more under the surface with you."

"I guess you gotta work on removing the layers, darlin'."

She bats my chest, and I catch her wrist.

Fuck, I want to taste her again. But I resist.

"Wanna see the rest?"

"There's more?"

"Hmmm."

I lace our fingers and lead her through the back.

My gym. My war zone. A steel cage center stage. Ice bath. Sauna. No distractions. No excuses.

"So you never need to leave this place?" she asks, eyes taking it all in. She pulls her hand away and wanders toward the rear door.

"What's in here?"

"Bodies."

"Ha-ha."

"A bedroom."

She tries the handle. Locked.

"Only special people can unlock that."

Beyond it, the woods. My second hunting ground.

"Right."

Her shoulders dip as she walks back to me.

"Special people? You mean like the instructor today? Would you let her in there?"

That spark in her eyes? It scorches me.

"Hallie," I warn.

My chest tightens.

"I don't want to fuck her." Blunt. Raw. But it's the truth.

She sucks in a breath.

"I don't care if you do."

Liar. My heart races and my palms start to sweat.

"I didn't want her to flirt with me. I was never going to entertain her."

The words fall out too fast. Too honest.

She twists her fingers together, her eyes locked on mine.

"You can do whatever. I'm not stopping you," she whispers.

I want her to stop me.

I want her to be as desperate for me as I am for her.

"I followed you to that class because I wanted to see you."

She bites back a grin, and some small relief pulses in my ribs.

"Right."

Fuck. I'm flustered.

And she's acting unbothered?

Except I can read every tell—the dilated pupils, the heat rising up her neck. It's a mask. She's hiding behind it.

"Hallie."

"Yes, Conan?" she teases, head tilted.

I step closer.

"I find it hot when you try to hide how much you want me."

She glances up through her lashes. "I want you, do I?"

"You're the one who grabbed my ass to stake your claim. You're down bad for me, trouble."

"Am not." Her chin tips in defiance.

"The hunt hasn't even begun, baby." I press my nose to hers.

She has no idea.

The thrill of the chase is my fucking religion.

Our silence is electric. I've never felt more alive.

"You can't chase something that isn't running, beastie."

A dark chuckle rumbles from my chest.

"Philosophical."

Her gaze flicks to my mouth, and I back away.

Soon. She'll run. And I'll catch her.

But right now?

Right now, I just need her safe.

CHAPTER 18

HALLIE

When he steps back, I feel like I've lost something.

"This reminds me, I need to get mine serviced soon."

I've put it off because, simply, I can't afford the expense. First I have to get on top of my bills, then I'll make sure my car is in tip-top shape before I start racing her again. This was something I used to help my dad with, but I am in no way qualified enough to do it myself.

"I'll do it."

"No." I blurt it out too fast.

"Don't trust me? I know what I'm doing. And there's a few scuffs on the paintwork I can fix too."

I hold up my hand.

"No, I don't mean that. I mean, one, I'll have no car, and I need to get to work. And two, I've got bills to pay that are more important, unfortunately."

Conan tuts.

"You keep the McLaren until I'm done. It won't take me

long. I'd like to work on her. See what's under that hood. And I don't want your cash. You can just owe me one."

My heart rate picks up.

"Owe you what?"

"I'll call in the favor one day."

I squeeze my legs together.

"I'm not a whore."

The words roll off my tongue before I can stop them.

He frowns.

"I-I don't mean— I was talking about patching me up most likely. Got a few fights lined up. I'm bound to need medical help. Might free up Finn if you can do it instead."

"Oh."

I let out an awkward laugh.

I want to hit my head against the wall. Sometimes my brain and mouth don't communicate fast enough.

"Sorry. And are you sure it's not too much hassle? You seem busy."

He shrugs.

"Not too busy for the right people, trouble."

A burst of excitement runs through me. I get to drive the McLaren.

I can't believe he trusts me with it.

Shame there aren't any races coming up. I'd wipe the floor with them in that thing.

"And this place, Hallie. If you ever don't feel safe and can't get hold of me, come here."

He pushes a key into my hand and holds it tight.

"Or, if you're bored and wanna help me fix up my Bugatti, you can always do that too."

He grins, and my heart races.

"Now that sounds like fun. Maybe you could teach me some self-defense too."

He rubs a hand across his forehead.

"That actually isn't a bad idea, trouble."

I offer him a small smile.

He's fun to be around. He gets me. He makes me laugh.

"I gotta go take care of your problem now. Want me to follow you home first?"

I press my hands on his chest.

"What exactly are you going to do to him?"

A darkness flashes across his eyes. It doesn't scare me, though.

"Depends how he reacts, Hallie. But he won't ever bother you again once I'm done. That a good enough answer?"

"I guess it'll have to be. And no, I don't need babysitting all the way home. I wanna drive your car for as long as possible."

He gives me a curt nod.

As I step back from him, it feels weird just leaving. So I wrap my arms around his waist.

He goes tense, but then his huge arms wrap around me and squeeze back.

"What's this for?" he asks softly.

"A thank you."

He rests his head on top of mine.

"No need to thank me, darlin'. I got you."

I didn't even realize I needed someone to catch me when I was falling.

And then Conan crashes into my life.

Making me see how fucking miserable I am, dragging myself through life.

The spark I lost seems to ignite again when I'm around him.

But he's just a friend.

"I'll give you a text when she's ready for you."

CHAPTER 19
CONAN

Driving the Range Rover feels dull compared to Hallie's Shelby. But I don't know how this shit's gonna go down. Never know when I gotta shove a body in the trunk.

I pull up next to Reggie and Rowan and kill the engine.

"Are we expecting a party?" I smirk, pulling out a cigarette.

"With you? Probably," Reggie replies, opening the trunk. "And here's your present."

I blow out smoke, eyes on the stash. Knives. Guns. Even some throwing stars.

I pocket a few.

"You know me so well."

We grab what we need. I go for a pistol, an easy choice and concealable. My pocketknife's always on me anyway. Most of the time, my fists are enough. But I gotta protect myself. Can't risk it before a fight.

Before we head in, I pull up the tracking app on my phone. Hallie's still out driving the McLaren. I grin watching the red dot move.

She better be safe.

"So what's the plan?" Rowan cuts in.

"We go in as normal customers. Ask for a booth, ask to see the owner. Business-related. Maybe slide 'em some cash. Or show them the guns. Quiet way first."

"And if that fails?"

"The Conan way. I beat my way through the doors."

Reggie nods. Rowan grins like he lives for chaos.

"I prefer the second option."

I lead the way, pushing into the club past the bouncers.

"Table for three?"

He sizes me up, then steps back.

"Sure. Stephanie will show you over."

A short woman in a gold glitter thong and no bra struts over.

"What kind of experience you after? You want to look or touch, sir?"

"Look," I snap.

"Really?" Rowan hisses behind me.

"Are you kidding me?" I throw him a glare.

She leads us to a booth, brings champagne, and slides her hand over my forearm.

"I'll be up on stage soon."

I smile at her. "Nice. Now, I do have to ask you a favor." I motion her close.

Her breasts brush my shoulder. All I see is Hallie.

"I need to speak to the owner," I whisper, pulling a fat wad of cash from my pocket.

"He doesn't see guests."

"It's important. I'll make it worth your while. No one will know."

She sucks in a shaky breath.

"Tell me what you want," I say, firm. I grab more cash.

She glances at the bar.

"Let me give you a dance. Make it less obvious. Gerry's watching me."

I nod and lean back. She straddles me, hips rolling.

Nothing.

My dick isn't even mildly interested.

"You're incredibly handsome," she purrs, dragging a nail down my chest.

I shove the money into her g-string. I've got shit to do.

"Where is he?" I ask quietly.

"He's not here. He never is since he started working with his cousins. But I know his schedule. He's at the downtown boxing gym, the shady one in the warehouse."

Her lips hover by mine. I resist cringing. But I got what I came for.

"Thank you."

She slides off me and struts back to the pole.

"Right. Let's go."

"You ain't even hard? Are you alright?" Rowan squints at me.

"I'm good."

"So, where we going?" Reggie asks.

"For a punch up."

I rise, the guys following as we head for the car.

"Call Drago. Tell him to hack the security cameras and wipe it," I order the twins as I pull up to the run-down boxing club. Tin warehouse. Four cars out front.

I pop the glovebox and pull out Delilah, my favorite pistol.

Reggie's already on the call. Rowan hops out and joins me.

"What's the plan?"

"Get everyone out. I'll deal with him. You keep watch."

He nods just as Reggie joins, grabbing my AK-47 from the trunk.

"Bit extreme?" Rowan asks.

Reggie's eyes burn cold. "We wanna scare them, right?" He loads the ammo like he's brushing his teeth.

"See? Psycho," Rowan whispers to me, and I roll my eyes.

"Let's go."

I lead us in. Reggie fires up into the ceiling.

Silence. Fear. My favorite combination.

"Everyone out. Now!" I bark.

Two guys sparring on the mats bolt past.

I spot Ben in the ring with some big blond dude. I head for the ropes.

"You," I point to the blond.

"I don't want trouble. I can pay you soon." He holds up gloved hands.

"I don't want your fucking money. I need half an hour with this dickhead." I jab my finger at Ben.

Big guy sighs with relief. Ben looks like he might puke.

"You're not with Faz?" Blondie asks.

I chuckle.

Faz runs the underground fights. We're good, but I keep my distance now.

"Not directly. But if you breathe a word of this, I can be."

He nods, backing toward the ropes.

"I've got amnesia, don't worry."

"Good."

At the door, he hesitates. "Uh... can you clean up any mess?"

"Fuck off," Reggie shoves him out and locks the door.

"You," I say, eyes on Ben. "Think you're tough for laying hands on a woman?"

"She's a liar."

I slam my gun into his jaw. He stumbles.

"Wrong answer."

I grab him by the scruff and shove him back.

"Fight someone who hits back. See how you like it."

He wipes his blood and grins. "It's too late."

"What is?"

"To save Hallie."

"From you? I'm right on fucking time."

He shrugs. No remorse. That lights the fuse.

I toss my gun and kick it off the canvas.

Before he can think, I punch him in the nose.

Shit, that feels good.

"Fuck!" He grabs his face as blood gushes.

"What do you want from me?"

"Nothing. I just want to hurt you. You left a mark on her. Now I'll leave a whole collection on you."

"All this over her?" he sneers.

I lunge, grab him at the waist, and slam him into the ropes. When he's on all fours, I swing my leg and kick his jaw.

He drops, face covered, curled up. Pathetic.

"Get up. Or are you too pussy to fight a man?" I kick his ribs. He grunts.

Blood drips from his mouth. He wobbles to his feet and takes a swing. I duck easily and chuckle.

"Jesus. You need a new trainer."

He stops. I jog on the spot. I could run rings around this asshole.

"I don't get your obsession with her. You're outta her league. She didn't satisfy me. Couldn't even stop me from sticking my dick elsewhere."

My vision goes red. Blood pounds in my ears.

"Is that what gets you off? Putting women down? Does it make up for your pencil dick?"

I grab him by the throat and lift him.

"You're gonna stay the fuck away from Hallie. This is your one and only warning. Touch her again, and I'll make sure you spend the rest of your life being fed through a tube. Or I'll bury you myself."

He gulps.

I drop him. He hits the mat hard.

"What, you her bodyguard now?" he coughs.

"Stop. Fucking. Talking about her."

His blood stained teeth emerge as he smiles. He's batshit crazy. Maybe I should just kill him. He's one of those pricks that will keep popping up.

"Did she suck your dick? Do that swirly thing? That mouth and her pussy—only good things about her. Miserable bitch. I wish I got to—"

I don't let him finish.

He makes me sick.

There's so much more to Hallie. She's brilliant. Smart. Funny. Sassy. Bossy. She lights up a room.

She makes my mind quiet.

She's worth ten million of him.

My mind blanks. My fists don't.

Punch after punch I demolish him. I jump on him, slamming my weight into every hit.

"You deserve every one of these."

His blood splashes on my face. His screams feed me. I thrive off his fear.

Until he goes limp. Even that doesn't stop me.

"Conan, fuck, stop!" Rowan's voice breaks through.

I blink. My lungs burn. I crawl off him, panting.

All I see is red.

"Is he dead?" I ask.

"I don't know. We ain't no doctors, Con."

I grunt. Not enough. I wanted to torture him more. His face is already starting to swell.

I guess it's time to call Finn.

"Conan. What have you done?"

I stare at the body. "What're the chances you can bring someone back to life? I wanna kill him again. Think I rushed it."

Finn chuckles. It cools my rage.

"I'm a doctor, not a fucking necromancer. Are you sure he's dead?"

"Lot of blood."

"Check his pulse."

I kneel, press fingers to his neck.

"Wait. You're helping me?"

Pulse—barely. Fuck, am I losing my touch?

"Yeah. I'm on my way. Wanna see what you'd do in round two. Cunt deserves it."

"How do you know who it is?"

"Con. I know everything."

"Nah. Twins ratted me out."

"Damn right they did. Call Drago. Get a cleanup crew."

"You taking him to the hospital?" I ask Finn.

"God, no. Got a setup at mine we can use."

I raise a brow, wiping the blood off my hand on my tee.

"Why the hell do you even need a medical room in your house? Should I sleep with one eye open in case you start needing test subjects or some shit?"

"Start?" he laughs.

"You better fucking—"

"Bye, bro."

My phone buzzes again. My heart skips.

HALLIE

Thank you again for fixing up my baby. I appreciate it more than you know. Speak to you soon. Have a nice night. <3

A heart. It makes mine race.

I look at the man at my feet and laugh. Told her I'd fix it.

ME

You're more than welcome. I'll text you tomorrow. Get some sleep. And it's safe to go home, trouble.

She replies instantly.

HALLIE

Do I want to ask?

Blood smears my phone.

ME

Probably best you don't. Just take my word. Night, darlin.

HALLIE

Sweet dreams, beastie.

I check the McLaren tracker again. She's nearby. A bar. Maybe I'll swing by.

I don't know what this is between us. But I know one thing.

Around her, it's calm.

"Get off your damn phone and clean the mess you made," Reggie barks.

I scowl. "You forgetting who works for who?"

He stands his ground as I stride over until I'm in his face, then we both crack up laughing.

"You think I wanna test you after that? You're good. Me and Rowan will clean. You keep sexting, buddy." He claps my shoulder.

Rowan nods fast. "Yeah, what he said."

"Pussies. Find his phone and wallet while you're at it," I tell them.

They might not be blood, but they're family.

The doors crash open and Finn strides in.

He kneels, assesses the body.

"Nice job, Con," he mutters, full of sarcasm.

"He hurt Hallie."

Finn's jaw ticks. "Elaborate."

"Attacked her in her home. She's scared. Got a nasty mark on her head."

Finn spits on Ben, then straightens.

"And you want me to keep him alive?" He asks.

I scratch my jaw.

"Stripper said he's working with his cousin. So maybe some family. He's a Brit."

Finn's eyes go sharp.

"You think—?"

"Nah. Too pathetic to be a Bowen."

London mafia. We lost Dad to avoid war with them. We owe them nothing.

"They'd be stupid to come near us now."

Finn nods. "Let's keep an eye on it. Killing a son ain't the same as killing a father."

I swallow.

I thought I could outrun the past.

But if it catches me, I'll kill it again.

CHAPTER 20
HALLIE

Lily is busy yapping away to the cute guy who bought her a drink.

I'm frowning at my phone, re-reading the message from Pete.

Twenty thousand dollars.

That would mean I could pay Lily back, catch up on my mortgage, and stop drowning in extra shifts.

But I promised her no more of this. And I don't even have my car to race.

"Hallie, what's up?"

I blink, look up at her, and quickly lock my phone.

"Nothing. Just waiting for you to finish flirting. He was hot." I wink, hoping it's enough to steer her away.

She grins, slipping into the seat beside me. "Yeah. He's got my number. Maybe once my new roomies move back home, I'll invite him over."

Guilt punches me in the chest.

"Lily, I'll be out of your hair soon. I promise."

Conan said it's safe, and I trust him. So tomorrow, I'll go home.

She leans across the table and places her hand over mine.

"I didn't mean that. I was joking. You and Bertie are welcome as long as you want. Forever, if you want."

I sigh. I should go home.

"Lils, you know we'll be bickering by next week."

We burst into giggles and clink our cocktails.

"That's why we're besties."

"Have you heard from Dickface?"

I shake my head.

"Good. Maybe Conan's already fixed your problem."

She fiddles with her straw, grinning like she knows more than she's letting on.

"Yeah. He said he has. The asshole deserves it."

I don't want to know the details, I just trust his word.

"Damn right he does. If your dad were alive, he'd have skinned him."

"Yeah, he would've." I stir my drink and stare into the red liquid, watching the ice melt.

My dad would've probably killed him and smiled the whole way to prison.

Lily's phone vibrates across the table. She curses under her breath.

"I gotta take this. I've been chasing this artist for months. His agent's finally giving me the time of day."

"Go. Answer." I wave her away.

She hurries off toward the exit, already muttering into the phone. I pull my phone back out, that damn message burning a hole in my thoughts.

And before I can talk myself out of it, I reply.

ME

Count me in. But I'll have a different car
this time. I will send over the plate later.

Pete replies immediately.

PETE

Nice one. I'll text details tomorrow.
Officially added you to the lineup. Be good
to see you, it's been a while.

ME

See you tomorrow.

I tap my nails against the table, heart thudding like a warning.

Lily returns, bright-eyed and bouncing.

"Good news?"

"Yes! He wants a showing next month!"

"I'm proud of you." And I mean it.

"And I am of you. Now—are you taking me for a proper spin in Conan's car or what?"

Just the sound of his name makes my cheeks flush.

"You really gotta bang him, Hallie. Get this flustery mess out of your system." She waves her hands at me like I'm some lovesick princess.

"We're friends. That's it. Let's not complicate it. And my boss is his brother. It's messy."

She rolls her eyes.

"I give it a week."

I tilt my head. "A week?"

"Yeah. Until you two finally bang."

I glance around before muttering, "Lily, I think he will literally ruin me."

She spits out her drink, laughing.

"Fuck. Off. That's the worst excuse I've ever heard. You want him to ruin you. That's the whole point. Jesus, Hallie. Your choice in men before Conan needs a goddamn case study."

"Hey! They were all hot."

She snorts. "Yeah, hot but shit in bed. Pointless. Now you've got hot and a sex god, and you're what, friends? That's not the Hallie I know and love."

I swallow the lump in my throat.

"It's been a rough couple of years. I'm trying to find my groove again. I like Conan as a friend. I don't want to ruin that. If we sleep together… I don't know. He might not want me around anymore."

"He's not a one-and-done guy."

"You don't know that."

"Does he look at you like he'd burn the city to the ground for one smile?"

I bite the inside of my cheek.

"I think so."

I know so.

"Don't you think it's time to do something just for you again? Stop overthinking for a second? And give him some credit. I think he's obsessed with you."

Lily's been with me through everything. The worst of it. Lily's the one person in my life who's never left. She'd drag me out of hell if she had to and never judge me for ending up there in the first place.

Everyone needs a Lily in their life.

"If I could turn off the four thousand thoughts in my brain, trust me, I would."

That's half my issue. My brain never stops. Sometimes it's amazing. I can juggle a million things at once, ace anything academic, and dive into any creative pursuit.

But the other side? Perfectionism. Self-doubt. Constant overthinking.

I'll talk myself out of something before I even give it a chance.

ADHD is like that. It's my sparkle, but sometimes, it dims everything else if I let it.

"Maybe," she says softly, "you just need someone who helps you turn it off."

I reach for the McLaren keys in my purse.

"Possibly. But for now, driving does that for me."

She stirs her straw, quieter now.

"Yeah. I get that. That's what ballet used to do for me."

"Are you ever going back to that? You were so good, Lil."

She freezes. Her expression shifts like a storm behind her eyes.

"No." Her response is quick and final.

I shut my mouth.

I watch her carefully. I've never pushed, never made her explain. One day she was at the peak of her ballet career, and the next, she was done. Her father opened her a gallery, and she never danced again.

"If you ever want to talk, you know I'll listen. Any time and about anything."

"Love you," she says, smiling a little too sadly for this place.

"I love you too. Wanna go for a drive, then?"

Distraction. That's one thing I've mastered.

CHAPTER 21

CONAN

Tapping my fingers on the table, the silence is thick between us. Enzo summoned the whole crew—everyone's here but Dr. Quinn. Usually, it's me who's late. But today, I raced from my garage and still made it on time. Might score some brownie points with Enzo for once.

Drago's tapping away on his laptop opposite me. I turn to Declan.

"Isabella still want to come to the gym with me after school?"

His little girl is my favorite person in the world. I love being an uncle. She's got fire like her mother and the temper of her father. Honestly, she's probably going to be a damn good fighter. Declan's not keen on it, though. Wants to keep her out of harm's way, always.

Though part of the deal is she teaches me to dance. Declan even bought me a pink tutu. So every Thursday, I'm spinning around in a fucking skirt. She gets these fits of giggles about it, and somehow that makes it all okay.

"Yeah. She did mention she wants to help you with the cars too. If you have time?"

I grin.

"I always have time for that little whirlwind. Actually, I think you need to pop another one out."

Declan coughs, and my eyes go wide.

"Is she?" I whisper.

"Shut it."

The door flies open, and the room falls silent again.

"This better be fucking good. I just had to call in some serious favors at the hospital." Finn storms in, slamming the door behind him.

I bite back a grin as Declan kicks me under the table.

I can't look at Enzo—he's got a short fuse, especially with Finn. But it goes both ways.

Finn's gray eyes meet mine; I discreetly nod toward the head of the table. He rolls his eyes.

"Afternoon, Enzo."

He yanks out a chair opposite me and Declan next to Drago, who, like me, is barely holding back a smile at Finn's outburst. Drago fits in well.

"Saving lives is more important than taking them, Dr. Quinn?" Enzo's thick Italian accent cuts through the room.

Finn glances at Declan, who scowls, then checks his Rolex.

"Yeah. In daylight hours. Remember, I have to keep my job at the hospital to make this whole fucking illusion real. But I'm here, aren't I?"

I clear my throat and get another kick from Declan.

"Do it again, and I'll throw you across the table," I whisper.

"Try me. I'll shoot you in the face."

"No. You wouldn't. Because you love your little brother. Finn is the one in trouble, not me."

I tease him.

Enzo's accent stops me from saying more.

"Yes. You're here. So quit the bratty complaining. This was important enough for me to fly in from Vegas."

Enzo leans back in his chair.

"Enzo. It's good. We're all here and listening," Declan cuts in.

Enzo nods, his eyes on me. I straighten my back and sit up straight.

"Conan. Your games are next. I've sent over the final contestants. This year you'll have ten."

I flick a glance at Finn. The more contestants for the Decadence Chase, the busier Finn is eliminating those who entered the women.

"Okay." I scratch my stubble.

"I do have a request, though," I tell them.

All eyes on me. Here goes nothing.

"What?"

"The reward will be two million, but no option for a submissive for a year. I need that in the contract."

I look to Drago for help. He's the guy drafting all the legal shit. A grey area of what he did for Vlad in Russia, but the guy knows everything—martial arts, law, business, cooking, and teaching Isabella. You name it, he does it.

"So what do you exactly get out of this?"

I shrug.

"You don't want a submissive?" Enzo arches a brow.

"Yes. Just one specific one who's not entering."

Finn rolls his eyes.

"You want to extend her an invitation?" Drago's deep Russian voice cuts through.

"No," I blurt.

I can't have Hallie knowing what happens in Decadence. Maybe one day I'll show her Inferno. We can have fun there. But the games? The Chase? No. Never.

We came up with these games when we were all single, trying to gain standing in the US with Enzo.

Five years passed. The Quinn brothers are solid here now.

The games are the pinnacle of maintaining order. But there's always another way.

"Don't fucking tell me this is your last year as well?" Enzo grits out.

I look to Declan. He must've told Enzo his games are done. Charlotte would chop his balls off if he continued with it now.

"It could be. Let's just do this year first and see."

I've never had a serious relationship. Don't know if I want that now. Or if it's even possible with my lifestyle. Hallie might wake up one day and decide I'm not enough. Or she might see who I really am.

My kinks aren't for everyone. My anger isn't either. But I'd never fucking hurt her.

Enzo tuts, shaking his head.

"Regardless of Decadence, even if they stop theirs, we've got my trials. Worst case, members start their own versions, or we get creative. There's always a way that won't ruin my brother's relationships," Finn cuts in.

I offer a smile to Finn. No matter what, he'll defend me until death—and I'd do the same for him.

We're family. Always. We owe it to our parents.

Enzo turns to Finn.

"How are you getting on? All families taken care of from Declan's games?"

Finn swallows.

"One more. He's out of state. Me and Drago are tracking him down. Think he's in Chicago."

Enzo nods.

Declan's contestants were daughters of Mafia bosses. Enzo targets a new pool of villains each game.

"Who are we going after with my Chase?" I ask.

He smirks.

"Rival club owners."

"As in clubs like Inferno?"

He nods.

"I've expanded fast in the industry. Need to whittle out the bad quietly."

"So my contestants… work at the clubs?"

"Some, probably. Others are daughters or partners. Their sacrifice has to be meaningful."

I swallow the lump in my throat.

"So their best earner, wives, or daughters."

"Pieces of shit," Declan mutters.

That's the point.

We let them think we're the worst. Pure evil.

But when they give up their women to Decadence, they sign away their lives.

And the women?

They don't meet that fate.

Maybe we're evil, but if it means destroying the real villains, so be it.

"Okay. Fine. Drago, I'm training for my fight. Can you go through the applications and arrange appropriate outfits? Matching masks?"

Drago scratches his head.

"Uh. I guess?"

I chuckle. He's still not used to the States, but so far, he's been damn helpful.

"Ask Reggie or Rowan if you need help."

Enzo clicks his knuckles, calling us back.

"I'm going off-grid for a while. Some things need sorting. I trust you to continue the games? No fuck-ups?"

"You have our word, Enzo," Declan confirms.

"No more ghosts coming out of the closet."

I frown. More ghosts?

Fuck, I have a graveyard full. Many ready to show up.

"Any ghosts we should know about?"

Enzo shakes his head and downs a scotch.

"None that concern you. But Arthur Bowen's asking questions. I assume he's pissed over James' death?" He pins me with a stare.

I look at Finn, who's poker-faced. We're keeping our suspicions about Ben quiet.

"I ain't heard shit from him, Enzo."

Declan shifts.

"He called weeks ago. I never returned. It was in the middle of my games and everything with Charlotte. He wasn't important."

I pull back and look at Declan.

"They know we're here?"

As much as I want to smash Arthur's head in, I have bigger fish to fry.

"No. He called my old line."

"Watch your back. I don't have much sway in the UK yet. If you have to eliminate the threat, do it quietly."

"They got their revenge for James. We owe them nothing."

My anger radiates. They took my father's life for my sins.

"We'll sort it, Enzo. Thanks for the heads-up," Declan says calmly.

As Enzo says goodbye and the door closes, I slouch back in my chair.

Finn grins. "Just send me and Con back to London. I'll make it impossible for Arthur to sniff us out."

I like that option.

Declan shakes his head.

"Drago, can you dig on him? See his movements?"

"Sure. Send info, I'll dust off my hacking manual."

I like this guy.

Our own Enzo, the Russian version who's less bossy.

I clap my hands.

"Now that the riveting meeting's done, anyone fancy a gym session with me and Isabella later?"

"I have to get back to the hospital."

My heart flutters. Hallie.

"Want a lift?"

Finn frowns.

"Why? What will I owe you?"

I fake hurt.

"Nothing. I'm heading to the garage. Gotta finish the Shelby."

"Hallie's?" Finn grins.

"Yeah."

I play it cool.

"You think I missed the half-million dollar McLaren at my work that belongs to you? Dumbass."

He stands, rounds the table, and smacks my head. I grab his wrist and squeeze.

"You can't work if I smash your hand to pieces."

I taunt him.

"I said watch out for her, not fall in love."

I release him.

"That isn't—"

He cuts me off.

"I see everything."

He backs away to the door. I clench my fists.

It's not love. I don't know how to love.

"Come on then, chauffeur," Finn calls.

"I guess me and Drago will go for a drink while we dig," Declan mumbles.

"You got a blade on you?"

"Yeah. Why?"

"Pass it here."

He places the cool metal in my palm. I flick it open.

The wound on my thigh is healing nicely. Hallie did good.

I push up my black tee and run the blade lightly along my skin—two inches, just above my left hip.

"Conan. What the fuck?" Declan jumps up and snatches the knife.

"What? It's part of my plan," I laugh.

"You need help."

Declan hits the side of my head.

"Yeah… that's exactly the plan. Medical help." I pull my top down over the cut. Can't let Finn see it. Don't want his help.

CHAPTER 22

HALLIE

I have this weird feeling gnawing at me. While I've got a few minutes to myself, I pull my phone out of my white coat.

Conan and I had a brief text exchange earlier, then radio silence.

I'm actually debating heading to his garage once my shift is over to see how he's getting on. I like being around him.

He's fun.

But the sexual tension may kill me off. I've never had to use my toys so damn much in my life. It's the only thing helping me sleep at the moment.

I've had a taste of him, and I crave more.

Yet, we're both resisting. Can we keep that up?

When is the right moment if it hasn't arrived already?

I sigh, slouching back in my chair.

Maybe I should keep some distance. I'll probably blurt out I've entered his car in a race, which is worth more than I will ever earn in my life.

Oh god.
My heart races.
What the hell am I doing?

CHAPTER 23

CONAN

I pull into the parking lot and spot my McLaren, so I take the spot next to it.

"Why are you parking up, Conan?" Finn asks suspiciously.

"I have something I need Hallie to look at."

He opens his door but stops to look back at me.

"Why couldn't I just look?"

"You're already late for work." I shoo him away.

"Don't distract her. I need her," he warns.

I hold my hands up defensively.

"Swear."

He huffs and slams my door shut, making the windows shake.

"Bastard," I mutter.

I head in through the double doors and straight to the reception area.

"Oh. Hi, Mr. Quinn," the redhead says sweetly, shoving her pastry to one side.

Placing my hands on the desk, I whisper, "Is Hallie free?"

She offers me a smile.

"Dr. Quinn already warned me you'd be here. Go and take a seat, she will call you out in a minute."

"Cool. Thank you."

I head over to the chairs and sit outside her door. Just as Finn comes out of his and calls for Mrs. Ellen Maple.

We lock eyes, and he glares, then switches to a smile for his patient.

Fucking psycho.

The little old lady trots past him and he holds back.

"Unless you want me to schedule you for heart surgery. I don't wanna see you in my hospital again." He points at me.

I clutch my hands over my chest.

"It hurts," I whine.

That gets the attention of the other patients waiting.

"Enough. Behave." He stomps over and leans down.

"Conan?" Hallie's sweet voice is music to my ears. Finn straightens himself.

"Me." I wave at her.

She looks between me and Finn with a frown.

"Everything okay?" she asks.

"Yes. Fine. I just need you to see my brother real quick. No idea what he's done, but here he is anyway. Sorry." He offers her an apologetic look.

He storms back to his office and closes the door.

"Don't know why he's got a stick up his ass today," I tell Hallie as I stand.

"Probably because we're here to keep people alive and ready for heart surgery, Conan." She lowers her tone, looking over her glasses at me.

Dear God, she's beautiful.

"You haven't even—" She holds up her pen to cut me off and turns her back, waltzing into her office.

She heads over to her desk and takes a seat.

I close the door behind me, but she doesn't turn around from her computer screen.

"Take your trousers off, Mr. Quinn," she demands.

I bite on my lip, my dick starting to twitch in my boxers.

"You haven't even asked what's wrong with me? You wanna see the goods?"

She slowly spins in her chair, pushing her glasses back with a smirk.

"I assumed you've lost your balls, sir. That's what you want me to look at?"

I blink at her, trying to ignore the fact that my cock is getting hard just looking at her.

Her caramel curls are pulled back into a bun. The black frames of her glasses just highlighting her brown eyes.

The clear gloss on her lips that I want to lick off.

The way her burgundy scrubs hide her curves that I know are under there.

Maybe this was a bad idea.

"My balls are perfectly fine, trouble."

She shakes her head.

"They can't be. Because if they were there, you'd have asked me on a date by now, rather than following me around and faking medical issues to see me."

Well, damn. She really did catch me out. Well. Not quite.

I slowly pull up my top with a smirk, revealing the cut on my stomach.

"A scratch. You came here for a scratch?"

I shake my head.

"Knife wound."

Her plump lips open, and she stands, taking a step towards me.

"It's clean."

Yeah. I should know; I did it myself.

"Does it need stitches?"

"Conan. That isn't what your brother's department does. We aren't ER. We're cardiovascular. I only patched you up that time as a favor for Dr. Quinn."

I look down at her and pull my top back down.

"Yeah. I know," I say quietly.

"Will I survive?" I whisper.

She giggles and grabs the hem of the T-shirt. I clasp my hand over her wrist.

"Maybe I just wanted to say hi," I tell her.

"You could have just texted me."

She looks up at me through her lashes, and I'm a goner.

"I prefer the real thing. And I like the chase."

Her cheeks flush and I lean down.

"You look beautiful today, Hallie," I whisper in her ear.

She clears her throat and taps my shoulder, so I straighten myself to stand.

"Sorry. Too much?"

She shakes her head with a smile.

"No. Just not at work, Mr. Quinn."

I take a step towards her, backing her into the cabinet, so I rest my hand above her head.

"So when?"

I glance down at her gripping onto the side.

"We will figure it out, I guess. Keep chasing and see what happens."

I pull away and nod.

"Whatever you want, trouble." I push a stray curl behind her ear.

Her breath hitches, and I stare at her shining lips.

No. I'll be good. For now. I just don't know how much

longer I can behave around her. I have to figure out what she wants.

But by the way she's biting her lip and blushing, I'd say it's the same as what I need.

"Your car should be ready in a couple of days, darlin'. I'll let you know when it's done. Me and Isabella are working on it tonight."

She frowns and chews on her nail. I can't help but smile.

"Isabella is my little niece. Declan's daughter. She's my little shadow at the garage."

"Oh. I wasn't—"

She's flustered, and it's so fucking hot.

"Yeah, yeah. I'll see you soon, trouble." I give her a wink as I head to the door.

"Your cut?" she asks, rushing back over.

"You know as well as I do, I need a band-aid at best for it."

"Don't cut yourself just to see me again, Mr. Quinn. Otherwise I'll send you to psychiatric."

I erupt into laughter.

"No shrink wants to see inside my head, baby. Trust me."

She offers me a small smile and hands me a band-aid.

"I kinda wanna see," she says quietly.

I grab hold of her hand, and we stare into each other's eyes.

"I don't think you do. I don't think anyone does," I tell her seriously.

It's a fucking mess in my head. Grief, anger, and rage.

"Right. Okay. Let me know when the Shelby is ready, and I'll swing by." She snatches her hand away.

Fuck.

Did I say the wrong thing?

"Yeah, will do."

As I open the door, I can't help but turn around one last time to look at her.

"Conan. Thank you for making it safe for me to go home."

"Anytime, darlin'."

She runs her thumb along her bottom lip and I squeeze the handle tighter. Everything she does is a tease. Unlocking this feral need for her.

Before I do something stupid, I head out and close the door behind me.

The quicker I fix her car, the quicker I'll have her at my garage.

And then I can do something about turning this friend situation into something much more beneficial to both of us.

CHAPTER 24

HALLIE

I kick my feet up on the table in the staff room and bite into my chicken salad sandwich.

Only a few more hours left. Then I need to seriously get to grips with racing this McLaren on the set track Pete sent over. There are a ton of corners, and she handles nothing like my Shelby.

But I keep replaying yesterday with Conan in my head.

The way he talks about himself makes me kinda sad. There's so much behind that tough exterior.

Maybe I should just ask him out. I want to learn more about him.

He makes me feel safe.

And when he looks at me, he actually sees me.

No one—not even my dad or Lily—has ever done that. Not even my mother. Who I haven't heard from in years, by the way.

Occasionally an odd text, one on my birthday. She's got her own new life in Ohio with Terry. Honestly, I'm fine without her. It's always been just me and Dad.

Even when he died, I didn't want to reach out.

Conan hasn't texted to say the car's ready, so I'm good for tomorrow night. Though I probably should double-check.

Because that McLaren could win me that twenty grand.

And deep down, I want to talk to him. He's becoming part of my routine—the guessing game of how he'll pop up.

A text? At work? My Pilates class?

I half expect him to knock on the door.

The door opens. I'm shocked to see Finn walk in with two cups of coffee. He never comes in here. He isn't social. At all.

He's either in his office or the OR.

He strides over and hands me a cup.

"Er, thank you."

"Wasn't me." He looks around the empty room, relaxing.

"Let me guess—Conan?"

"Yeah," he huffs.

"He's at my workplace far too much, Hallie."

"I can't stop him."

"Oh, I know. Once he sets his sights on something, you're screwed."

"We're just friends, Dr. Quinn. He'll get bored soon enough."

Finn frowns and sips his coffee.

"Read the note on the cup. Don't bet on that. Anyway, see you in OR in…" He checks his fancy watch. "Twenty-four minutes. Should only be an hour or so. Pacemaker. Then you can go home."

I fight the urge to read the note while Finn's here.

"Okay. Tell Conan I said thanks!"

"Nope. Not getting involved."

He waves behind him as he walks out.

When the door clicks shut, I turn the cup and see his scribbled handwriting.

Does this count as chasing, trouble?

I giggle at his words and press dial. I want to hear his voice. It's been a whole day without it.

He picks up on the first ring.

"I take it you got the caffeine?" His husky voice sends shivers through me.

His accent does things to me it really shouldn't.

"I did. Thank you."

"Hmm, mmm. You seem to thank me a lot, trouble."

I bite my lip.

"Because you do nice things."

"Yeah? You like that?"

Fuck. Is it getting hot in here?

"Yeah. I do."

"Good."

My knee starts bouncing. I'm not sure if I'm excited or nervous.

"Oh, by the way. Getting coffee delivered to my work by my boss is technically still chasing."

His deep chuckle makes me clench my thighs.

"Ah. Okay. Looks like I'll keep delivering things to you then."

"Conan!"

"What? Are you smiling?" he asks.

Like an idiot—to the point my cheeks hurt.

"Yes, Conan. I am."

"Then I shall continue my quest."

There's a pause.

"Hallie… Are you free tonight?"

I suck in a breath.

"I—I have plans tonight. Sorry. Another night?"

"Tomorrow?"

My stomach drops.

"Okay. Not tomorrow night either. The one after. Wait, I'm working. Shit."

He laughs, easing my tension.

"Want to just sync our calendars up?"

"Pfft. You think I'm organized enough to have a calendar? I just go with the flow and hope for the best."

I can thank ADHD for that. Late to appointments, missing them completely. A hot mess. But most of the time, I wing it.

"Yeah. Me neither. Just text me an evening you're free, and I'll make sure I am too."

I pout. He's so damn cute.

"Okay, beastie. I can do that. I gotta go into surgery now. I'll speak to you later."

"Surgery?" There is panic in his voice.

"I'm assisting your brother. Don't panic."

"Oh, shit. Yeah. My bad. You got me there."

I giggle. He's funny without even trying.

"Break a leg."

"I'll really try not to break the patient's leg, seeing as we work on hearts."

"Ha. Have a good day, darlin'."

"You too."

I cut the call, butterflies swirling in my stomach as I look at his handwriting again.

What happens when the chase is over, though?

CHAPTER 25

CONAN

"**G**et up, fuck face, Declan's got a surprise for you," Finn shouts as he tosses a t-shirt at my head.

I groan as I roll over and find him at my door.

"It's seven in the morning. What could he possibly need this early?"

"You'll see, little bro. Now get in your training gear, I'll make you a smoothie."

"Coffee," I correct him.

"You need fuel, not caffeine. Doctor's orders."

He flips me off and slams the door behind him. The first thing I do is grab my phone and scroll through my notifications.

I'm only looking for one name.

Hers.

And I'm smiling like a maniac when I see it on my screen. A message from 5 A.M.

TROUBLE

Hi, beastie. I'm just heading into work. Do
you need your car back later today, or can I
drop it off tomorrow morning when I pick
up the Shelby? (I'd really like one more
night with her.)

I type out a reply and ignore my raging hard-on for her. I watched her last night on the tracker, doing the same route, over and over. Each time, slightly quicker. She's certainly making use of the McLaren.

ME

Tomorrow morning works fine. I, too,
would like one more night with her.
She's all finished, so I will take her for a
spin.

I mean Hallie. I want another night to explore her. Stretching my arms above my head, I kick off my blanket.

"Calm down, boy. You can't have this one."

I rub my cock to try and relieve some of the pressure.

The memories of her shaking around me. The way she tasted.

Fuck. I let out a grunt and shove my hand under my boxers.

It's not just her memory that gets me going, it's the thought of the future.

What if she was into my kinks?

Her running, scared and turned on, in the woods while I chase her.

Her screaming for me as I bite and scratch her.

Tugging on my dick, I picture throwing her to the ground and ripping off her bra. Her nipples erect and begging to be sucked.

There's fear in her big eyes as she tries to shuffle away from me.

But she's soaking wet as I thrust inside her tight cunt.

Squeezing my eyes shut, my thighs clench as I imagine flipping her over on all fours and tugging on her hair.

Using her and claiming her.

But with every thrust, she's stealing a part of me too.

"Fuck!" I cry out as my cum spills over my hand.

I'm breathing so heavily as I open my eyes, and my phone pings.

TROUBLE

Okay, it's a deal. One more night.

I chuckle to myself.

One more night? As if.

"JESUS FUCKING CHRIST, DECLAN," I whisper over my shoulder.

"What? He's the same size as you."

"You didn't tell me it's Keller Russo, though. Did you? You never seen him fight? I brawl, he punches to kill. I'm about to have my head knocked clean off my shoulders."

Finn laughs beside me and I turn to face him.

"I can't stitch that back on. Neither can Hallie," Finn replies with a straight face.

Great.

As Keller approaches with an outstretched hand, another beast walks through the doors, followed by a curly haired guy that looks like he's ready to run at me with a right hook.

"Honor to meet you, Keller."

I shake his hand, and I swear to God it feels like my bones are crunching from his grip.

What a dream. Wait. Am I fangirling my idol?

"I've heard a lot about you, Conan. I've had Grayson here knock me into shape to fight you. Can't have you caving my skull in. I got a lot of kids to get home to."

There it is.

I might faint.

Keller fucking Russo thinks I can KO him.

"We aren't underground anymore. No one dies in the ring," the blonde one cuts in and holds out his hand for me to shake.

"I'm Grayson. I'm here to kick your ass until you're fight ready. And this here is Jax. If you can keep up with him and take Keller's blows, you'll be unbeatable."

A smirk creeps up on my lips. Now it's clicking into place.

"The King of Chaos? We've met before, right?" I ask him.

How didn't I realize? I was probably too busy trying not to get shot in Russia.

"Yeah. We didn't really have time to catch up, though."

He clicks his tongue piercing against his teeth and cracks his knuckles.

Now isn't the time to talk about our recent Russian mission to save Declan's wife and kid.

From what I've heard, Jax is similar to me. He can switch to become a killing machine in the ring.

"So we've got three days?" Grayson asks.

"Yep."

"And why did your last trainer quit? Declan was a bit sparse on the details."

I scratch my head.

"I might have knocked him the fuck out."

Jax sniggers and Grayson turns to Keller.

"You're up first with him," he tells Keller, who simply shrugs, unbothered.

"We're doing boxing rules only first. That's why we're here. Your opponent is first and foremost a skilled boxer. The other parts, we know you got that down. We need to make sure if this asshole starts pulling professional boxing moves, you can handle it and return it."

"Sounds good. I used to primarily just box as a kid. It's not until I got older that I thought the cage was less rules, more kicking, so I went to that."

Grayson nods.

"You're lacking the discipline boxing will give you." He tosses a rope at me.

"So to start, you got fifteen minutes of skipping to warm up."

I shrug.

"Alright."

I start to jump the rope while they watch.

"You think you two are here to watch? Grab a rope and join him," Grayson orders Keller and Jax.

After that is over, we're up in the ring and gloved up.

"Let's change it up. Jax, get your ass in there and run rings around him. Conan, I wanna see your speed. I'm guessing, like Keller, being big comes with its negatives."

I arch a brow.

"I disagree. I've never had any complaints about being too large, Grayson," I say back.

That earns a chuckle from Keller.

"You and Keller wanna compare dick sizes after?" Jax taunts.

"Trust me, Conan. You don't wanna do that. He's a fucking monster," Grayson tells me, keeping a deadly serious expression.

I turn to Keller.

"Come on, you gotta tell me now. How monstrous we talkin?"

"Look, if you can take a right hook from me and still stand, I'll tell you."

"Deal."

Is it weird that I'm excited for Keller 'The Killer' Russo to right hook me?

Grayson claps to get our attention.

"Great. Glad we cleared that up," Grayson grunts, ducking under the ropes. He and Keller stay at the corner while me and Jax circle each other in the center.

He takes a quick jab at me, I duck easily and throw one back, managing to just scrape his jaw.

"Nice, Conan," Grayson shouts.

It's Jax's turn to unleash his full force, throwing a barrage of punches my way. He's so fucking quick; when I retaliate, he's already fucked off out of the way.

He lands a blow straight into my gut.

"Fuck!"

"I thought we were following boxing rules?" I grit out.

Jax shrugs, holding up his gloves with a smirk.

"My bad. I don't really play by any rules."

"Good."

I push myself up straight and lunge at him, grabbing him by the waist and shoving his back into the corner post.

Now it's my turn to let him take some hits.

"Enough, you two!"

Grayson grabs me by the shoulders, and Jax laughs.

"I wanna cage fight, this shit is fun."

"Now you get it," I tell him.

"Jax. Fuck off over there." Grayson points to the opposite corner and Keller strides over.

"Okay, this time. You're going to just hit each other. One for one. Let's see how you take a punch."

Keller shoots Grayson a look.

"I'm going to punch you in the head in a minute," he tells Grayson.

"You agreed to do whatever it takes. Suck it up, I'm sure Sienna would like a few scratches on your face."

Standing in front of Keller, gloved up and ready to punch, is surreal.

We touch gloves before we start.

"Show me what you've got then," Keller tells me.

I draw back my right hand and launch it into his face as hard as I can. His head twists with the force and he grunts. But his feet don't move.

He's like a block of steel.

He rubs at his jaw and slowly turns to face me. When he's grinning, I kinda feel relieved.

"Nice shot. Powerful. My turn."

I tense up as I await my fate. I'm giddy with excitement.

As his red glove hurtles towards my face, I squeeze my eyes shut, and the impact has stars shooting in front of my eyes, the fucking pain searing into my skull. It's so powerful, I can't cry out in pain.

My brain is rattling around in my head… I think.

I blink a few times. Did I black out? What the fuck?

The room is fuzzy and bright. I look up, and Keller is staring back at me, amused.

"You stayed up on your feet. Pretty decent."

My ears are ringing, so everything is a bit faint.

"Cool. Thanks. I need to go sit down."

"Don't be a little pussy, Conan. You've gotta take them both on. We've got four hours of this," Grayson warns.

I'm determined to win this fight. I want that shot at the championship. And if that means getting the shit beaten out of me by two world famous fighters, then so be it.

"Just make sure my face isn't too swollen. I've got a date," I tell them, and they all smirk.

"Another fighter lost to a woman, ey?" Grayson asks.

"Maybe. I kind of hope so."

Jax taps me on the shoulder.

"It's the best loss you'll ever have."

I TOSS my clothes in the laundry and hold my breath as I submerge myself into the ice bath.

"Jesus, fuck!"

I'm shivering by the time I'm sat down, but my muscles need this to survive another day.

My fight is in two days.

Grayson thinks I'm good enough. And they'll all be there on the night. Maybe I really do have a shot at turning my career around.

It feels good—doing something the right way for once. I think Mom would be proud of me. If she could look past my other activities, I'm doing one thing right, at least.

After a few minutes, before I go completely numb, I jump out and wrap myself up.

All I can think about is Hallie saying she was busy. Too busy for me? Or is she avoiding the whole date thing?

Fuck it.

Let's see where she is.

Maybe I'll have to keep her Shelby a little longer.

CHAPTER 26

HALLIE

Nerves consume me as I slip into the parking lot.

I hold my breath. This car is so damn loud it's like a beast waking up.

Hundreds of people are here. Every single one of them is watching.

Well, the blacked-out windows help.

She's a stunning car—sharp edges, aggressive stance. But I'm nervous.

I tried the corners over and over last night. Some are so tight, they almost bite back.

I'm used to my Shelby. She's not easy, but she's powerful, wild but loyal. When I drive her, we become one.

Corners I used to lose the back end on? I've perfected them.

This? She's different. Delicate but fierce.

For twenty thousand dollars, it's worth a shot.

I ease her into the space next to Pete's car and kill the engine.

That's when the nerves flip to pure excitement—the roar of engines, the screech of tires.

191

I spot Pete and his man bun, leaning against the hood of a Bugatti, chatting with some tall guy.

I walk over, squeezing the keys in my hand.

"Nice ride!" the blond guy says.

"Uh, thanks," I reply quietly, feeling small under their stares.

Pete turns toward me, worry carved deep into his face.

"Hey," I say.

He nods, eyes flickering past me to the McLaren. Fingers brush his beard.

"If you stole that, return it before you end up dead, Hallie," he says bluntly.

My heart stutters.

"Stole?"

I pause.

"Dead?" I can't hide the shock from my tone.

"Are you shitting me? You don't know who owns that monster?" Pete says.

Confusion hits me.

"Yeah. Conan?"

"Oh, holy fuck. Hallie. Seriously, leave him be. You're way out of your depth on this one."

I shake my head hard.

"He knows I have his car. He gave me it. Stop panicking."

Pete rubs the bridge of his nose like he's trying to will calm into existence.

"You sure you wanna race it? Seriously?"

My stomach flips.

"I mean, I'm slightly worried that if I scratch it up, I won't be able to afford the paint job. But, other than that, I'm certain. How can I not race this thing?"

I glance back at the car, a slow smile spreading.

"Okay. Your funeral, I guess."

"Why do you keep saying that? He's my friend."

I nervously twist my rings.

"Friend?" His tone is thick with surprise.

"Yeah. Friend."

"You keep some interesting choices for friends, Hallie. Be careful."

I swallow hard, the words heavy in my throat.

"Sure."

Conan makes me feel safe. Why would I be scared of him?

Shit. Is he going to be mad if he finds out I've raced it? Or that I race at all?

Out of everyone, I think he'd get it.

The adrenaline. The quiet mind.

The danger.

"Look. He doesn't know exactly that I'm racing her. So we can just keep that between us. I'll tell him tomorrow."

"For fuck's sake, Hallie," Pete hisses.

"You think all these people can keep quiet?"

I look around at the crowd—men and women, some circling the McLaren like sharks.

"Uh, yeah?"

I've never heard his name dropped at a race before.

"Whatever. Head over to the starting line, be careful with that thing. She isn't a Shelby."

"I know."

Just because I'm a woman doesn't mean I don't know cars.

I grew up surrounded by them. Helping Dad fix them up.

I've been racing for two damn years.

I've won a few. I'm not the best, but I keep up.

But in this car? I have a shot.

With a sharp breath, I push through the crowd, shoving people aside to reach my car.

"Damn. How many dicks you gotta suck to earn one of these?" a sleazy, tatted guy asks.

"Just the one." I flip him off and slide behind the wheel, letting the engine roar alive.

"Be good for me, please," I whisper as I shift into first and pull away.

Ten of us are in the race. I'm starting sixth.

But looking around? My car will piss all over theirs.

It all depends on the roads and my driving.

No distractions.

Except the fear still buzzing in my brain, Pete's eyes when he mentioned Conan.

What am I missing?

The girls line up at the starting line, red flags waving like a challenge in the air.

My heart hammers as the cars around me rev, a beautiful, terrifying symphony.

The crowd counts down.

And go.

We launch down the first straight.

My car screams, hungry for more, but I hold back—I need more space first.

Fuck. This might be harder than I thought.

CHAPTER 27

CONAN

I watch the dot on my screen obsessively.

She's pushing nearly a hundred miles per hour.

My stomach twists. It's the same route as last night. I should've fucking known.

I scroll through my texts. Hundreds unopened, all just shit I don't care about.

I search Pete's name.

There it is.

Entry for the race tonight. That motherfucker.

I don't race anymore. It's fucking dangerous.

I've got enough shit I could get caught for, I don't need to be locked up for illegal street racing.

Not when I've got enough blood on my hands for the death penalty.

Though, the few times I did race when I first moved here?

God, it was fucking exhilarating.

My fist shakes.

I call Pete. No answer.

So, I try again.

This time the asshole picks up.

"Conan?"

"Yeah," I growl. "Wanna tell me why my car is in a race and I'm fucking not?"

I can't hide the edge in my voice.

I don't give a shit about the car, but the woman driving it? That's another story.

Not just driving. She's illegally goddamn racing it.

"I had no fucking idea, didn't know she's your girl. But, Con, I might have said too much."

My girl? I wish.

"Too much, how?"

Fucking Pete and his big mouth.

I push my whiskey away. I need a drink, but now I've got a sassy nurse to deal with.

"Look, I thought she'd stolen the car from you. Wanted to warn her, so I told her she might end up dead."

I pinch the bridge of my nose.

"You told Hallie I'd kill her?"

Of all the things I want to do to her, killing isn't on the list.

Punishing her? That's climbed to the top three.

"Yeah… thought it might make her return the McLaren."

"If anything happens to her, you, Pete, will be the one I kill with my bare hands."

He mutters under his breath.

"I told her not to race it. She was so sure."

The corner of my mouth twitches into a grin. Sounds like her.

"You know Hallie well?"

"Yeah. She's been on the scene a couple of years now. She's good. Not sure about letting her loose in your McLaren, though."

That sick feeling crashes down.

A McLaren races nothing like a Shelby.

But I guess that's why she spent all last night practicing.

"Fuck. I'll be at the finish line."

"Great."

I cut the call and throw on some clothes.

There's going to be a lot of people there.

I need backup.

Just in case.

CHAPTER 28
HALLIE

I shift down a gear as I hit the corner I've been dreading.

I'm in third place now, close behind the leading two cars.

I've gotta overtake a Bugatti and a Corvette.

My car could clear these two easily, if it weren't for the traffic and these corners.

I'm understating, being cautious. I'm used to over-steering in my Shelby so I don't lose the back end.

In this, it's different, smoother. But it's not mine.

My ass has been clenched this entire race.

I've lost a few seconds on taking that corner like a baby, so I shove my foot down on the gas.

The wind blows through my hair as their taillights get closer.

The Corvette tries to make a move on the Bugatti. I keep closing the distance. I need to stay in this race till the end.

The Bugatti hits a new level as it shoots off, leaving the Corvette behind.

I check my mirrors and crawl up behind him, at the last minute, undertaking him and slotting back into place in front of him.

"Yes!" I scream.

Excitement floods my veins. My spark for life returning. My heart pounds, but I'm smiling.

One more car to go.

Come on, Hallie. You got this.

Gripping the steering wheel tighter, we turn right; I do that easily, losing no time.

Shifting back up the gears, the car is screaming for more. I'm closing the gap quicker than I thought I could.

Dodging in and out of the traffic, the streetlights become a blur; all I can focus on is this Bugatti in front of me.

We've got the final corner coming up, my nemesis. Then we're on the home stretch.

As we approach the turn, the front of my McLaren is halfway up the Bugatti.

"Come on, come on, come on," I whisper.

Carefully, I turn the wheel to the right.

CHAPTER 29

CONAN

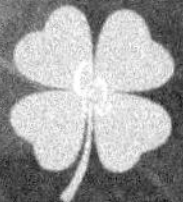

My heart is in my fucking throat.

I can hear the rumble of the engine before I even see her.

That sound, that's my girl.

She's in the top two.

"Come on, baby."

I bite down on my fist, hard enough to bruise.

Then I see it. The mean headlights. My McLaren.

And in the next second, they're gone.

Not turning. Not slowing.

She's flying straight through the fucking corner.

My blood freezes.

I don't breathe.

Don't blink.

Every fucked-up image I've ever seen comes back at once—metal flipping, glass exploding, her body…

I squeeze my eyes shut.

I can't.

I can't lose Hallie.

Not like this.

When I open them again, the air slams back into my lungs.

She's on the track.

She's okay.

But the Bugatti's almost at the line.

"Under fucking steer," I hiss.

My fist cracks against the hood of my Range Rover.

She was right there. Inches from taking it.

But none of that matters.

Because for three full seconds I thought she was gone.

And now all I feel is pride burning a hole in my chest as she crosses the finish.

The crowd loses their minds.

But no one goes near the McLaren.

They know better.

"Con… you ain't going to explode here, are ya?" Rowan mutters beside me.

"Me? Explode? Never."

I cross my arms, lean on the Rover, eyes locked on her.

Hallie pulls into a space like she owns the whole damn night.

She kind of does.

"Nah. I'm not mad. That was fucking hot," I mutter.

I tap Reggie on the shoulder, jaw still tight.

"Stay by the car, I'll be back."

CHAPTER 30

HALLIE

Second place. It's still five thousand. Enough to pay Lily back.

And the thrill? That was priceless.

I cut the engine and climb out, breath catching as the high starts to wear off. I need to find Pete. Cash first, consequences later.

But the second the door shuts, the hairs on my arms rise.

"Hallie. What the actual fuck do you think you're doing?"

That voice. That accent.

Oh, shit.

I turn slowly, hands protectively cradling my stomach like they'll shield me from the storm stomping straight toward me.

Conan.

He's furious, his jaw locked, eyes burning. Rage radiates off him like heat from asphalt.

"I'm sorry," I whisper, unable to meet his eyes.

He stops in front of me, towering, and I brace for the explosion.

"Sorry? You nearly gave me a damn heart attack on that last fucking corner. A McLaren handles way smoother than your Shelby. Remember that for next time."

Next time?

My head jerks up. He's grinning.

"You're not mad at me? For using your car?"

He shakes his head, stepping in closer.

"I'm mad you didn't invite me to join."

His fingers brush my hair over my shoulder, knuckles grazing my neck. I shiver.

"The fact you took my car to illegally race it is one hell of a turn-on. And you would have won if you didn't under-steer that corner at the end. Fuck, if you'd have won, I probably would've made a mess in my boxers."

I squint, trying to gauge if he's joking. He isn't.

"So just to clarify. You don't care about me racing? I'm not about to get a spiel on how dangerous and illegal it is? And you're not going to demand I stop?"

His hands settle heavily on my shoulders.

"I'm far from an angel. You've got skill. It clearly makes you happy. That's what matters. That beautiful smile of yours is worth the mini heart attacks you give me."

My whole face warms. I smile so wide it hurts.

"So I can keep the McLaren? Do a swap?"

I bat my lashes, pushing my luck. His smile falters.

"No."

That catches me. He's not mad about the car. It's something else.

"So why are you in such a grump? Worried I might've smashed up your car?"

He steps back and runs both hands down his face, pacing a second before turning on me again.

"What the fuck? No! I couldn't give a shit about a bit of metal. You, Hallie. I'm worried about you."

"Really?"

He exhales like it costs him, then pulls me against his chest. My tension drains as I settle into his embrace.

"I'd give up every single car I own in a heartbeat if it was a choice between you and them. Hell, I'd give up everything. You just need more practice in the McLaren before you race again. And I would never dream of taking your Shelby from you in return."

Tears well in my eyes, and I wrap my arms tighter around him.

"You did good, trouble. I'm proud of you."

Those words crack something open. I haven't heard them in two years. Not from someone who meant it.

A sob punches out of me.

"Baby, please don't cry. I promise I'm not upset," he murmurs.

I tip my head up. His brows pinch, like he doesn't know what to do with the mess I've become.

"I'm not sad." I sniff. "I'm happy, I think."

He looks at me like I've grown a second head.

"You want me to drive you home? I'll have my men follow behind and drop the McLaren off?"

Pete clears his throat behind us. I flinch, but Conan doesn't let go.

"Well done, Hallie. Here." Pete hands me the wad of cash, eyes darting nervously between us.

Conan glares at him like he wants to rearrange his face.

"Conan. Good to see you." Pete backs away slowly into the crowd.

"He's scared of you," I whisper.

"Fucking right."

He takes my hand and guides me to his Range Rover. Two men, who are absolute giants, wait beside it like they were built in the same lab.

Conan tosses the keys to one. The other groans.

They nod silently and disappear with the McLaren. Conan opens the passenger door for me, but I don't move. I have something on my mind, and I have to blurt it out.

"Are you hiding who you really are from me, beastie?"

His jaw twitches. One second later, he's right in front of me, my back pressed against cool metal.

"Fine one to talk, Ms. Adrenaline Junkie."

Okay, fair.

"There are a lot of parts to me, trouble. You gotta stick around to see them all."

He leans in, green eyes wildfire hot.

"Should I be scared of you?" I whisper. "Everyone makes it out like I should be. Like I'll end up dead with you."

He doesn't answer. Just grabs my throat and pins me against the door.

My breath stops.

His eyes darken.

"Are you scared of me?" he growls. "Or scared of what you feel for me? Because you know damn well I'd never hurt you. Does it matter who they think I am? The only version of me that matters, is the one I am with you."

His grip loosens. My lips part on a shaky breath.

God help me, I believe him.

"I-I didn't say I'm scared of you. I asked if I should be."

He lets go, and I miss his touch instantly.

"Get in the car, trouble."

He grabs my ass and helps lift me into the seat.

I don't know what this thing is between us. But I know one thing—being just friends isn't going to cut it.

We ride home in a comfortable silence, with his hand on my thigh the entire time.

"Are you coming in?" I ask when we pull up at mine.

The McLaren's already there. The twins waiting beside it like statues.

"I can't, trouble. I gotta get those assholes home. But your Shelby'll be ready tomorrow. I'll see you then?"

A lump lodges in my throat. Disappointment swallows me whole. Something has shifted between us.

"Okay. Fine. Thanks for the ride home."

As I reach for the handle, his hand clamps around my shoulder.

"What's the attitude for, darlin'?"

"Nothing."

"You going to lie to me? Hmm?"

"No. I'm just tired, let's leave it at that."

I shrug him off and step out.

Maybe I read too much into this. Maybe I'm just a hormonal mess disappointed he doesn't want to rail me.

"Night, trouble." He blows me a kiss.

"Night, Conan."

Inside, I barely make it three steps before I hear footsteps behind me again.

"Hey, you need the key."

I turn to one of Conan's men; I don't look at him, just grab the keys.

"Thanks."

I run inside, slam the door, and lock it.

The cash spills across the counter when I dump my purse.

I definitely rattled him. He's hiding something. And he's scared, maybe not of me, but of what he feels.

Same.

Bertie barrels down the stairs and jumps on me.

"Hey, baby boy," I coo, petting him.

I let him out into the garden and step out after him, the sky wide and black and full of stars.

I miss you, Dad.

I blink the tears back, go inside, and pour myself one of his favorite whiskeys. I can't help thinking that even that is a strange twist of fate. Of all the distilleries, all the whiskeys, my dad was obsessed with the one Conan's father created.

Grabbing my phone, I debate texting Conan to apologize. But, before I can do that, his name pops up.

I answer. Of course I do.

"Hallie…"

I'm already smiling.

"Conan…"

"I can't go to bed knowing you're upset with me. Can we talk?"

"I'm not mad, I promise. I was just disappointed you didn't want to…" I trail off. I sound like a ho.

"Didn't want to?"

"Come into my house. Kinda felt like you were brushing me off after I asked if I should be scared of you."

He sighs. Long. Heavy.

"I didn't mean to do that, baby. I'm sorry. I've… not ever had this kind of friendship with a woman."

Friendship. That stings.

I toss back the rest of the whiskey.

"If you want to just be my friend, maybe don't call me baby. Or darlin'. Or trouble."

He chuckles low.

"Darlin', you have no idea. But I think we're on the same page about one thing."

"What's that?"

"That being friends ain't enough."

I blow out a long breath, feeling the heat start to rise.

"I-I think you might be right, beastie."

I twirl my hair through my fingers, waiting anxiously for his answer.

"Tomorrow? Let's talk about it then? Yeah?"

He seems a bit nervous, and that just makes me fall harder.

"Let's do that. Thank you for calling, checking in on me. I appreciate that. I'll come to the garage after my shift."

It makes me feel secure and validated.

"I don't want you to be angry with me. Get some rest, my racing queen, I'll see you in a few hours."

I giggle at that. I'd love to race him.

"Night, night, Conan."

CHAPTER 31

CONAN

Song, Dangerous, Sleep Token.

I want it to be perfect for her. Rifling through the shelves in my garage, I find the right oil for her beast just as I hear the rumble of the Mclaren come to a stop.

As I turn, there's a knock on the metal.

My eyes lock with hers. The wind teases her shiny caramel hair, the soft waves catching the late light like it's trying to show her off. My gaze drops to that tight little blue sundress, clinging to her like a fucking secret.

Stop it.

I don't do girlfriends. I fight and I fuck. That's it. No room for softness in a world like mine. She doesn't belong tangled up in my bullshit.

"Hi," she whispers, wearing that sweet little grin. My chest fucking stirs as she holds onto the doorframe, crossing her legs like she's not aware she's been living in my head rent-free. She seems nervous. Or maybe that's just wishful thinking.

"Hi, trouble."

She steps inside, fingertips brushing the new shimmering paint job on her Shelby.

"She looks perfect."

I nod. "Like her owner."

The words slip before I can pull them back.

The tension between us tightens, electric. She's too close. She always is.

I clench the bottle of oil tighter.

"She needs more oil?" she asks, tilting her head.

"Just a top-up. I wanted her in top shape for you. You know, for your naughty nighttime activities." I wink.

Damn. I exploded in my hand last night, jerking off to the thought of her racing my McLaren with that wicked smirk on her lips.

Hallie grins and takes a step back, giving me space, except all I can breathe in is her sweet scent. It's wrecking me. Tempting me.

"Don't let me get in your way. And about the street racing…" She trails off.

I bite back a grin. "Secret is safe with me, baby," I tell her, twisting off the cap and checking the stick.

"You look hot when you're concentrating," she blurts out.

I steal a glance in her direction as I pour the liquid in.

"Is that right?"

She nods as I twist on the lid to the bottle; I catch her watching me. Not just looking. Watching. Like she's studying a creature she doesn't quite trust not to bite.

I toss the oil back onto the shelf and slam the hood shut, the sound cracking through the air.

"What are you thinking, trouble?" I ask, raising a brow.

"You've got huge hands. Must be hard to get into all the tight spaces."

I chuckle, holding them up. Tattooed, calloused, capable.

"They fit right where they need to, trouble."

She flushes a brilliant red. I take a step closer.

"They even make the perfect necklace," I murmur, dragging my own hand across my throat to demonstrate.

Her plump lips part. Fuck. How far do I want to push her?

"They'd look much prettier wrapped around your throat, Hallie."

She flutters her lashes. That grin? All teeth and sin. "Show me, beastie," she breathes.

I'm a fucking goner.

I lunge forward, grip her throat, and spin her, pressing her back against the side of her car. Her pulse pounds under my palm. I squeeze. Not enough to hurt. Just enough to claim.

"Fucking perfect, baby." Her eyes go wide as I slide my phone from my pocket.

"Wanna see how beautiful you look?"

"Y yes."

I snap the photo. My cock is throbbing as I sneak a look. Mine.

I turn the screen to her. Her eyes glisten. She's hungry for it.

"What do you think about your new accessory, Hallie?" I ask, brushing my nose along her cheek.

"It looks hot. It feels even better."

She parts her legs. I step between them, pressing tight.

"Is this what friends do, baby?"

She shakes her head. I drag my face back to hers.

"You gonna tell me to stop?" I would. I'd stop. But God, I don't want to.

"Stop what?"

I tighten my grip.

"Me bending you over the hood and finally taking what's mine."

She gasps, and I chuckle.

Darkness flickers in her gaze as she slides her hands under my shirt, dragging her nails across my abs. It sets me on fire, but I don't flip my switch. Not yet.

"I don't have any panties on."

"Fuck, Hallie."

She bites her lip. My gaze zeroes in.

"Yes. That's the idea. Conan fucks Hallie senseless. Can you do that for me, beastie?"

I blink. That challenge in her voice knocks the wind out of me. I'm used to control. No talking. No feeling. Just a fuck.

This? This is something else. Hotter. Deadlier.

"I wouldn't test me, trouble. I don't know how much you can handle of me yet."

I grab her hand and press it to my cock. She wraps her fingers around it, rising on her tiptoes, nose brushing against my stubble.

I slip my hand beneath her dress, dragging my fingers through her slick heat.

"Is this what I do to you? Hmm? I turn you into a good little whore for me?"

Her breath hitches. She spreads her legs wider. Her little breathy pants by my ear makes my skin crawl in the best way.

"Be a good boy and show me what I've been missing. Show me how you really like it."

Holy. Fuckin'. Shit. I've met my match.

"There's nothing good about me, darlin'," I growl.

She pulls back, sliding her hands up under my shirt, tracing each line of my abs.

"Yeah, there is. Deep down, you're a softie, really."

I laugh low and dark, shaking my head. Wrong. So fucking wrong.

I grab her throat again, lifting her and settling her ass on the hood. I step between her thighs, boxing her in.

"Wrong. And you're about to find out just how fuckin' dark I am, Hallie."

She swallows hard. I smirk, feeling her heart hammer against my palm.

"Yes. You seem to bring out another side of me. But that ain't the man I am deep down. You really want to see him?"

"I do," she says, confident. Steady.

I release her and take a step back, running a hand down my face. Testing her. Watching her.

"Fine. If you want me to fuck you, you gotta earn it, darlin'."

"How do you suggest I do that then?"

I grab her cheeks and stare into those wide eyes. "Run."

She blinks. Then looks toward the door.

"What do you mean 'run'? You think I'm going out in those scary-ass woods in the pitch black? A leisurely jog isn't what I'm after from you, beastie."

I laugh, digging my fingers into her thighs.

"Nothing leisurely about what I'm going to do to you once I catch you."

She studies me now. Eyes flicking between curiosity and something darker.

"What is this? Some sort of chase kink?"

I shake my head, keeping my face hard.

"No, trouble. This isn't me chasing you… this is me hunting you."

I lean in, tongue sliding along her jaw. She sucks in a breath, head tipping back, so damn responsive. Too perfect to just be my friend.

But if I let her in, I might never let her go.

"Now fucking run," I whisper, stepping back.

She slides off the hood. Staring between me and the door. Her chest rises and falls fast.

There's a hesitation in her. The kind that tastes like adrenaline. Like she's balancing on the line between fear and arousal. That mix drives me wild. I want her to feel it. I want her to see me.

"What will you do if you catch me?" she asks, voice barely audible as she smooths her dress.

"It's not if. It's when. It's up to you to decide if you want to find out."

She chews the inside of her cheek.

"Do I need a safe word?"

A slow, dangerous smile spreads across my face.

"You think a safe word will save you? Sure. Go ahead."

Her brows knit, and I shrug.

All she has to do is say stop. And I would. For her, I would. But this game? It's mine.

"You know what? I don't want one."

I lean back against the hood of her Shelby, arms crossed, waiting.

"Good girl."

CHAPTER 32

HALLIE

A flash of darkness crosses his eyes as I stumble back toward the door. The way he told me to run lit a fuse under my skin.

So that's what I'm doing.

I cut a sharp left, skirting the edge of his unit and bolting for the tree line. No footsteps yet. Just the wind needling across my face, cold against the fire building in my chest.

The second I cross into the woods, the air shifts. Branches scrape past my arms as I weave through the trees. Everything's shadows and movement, like the forest is watching. But all I feel is him.

My blood's roaring in my ears. My lungs burn. I'm not built for sprinting like this, especially not with a six-foot-six beast chasing me down like prey.

Then I hear it. A crack that sounds like a punch landing hard against bark.

I freeze. Leaves crunch underfoot as I slip behind the nearest tree, my back pressing flat against its rough trunk.

"Hallie, Hallie, Hallie…where are you?" His voice floats through the trees.

I bolt. Again. Deeper into the woods, deeper into the dark. The moon spills in through the gaps in the canopy, a silver blur through the branches.

My foot sinks into a puddle, sending me sprawling.

"Fuck," I hiss, palms slamming into the dirt. Mud sucks at my sandals as I clamber upright, soaked and panting.

A pain radiates in my ankle, but I try to ignore it. I have to run.

"You better still be running, trouble."

His voice is closer now. So close it sizzles down my spine.

I spin, breath ragged, eyes flicking left and right. No end. No clear path.

Panic and anticipation twist into one as I dart left, weaving through the trees. I hear his footsteps now.

A thick arm wraps around my waist.

I scream, kicking back. But it's too late.

I look up. All I see are his green eyes, wild and glowing in the moonlight. The rest of his face is hidden beneath a black balaclava.

He tosses me to the grass like I weigh nothing. I scramble backward, chest heaving, but he just stalks forward. I've never been more turned on in my damn life.

"Looks like I caught my prey. Too easy."

I shake my head. No way. Not like that.

I leap up and tear off again, bare legs pumping, dress flying. I can still feel his hands on me. I can smell him— dark spice and danger.

I don't care. I'm not giving him the satisfaction.

This is foreplay. Twisted. Raw. Addictive.

He's right behind me again. I zigzag through the woods, whipping a branch behind me, hoping it smacks him across the face.

This is the most alive I've felt in years. No rules. No walls. Just heat and adrenaline. It's like being on the track, but hotter and hornier.

"Come on, beastie. I thought this was your thing?"

I don't hear him. I risk a glance over my shoulder, and my body slams into something solid. Stone? No...*him*.

His hand wraps around my throat before I can recover.

"What were you saying?" he rasps, voice low, lethal.

Fuck.

I claw at his grip, nails scraping his black shirt, desperate. He doesn't let go.

"Make me bleed, trouble. I dare ya'."

I scream as he slams me back against the bark of the nearest tree. I dig my nails into his throat, leaving marks.

And he groans. Like he fucking loves it.

His body pins me tight.

"I can't breathe," I gasp.

"Good."

My eyes widen. There's something wild in him that I don't want to tame.

How far is he going to take this? How far do I want him to?

His hand slips up under my dress, fingers sliding into me so deep I gasp out loud.

"Fuck. So tight. So fucking wet. Such a little slut for me."

I nod, moaning, back arching as he fucks me with his fingers.

Cold air hits my skin as he rips my dress clean off of me. I gasp.

"Much better."

He leans in, lips grazing my ear.

"That was too easy, trouble. Next time, fight me off.

Don't let me get you. You only submit once I get my dick inside your tight pussy."

He curls his fingers and I whimper, legs shaking. Then he withdraws, grabbing my chin, holding me in place.

"Do you understand the rules?"

I'm naked. Panting. Mud-covered. And my ankle really fucking hurts.

And soaked in more ways than one. I should be scared. I am.

I stare into his eyes. That fire. That need. It's all for me.

"Got it, beastie. Chase me. Fight me. Fuck me. Good luck catching me this time."

I tap his cheek. He catches my wrist, holding it there.

"That was just our warm-up, darlin'. Now I know how soaked you are... that's just given me the green light to show you what I really want to do to you."

He releases me and takes a slow step back. The hunt's not over. It's just begun.

CHAPTER 33

CONAN

She bolts again.

Fucking barefoot, bleeding, and naked—and laughing like a damn siren as she disappears between the trees.

I let her get five seconds ahead. Ten. Let the illusion of control sink into her pretty little bones.

Then I move like a shadow with a hard-on.

Her footprints in the dirt tell me everything I need to know. She's limping slightly. Right foot's dragging. But she doesn't stop.

Good.

She's fighting. Just how I like it.

The scent of her—sex, fear, and defiance—is thick in the air by the time I reach the edge of a ravine. She's nowhere in sight, but I hear her muttering "fuck" under her breath.

I tilt my head back and breathe deep. Goddamn. She smells like prey. But she runs like a queen.

I catch the movement in my periphery; her silhouette flickers between trees, backlit by moonlight. She turns, glances over her shoulder…she runs right into me.

She smacks into my chest with enough force to stumble back, but I catch her.

Now with both arms around her waist, I lock her in. And I don't let her scream this time. I spin her, shove her hard into a tree, my hand clamping over her mouth.

"You wanted a fucking monster?" I growl against her ear. "You got him."

She bites me right into the meat of my palm.

I hiss, but I don't let go. I shove my thigh between hers, pinning her in place as I drop my mouth to her throat, teeth scraping skin.

She thrashes against me, her knees bucking, her hands scrambling across my chest.

Feral. Just how I fucking wanted her.

But I've got her. I've always got her.

I yank her wrists above her head with one hand, hold them tight against the bark, and grind my cock against her ass through my jeans.

"Still want to play, trouble?" I rasp. "Game's not over until my cock is in your pussy. You can still try and run."

She moans behind my hand, arching into me like the little masochist she is. My other hand grabs her hip, grinding her back into my cock. Fuck, she's soaked. I can feel her heat from here.

"You should've fought harder." I bite, dragging my teeth across her jaw. "You should've screamed louder. Should've kicked me in the fucking balls. Because now?"

I drop my hand from her mouth, just long enough for her to spit in my face.

"Go to hell."

I laugh, wiping my mask. She's shaking. But not from fear. Her pupils are blown wide and her chest is heaving. She's so fucking ready for me.

"Darlin'," I whisper, dragging my tongue up the shell of her ear. "I'll take you there."

I release her wrists just to spin her around. But before I can, her hand flies towards my cheek, and she slaps me. Hard.

My head snaps sideways with the hit. And I grin like a fucking maniac.

"Atta girl."

I grab her by the throat again, lift her clean off her feet, and slam her back into the tree hard enough to shake the branches.

She gasps, legs kicking, and she's screaming at me.

I lower her just enough for her toes to scrape dirt, then rip open my jeans, my cock already leaking.

"Tell me no," I growl, lining up.

She stares at me with her mouth parted, heaving for air.

"No." Her voice trembles. But her eyes, fuck, her eyes dare me.

I stay still, assessing her next move before I make mine.

And then she smirks and starts to roll her hips, rubbing her bare pussy against me.

She wants a taste of the real Conan. Well, she's just summoned him.

I thrust in one brutal, claiming stroke, pinning her to the tree like she was made to be fucked by me and only me.

She screams so loud my ears ring.

Her back arches, her nails dig into my neck, and all it does is make me fuck her harder.

"Still think you can run?" I pant, slamming into her, each word punctuated with a thrust.

"Still think you're in control?" I whisper.

She wraps her legs around me, her cunt clenching so tight I nearly lose it. Her lips brush mine.

"Harder," she whispers.

I lose it. One hand on her throat, the other gripping her thigh, I fuck her into the bark until she's sobbing, begging, biting down on her own fist to stay silent.

I rip her hand away from her mouth.

"Scream for me, baby. I want to hear how much you love it."

Or how much she loves me like this.

She shatters around me. And I don't stop. Not until I'm buried to the hilt, spilling inside her, growling her name like a fucking prayer.

When I finally pull back, she's limp in my arms, scratched, bruised, and smiling like a devil.

Her voice is a wrecked whisper.

"You call that a monster, beastie?"

I kiss her hard. "I'm just getting started."

Holy fuck. I can barely breathe. My skin stings from her scratches and bites. I pull off my now ripped t-shirt and put it over her head.

"That was fun," she tells me.

"Yeah, baby. That was fucking perfect."

My cock still throbs inside of her. The fact she's so into this—something we can enjoy together. Fuck. She really is perfect for me.

"Let's go back and clean up, get you warm."

She bites on her lip and bats her lashes.

I'm obsessed with her. I can't deny it any longer.

"I can think of lots of ways you can warm me up, sir."

Damn.

I'll lose my mind soon, I'm certain of it.

AFTER WE HAVE a shower in my gym, I give her another sweater that fits like a dress on her. She looks cute as hell.

"So, you going to take me back to your bedroom here?" she asks, biting her nail.

Fuck. I want her. Not here. She's better than being shacked up in a tiny room in my garage.

But I can't take her to Decadence. Not yet. Not until the Chase is done.

"You got enough room in your bed for me?" I whisper, tucking her hair behind her ear.

"If Bertie allows you in, then yes."

"Good girl. Now, how about that race?" I tease.

Her eyes light up, and a naughty smile dances on her lips.

"Whoever wins gets to come first," she tells me, wiggling her eyebrows.

I slide my hand down her back and grab her ass, pressing her tighter against me.

"Oh, yeah?"

Maybe I'll lose on purpose so I have her pussy on my face first.

"Yeah," she breathes out.

She pushes herself up on her tiptoes and runs her nose along my jaw.

"Maybe I want to lose so you can fuck my face and come all down my throat."

I choke on a cough and all the blood rushes south.

"This is about to be the slowest race in history then,

darlin'. Because all I want is another taste," I tell her, yanking her back by her hair.

A soft moan leaves her lips as I dip my head down and run my tongue along her throat.

"Or perhaps, we change the rules. Whoever wins gets to go down on the loser," I mutter against her skin.

"Yeah. I like that one better. I've been dreaming about tying you up and making you watch just how pretty I look sucking your big cock."

"Jesus fucking Christ, Hallie," I hiss.

Her hands glide past my hips and around to my ass, and she squeezes.

"You'd like that, wouldn't you, beastie? Being a good boy and letting me do whatever the hell I want to you."

I sink my teeth into her skin.

"For some damn reason, yes. I want all of that. I don't know what you're doing to me, trouble. But don't stop."

CHAPTER 34

HALLIE

Song- I Like You Best, Ella Red

We stumble through the door, our lips locked, our hands roaming each other's bodies.

"I won," I pant against his mouth.

He picks me up by the hips and slams me into the wall. Just like he did that first night.

But this time, it's for real.

"I know, darlin'. Trust me, I know." He presses his hips against me, his hard cock pushing against my aching pussy.

That race over here, the adrenaline. With every shift of the gear, the tires screeching, watching the needle hit over one hundred.

Knowing he was just behind me, racing with me, really, not against me.

Electrifying.

Running my hands through his thick hair, I deepen the kiss.

"Fuck, baby," he murmurs.

"Fuck my face," I correct him.

He pulls back, searching my face with a sinister grin.

"I'm going to fuck every hole of yours tonight. But this first round is all yours." He steals one last kiss before stepping back.

He leaves me breathless.

He holds his hands up in the air, the room crackles around us.

"Tell me what you want to do to me. Boss me around, baby. I'm all yours."

My heart pounds and my hands shake.

"All mine. Hmm." I tap my lip.

"Follow me, beastie." I hold out my hand to him, and he links his fingers through mine, and I lead him up the stairs.

Opening up my bedroom, I flick on the lights and stop by the bed.

"Welcome. This is where all the naughty things happen."

Conan scans the room. The baby blue covered walls, the fluffy white pillows, and of course, the piles of laundry I've yet to put away.

"The cuffs better be fluffy," he whispers.

"Maybe. But they aren't pink." I wink.

Everything is blue in this room because at the time that was my fixation of color.

I haven't redecorated since Dad died.

"It's cute. Just like you."

My cheeks blush.

"Clothes off." I point at him.

His eyebrow raises, but he doesn't pause. He rips the top over his head and pushes his sweatpants and boxers down, kicking them towards one of my laundry piles.

His dick stands to attention and I lick my lips, taking a step closer and wrapping my hand around his shaft.

Using my thumb, I wipe away the pre-cum, locking my eyes with his as I bring it up to my mouth and lick it clean.

"I want more," I breathe out, starting to gently stroke his cock.

He grunts, closing his eyes.

"Hallie."

"Hmm?" I say with mock innocence while cupping his cheek and turning his face to mine, capturing his lips.

I slowly kiss him as I jerk him off.

His hand lands on my ass and I shake my head.

"No touching, beastie. You be a good boy for me and just let me make you feel good."

He groans.

"I-I don't know if I can. Fuck. Hallie, I need you."

I bite his bottom lip and circle the tip of his dick with my thumb.

"You lost. These are my rules. You break them, you leave."

His eyes fly open, almost in horror.

"I'll be good. I'm being good. I promise." His voice is husky, making his accent thicker.

Fuck. I'm soaking for him.

But I want him desperate for me. This element of control, or power even, I've never experienced. But having this man at my mercy, ready to beg for more, makes me come alive.

"You think if I get on my knees and suck your dick, you'll be able to stop yourself from grabbing my hair?" I ask, stepping back.

"Honestly? No."

His fists clench, and I take another step back. This time removing the sweater over my head, leaving me completely naked for him.

He bites down on his hand, his gaze scanning my entire body.

"Absolutely no way. You're gorgeous, baby. Like, I could come on the spot just looking at you."

With an extra sway in my hips, I close the distance between us and push him back onto the bed.

"Hands up by the headboard," I command.

He shuffles back and puts them between the metal, while I rummage for the blue fluffy handcuffs.

Working on the first wrist, I'm unsure if they'll work.

"Might be a bit tight," I tell him.

"I don't fucking care if I bleed."

I suck in a breath and try again with more force, finally securing the cuff.

I do the same with the second.

"You look so hot, beastie. Want to feel how wet I am?" I grin.

"Oh, wait. You can't." I spread my legs, sliding my finger along my pussy, retrieving some of my wetness.

"I bet your cunt is soaking for me, Hallie."

Climbing onto the bed, I straddle him and push my fingers into his mouth while my pussy rests on his pulsing dick.

He sucks them clean and moans, jerking his hips up, making me squeal.

"Conan," I warn.

He tips his head back.

"I can't help it, baby. I need you. This teasing is going to make me lose my damn mind."

Pressing my finger against his lips to silence him, I trail the other hand down towards his abs. He tenses under my touch.

"Where's your phone?" I ask him.

"In my pocket." He nods to his pants on the floor next to the bed.

As I climb off him, I scramble to the pile of clothes and retrieve the cell.

"Code?"

He rattles off the numbers and it unlocks, revealing a cute picture of him and his brothers. They all look similar, yet so different.

"You trying to see how many other women are texting me?" he teases.

I snap my eyes up to his and glare.

"No. I don't care."

I swallow the lump in my throat. I do care. More than I'd like to admit.

Getting back onto the bed, I lift my leg over his huge frame and start peppering kisses along his jaw, moving south down his body.

"You're so fucking hot, beastie," I mutter, before running my tongue along his chest, swirling it around his tattoos.

"Trust me, baby. You're way fucking hotter."

As I settle between his legs, I pull up the camera on his phone and turn it for a selfie. When I'm happy with the angle, I slowly swirl my tongue over the tip.

"You're being such a good boy, Conan. I think you've earned yourself a reward. Don't you?"

I snap a picture as I take him in my mouth.

"Yes, baby. I've been so good for you."

With my mouth now fully on his cock, I keep my eyes locked on his as I take him as deep as I can go, randomly taking action shots as I do.

When my eyes start to water, I slowly suck back to the top, digging my nails into his thigh.

"You taking pictures for me, trouble?" he asks, almost breathlessly.

I change to running my tongue along the shaft.

"Mmhmm. Now you get to see how pretty I am with your dick in my mouth whenever you want."

That pure, feral hunger returns in his eyes and he starts to pull on his restraints.

"You misbehave, and I delete them."

He clenches his fist. I don't know how much longer those handcuffs will last.

"And trust me, you're going to want to save this collection."

A whimper escapes him and that sends ripples through me. Holy shit. I've never been more turned on in my damn life.

"Fuck!" He roars out, bucking his hips, thrusting himself deep enough for me to gag.

I let him take back some control, using my mouth how he needs. My own juices start to soak down my thighs. As soon as he tenses up, I pull off him and sit on my heels, watching the heavy rise and fall of his chest.

"Let. Me. Out. Hallie." His husky voice tears through my resolve.

"Fuck it," I hiss.

I clamber up his body, settling my needy pussy over his huge cock, lining it up, but I don't sink down, not yet.

Holding the phone up, I find my favorite picture and show him.

He blows out a breath.

"My new fuckin' wallpaper right there. Beautiful. Fuck. I'm about to come."

The desperation is thick in his tone. I love that I can do this to him.

"Maybe I should send it to all those women in your contacts?" I tease, chewing on my lip.

His eyes darken, and I jolt back as he rips one of his restraints clean off and grabs my throat, bringing my face down to his.

His hot breath beats against my cheek.

"If that's how you want to claim me, do it. I don't give a shit. I'm not interested in anyone else. Only you, Hallie. And I'm going to stare at those pictures of those pretty lips wrapped around my cock the second I wake up and every free moment I have in a day. That's what you do to me."

All the breath is knocked from my lungs as he crashes his lips over mine.

"But if you get to claim me, then I'm sure as fuck marking you as mine."

He pulls back and stares into my eyes, setting my body alight.

"I'll claim you in other ways, beastie," I breathe out, throwing his phone down beside me.

He casually yanks the other handcuff off, gripping my cheeks.

"I'm taking back charge now. Understood?"

He slides two fingers into my mouth, and I nod.

"Good fuckin' girl."

Just as he's about to kiss me, he pulls away and lifts me off him, tossing me on the bed as he gets off of it. Before I can even figure out what's happening, he's spinning me so my legs are dangling over the edge of the bed and I'm flipped onto my stomach.

"Spread them wider, let me see that gorgeous cunt I get to sink into."

I push my legs apart and he tugs me towards him by the calves.

His rough hands grip my ass, and stars fill my vision when his hand slaps my cheek so fucking hard.

"You think you can edge me?" he hisses.

Smack.

"Fuck! Conan!" I cry out.

"Pretending you don't enjoy a bit of pain? Pretending to be a good girl?"

He thrusts his fingers inside of me; my walls clench around him. I'm dripping all over his hand.

"Hmm. Feels like you fucking love being dominated."

I dig my fingers into the blanket.

"Please, Conan," I beg.

He chuckles, teasing my entrance with the thick head of his cock.

"Oh, such a beautiful noise. Beg louder."

He pushes himself in just a touch.

"Please, Conan. Sir. Please. Fuck me. Rough. Fuck me like an animal. Make me scream your name. Make me come all over your dick. Please. Make me yours. Claim me."

CHAPTER 35
CONAN

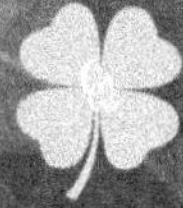

Song, Kool-Aid, Bring Me The Horizon.

That's it.

I can't hold back anymore.

I thrust into her as deep as I can, crying out her name as I do. Her pussy strangles my cock. She screams, clawing at the bedsheets.

I don't give in, I don't let up. I fuck her, like the feral animal she wants. Sliding my hand into her hair, I yank her head back by the scalp.

And when I smack her ass, she fucking floods all over me. Heaven.

"You take me so damn well, trouble." I look down at her stretching around me.

"Y-yes. More!" she cries out.

"My good girl. Letting me fuck you raw."

As soon as I say the words, my heart hammers. What the fuck am I doing?

"It feels so good, Con," she pants out, her voice husky and almost making me come.

"It's perfect," I grit out, tugging her hair even tighter.

Her warmth, the way she's squeezing me—I couldn't stop now even if I tried.

"Mine," I grunt.

"Tell me you're mine, and I'll let you come."

I push in deeper, holding her in place by her hip, my fingers digging in deep enough to leave marks.

"Tell me."

"I'm yours, Conan. Please let me come."

Her body trembles, her pussy suffocating my cock. I quickly pull out so I can flip her onto her back, and within seconds I'm sinking back inside her.

Pushing her leg back to deepen my thrust, I grip her throat. Her eyes glistening, a single tear rolls down her cheek, so I lean in and lick it.

"You look so fucking pretty when you cry for me. Now come all over my cock, trouble. And let me hear you scream."

I pinch her clit and fuck her relentlessly. Her body convulses, her eyes now almost black, and she climaxes so hard it takes me over the edge with her.

While she screams out my name, I cry out hers. I let it rip through my entire body, like all the blood is being drained from me as I fill her up.

Every last fucking drop is hers, to the point my head spins.

My chest heaves as I lean over her, resting on my forearm, and swipe her hair away from her face.

"Holy shit, Conan. I've never come like that before. I thought I was going to pass out."

"So did I." I nuzzle my face into her neck.

"Really? It was that good for you too?"

I pull back and cup her face, my cock still twitching inside her.

"I wasn't joking, Hallie. I've never experienced anything the way I do with you. And I don't just mean sex. This is new, different, but really fucking cool."

She leans into my palm and her eyes flutter closed.

"Yeah. It is, isn't it?"

She sounds exhausted.

"You got room for the both of us in your shower? Let me take care of you now?"

She nods.

"We can make it work."

I hope she's right. And not just about the shower.

About everything.

I BLINK my eyes open as Hallie wiggles her ass against my crotch.

"Morning, trouble."

"Morning, sexy."

"Oh, your voice when you wake up is so hot," I tell her, pressing my hardening cock against her ass.

"So is yours."

She turns to face me, wrapping her arms around my neck.

"I have work soon," she pouts.

"I know."

I may have demanded her schedule from Finn after the street race saga so I can "keep an eye on her".

"Maybe we could do this again? Or is that not—"

I chuckle.

"God, woman. I've just woken up, and you're already questioning me. This was never going to be a one night thing. And actually, I've been meaning to ask you something, but it turns out I had to have my balls checked first."

She grins.

"Oh, yeah?"

Jesus, why is my stomach doing somersaults?

"Well, this isn't just about sex. Not for me. I like you, Hallie. You as a person. I want to get to know you, all of you, properly. Your little quirks, what makes you laugh, and what makes you tick. So, will you go on a date with me? For real?"

She runs the back of her hand along my stubble. Fucking hell, am I about to start sweating? Why is it so hot in here?

"Yes, beastie. I'd love that."

I lean in and capture her lips, letting my kiss speak the volumes that I can't voice out loud. I am so out of my depth here, but this woman, she's keeping me afloat.

So I'll do anything possible to keep her beside me.

I pull back and study her eyes. My mom always said they're the gateway to the soul.

And when I look into hers, I feel that.

"Tonight?"

I know she's not working after six.

"I can do that. What shall we do?" she asks.

"Well, I have my fight tonight. I'd like to have you there, and then maybe I'll have a surprise for you after I win."

Her eyes go wide.

"W-with your family?" she stutters.

"Shit. Is that too much?"

She giggles.

"For a first date? Maybe. But I'd love to. Dr. Quinn will be there?"

"He will. Nothing bad will ever happen to you when you're around us."

She frowns.

"What if I get all horny watching you beast it out in the cage? Ugh. I bet you're hot as fuck." She fans herself and tips her head back.

I take the opportunity to sink my teeth into her neck.

More marks.

Mine.

"Oh, I'll let that thought fuel me to win quicker so I can get to you faster."

"I'll be waiting for you."

She kisses my nose. I groan as my phone vibrates on the bedside table. Picking it up, I see a chain of messages from Keller.

"Oh, shit," I grumble.

KELLER

you're fucking late. Get your ass here now.

I type out a quick reply.

ME

won't be long, just doing some business.

Hallie rests her head on my shoulder and I grin, pulling up my contacts list.

"See? No other women on here, well, other than my brother's wife, Charlotte, and our housekeeper."

She eyes me suspiciously.

"Did you delete them while I was asleep? And why is Charlotte saved as Crazy Bitch?"

I chuckle. I'm not sure now is the time to elaborate on

the fact my sister-in-law tried to shoot me. We've moved past that, she's one of us now. So, I'll breeze past that question.

"Nope. Deleted them all after your race. But I've not slept with anyone since before I met you that first night. I swear. I've not even thought about anyone else."

Her nails graze up my stomach.

"Good boy."

My dick stands to attention. Keller and the guys will have to wait.

"Fuck. That'll do it."

I roll on top of her, kicking open her legs.

"Conan, I don't think I can. I'm so sore," she whines, yet her hips roll against my dick.

"I'm sorry, baby. Let me make you feel better. I'll be gentle."

I nip at her neck and she wraps her legs around me, pushing me tighter.

"I'm such a slut for you, aren't I?" she whispers, and a blush spreads up her neck.

"My slut."

I lick my way up to her jaw, using my free hand to slowly circle her clit, getting her nice and wet for me.

"I thought you don't do gentle?" she asks, raising an eyebrow.

"For you? I'll do anything. Now close your eyes and relax," I whisper against her lips.

CHAPTER 36

HALLIE

"**W**ell, what do you think?" Lily asks.

I tap her hip and laugh.

"I'd tell you if I could actually see in the mirror."

"Oh. My bad." She jumps out of the way and steps behind me.

"I look…"

The shimmer of the gold eyeshadow brings out the browns in my eyes. The bouncy curls shape my face. And my skin, it's glowing.

"Beautiful," she finishes my sentence for me.

"Yeah. I kinda do, don't I?"

She places her hands on my shoulders.

"Whoever made you doubt how fucking stunning you are, I want to hunt down and beat the shit out of."

"Scary Lily."

Her eyes darken.

I often forget her Russian mobster heritage. Her and her mom moved over to the US when Lily was only young. But she keeps in contact with her father, I even met him once.

Scary as fuck. But Lily, she hides her accent so well, you'd think she's never left the States.

"I can be. Or I know people that can be."

I shiver; I know she isn't lying.

"Good to know, but I think Conan has taken on that role."

My cheeks flush just talking about him. As I look at myself in the mirror, I actually look happy.

"I assume he didn't ruin you?" she asks playfully.

"Well, no. But it's an adjustment. He took care of me after too."

She chews on her gum and has a confused expression.

"Yeah? Hallie, you know every guy should do that after? Right? That's just standard?"

I swallow and shake my head.

"I did not."

"You have a lot to learn, my little berry."

"I know. I'm trying."

She offers me a sincere smile.

"I'm proud of you. I've not seen you this giddy in a long time."

A warm fuzz envelops me as I stand up and turn to face her.

"You won the bet," I whisper.

"I'll take my payment on our next night out. Now go get that killer black dress on, you're getting picked up in twenty minutes!"

She ushers me towards the wardrobe before she heads out of the bedroom.

"And go for the deep red lipstick, that'll make him wild for you."

As the door closes, my phone pings. I run over so quickly I almost fall on the bed.

BEASTIE

I can't wait to see you. My brothers are on
their way.

ME

You better win for me, Conan. I want to
celebrate with you.

I snap a quick picture, pushing up my bust to make them almost fall out of my robe.

BEASTIE

… I'm malfunctioning. I need another one
with everything off… so I can think of it
while I fight.

Biting on my lip, I push the silk over my shoulders and let it drop to the floor. Positioning myself in front of the full-length mirror, I cross my legs and cover most of my boobs with my forearm, but leave enough showing to give him an idea.

Once I'm happy, I hit send.

BEASTIE

Brb, now I have to jerk off to this.

Another text pops up immediately.

BEASTIE

Sorry, what I meant was, you're so fucking
hot. I can't wait to get my hands on you.

I let out a giggle.

ME

I'm already wet just thinking about what
you'll do to me.

BEASTIE

Drop to my knees and eat you out. Come
all over your tits. Fuck your face. Eat you
out again. Fill you up. Tie you up. And
that's just the first round.

Holy shit.

ME

Can I touch myself?

His name flashes up on the screen and I accept his call.

"You're in my earphones, I'm in the changing room. You can, baby. But I want to listen while I warm up."

"Holy shit, this is hot," I whisper, suddenly aware that Lily is downstairs.

"Yeah, I know. And it's too busy here for me to do anything about it." The frustration in his voice is clear.

"This won't distract you?"

I quietly lock my door and lay down on the bed, spreading my legs.

"No. Please, trouble, I gotta hear it. Those little whimpers."

Circling my clit, I melt into the feeling.

"I wish it was you doing this."

He grunts down the line.

"You got any toys?"

I scramble for my bedside drawer and pick my favorite red one out.

"I've got the best one, she makes me finish in record time."

"Quicker than me?"

"God, no. But quick enough for you to get back to training."

"Good girl. You lying down?" he asks quietly.

"Yes. I'm imagining it's your tongue."

I put him on speaker and rest the phone on the pillow next to my head.

"Let me hear you whimper for me, Hallie. And I'll let you know when you can come."

I let out a gasp as I slide the cool toy inside of me.

"Ah. There it is. That sweet, sweet noise."

I push it in as far as I can and turn it on, letting the vibrations take over.

"Fuck, Conan."

"How close?" he asks.

"Very."

My toes start to curl.

"Take it out," he commands, and my blood runs cold.

"W-what? No."

"Hallie. Take. It. Out."

Reluctantly, I do as he says.

"You're going to pay for this, beastie," I fire back.

"I'm counting on it, baby," he chuckles.

"I'll see you soon."

He blows a kiss and cuts the line. I stare at the toy on my bed.

I could just ignore his order.

I shake my head. Nope. This is way hotter.

As the Mercedes pulls up outside my house, nerves take over.

"Here." Lily hands me my leather jacket. "She's a stunner."

"Thank you."

I give Bertie one last head pat.

"I'll see you tomorrow morning?"

Lily grins.

"Don't rush home tomorrow. Me and Bertie will be having loads of fun. Enjoy your time with Conan."

"You're the best," I tell her.

"I know I am. Now go." She points to the door. I rush out in my heels down the steps, and Dr. Quinn gets out to greet me.

"Hallie."

"Dr. Quinn."

He shakes his head.

"Outside of office hours, I'm Finn." He opens up the door for me.

"In there is Declan and Charlotte."

As I go to get in, Finn clears his throat, which makes me pause.

"This isn't weird. Right? I know we work together, but your brother makes me happy."

Finn chews on his lip with a frown.

"Hallie, what or who you do in your spare time has nothing to do with me. I just don't want this to impact our working relationship if it goes wrong."

"Oh." I drop my gaze.

"Not that it will. But Conan is Conan."

"Finn. Shut the fuck up," a deep Irish voice shouts from inside the car.

"It won't," I assure him. "We're just friends."

I don't even know why I bothered with that lie.

He raises his eyebrows.

"Fucking hell, you're both shit liars," he mutters as I get in the car, sliding in next to Charlotte.

And my god, she is beautiful.

Stunning blue eyes and dark purple hair. Tattoos that span her entire arm.

"Hey. I'm Hallie." I hold my hand out to her.

"I'm Charlotte. I've heard a lot about you." She pauses. "Actually from my daughter. Conan talks about you a lot to her."

"Aww. That's sweet."

She smiles and I relax.

"Yeah. It is very."

Declan turns in his seat to face me. His eyes are an even more striking blue.

He has similarities to Conan, like the nose and face shape.

But he doesn't have Conan's cheeky look.

"Declan?" I ask.

"Yep. Nice to meet you. Whatever Conan had said about us, it's all bollocks."

"He's only ever said good things."

"Oh. Well then." He shuts up.

I laugh, and so does the rest of the group.

I turn to Charlotte as she eyes her husband, and Finn starts to weave in and out of traffic.

"Even Charlotte?" Declan quizzes.

"Hey!" She leans forward and smacks his arm.

"What? He has you saved as Crazy Bitch on his phone."

I hold in my laughter. He never did answer my question about that.

Charlotte pouts.

"I didn't shoot him though."

My heart hammers and my eyes lock with Finn's in the rearview mirror.

"Shoot him?" I question.

Declan and Charlotte make a silent exchange.

"Yeah. We had a little disagreement, so I stole his gun and shot him. No ammo in it though, he was fine. As you know, he's still alive."

My mouth drops open. This only makes my mind race thinking about Pete's warning.

"Okay," I say quietly.

"Don't worry. You're safe with us." Charlotte smiles sincerely, and it puts my racing mind at ease.

Conan has never not made me feel safe. I know there's more to him, and he's actively inviting me to be part of it.

To see this, maybe, darker side to his life that he's alluded to.

"I know," I tell her.

Charlotte leans in.

"The world is full of monsters, Hallie. But these guys? They're the good ones disguised as the bad. Just remember that."

I frown as she pulls away. I just want Conan as he is. I don't care about anything else.

"Are you excited to see Conan fight? He's an absolute animal in the cage." She switches conversation so easily.

"Yeah. I've never been to one of these either."

I leave out the part about how excited I am to see my sexy man doing something he loves.

I twirl my thumbs on my lap.

"Just remember, he knows what he's doing, okay?" Declan chimes in.

"Hallie is a nurse, Dec. She can cope with a few cuts and some blood," Finn counters.

I don't want Conan to get hurt.

As we pull up outside the stadium, Finn helps me out of the car and I walk in beside him.

The place is buzzing, mainly with men. Crowds of people chanting and cheering. I look over to the big metal cage in the center.

The two guys in there are beating the shit out of each other. Blood sprays from the smaller one's nose. I stand still, transfixed on the violence.

"Come on, we gotta get up front." Finn ushers me along.

A bottle flies past my head and the group surrounds me. They're like my own bodyguards; even Charlotte has a scary look in her eyes, like she could take down any one of these men.

Declan and Finn push their way through so we're at the front, past the barrier, and finally I can breathe.

"This is crazy," I mutter.

"Crazy for a first date, yeah," Declan says under his breath, and Finn jabs his elbow in his ribs.

"What?"

"Oh, just to warn you, all three of them argue constantly. Out of love, apparently," Charlotte whispers.

"It's kinda cute."

Both the men glare at me and Charlotte giggles.

"I'm going to go check on Con. I'll be back," Finn announces as he strides away.

Charlotte and Declan stay on either side of me, again, like they're protecting me.

Conan's face flashes up on the huge screen. Videos of him training, clips from his previous fights.

My jaw is on the floor.

Fuck. He's hot. But he looks so angry. I almost don't recognize him.

Nerves wash over me. I can hear what feels like every person talking in the room, and the flashing lights are making me dizzy.

CHAPTER 37
CONAN

"Is Hallie okay?" I ask as soon as Finn barges into my room.

"Yes. She's fine. We said we'd look out for her."

I nod, adrenaline already burning through my veins as I jog on the spot.

"You ready?" Finn asks, stepping aside as I punch the air.

"Ready as I'll ever be."

He nods, sliding on his cap.

"I'm saying this out of brotherly love—and because, for some reason, I think Hallie's good for you—but don't lose your head in there. She's watching."

I freeze and swallow hard.

"I'm trying."

But I can't help it when that switch flips. When that fury eats through everything.

"You need to give yourself more credit. You control the switch, not the other way around."

I nod.

"You want that championship shot? Go fucking get it, brother."

He grips my shoulder hard. Sometimes he reminds me of Dad so much it guts me.

Fuck, I miss him.

"I will."

"Now, please get back out there with Hallie. I'm starting to question if bringing her was a bad idea."

Finn chuckles. "Too late now, Con. You realize the more time she spends with us, the more she's going to start working us out? She's clever, that girl."

Chewing on my lip, I nod.

"I want her to know all of me."

Except the Decadence Chase. That part stays buried.

"She's not like Charlotte, Con. She might not be as accepting of our lifestyle."

I clench my wrapped fists.

"I guess I'll just have to see how far I can push her before she runs."

"That's the spirit. Good luck, bro."

As the door shuts behind him, I sit on the bench, waiting for my name to be called.

How much will be too much for Hallie?

If she knew who I really was, would she still be here?

I slam my fist into my thigh.

"Con. You're up." Grayson strides into the room.

I stand and pull on my competition gloves.

"Use your head. Stay light on your feet. Then unleash the beast. You've got this easy."

He taps my back as I walk toward the tunnel.

I won't lose my head.

Not this time.

CHAPTER 38

HALLIE

My heart climbs into my throat as the music blares and the crowd roars.

Then he steps into the cage—my Conan—in those shimmering green shorts.

His body gleams under the lights, muscle carved like a god's.

I press my lips shut to stop myself from salivating.

When his opponent enters the ring, Conan's eyes find mine.

And in that second, nothing else matters.

When he winks, I melt.

I blow him a kiss, and he chews on his lip, giving me that look.

The one that says he wants to rip my panties off with his teeth.

"Good luck," I mouth.

The bell rings. The crowd goes feral.

His opponent, smaller but fast, launches at Conan, who grapples him and slams him against the cage wall.

He lands with a brutal thud.

"Fucking come on then!" Conan beats his chest as the man scrambles to his feet.

Conan lunges without hesitation, slamming into him like a truck.

As he grabs on, he drives a punch into the guy's gut.

"Cover, Conan!" A huge blond guy pounds the metal.

The other fighter brings his knee up—smashes it into Conan's jaw.

Conan stumbles and shakes it off. Then they're back at it, brutal and relentless.

Like two wild animals tearing at each other.

Punches, kicks, sweat, blood.

The guy swings. Conan ducks. Drives his foot straight into the guy's stomach.

My pulse won't calm. I'm chewing my nails like they'll anchor me.

"You can breathe, Hallie. Nothing's going to happen to him," Finn says beside me, eyes locked on his brother.

"Fucking hit him harder!" Declan shouts, making me jump.

The bell rings again. The ref pulls them apart.

I finally breathe.

That five minutes felt like a goddamn eternity.

Conan wipes sweat and blood from his face, eyes locked on mine as he blows me a kiss.

I hope I don't look as pale as I feel.

CHAPTER 39

CONAN

Song, Coming Undone, Korn.

I stride to my team. Keller's already on me, wiping blood from my face.

I spit out my mouthguard and gulp water.

"You're doing a good job, Con. Use that brute strength. He can't take it. And those kicks? Beautiful."

"Thanks." I rub my jaw. "That fucking knee to the jaw hurt like a bitch."

"Yeah, I bet. Don't leave yourself open like that again."

Before the bell rings, I glance at that beautiful girl in the front row.

"I need to finish him this round," I tell Grayson.

"You know what to do."

I nod.

For five minutes, I need to be the man I don't want Hallie to see.

The faster I end this, the faster I get to my date.

"I'm on it."

Grayson slaps my bicep.

"Not too far, Conan," he warns.

"I'll try."

I head back to the center of the cage. Dan's eyes lock with mine—cold, dark, smug.

"That your girl?" He smirks, glancing toward Hallie.

"Oh, I wouldn't go there," I hiss.

"I can. I'll knock you clean out and take your girl. I bet her pussy tastes—"

He doesn't finish.

A clean uppercut shuts his mouth and drops him to the mat.

Seconds later, I'm on top of him.

The more he tries to fight, the harder I hit.

Fist after fist after fist.

I grab his throat. He gasps, flailing. His hits go weak.

I let go.

It's not enough. I want him to hurt more.

He charges. I kick his thigh out from under him.

"I'll still fuck your girl and make you watch. Might even share her with my friends," he spits.

There it is.

The switch flips.

I'm going to kill this man.

"Oh, fuck. Fuck. Fuck." Finn says each word louder.

"Conan, no!" Declan screams.

"W-what's going on?" I grab Finn's arm, but I don't take my eyes off Conan.

Blood pours from the guy's mouth as Conan drives a kick into his face, the thud echoing around the arena. Before the man can drop, Conan's thighs clamp around his neck like a vise. He taps weakly on the canvas with one hand, the other flailing. His face drains of color while Conan hammers punch after punch into his skull.

He's going to kill him.

"Conan!!" I scream.

Those eyes, dark and wild, I don't recognize them. But when they meet mine, his chest heaves slower. And he lets the guy go.

My hands tremble as they fall to my sides. I step back. Everything's a blur.

Conan is announced the winner. His team swarms him. But all I can do is stand there, stunned.

That wasn't a fight. That was a brawl to the death. And Conan looked like he wanted it.

I didn't recognize the monster in there.

My chest feels like it's caving in. I can't breathe. "I-I need some air," I whisper to Charlotte.

"I've got you."

She grabs my hand and leads me past the crowd, shoving open the metal doors.

The cold night air hits me like a slap. I plant my hands on the wall, sucking in lungfuls. I'm overstimulated as hell.

"Hallie, it's okay. It's just a cage fight. It's what they do," she says softly.

I shake my head.

"He could've killed someone."

Charlotte laughs. "Hallie, that's something you'll have to get used to, being involved with the Quinn family. Death comes with it."

"Even murder?" I whisper.

"Uh, yeah. You really need to talk to Conan. Or leave. Before he falls any harder for you. I don't know what to say, Hallie."

My head spins. "Can you take me home?"

Her eyes dart left to right. "I need the keys. Come with me?" She holds out her hand, and I take it.

She leads me down a corridor and pushes open a door. All the air is knocked from my lungs.

Conan's there. Bloodied. Looking sorry as hell.

"I'll leave you guys to it," Charlotte says, disappearing before I can stop her.

I step inside and close the door.

"Are you okay?" he asks quietly.

"No. Not really. That was… a lot. So is everything I'm learning right now."

He runs his hands through his hair, fidgeting like a boy who knows he's done wrong.

"I'm sorry if I scared you." There's honesty in his voice. Sincerity that softens my gut.

"Who are you, Conan Quinn? Who are you really?"

His Adam's apple bobs. "I'm an ex-underground, turned professional MMA fighter. I run a garage to fix my cars. And I'm a Quinn. Which means Irish Mafia. Born and bred."

I let out a shaky breath. "Mafia?"

"Yeah. I'm sorry I didn't tell you, trouble. I didn't know what you'd say."

My eyes trace the ink on his skin. The blood. The bruises.

And that face—raw, pained, aching.

"I didn't want to lose you. I thought you'd hate that part of me."

I step in close, resting my hands on his sticky chest. "I'm annoyed you thought I'd run from you, beastie. I knew something was off. I just didn't expect that."

He lets out a quiet laugh and wraps his arms around me. His grip's tight. Protective.

"Are you mad at me?" he murmurs into the top of my head.

"I'm more mad that you've been edging me for hours."

He pulls back, cupping my face.

"I'll resolve that for you, baby." He presses his lips to mine.

"Am I safe with you?" I ask, staring into his eyes.

He doesn't hesitate. "Always. It's not as bad as it sounds. It's business."

"You don't hurt kids, women, or animals?"

"Fuck no. We try to stop the ones who do. That's the goal, in a roundabout way."

I slide my hands up his chest and wrap them around his neck.

"We've gotta work on your temper, Conan. The way you flip—it's unsettling."

He sighs, resting his forehead against mine.

"I'm trying, Hallie. I really fuckin' am. A few years ago, I killed a guy—a rival family's son. That cost my father his life. And I'll never forgive myself."

I close my eyes and hold him tighter. "How can I help you, Conan?"

I see him. The man under the blood. And I want to be his anchor.

"Just by being you, Hallie."

I lean back and run my finger across the cut on his eyebrow.

"Want me to clean you up?"

He smirks.

"Oh, yes, please."

He lets out a groan as I run my tongue along his jaw.

"So what am I now to you? Your on-call nurse, your fuck buddy, your friend, your cheerleader at fights?"

His fingers squeeze my throat.

"You forgot the comedian," he whispers against my ear.

"I am kinda funny."

His free hand grips my ass.

"Funny. Beautiful. Sexy. Smart. Kind. Caring."

I start to blush as he reels them out.

"You forgot horny."

"Hallie, I know you're horny as hell. But, we have a booth booked at a bar. The quicker we do that, the quicker I get you back to that penthouse."

His breathing quickens as I grab his dick through his shorts.

"Is that a promise?" I bat my lashes at him.

"Damn fucking right."

I let out a squeal as he lifts me by the waist and pushes my back against the wall.

"You look fucking divine, darlin. And we have a win to celebrate."

I grab his face and he smiles.

"I'm proud of you."

He blinks at me but remains silent.

"You were a beast in that ring. You owned it. And you won fair and square. You just about managed to contain the anger this time. I think that's a pretty big deal."

"You're not just a fuck to me, you know that, right?" he tells me.

"I know, beastie. Because if I was, you'd have had sex with me here already."

Wrapping my leg tighter around his waist, I roll my hips over his cock.

"We could, just quickly," I whisper against his lips, biting back my grin.

"You think you can tell me what to do?"

He squeezes his hand tighter around my throat, but I can't help but smile.

He's making me crazy.

And I love it.

"Eat me out."

He blows out a breath.

"Alright. You win. Tell me what to do whenever you want, trouble."

He drops to his knees and grabs my leg, putting it over his shoulder.

I hold onto the wall for support, a soft moan leaving me as he runs his tongue all the way up the inside of my thigh.

I hold my breath with my eyes closed, waiting for him to feast on me.

But it never happens.

As I look down, he's grinning wildly.

"You're soaked for me, darlin'. And I want to enjoy every second of seeing you squirm tonight. That anticipation will make you scream so loud for me later. Trust me?"

"Fuck." I hit my head back against the wall.

What was heat is now ice running through me.

"Please?"

He nips at my sensitive skin.

"Trust. Me. Trouble."

CONAN

I blow out a breath as Hallie and Charlotte head to the ladies' room.

"You good?" Finn asks.

"Yeah. That was fucking close. I scared her. I could see it in her eyes."

I knock back the rest of my scotch. I'm only having one because I want to be high off Hallie, nothing else.

"It's better she knows now, if you're serious," Declan chimes in.

"She took it fine."

"Does she know about Ben?" Finn asks with a grin.

"Fuck no. But she knows I sorted it. She's a smart girl. She'll put the pieces together."

Finn nods.

"Her and Charlotte seem to get along well." I nod toward them laughing as they re-enter the room, and just about every guy's head swivels to watch them.

"Charlotte is a good girl, under that murderous exterior," Declan says, admiring his woman.

I want what he has.

At first I thought he'd lost the plot being so head over heels over a woman.

Now? I get it.

That life, that little bubble of calm he's built, means everything to him.

Maybe I can have my own version of that.

Hallie sets her sights on me with a bright smile, and my heart stutters, then pounds.

Yeah.

She is my happy place. I'm certain of it.

I slide over in the booth to let her in, but this little minx is out to make me pay.

I can tell by her smile.

She shuffles in and then jumps on my lap, pressing her ass right against my dick.

Wrapping my arms around her waist, I brush my lips over her shoulder.

"Naughty girl. You have no idea who you're messing with," I mutter, only loud enough for her to hear.

"Oh, I have a good idea."

She wiggles her ass, and I tighten my hold.

As she sips her champagne, joining in the conversation with my brothers, I just watch.

She fits right in with us.

As she leans back, resting herself against my chest, I rest my head on her shoulder.

"To Conan on getting his championship spot," Finn announces, and we all raise a glass.

Hallie turns her head to me.

"You didn't tell me how important it was! Championship spot? Conan!"

I shrug and take the glass from her hand.

"Gotta win my next fight to be declared Champion."

She frowns and pouts.

"Don't pout like that unless you want me to lay you over the table and kiss the life out of you."

Her eyes go wide and that blush spreads up her neck.

"And that's a problem, because?"

She is taunting me.

My blood rushes south and I don't trust myself to keep it together.

"Hallie," I warn.

She digs around in her purse, and then her hand slyly dips into mine.

Her fucking panties.

I throw my head back and groan.

"You're killing me, trouble."

"You deserve this."

She smiles sweetly and then turns back around to the table.

I glance down at the lace in my hand, rub it between my fingers, then shove it in my jacket pocket.

My hand slides over her thigh. She tries to close her legs, but I keep them just inches apart.

With each breath, I move higher, slipping under the hem of her dress.

"Conan," she hisses.

"Yes?"

I run my nose along her shoulder blade.

As discreetly as I can, I press her clit with my index finger.

"Fuck," I hiss.

She's soaked. I can't take this anymore.

CHAPTER 42

HALLIE

Song, southbound, Artemas.

I feel him hardening under me, and I bite my lip, trying to navigate the conversation Charlotte and Declan are having with me about my job.

It's as hard as Conan's cock to concentrate.

"Excuse me. I have to go to the ladies' room," I blurt out.

If he won't relieve me, I'll have to do it myself. I feel like I'm about to spontaneously combust.

"Where do you think you're going?" Conan growls in my ear.

"Chase me."

He groans as I shuffle off his lap and make a dart for the toilets. Before I grab the handle, he grips the back of my neck, spins me to face him, and kisses me.

"You're driving me crazy, Hallie," he mutters between kisses.

"Well, do something about it," I challenge.

His eyes darken as they flick upward.

"In a bathroom? You want to get fucked here when we

have a suite waiting for us?"

I grab the collar of his shirt and tug him down to me.

"Conan. I desperately need your dick inside of me. Call it an appetizer or something. Do what you want with me after. I just cannot think straight until you make me come. I'm losing my mind here."

He's making me insane, but it's in the best possible way.

Conan twists the handle and we fall into the ladies' room, our lips locked, my fingers fumbling with his belt.

The door clicks shut behind us.

His hand grips my jaw, forcing me to meet his eyes.

"You've been such a good fucking girl for me, baby."

He spins me around, and I grip the basin as he kicks my legs open and yanks up my dress.

His hands slide over my ass.

"Fucking perfect."

Our eyes lock in the mirror and the room goes molten.

He unbuttons his pants and frees his cock, making me lick my lips.

"This what you want, darlin'?" he asks, stroking his dick.

I nod eagerly.

"You've been teasing me all night, trouble. Now I get to give you a taste of how it feels. Be quiet, my brothers don't need to hear how loud you are when you come."

My mouth drops open. He gives me a smirk.

"I—I can't be quiet."

He chuckles and thrusts his fingers inside my needy pussy.

"Oh, I know."

As he pulls his fingers out, he steps behind me and runs his hand up my throat, then shoves his soaked digits into my mouth, deep.

"Problem solved." He winks at me in the mirror.

My muffled cries echo as he slams into me.

"God, baby," he grits out.

I keep my eyes on him. With every thrust, I watch him go deeper, lose more of his control.

He's losing his mind, just like I am.

"You want to be filled up with my cum?"

"Y-yes."

I bite down on his fingers as he slaps my ass and fucks me into oblivion.

"I can feel you're close."

He presses down on my lower back and lets loose.

"Come on, baby. Give it to me."

He slaps my ass and I scream, but he shoves his fingers deeper into my mouth.

"Now."

He spills inside me and I follow, letting the orgasm tear through every nerve ending.

He keeps thrusting until I'm wrung out and trembling.

As he brushes my hair off my shoulder and plants a kiss there, I melt.

Then he turns me to face him.

"That better, trouble?" he whispers against my lips.

"Much better, beastie."

I straighten his tie and pull him in for a kiss.

"Can we leave yet?" I ask.

He licks his lips.

"You don't like my family?"

My eyes widen in horror.

"Oh my god, it's not that. They're great. It's just, I want to spend time with just you."

He steals another kiss and slips a set of keys into my hand.

"You wanna drive? I brought the Bugatti."

I gasp.

"You fixed it?"

He nods. I kiss him hard.

"It would be an honor. Can I race it one day?" I flutter my lashes at him for full effect.

"If you behave. Now, shall we escape?" he asks.

That word flicks something in my brain I think he might enjoy.

I slide off the basin and duck under his arm, sprinting straight for the door.

I shoot left toward the back exit, bashing through the double doors into the dark.

"Shit."

I run for the parking lot, his footsteps heavy and closing in behind me.

I spot it under the lights and make a dash, unlocking it just before I reach it.

A burst of giggles escapes me as he grabs me and lifts me, planting my ass on the hood.

"Gotcha." He winks.

Darting my eyes around, I realize there's no one here. Slowly, I spread my legs open for him.

His gaze zeroes in on my pussy. He runs a hand down his face and lets out a ragged breath.

"Be a good boy and clean me up so I don't make a mess on your seats."

He drags me closer and drops to his knees.

"This pussy is mine. No one else ever gets to see it, touch it, taste it, or fuck it again. Understood?"

I swallow, instinctively trying to close my legs, but he only pushes them wider.

"If my face is between your legs, no one can see your

sweet pussy. Only me. I'll do as you demand, darlin'. Then you're my good little slut tonight."

As soon as his tongue connects with my clit, my legs quiver.

"Let me hear you. No need to hold back now."

Holy shit.

I'm getting eaten out on the hood of a Bugatti in a parking lot.

I've officially lost my mind.

And I don't care about anything except what Conan's tongue is doing to me.

"More, Conan," I beg.

He answers with the addition of his fingers, fucking me deep.

It doesn't take long for my climax to build, the pressure unbearable.

When he curls his fingers just right, my hips buck, but he holds me still.

"C-Con, I'm close."

My soft moans become frantic, my breathing scattered.

I can feel it rising in me, pulsing through every limb.

Running my fingers through his hair, I hold him in place and ride his face.

His groans against my pussy only drive me closer.

"Oh my god."

I throw my head back and scream his name as a warm gush escapes from me.

"What the—"

I look down, panting, blood whooshing in my ears. Conan is still licking up every drop of my mess.

As our eyes lock, my heart stutters. I've soaked him.

He grins as he pulls back and wipes his mouth with the back of his hand.

"Baby, you just squirted all over my Bugatti."

He adjusts his crotch as I close my legs.

"I—I did?" I croak.

He leans in, grabs me by the neck, and kisses me. I can still taste myself on his lips.

"Yeah. And that was the hottest damn sight I've ever witnessed. Shame I can't ever clean my car again."

I giggle, and he kisses me again.

"I've never squirted before," I whisper.

"Fuuuuuck," he groans.

"You're serious? Never? I'm the first?"

That excitement in his voice makes my chest bloom with warmth.

"I saved it for you. Now take me to bed, baby," I whisper.

"I can't wait to see what else I can make you do." He grins, pulling away and lifting me off the hood to help me into the passenger seat.

"Such a gentleman. Hey, I thought I was driving?"

He chuckles.

"After how hard you just came? I don't think your legs can take the drive." He pauses and licks his lip.

"And I'm a gentleman most of the time, yes. But what I'm going to do to you all night is far from that, trouble."

I snap my mouth closed and squeeze my thighs together, which makes him chuckle.

That's what I love.

We can flit between laughing, making each other come, being emotional, and peeling back our layers. And every single part we expose only connects us deeper.

He's the match.

And I'm the spark.

Together, we burn bright.

CHAPTER 43
CONAN

Song, I Feel Like I'm Drowning, Two Feet.

The sun shines bright through the windows, warm and unrelenting, and I pull Hallie tighter against my chest.

"Morning, gorgeous."

She stirs against me, her body a perfect fit, her voice husky as sin.

"Good morning, beastie."

The sound of it, rough and ruined from how hard I made her scream last night. It sends electricity down my spine. She's wrecked and still radiant. And fuck, all I can think about is how much I need to wake up like this again.

Preferably every damn day.

I exhale slowly, heart thudding, a wave of nerves crashing over me.

"Hallie…"

She sits up, tugging her messy bun loose and shaking out

her hair like a goddess. Like mine. She's so beautiful it hurts.

"This sounds serious."

I cup her cheek, grounding myself in her.

"In a good way."

Clearing my throat, I stare into her eyes and let silence speak. I'm a fucking asshole. If she ever finds out the truth, the whole truth, I'll lose her. And I'm not sure I'll survive that.

One lie can't destroy everything we've built…can it?

"I'm going away for a few days next week."

My stomach twists.

"Are you going anywhere nice, beastie?"

She smiles, and it's like a goddamn knife to the heart.

"Just to train with Grayson in New York."

"That sounds fun. You gonna miss me?"

I tug her bottom lip with my thumb, memorizing the softness there.

"Of course I'll miss you. I'm gutted I have to go, when things are finally falling into place," I sigh.

I watch as she traces the tattoos on my chest with her finger. Damn it feels nice.

"Wait. Why are you saying it's good you're leaving me?"

I said that? What? Oh…

"I'm not leaving you. Shit."

I sit upright and pull her onto my lap, needing her close —needing her to know this isn't goodbye.

"I'm just teasing you, beastie."

She pouts at me and I blow out a breath.

"There was something else I wanted to ask…"

God, I'm nervous.

"Well?" she prods, her eyes searching mine.

"I was wondering… if maybe you want to do more of this when I'm home?"

She gives me a confused look, her stare searing into my soul.

"This? As in, fucking?"

I thread my hands through her hair and pull her into a kiss. One that says everything I've never said. One that's deep and slow and full of all the unspoken things I've kept buried.

A promise.

"More than that, baby. I was asking if you'd like to go on more dates with me."

Her eyes glisten. She cups my face, her voice trembling with excitement.

"You have no idea how much I'd love that. We can have so much fun. We could go travelling? What about Germany? Race some cars on a track? Or Dublin, show me where you grew up? I'm trying to save, so we could do some vacations?"

I want all of it. Every damn thing. With her.

"Darlin', I've got more than enough money for us to travel the world and never work again. And a private jet to take us wherever we want. Don't kill yourself saving. I've got you."

She opens her mouth to argue, then snaps it shut.

"You're rich? Wow. I really did hit the jackpot. Treat me like a queen, beastie."

I blink, startled. But at least she's honest.

She could drain every account I have, and I wouldn't care; she'd probably just buy badass cars and book trips to racetracks. And I'd be right there with her.

"I'm joking. I'd still date you if you were broke. I fell for you because you're funny… and very, very persistent."

I link my fingers with hers, grounding myself in the feel of her.

She pouts, mind clearly spinning. She's too fucking cute.

"Oh, and you're probably the hottest man I've seen on this planet. That helps. Even if the money goes, you'll still be fine as hell and know how to fuck."

The shit she says. It kills me, in the best way.

"You fell for me, hmm?"

"Yeah. I dived headfirst off a fucking cliff for you, Mr. Quinn. Straight into the sea of madness and obsession."

"Trust me, baby. I'm swimming right there with you."

She bites her lip. "So how many days are you away, exactly? I might pick up some extra shifts. Wait—is Finn going with you? He's off next week too."

Fuck. Sometimes I forget he's her boss.

"Yeah. He's my punching bag."

"I doubt that. Hang on...is my boss part of the mafia too?"

She whispers mafia like it's a sin.

"Yes, trouble. Dr. Quinn is very naughty outside of hospital hours."

I press my finger over her lips, teasing.

"Our little secret. You tell anyone, and I'll have to kill you."

Her eyes go wide. I try not to laugh.

"Make it painless. I might have to tell my best friend, Lily. But it's okay—I'm certain her dad is part of the Russian mafia," she rambles.

What the fuck?

I need to ask Drago about that.

"Jesus, Hallie. I'm joking. I'd never, ever, ever hurt you. Nor would Finn. None of us would. No matter what. If I break that promise, I'll let you kill me. Okay?"

She goes quiet. That silence cuts deep.

"I can't tell if you're fucking with me. I'm going to need diagrams on how this mafia stuff works. Do I need a bodyguard? Is Declan your boss? Who is his boss? Do I have to work for you too?"

I slap my hand over her mouth before her questions spin me into a full-blown panic.

"I am your bodyguard. The rest doesn't matter. I'm keeping you far away from that side of my life. I just need you to know it exists. That it's part of me."

"Okay, beastie. I trust you." She grins and squeezes my biceps. "My protector."

Damn right I am. And I always will be.

"So… want to spend tonight with me again? And then we can date once I'm home?"

I rub my nose against hers, needing her like air.

"Lily's dropping Bertie back home this afternoon. Stay at mine?"

I can't take her back to Decadence anyways. Not yet. That's a whole other world I'm not ready to explain. In time…maybe.

I probably need to buy a house outside the chocolate factory. Somewhere that's just mine. Just ours.

Maybe I'll do that after the Chase is finished.

"Sounds perfect to me, trouble."

Because as long as I'm with her, it doesn't matter where we are. She's home.

CHAPTER 44

CONAN

"Why so glum, brother?" Declan asks, already pouring me a whiskey.

I take it and knock it back in one gulp.

"I feel like shit," I mutter, sinking into the chair opposite him.

"You get injured in the fight?"

I run a hand over my face. If anyone can understand, it's my madly-in-love brother.

"No. I just had to lie to Hallie about the Chase. And I can't see her all week." I sigh, heavy and hollow.

Declan chews on his lip, reading me.

"You know we can't call the games off now. It's too late. But this can be the last year, you know…if you and her end up together. If that's what you want."

I snatch the bottle of Dad's whiskey and take another swig straight from the neck. I know exactly what he and Mom would've said. Mom would've loved Hallie. She's a good girl. Good for me.

"Yeah. That's what I want. But if she ever finds out the truth about me—or this whole fucking thing—" I throw my arms up, gesturing to the goddamn sex club we own. "She'll run for the hills. And that's not the Chase I want."

I drag my hands down my face, the dread sitting deep in my gut, gnawing. Declan's right—we can't afford to lose Enzo or our position in this world. We've bled too much for it.

"She might not," Declan says quietly. "I saw how she was watching you fight, Con. You know what she did do, though? Something none of us have been able to do. Not even Mom…"

My head snaps up. "What did she do?"

Declan's lips curl around his glass, a slow, knowing grin spreading across his face.

"She tamed the beast in you."

I frown. "Tamed me? How?"

He rolls his eyes and throws back the rest of his whiskey.

"Fuck me, do I really have to spell this out for you? Last night. In the cage. You lost it. Mentally tapped out. You were about to kill that guy. Am I right?"

The knot in my chest tightens. My throat closes.

"Yeah. But I didn't kill him."

Declan taps the side of his head.

"Because…"

I close my eyes and drag myself back to the fight. It's a blur, just like every other time rage hijacks my brain. But then…

That flash.

Locking eyes with Hallie.

I didn't want her to look at me like I was a monster. I wanted her to be proud of me. Not terrified. Not running.

"Fuck," I whisper.

"Fuck indeed, little bro. She's the one."

I slide my glass away and pour more whiskey. Let the burn anchor me.

"What do I do, Declan? I've never—"

"Had a relationship longer than one night?" he finishes for me.

I nod. Not quite how I would've phrased it, but he's not wrong.

Until Hallie, I never let anyone get close enough to matter. I've always been better alone.

But now?

Picturing a future without her in it?

Unthinkable.

"You do the Decadence Chase. One last time," he says. "And then you follow your heart. You don't let her get away. The games start Monday. It'll be a few days, max. Then you're done. We'll find replacements. No issue. Rowan and Reggie have been frothing at the mouth for a chance to host. They'll make good Masters of Inferno."

My stomach turns. It's real now.

And she's the only thing I've ever wanted to fight for.

"I can't let her go," I say, my voice hoarse. "She's mine."

She's not just a woman.

She's an obsession.

A fire under my skin I'll never be free of.

One last Chase.

That's all that stands in my way.

CHAPTER 45

HALLIE

Day one of Conan being away. Five more to go.

I miss him.

Holding back a yawn, I glance down at my phone, my heart softening the second I see his name lighting up my screen. Just a text, but it's enough to make me smile like a fool.

Beastie: I can't stop thinking about you.

I reply quickly, feeling Lily's stare at the side of my head.

Me: Same goes to you, beastie.

When I look up again, Lily's quiet. Not because she has nothing to say—but because she's watching me. Studying me like she already knows the truth before I do.

"You're really falling for him fast," she says, a small smile playing at her lips. "It looks good on you."

I nod.

She's not wrong. I haven't felt like this in... God, I don't even know how long.

That kind of dangerous, all-consuming happy—the kind

that makes you start bracing for impact, waiting for it all to fall apart.

"Yeah," I murmur, voice light but real. "I guess Conan's been able to show me in just a few weeks how I should be treated…when others couldn't manage that in a year."

I set my coffee down, the ceramic clinking softly against the table, and turn toward her, crossing my legs.

There's a tension in my chest I didn't realize I'd been holding until I speak again.

"So you don't think I'm crazy? For dating him? After everything that happened with Ben?"

Lily doesn't even flinch.

"Hallie, sweetie. You are—and always have been—a little crazy."

She grins. "But Conan seems like the same kind of crazy. And you're good for each other. That's all that matters."

And that right there? That's why she's my best friend.

She loves my chaos, even when it drives her to the edge.

She leans back and lifts her coffee, dramatic as ever.

"And fuck Ben. Not literally. I mean, I hope he dives headfirst out of a plane and his parachute fails."

She presses a hand to her chest like she's making a vow.

"And I say this with every ounce of hatred I possess in my tiny, furious body—Fuck. Ben. If I ever see that bastard again, I swear to God, I'll go full crazy and drive my stiletto through his eye."

And that right there? Is the other joy of having Lily as a best friend.

She hates my exes more than I do.

"Ugh. I don't want to talk about that asshole ever again." A shiver runs down my spine; I will never forget how wild Ben was when he attacked me.

Bertie jumps up between us and rolls onto his belly.

"So needy," I tease, stroking him.

"So what are the plans for this week?" Lily asks, leaning over to grab the bowl of chips.

"Working mainly. Might clean the car. Potentially sort my laundry out."

Her mouth falls open.

"Fuck. Is he trying to domesticate you too?"

I scowl at her.

"No. No one could ever do that."

I hope that isn't what he expects from me.

"What if he's as messy as I am?" I gasp in horror.

Lily chuckles and shoves some chips in her mouth.

"Hire a cleaner."

"True."

Not on my wage we won't be. I snuggle up with Bertie and start scrolling through the TV to find a film with a smile on my face. I'm really fucking happy.

By the time I can hardly keep my eyes open, I glance over and find Lily sound asleep beside me. I've been utterly exhausted today, probably after spending the weekend with Conan, I need a week's rest. I look at my phone and it's nearly midnight.

Conan's nickname appears on the screen.

BEASTIE

You still awake? Are you sure you're okay?
You've been quiet.

That pulls at my heart.

ME

I'm fine, I promise. I'm just tired.

I see the little dots keep appearing and disappearing. Until it pings.

BEASTIE

Tired of...not me, I hope.

This man. He will be the death of me. But I love how much he needs me.

ME

No, beastie. When I feel like this, all I need is you xx

His reply is instant.

BEASTIE

Fuck. I wanna drop everything and come back to you.

And the thing is, he probably would, just as I would for him. But he can't. This week is important.

ME

Nope. You do what you have to do. I'll still be here waiting for you to come home.

And that is the truth. I want to be all in with him. I like how I feel around him, how safe I am, how obsessed we both are. I've never laughed around a guy so much in my life. I want this.

I want it more than anything.

CHAPTER 46

CONAN

Shoving my phone into my back pocket, I do one final walk through the woods.

It's just a game of chase.

Nothing more.

I can't stop thinking about my texts with Hallie last night. She will be waiting for me. That she needs me. It's like an arrow through the heart.

"Conan, do you think we should put some more rope out?" Reggle calls out from my left.

"Yeah. Can do."

Finn tuts behind me.

"I've never seen a Quinn brother more glum before his own Decadence Game. What's up?"

I look up at the trees, rustling in the breeze.

"I *want* to chase. Just only with Hallie," I sigh.

His hand claps down on my shoulder.

"I understand, brother. I do. But you gotta get that stick out of your ass and play the game. No one is asking you to fuck these women. They're here to be hunted, remember? Not fucked. That was just if they wanted it. Those are the rules. That applies to you too. You don't do it if you don't want it."

I scratch my head.

Okay. He's making sense here.

"You're the game master. It's a game of survival. Treat it as such. What Hallie doesn't know can't hurt her right now. Just relax. You might have fun,"

Reggie, Rowan, and Drago join us.

"All set?" I ask.

"Yeah. So talk me through what you want us to do?" Drago asks, pulling out his cigarettes and handing one to each of us.

"Well, usually, every year only I chase and hunt the contestants. But this year, I want the three of you as hunters too to assist me. Drago, you'll be on Intel with the drones. I have to be the one to capture the contestant, but Reggie and Rowan will be there to help; perhaps send them to me."

Rowan rubs his hands together.

"You'll also be involved in orchestrating the endings for the captured women. We have to make it look real to the remaining contestants. Get creative. We've got enough huts placed around that we can drag them to and then take a shot into the air. When it's safe, the losing participants can be taken to the holding cabin until the end."

Drago takes a long drag.

"So, they don't die? It's not a game of survival?" His Russian accent cuts through the air.

"No. We don't hurt women here, Drago. We just have to make it believable. The competition is real. The kinks are real. And they will be dead to their original lives—they can never return."

He nods.

"Nice. Saving them from the shits that entered them?"

"Exactly. Illusions of the villains." That's what Declan describes us as.

"So your kink is running?" Drago shoots me a look.

I shrug.

"Hunting. Primal."

"And you're not going to be doing that this year?"

"I'll hunt. Just no fucking."

Roman's eyes go wide.

"What if the women start turning on each other? There could be another Charlotte again."

I chuckle, she certainly threw a grenade into Declan's games.

"I'm hoping Enzo won't let in an assassin." I look at Drago.

The problem is, Enzo sends in the contestants under alias names. No pictures. Nothing.

Especially with my game, the element of surprise is key.

"We will all be masked, and so will the women."

"Nice," Reggie chimes in.

"Finn, you'll be waiting for the losing contestants? Correct?"

He nods.

"Yes. I need to find out everything about their families before I end them."

I take a drag of my cigarette and tip my head back to exhale.

"We've got a team ready for collection?" I ask Drago.

He checks his watch, his blue eyes returning back to me.

"Yes. Scheduled to start in five hours. Good to go."

That's one less thing to worry about.

"Check over the contracts. I've left a copy in your cabin. Make sure you're okay with the terms. I removed the submissive clause. Or it should have really been the prey clause."

That earns a chuckle from Finn.

"Good. The keys have been planted. And each of the huts has been set with the challenges."

Clapping my hands together, this could actually all work out.

"What's your challenge this year?" Reggie asks.

"Survival of the kinkiest. They find a key, they track down the hut without getting caught, and then they have to complete a challenge. Each cabin has a different task for them that gives them a pass to The Chase. They fail the challenge, they're eliminated."

"Nice."

"So how does someone win?"

"Whoever is still standing at the end after I enter the hunt in phase two will be the winner of The Chase."

I can see Rowan's brain ticking.

"Questions?" I ask him.

"If you don't want to keep the winner… can I?"

I let out a laugh.

"We gotta talk to Declan about letting you have your own fucking games."

The twins would do well as a replacement for me. Because I will be chasing Hallie to the ends of the earth once this is over.

"Shall we drink? To the final Decadence Chase?" Finn asks.

"I guess. Why not? We've got a few hours to kill before we begin."

As we walk back to my cabin, I can't help but check my phone.

Every time I get a text from Hallie, the guilt gnaws at me more.

"I didn't particularly enjoy lying to her either," Finn tells me under his breath.

He also had to make out he's in New York with me. But knowing Ben is in a coma in Finn's house relaxes me.

She's safe from the monsters in this world.

"Trust me, I'm never fucking doing it again to her."

CHAPTER 47

HALLIE

Letting out a yawn, I call Bertie in from the yard.

"Come on, boy. Let's get some sleep."

I've got an early shift tomorrow.

"You get to spend the day with Lily tomorrow." He wags his tail.

I shoot Conan a quick goodnight text, he replies fast, telling me to sleep well and how he misses me.

I've still got a smile on my face after showering and getting into bed. I can't help but pull up Conan's contact and call him.

He answers immediately.

"Hi, trouble." His raspy voice drives me crazy.

"Hi, Beastie. You have a good day? It's weird not hearing your voice at least once a day."

He chuckles.

"I've missed hearing your voice. I've never felt like this before." He trails off.

I snuggle the comforter around my neck.

"Have you ever felt like this? About a guy?"

"No," I answer quickly.

"Not even Ben? Like at the start?"

I blow out a breath.

"I knew very early on I was forcing it. I was just kinda lonely, I think. I've had boyfriends in the past who I've liked more, but again, I never felt this. Whatever this is. It just feels special."

"Yeah. You know, my mom always said, when I found the girl, I'd just know, probably when I'm least expecting it."

"Sounds like a smart woman."

I know, just by the rawness in his voice, how much he misses her. And I can relate, I feel the same about my dad.

"Do you see your mom? You've not mentioned her."

I sigh and roll onto my side. This isn't the conversation I really wanted, but I feel safe opening up to him.

"She's only my mother because she gave birth to me. She's never been a mom. My dad left her when I was young, and I begged to live with him. She quite happily gave up custody, moved to a new state, and got remarried. Occasionally, I'll get a birthday text. I don't care, though. I'm fine without her. She was just someone who shouldn't have had kids, you know?"

"Oh, Hallie. I'm sorry. You deserve better."

"I had better. My dad was incredible, Con. I never wanted for anything. I was his shadow." I stop when the pain starts to return and the lump lodges in my throat.

"You okay, baby?" he asks softly.

"Yeah. It's just so hard to talk about him without breaking down. I-I don't know if I ever will be able to. But I feel bad, because he deserves to be remembered and spoken about."

I hold in the sob that begs to escape.

"You don't need to feel bad, baby. I promise. I feel the

exact same way about my parents. I bury it and try to forget it happened, but then it weighs down on me so bad that I force myself to remember. But it's hard. You can always talk to me, if you want to? I'll listen."

I hiccup, and he brings a smile out on my face.

"Maybe I can try. I've gotten better. The first year I actually hid all of the photos, I now have them back up on the walls."

"It just takes time. Grief sucks. It hurts. And I don't think it ever goes away, we just hide our pain better every day. Or find new ways to distract ourselves."

"You can talk about your parents whenever you want too, Con. You know that, right? I want to hear all about your Dad's whiskey. And your mom. She sounds cute."

He chuckles.

"She was cute. But she was also a little ball of rage. Don't tell my brothers, but she used to call me her favorite. I think it was because we were so similar. I got my anger from her. Shit, I used to dread going home when I'd been in trouble at school."

I giggle.

"I can imagine. I told you before, you're a softie deep down."

"No. Hallie. I'm not. Not really. You, however, have a way of making me that way. What can I say? I'm down bad for you, trouble."

"Ditto, beastie."

"Are you training tomorrow?" I ask.

The line falls silent, and he clears his throat.

"Yeah, busy day tomorrow."

"You'll be amazing, I'm sure. When is the championship fight lined up for?"

"My promotion team is just ironing out the details. Probably in a few months, so I have time."

"Nice. I can't wait to see you win that."

"Yeah. The first legal thing I've done in my life."

"Conan! Seriously?"

"Probably. I'm a naughty boy, Hallie. You sure you can cope?"

I roll my eyes.

"I can handle you, don't worry."

"Good. Now you need to get some sleep, you've got an early shift, right?"

I blink, feeling the blush spread up my cheeks.

"You think you can order me around, beastie? Hmm?"

"Don't think so, know so. But it goes both ways."

I tap my finger against my lips.

"I order you to come back home and snuggle up in bed with me," I tell him.

"Cute. And I wish I could. It won't be long. Only a few more days. I'll have a fun date planned the second I step foot back in Pennsylvania."

"Hmm. I might be busy that day," I tease.

"I don't care. I'll just steal you from wherever you are and take you on the date anyway. I need my fix of Hallie the second I'm home."

"I'm joking. I can't wait."

"Night, trouble. Sweet dreams, and say hello to Bertie for me."

I sit up, and Bertie whips his head up to me.

"Will do. Night, night, beastie."

When the call ends, I tap the bed and Bertie snuggles up beside me. I drift off into a peaceful slumber.

For once, everything is going okay.

CHAPTER 48

CONAN

I knock on Finn's door, and I'm nervous—that sweaty palm kind of nervous. I've never been here in the past five years.

It's a no-go area. Probably for my own sanity. It's pretty damn clear that my brother is psychotic, I just don't necessarily need to witness it with my own eyes.

I know it's a place he built for when he was training to be a surgeon. But I also know it's now where he hosts his Decadence Trials.

Me and Declan always joke that it's where he holds medical experiments on his torture victims. Now standing in front of the secured metal door, it kinda feels like I wasn't wrong.

It's clinical. The white walls, the chemical twang in the air. It makes me shiver. It's a relief when the door swings open and Finn stands there.

"Are you sure you want me to come in?" I ask.

He frowns and runs a hand through his hair.

"Stop being a baby."

I hate hospitals, despite the fact I keep managing to land

myself in one. And this feels like a fucking at-home version.

He leads me through the corridor; there's two rooms on either side and one in front of me. He unlocks the middle one with a set of keys.

The monitor beeps steadily, and Ben lies in the center on a bed. The swelling looks better on his face, even with the tubes coming out of his mouth and attached to his hands.

"The dead is coming back to life," Finn tells me, turning the monitor to me, showing me his normal heart rate and blood pressure.

"His vitals have leveled. I've kept him under for now until we're ready. I guess then we will see if there's any lasting damage. Or if he can even speak. He's missing a few teeth too. I don't have any way to scan him, so it's a guessing game, but I've kept him alive. His injuries looked worse than what they really were."

I chew on the inside of my mouth.

"I've always wanted to smother a patient with a pillow, like they do in films."

Finn chuckles and shakes his head.

"First it was the damn map on the desk, now it's smothering. You need to watch less TV."

"Have you done that before?" I ask.

"No. I'm much more creative than a fucking pillow."

"Oh."

I'm kinda disappointed.

Maybe I'll do it on Ben for his second death.

"So once I finish The Chase, we see how this bastard is doing and try and get our answers? Then I can kill him."

We sent Reggie and Rowan back to the boxing gym to see if they could locate his phone, but nothing. Which is weird. Who the fuck doesn't take their cell out with them?

Someone that doesn't want to be tracked I'd assume.

"Yes. I've got everything linked to my phone and security footage. I'll be able to help with The Chase if you need, and start to bring him round."

I swallow.

"Yeah. Okay. The contestants are arriving soon. I best get going. But, thank you."

"Anytime. That's what older brothers are for…" He smirks.

"Bringing your victims back from the dead."

I let out a laugh.

"Usually I want them to stay fuckin' dead."

AFTER PUTTING on my camouflage sweatpants and tight black, long sleeved tee, I finish off with my black balaclava and gloves.

Ready to hunt.

To the women, I'm completely unrecognizable. That's the idea. We never want it getting out who runs these games, the element of secrecy adds to the illusion.

Unless they know my eyes well, no one would guess.

"First contestant is entering the woods now. She's feisty," Asher, one of our newer recruits, tells me through the radio.

"Okay. Continue as planned to the intake cabin. The contract is on the table."

I log into the security system and pull up the first cabin. Each girl is taken there first to sign the contract and is given their outfit and rucksack of basic survival supplies.

The second year I did this chase, the winner actually

lasted six days in the woods, the master of hiding. So, I've had to dial it back as I don't have six full days to hunt.

Instead, this year, I've opted for a scavenger hunt style to eliminate the first round, speeding up the time to get to the real chase. And this year we've got Drago on the drones, my eye in the sky to hunt these women.

I send one last text to Hallie, it's like a kick in the teeth. I'm a fucking asshole. A selfish one.

ME

Have a great day at work, trouble. I'll be busy training today, but I'll call you when I can. Miss you.

It's midnight, she will be sleeping. I know she has an early shift.

I put my phone on silent and put it on the desk. No more distractions.

I keep my eyes locked on the screen as the first partici-pant is led blindfolded through the woods. Once inside the cabin, Asher removes it, and I screw my nose up as this fire-cracker of a brunette launches her fist into his chin.

I can't see her face, since she's covered by the deep green full-face mask. "Ouch," I mutter.

He safely restrains her and guides her to the table, pulling out her seat and sitting her down, with a gun to the side of her head.

Great start.

I pull up my script on the screen as Dean, the second guard, places the contract in front of her.

She scans the room and I can smell her fear from here. But it doesn't spark anything in me. Not this time.

I need to get that hunting blood flowing through my veins, just like I did when I chased Hallie.

CHAPTER 49
HALLIE

I bolt upright as my front door crashes open; it's like a bomb has gone off. Bertie erupts into a fit of barking as I launch myself to my bedroom door and lock it.

Before I can even move away from the door, I hear deep voices getting closer. I suck in a breath, Bertie's barks are bound to give me away.

"Shhh," I warn Bertie.

As I sprint to the bathroom, my door is kicked wide open. Three armed, masked men barge in, blocking my exit.

Am I being arrested?

Is this for the racing? Or because I'm now seeing someone in the mafia?

I glance over at my phone. The tall one in the front clocks it and aims his pistol directly at me.

"You have been summoned to participate in a game. All of your questions will be answered on arrival. But we need you to come with us."

I can't place that deep accent. Maybe southern?

"I-I haven't signed up for any games? Is this a joke?"

My hands tremble, and I push myself against the wall.

Bertie stays protectively beside me, barking with all the aggression that big softie can muster.

"Miss, this isn't a joke. If you don't come willingly, we will have to use other measures, which we would rather avoid."

I look at my phone again.

"Don't make any stupid moves." The one at the front steps forward.

I need Conan.

"Hands behind your back and turn around."

"Am I being arrested?"

He chuckles as I do as he says. He clasps them together with cuffs and places some black material over my head. A mask of some sort?

As I blink, it all goes dark when he fastens some kind of blindfold over my eyes.

"We're heading to a secure location. Time to go, Contestant Ten."

My blood runs cold. Maybe this is a reality TV show of some kind that Lily has signed me up for.

But they looked so scary. And those guns were real.

"I need to tell my family." My voice shakes as he turns me around and leads me abruptly through the house.

"No. You don't. You belong to Decadence now." His voice is lethal.

Silent tears roll down my cheeks. I think I'm going to die.

I'm escorted into a car and he presses on the top of my head to guide me inside.

And then it's silent.

As the car comes to a slow stop, a door opens and slams shut. And then cold air whips over my skin as my door is opened.

It smells earthy. Like the woods. I'm bundled out of the vehicle and led down a gravel track.

A door creaks open and I'm escorted inside, the lock clicks behind.

My eyes are blurry as the blindfold is removed. All I can see is wooded walls and a single table and chairs in the middle.

"Sit," he grunts.

I do as he says, my leg bouncing erratically. I'm cold and terrified.

"Your hunter will provide clear instructions shortly," he tells me.

As I look into the left corner, I see the red dot of a camera flashing. Below it is a small round table with a black rucksack and a green underwear set.

What the hell is going on?

Pulling the paper up on the desk, it's as if I'm looking at another language.

Congratulations, Contestant Ten. You have made it to the Decadence Chase.

Now that you have entered the woods, you have become both the hunter and the prey.

This is a game of survival with a twist. It's survival of the kinkiest.

Are you prepared to give yourself to The Chase for the chance to earn the ultimate reward?

What would you give for two million dollars?

If you are inclined to play, you will find the contract on the next pages. Read it carefully. The rules must be followed in Decadence.

The stakes are high. Your life's on the line.

My hands tremble and I drop the papers on the desk.

"Let me go," I beg the guard.

He ignores me.

"Please. I don't want to play."

My head starts to spin.

"If you don't want to play, that is an option, but you'll meet the same fate as you would if you lost The Chase. Read the contract and then make your decision."

As I go to stand, I feel him shift. I glance up and find the gun pointed at me again.

So I sit firmly back on my ass, picking back up the contract. Trying to read the words through my burning eyes that threaten to spill.

The Decadence Chase Contract

The agreement is entered into between The Hunter of Inferno **(hereby referred to as 'The Hunter')** and Contestant Ten **(hereby referred to as 'The Contestant')**

PARTICIPATION:

This contract binds The Contestant to The Hunter. Once The Contestant enters the gates to the property, they willingly give full control to The Hunter.

The Contestant understands this is a game of survival. She shall compete with NINE other women.

There are two phases to complete this Chase. You must survive the challenges in Phase One to be given a spot for the Final Hunt.

The games shall take place in the Woods of Decadence. The Contestant understands that this is the wilderness. You have to survive out there. The Contestant shall be given a small supply of the bare essentials.

The Contestant MUST wear their mask and outfit the entire time, unless explicitly instructed otherwise by The Hunter or his men.

THE REWARD:

The winning Contestant shall receive the sum of TWO MILLION DOLLARS.

CONSENT:

The Decadence Chase is designed to establish and test The Contestant's hunger to survive and thrill to be chased.

This isn't just a game of who can stay alive the longest.

This is survival of the kinkiest.

The Contestants may use a safeword to stop it at any time, however, the consequence is elimination.

This Contestant's safe word is **STRAWBERRY.**

Therefore, The Contestant consents to the below, but is not limited to:

- Hair pulling
- Restraints (of entire body)
- Use of sex toys
- Sensory play
- Branding
- Anal
- Vaginal penetration
- Choking
- Biting
- Spitting
- Rough play
- Role play
- Self-gratification
- Edging
- Orgasm denial
- Torture

- Degradation
- Cold conditions
- Extreme temperature play
- Being hunted for sport
- Humiliation
- Death

The Contestant agrees to allow her designated guard/handler to lead her around the woods. She **must not** go anywhere without her guard.

She must follow orders.

She **must not** climax in the games unless specifically instructed to by The Hunter.

She may use violence upon another Contestant for survival purposes only. However, only necessary force may be used. The Contestant may **NOT** end the life of another in these woods.

No weapons are to be used, including handmade weapons, such as branches, sharpened sticks, and/or rocks.

CONSEQUENCES:

The Contestant understands the survival element of these games.

Therefore, The Contestant understands that once she enters the gates of Decadence, if she is unsuccessful in either phase of The Chase, she consents for her life to be ultimately terminated.

If The Contestant makes any attempt to harm a member of Decadence or escape her fate, she is also consenting to a punishment of death.

Once you enter the woods, you are both the hunter and the prey.

Full instructions for each phase shall be given to The Contestant at the required time.

SIGNATURE AND DATE:

By signing this agreement, The Contestant understands she is signing her mind, body, and soul over to Decadence.

The parties hereby agree to the terms and conditions set forth in this agreement, as demonstrated by their signatures below:

....

If I sign, I could change my life. Two million dollars. The cars. The house. No more scraping by.

But if I lose, I die.

If I say no, it looks like I also die.

Visions of Conan play in my head. Would he understand? I have to get back to him.

The only way to do that is by being like him. By fighting, hunting, and winning.

I pick up the pen and can't hide my trembling fingers as I sign my life away.

I'm petrified. But that isn't going to save me. I can't let my fear win.

CHAPTER 50

CONAN

"**B**oss. The final contestant has signed the dotted line. She's getting dressed now. It's time to explain the rules." Rowan keeps his disastrous American accent.

"Got it."

It's easier for them to retain the information if I speak it clearly. Reading them when they're in a state of shock can lead to issues.

I zone in on the security feed for the intake cabin and press the speaker. But my eyes are fixed on the shaking woman standing in the middle of the room.

I can't see the fear in her eyes from here, but I can feel it. But the way she stands with her spine straight and her chin up tells me she's defiant. She's up for the challenge.

Her build is similar to Hallie's. I rub the ache in my chest. She's all I can think about.

I press the button on the speaker, which distorts my voice to the contestant.

"Welcome to the Decadence Chase. I am the Hunter of

Inferno. As of now, you belong to me. But whether you walk out of these gates is up to you."

She remains still and I take a breath.

"The Chase is conducted in two phases. Should you survive phase one, you shall enter phase two. Only those worthy will have the opportunity to be hunted."

I can't help but imagine Hallie being put in this situation. It makes the guilt kick in even more. I know the truth behind the games, but the girls don't.

Fuck.

I think she's brought out some kind of humanity in me, and I'm not sure if it's a good thing or not.

CHAPTER 51
HALLIE

I remain frozen in place. My life is on the damn line, and I need to concentrate on what this robotic voice is telling me.

I'm thinking of this like a race.

"Phase one will start as soon as you enter the woods, as you are the last contestant. The first eight girls to find a key must then find the cabin with the corresponding number to the key. The two losing contestants shall be eliminated. Once inside, you will find your challenges to complete. And remember, this is crafted to test your survival skills in various ways, but also to open your eyes to the rush and the kinks that can come alongside that. Don't hold back. Let your primal fantasies come to life. We were animals put on this earth, and that's how we behave here."

The robotic voice altering is terrifying. Only adding to the fear running through me.

Closing my eyes, I recite the rules: find the key, find the cabin to match the number.

"As for rules on finding the keys: You are now all hunters for this phase. You may fight your way to a key, but

347

you must not harm the other contestants beyond what is reasonable. Weapons are not permitted. Remember, you are always being watched in Decadence. You break that rule, you shall be eliminated."

I'm a nurse. I dedicate my life to trying to save people. The thought of killing someone makes me feel sick. But I'm not a fighter either. I'm fit, I'm strong.

But if it really comes down to me against them, what am I really capable of?

I'm on my own here. I have no Conan and Lily fighting in my corner.

"Do you understand so far? Nod or shake your head." The voice breaks me back to reality.

I nod my head slowly.

"Very good. Should you find your key and cabin, inside you will find instructions for your challenges. You will be watched by a guard. Say your safe word, and you'll be removed and eliminated from The Chase. Successfully complete them, and you will be taken to phase two."

I open my mouth to speak, locking eyes with the guard who shakes his head.

"Eager to hear?" The voice chuckles.

I clench my fists. This is fucking sick and twisted. I'm angry and also confused. I'm just a cardiac nurse who lives with her dog. What have I done to deserve this?

"Phase two is where I enter The Chase. You'll spend the night in the woods. Survive. That's all you need to do. Rest, recover, and get ready for nightfall. Because that is when I will be hunting my prey. If I catch you..." He takes a purposeful pause.

I get the gist.

I swallow the bile rising in my throat. I can't imagine

another man inside of me other than Conan. All that means is I cannot be caught.

"The contestant who is last to be caught, or remains to be, will be the winner of The Chase."

How is this legal?

Tears threaten to erupt. Less than three hours ago, I was the happiest I've been in years. Life was falling into place. And now? Now it's going up in flames.

All I can do is try not to end up in the ashes.

"You're never alone in the woods of Decadence. Even in phase one. Show me your skills to survive. I want to see your hunger to live."

I look down at the flimsy green lace bodysuit I have on, down to the black lace-up boots. Like some sort of sexy military getup.

I'm hoping this is all a fucking nightmare I wake up from soon. This cannot be reality.

"Good luck, Contestant Ten. Hopefully, I'll see you in phase two, and I'll be chasing you soon."

My eyes flutter closed, picturing being in the woods with Conan. How good that felt. How alive I was with him.

The thought of never seeing him again is so excruciating, but it's also my fuel.

I will win this game.

I will find Conan.

And we will burn this place to the ground.

CHAPTER 52
CONAN

Reclining back in my seat, I let out an exhale.

Hallie hasn't replied, I guess she's getting ready for work. Declan strides into my cabin and tears off his mask. We take extra precautions during our Decadence Games to remain anonymous.

"You ready?" he asks, grabbing the whiskey.

"Yeah," I answer, glancing down at my phone on the desk.

"Pass that here." He holds out his hand.

"What? No." I grab the phone.

"Conan. You can't concentrate if you're constantly thinking about Hallie. Or trying to contact her. I know you, brother. I haven't seen you like this over a woman before in our whole life. The more you speak to her, the deeper you're treading into lying to her. It's just a couple of days. Just send a quick text saying Keller is taking your cell so you can concentrate on training. Then after this is done, we move the fuck on and never talk about it again."

I swear to God I'm almost sweating at the thought. No contact? Sounds like hell. But I know he's right.

Damn, Declan is always right. That's why he's the boss.

"Fine," I huff.

Declan chuckles.

"It's like we're kids again. You want me and Finn to go beat up some bullies for you again?"

I roll my eyes.

"That was one fuckin' time, and I was six. You two were older. Shall we talk about the times I've saved your ass? Hmm?"

Declan shakes his head and motions for me to give him the phone.

"I swear to God, since Dad died, I've inherited two new ones."

"Because you behave like our child."

Touché.

"You seem calmer now, though. I like seeing you more settled, Con. It suits you."

"It's Hallie. Honestly, I am convinced she has some sort of chemical effect on my brain. When I'm with her, I'm like a goofy teenager, desperate to please her. To make her laugh."

Declan nods.

"That's called being in love, brother."

Fuck, that pain in my chest is back. I think I knew early on that she was stealing my heart, and I didn't do a damn thing to stop her. I hope she feels the same way.

I ignore his comment and type out the message.

ME

> Hi, gorgeous. So, Grayson has demanded
> that my phone gets locked away for a
> couple of days so I can concentrate on the
> boot camp. As soon as I get it back, I'll call
> you and be on my way back to you. If you
> need anything, call Finn. He will have his
> phone still. I miss you. XX

As soon as it goes through, Declan swipes the phone out of my hand and pockets it.

"I'll keep it charged and safe at mine. Okay?"

"Yes, Dad." I fake a grin.

"Don't make me beat your ass, Conan."

I bite my lip to hold back the grin.

"Try me."

CHAPTER 53
HALLIE

The trees rustle in the breeze. Why are the woods so damn scary at night? I've seen enough movies to know this is where the monsters hide. That in itself sends shivers down my spine.

As I look left and right, that's all I see. Trees and more fucking trees, spanning for miles.

I'm already exhausted. The adrenaline's wearing off. I'm not sure how long I've been walking now. It feels like forever, but it could be just an hour.

Now I'm just wandering aimlessly in the dark woods with only the moonlight for company.

A key.

I need to find a damn key.

Arms curled around my chest, I walk with my nerves lit like tripwires. What monsters live out here after dark?

A tree looms ahead, and I lean against it, drop my backpack, and start digging through it blindly. My hands fumble, clumsy in the dark, searching for anything useful—

A flashlight.

Flick.

355

The beam slices through the night like a blade, and I exhale as light floods the space around me.

I check the supplies:

Protein bars.

A bottle of water.

One Liquid IV packet.

A pathetic first aid kit.

Matches.

Great.

Bare bones survival.

No sweater. No real food. No comfort. Just enough to stay breathing.

But I don't need comfort. I need that fucking key. I'm trying to get my brain to focus on this one task so I don't think too wildly about the rest—or the consequences for losing.

With the light in hand, I push forward.

Then I hear faint footsteps up ahead.

I kill the flashlight. My back slams against a tree, chest rising slow and shallow. I don't breathe.

The steps aren't heavy. Not a man.

A woman.

I creep forward, slow as death, waiting for a glint of her in the moonlight.

And there—a silhouette, feminine, about my size.

I flick the flashlight back on.

She whips around and freezes.

And I see it.

The key. Hanging from her hand on a chain.

I remember the rules. I can fight her. I just can't kill her. Can I really be this woman?

I'm Contestant Ten. The last woman left. This might be

it. My shot. I've probably been dropped in this part of the woods for a reason.

She tightens her grip on the key and takes a step back. We're evenly matched.

She bolts.

And I go after her. Fight or flight, I chose to survive.

My legs scream as I push harder, faster, the flashlight shaking in my grip, tracking her. I'm trying to be quiet, but every branch I snap sounds like a gunshot in the silence.

She veers left and trips on some low branches.

That's all I need.

I lunge at her, putting all my force behind it.

My weight crashes down on her and I slam her to the forest floor.

One hand on her face, the other fighting to keep her down as she thrashes, panicked.

She's strong.

But I'm desperate.

I grab the key. Yank it free.

And I'm gone.

Running. Blind and reckless and breathless.

My lungs burn, throat raw, but I don't stop. Not until I'm sure no one's chasing me.

Only when silence returns do I slow. I kill the light, clip the chain to my bra strap, and shove the key deep into my bra.

Lesson learned.

Hide the key. Don't advertise your target.

The woods stretch deeper and darker, but I keep moving. The air shifts around me—

Still. Watching.

I don't know if I'm alone.

I don't know if I ever really was.

At a break in the trees, I drop my rucksack and collapse onto it. I flick the flashlight back on and let the beam land on the metal.

Number six.

That's the cabin I need.

But I haven't seen a single one yet.

It has to be out here. Somewhere.

My eyelids grow heavy. I yawn. Tempted.

But no.

No sleep. Not here. Not yet.

As I steady my breathing, I glance up.

A red light blinks above me.

A drone, maybe?

It hovers over me and I glare up at it.

Fuck whoever's behind it.

Fuck this whole twisted setup.

They named this place after *Decadence Chocolate.* America's sweetest luxury.

What a joke.

This isn't sweet.

It's hell.

The drone drifts off, and I'm left swallowing rage.

My fingers twitch toward my mask. I want to rip it off. I can breathe, I can see—but it's still suffocating.

But I hesitate.

If I'm being watched, if every moment is being judged, would taking it off break a rule? I vaguely remember the contract saying something about having to wear this flimsy uniform and mask at all times.

I can't risk it. Not now.

This ridiculous costume, the mask, the lingerie—it's all part of their game.

A trap, maybe.

Or a test.
I stand and strap the rucksack back on.
One goal left.
Find the cabin.
And don't get caught doing it.

CHAPTER 54

CONAN

"Y"ou missed a good fight between two of the contestants," Drago says as I approach the screen, peering over his shoulder.

I recognize the contestant on the screen, the only one that stood out to me in the intake. Contestant number ten. Nervous yet defiant.

"Has she got the key?" I ask.

"Yep. She stole it right from Contestant Eight. Chased her down, smothered her, and then legged It."

"Nice."

"Contestant Eight remains unharmed?" I ask.

"Yeah. She's chasing her own tail now in the woods. She won't make it to phase two."

I scratch my head.

"How far is Constant Ten from the cabin? Which key does she have?"

"I'd assume it's key six. And if so…"

He zooms out on the drone.

"She's less than fifty meters from it."

I nod.

"Who is manning that cabin?" I ask, and Drago pulls up the time schedules on the other screen. I scan to find cabin six.

"Reggie."

"Oh."

That is a difficult cabin to complete. A true survival task.

"Let's see if she makes it first. Contestant Nine is right on her tail."

I squint as I lean in on Contestant Nine.

"Is she holding a bat?"

How the hell?

He zooms in closer.

"No. But that's a huge fucking branch."

Anger fizzles inside of me, I don't know why.

"I'll take care of her. No weapons is quite clearly in the rules. We gotta stop her."

I can tell by the way she's stomping through the dirt that she means business. And I'd take a bet she is willing to kill to survive. That is the risk of this game, that is why we have to monitor it so closely.

It looks like she will be reminded why it's important to listen to the Hunter of Inferno.

And for some strange reason, I want Contestant Ten to make it to phase two.

CHAPTER 55

HALLIE

A branch snaps under my boot.

I freeze.

The air shifts around me. My hand instinctively clicks off the flashlight. The cabin is just ahead. Close enough to taste.

But there's a prickle crawling up my spine, a whisper behind me that doesn't belong to the wind. I don't know if it's paranoia or instinct screaming, but I press myself to the tree beside me and hold my breath, eyes locked on the cabin like it's my salvation.

Just one more sprint.

I launch forward.

The scream tears from me as something slams into the backs of my legs, sending me crashing down into the dirt. My palms sting. My knees burn. I brace, heart racing, waiting for another blow… but it doesn't come.

One eye cracks open.

She's there. But then I see *him*, standing behind her. Towering. A shadow carved in armor and menace.

"P-please. I wasn't going to kill her." Her voice breaks like glass.

I don't flinch. I have no pity. The bitch tried to end me.

"Weapons are forbidden. You broke the rules. Now you must pay the consequences." His voice is like gravel and steel, thick with an American drawl, distorted by the mask stretched over his face.

I scramble backwards, watching in horror as he grips her and drags her into the darkness.

As soon as they vanish, I bolt for the cabin, fingers trembling as I fumble with the flashlight.

Then her screams cut through the night.

A gunshot follows.

And my entire body turns to ice.

My breath staggers. My bones quake. This isn't a twisted prank or some sadistic simulation. This is *real*.

I yank the key from my bra, shoving the flashlight between my lips, hands shaking so badly I nearly drop it. The moment the lock clicks and the door swings open, a wave of relief slams into me so hard I almost sob.

But that relief dies the second the light flickers on.

Another man stands in the corner of the room.

Massive.

Silent.

Just like the guy from outside.

His black t-shirt stretches over stacked muscle, arms relaxed at his sides—but his pistol is gripped, visible and ready. His face is hidden behind a matte black mask, and his dark eyes drill into mine, unblinking.

My feet are locked to the floor.

To the left, a steel bath glistens, packed with ice. To the right, a narrow wooden structure—like a sauna, barely big enough for one. Center of the room: a table. On it, a deep green box and a white envelope, clean and waiting.

My legs carry me forward before I tell them to.

I lift the lid.

My breath stutters.

Inside, a slim green wearable vibrator. Next to it, a butt plug and a small tube of water-based lube.

"What the fuck…" I whisper.

Glancing at the guard, he hasn't moved. He's just watching. Does he expect to watch me *use* them? Or worse… make me?

I swallow back the nausea clawing up my throat and shove the box aside, ripping open the envelope with trembling fingers.

Welcome to Cabin Six.

Here, your challenge is to survive the extremes. If you look up at the wall, you'll see a timer. Every element of this challenge is timed. First you must insert both toys to start the games.

Remember, this isn't just about staying alive. It's about being able to get off on survival.

These have remote access. I will know if they have been put in correctly. Don't try and beat the system. The punishment will be elimination.

Once you have completed that, you are required to do the Ice Bath Challenge first.

You must simply submerge yourself in the ice water and sit there for two minutes.

The timer will go off when you have completed this. Then, you shall test your tolerance to heat while dealing with some internal heat.

A test of endurance, strength, and orgasms. You will give me your climax in return for your freedom from the heat. Only once I see you cum will the doors be opened.

You may use your safe word at any time, with the consequence of being eliminated.

You can choose to not take part in the challenge—again, you will be eliminated.

Keep an eye on the clock.

Should you wish to partake, please instruct your guard to leave while you insert them. That will begin your game.

I look forward to seeing you soon.

Love,
The Hunter of Inferno.

The paper falls from my hands.

My jaw drops. A scream lodges somewhere between disbelief and dread.

Above me, the timer flashes. Thirty seconds and counting down.

What?

I grab the toys. My heart slams against my ribs. I can't seriously be expected to—? *This?*

Two million dollars or death, Hallie.

The guard clears his throat.

Five seconds.

"You can go," I say, breathless.

He nods once, turns, and shuts the door behind him with a sound that feels like finality.

I let out a strangled breath, using the table to hold myself upright. My eyes sting. But I won't cry. I won't fucking cry.

The timer resets—now two minutes.

To insert the toys.

Jesus Christ.

The lube slips from my grip, landing on the table with a pathetic splat. My hands won't stop shaking. I force myself to try again, coating my fingers with it and slicking the vibrator. I glance at every corner of the room. No cameras. But I feel *watched.* Like the guard left his shadow behind to haunt the space.

I drag the chair over, plant my foot, and push my lace bodysuit to the side.

The moment the vibrator pushes inside, I hiss.

"Fuck!"

My walls clench, but I keep breathing, forcing my muscles to relax. Once it's seated, I adjust the angle so the top rests over my clit.

It doesn't vibrate.

It just exists—and it's all I can feel.

I glance at the timer. One minute left.

I pick up the butt plug next and lube it thoroughly. My throat tightens.

It's been a while. Not since I saw Conan's dick and

wondered if he'd ever want to do ass play, and if so, how badly that would hurt.

A tear slips free.

I wish I could tell him. I wish he knew what was happening to me. That he could come crashing in, wrapping his arms around me and promising it's all going to be okay.

Just once more. That's all I need.

But this pain reminds me what I'm fighting for.

Conan. Bertie. Lily.

So I bend. One hand pulls myself open. The other positions. I exhale slowly and let the plug slip inside, picturing Conan—his Irish lilt coaxing me through it, his voice steady and low, calling me his good girl.

His green eyes, fierce and gentle.

I stand and shift, making sure everything's in place. Then I re-adjust the bodysuit.

Ten seconds left.

I bolt to the door and yank it open.

"Done," I whisper.

He enters, silent.

Not a single word.

His footsteps are heavy but unhurried, boots sinking into the wooden floor as he returns to his post in the corner of the room. Watching.

Always watching.

I force my eyes away from him and turn to the bath.

The ice gleams under the overhead light, glittering and sharp. Almost mocking me.

I move toward it, every step slower than the last, as if my body is already grieving what it's about to endure. The water is full to the brim, surface still, waiting like a predator with teeth made of frost.

The timer on the wall flashes again.

ICE BATH INITIATED: 2:00

It starts the moment I lower my foot over the edge. The sting is instant, like knives slicing open my skin. My gasp echoes too loud into the silence.

I hesitate. Just for a heartbeat.

Then I grip the edges and plunge.

The cold is violent.

It punches the air from my lungs and rips a scream from my throat, muffled behind clenched teeth. My body tries to escape. To thrash, to run, to crawl out of the frost—but I stay.

I stay. I want to survive.

My thighs cramp as I force them beneath the surface. My teeth chatter uncontrollably. My arms pull tighter to my chest, but it does nothing. There is no warmth. Only burn.

The kind of pain that feels like death in slow motion.

I look up.

He's still there.

Still silent.

Still watching.

His arms are folded now. The pistol still resting in one hand, casual as if he's done this a thousand times. His dark eyes behind that black mask don't waver. He doesn't move.

And that somehow makes it worse.

Because I'm completely alone. Naked in the ways that count. Drenched in agony, holding myself together while some stranger stares like I'm a science experiment.

The first thirty seconds crawl by like molasses. I count my breaths to keep from screaming. Every nerve screams. My nipples are pebbled and burning beneath the thin lace of the bodysuit. My skin pulses with pain.

Forty-five seconds.

Tears burn at the corners of my eyes.

My fingers have gone stiff, fists clenched beneath the water. My toes feel like they're splintering.

I want to quit. God, I want to get out.

But I can still hear her scream.

And the gunshot.

And I know—if I leave this bath before it ends, I won't just be cold.

I'll be dead.

Sixty seconds.

I grit my teeth until my jaw aches, pressing my palms against my thighs to keep them from shaking. My body wants to shut down. Go numb.

It doesn't.

It just hurts.

Ninety seconds.

I make the mistake of looking at him again. He tilts his head slightly, studying me like I'm being graded. Not cruel. Not kind.

Just... a man who's seen this before. Who's waiting to see if I'll break.

I won't.

I can't.

Not when there's so much more on the line than just my life.

Conan. He is my fire in this frost.

One hundred seconds.

I feel nothing now. Not in a good way. My skin is red and splotched and going pale at the edges. My mind starts to drift, dizzy from the ache.

But then—

BEEP. BEEP. BEEP.

The alarm sounds overhead.

I've done it.

Two minutes.

I gasp as I launch upward, sloshing water and ice over the sides of the tub, slipping against the metal rim as my feet fumble for purchase. My lungs seize from the sudden movement, my body shrieking in protest as I climb out.

I collapse to the wooden floor, my limbs shuddering, my breath ragged.

My lips are blue.

My fingers refuse to close.

But I'm alive.

I did it.

I glance toward him, expecting a nod, a word, something.

But he doesn't move.

Just watches.

Still.

As I lie there, shivering, frozen, and burning all at once, I realize…

This was only the beginning.

CHAPTER 56

CONAN

I race back to my cabin after delivering Contestant Nine to the elimination zone run by Declan. He explains what will happen next as the girls arrive one by one. He's got the easy job.

He will also work with Enzo to initiate the next part of the games.

The one where they get to start a brand new life, well away from the abusive assholes who sent them to us.

I, however, need to get back on the computer and pull the security feed up from Cabin Six.

Because the way the air crackled and my heart raced when I was in the same space as Contestant Ten is not normal.

It's only happened one time. Around one woman.

But it can't be.

I just need to see her. I need to watch. My gut is dragging me to this, kicking and screaming.

The camera feed loads slowly, grainy at first from the steam.

Another contestant. Another challenge. That's what I'm telling myself.

I don't flinch anymore. I've trained myself not to. Told myself I built these tests for strength, not cruelty. But some nights…like this one…something creeps under my skin.

The girl is trembling as the guard leads her into Cabin Six's sauna. Her arms are wrapped tight around her stomach like she's trying to hold herself together. Soaked and shivering, her skin flushed red from the ice. She's hugging herself, legs trembling beneath her as Reggie leads her toward the sauna door. She stumbles once. He catches her elbow, just long enough to keep her from falling. No tenderness. Just protocol.

I squint at the screen. Am I just looking for similarities? Trying to hurt myself?

He follows her in, lifting a thick leather collar from the wall and fastens it around her throat.

I flinch.

She doesn't.

Her chin tilts up defiantly, and the collar clicks into place with a magnetic lock and snaps to a chain bolted to the wall. It allows just enough slack for her to sit down on the bench, but not enough to move freely.

She's trapped.

Exposed.

My thumb hovers over the button.

The remote in my hand is small. A polished green that matches the toy.

Control Unit 6 reads the screen, and the timer begins to count down from ten minutes. That's all she has to do: climax within that time frame.

She shifts uncomfortably, tugging at the collar, then

glances toward the glass window that separates the sauna from the rest of the cabin.

She can't see the camera. But she knows.

She knows someone is watching.

My thumb hovers over the button.

Just procedure.

I press it.

The moment I press the button, her back arches.

It's not violent. Not yet. A slow hum. Barely a pulse.

But it makes her squirm. Her thighs press together instinctively. Her eyes slam shut. I wish this feed was better quality in that lighting so I could see her eyes beneath the mask.

I start to feel it burning up inside of me, watching her already squirming under my control.

I don't want to get hard for this. I hate that I am.

Because this isn't sex. It's not pleasure. It's survival dressed in sadism. If Hallie could see this, she would hate me.

The timer on the wall starts ticking down from ten minutes.

The moisture in the sauna fogs the screen, but I don't take my eyes off her. Every twitch. Every tremble. I see it all.

She shifts her hips. She's already flushed from the ice bath, but now her skin is blooming pink for another reason.

Her head tips back against the wood behind her, and she lets out a low, shuddering breath.

The vibrator pulses.

Not hard. Just enough to tease.

One minute in.

She grips the edge of the bench, knuckles white, legs

tense. It's like I can feel the heat and the ache building inside her, a cruel contradiction. Her muscles would have already been strained from the cold. Now they're melting, giving her no relief. Just the slow burn of heat meeting the simmer of arousal.

The screen shows her trembling. A drop of sweat rolls down the valley of her breasts. Then another down her stomach.

She whimpers. A broken sound, half sob, half plea.

And it shatters me.

Because I know that sound.

I know it too fucking well.

My spine locks. My thumb slips off the remote.

"No…" I whisper.

A raw cry tears from her throat as her body arches.

"Conan."

It's not a whimper. It's a prayer.

And I feel it like a bullet to the chest.

"No. No, no, no, no."

I scramble for the controls, but it's too late.

Her body jerks. Writhing in a storm of heat and shame and goddamn survival. But she's doing everything in her power to stop herself from orgasming.

My name still echoing from her mouth.

Hallie.

My. Fucking. Hallie.

She has to finish. I have to do this to her to get her through to the next phase. Fuck, it makes me feel sick.

I turn the power up on the vibrator, her body now shaking relentlessly. The more she fights, the harder it's hitting her.

Her fists clench and she lets out a scream. It rips through me and drags my heart out with it.

I hate myself.

I hate this game.

I'm a fucking evil monster. Just like the ones I vowed to protect her against, I've become. All I can do is stare at the screen and watch my future crumble in front of my eyes, by my own hand.

This is the end of everything, I know it is. At least if she wins, she can take the money, that's the least I can do. Because I can't take back what is done. It's too late, she's here and she's playing the game.

But I can help her win. I can give her something.

A climax shatters her, leaving her breathless and broken. Shutting off the vibrator as soon as she's done, I toss the remote, full force against the wall.

"Fuck!" I shout.

I fall back in my chair, blood drained from my face. I made her do this.

I controlled her. Watched her break.

I want to end this. Burst through that wall and rip the collar off her. Carry her out of there and wrap her in every piece of warmth I have to offer.

End the games and forget this part of my life ever existed.

But I can't.

We are in Enzo's debt. The Chase has to finish, and there has to be a winner. We have strict instructions not to fuck this up like Declan's games.

And here? If she's here, I know I can keep her safe. Because the only monster that can hurt her is me now.

A sound claws its way out of my throat. Something feral.

The timer blares. Ten minutes. To her, it must be the ultimate relief, but to me, it makes me feel sick.

Reggie opens the sauna door and removes her collar.

Hallie slumps forward and I'm frozen in my seat, hand shaking, chest heaving, staring at the woman I was supposed to protect…barely surviving the hell I created.

Oh my God. What have I done?

CHAPTER 57

HALLIE

I'm a trembling mess. My body is an inferno, but inside? I'm cold as fucking ice.

I was so close to losing everything there. And in a way, I did. I came so hard. Whoever had control of that toy knew how to play me.

And I feel disgusting. Like I've betrayed Conan and myself. I might have gained a sliver of freedom, yet it's only trapped me inside my own mental hell harder.

I stumble towards the table to catch my breath.

Everything is becoming a fucking blur. Why are they doing this?

The guard strides over to me and hands me a bottle of water. I snatch it out of his ginormous hands and pull the bottom of my mask up.

Oh my god, it feels so good to breathe in just air.

That sauna was so claustrophobic in the mask, I'm surprised I didn't pass out. The distraction from the toy was my only savior there.

I gulp it down in one go. The nicest water I've ever drank.

It's eerily quiet. My heavy breathing is the only noise.

I don't want to leave this cabin. It feels safe here.

I should be elated. I'm through to the next round, another step towards winning. But all that consumes me is dread.

Being chased. Fighting to survive.

I could die.

The guard opens the front door, and a gush of cold air envelops me, making me shiver.

Taking a deep breath, I walk out of here and back into the dark night, following this stranger into the depths of the woods.

Not a single word is exchanged. I have nothing to say to him. Because, what I've realized is, if I could, I would kill him with my bare hands.

Does that make me a monster too? Just like the ones who run this game.

Are we all just evil deep down?

I shake my head. I know I'm not. I try to be a good person. Even when my world is ripped apart.

But the woman who walks out of here, if she ever does, is not going to be the same Hallie that entered.

CHAPTER 58

CONAN

I nearly kick Drago's door off its hinges.

"Drago!" I shout, storming down the hallway like a fucking bomb about to blow.

"In here," he calls from the left.

I spin around and burst into his office—red-faced, heart jackhammering, breath all over the place.

"Can you pull up all the applications Enzo sent and the addresses the men were sent to to collect the contestants?"

Drago squints. "Yeah. What's going on?"

I rub my temples, trying to push back the pounding in my skull. My head feels like it's about to crack open.

"Hallie. My girlfriend? She's a contestant."

His eyes widen and my heart is threatening to explode.

"How?"

"I have no fucking idea." I throw my hands up. "Enzo said this was about sex clubs. That the contestants were either the partners of or worked for the men who frequented them. Hallie is neither. As far as I know, she's not involved in anything like that. Not even close."

"This doesn't feel right, Conan," Drago mutters, already typing.

I collapse into the chair beside him, my gut twisted in knots.

"Okay," he says, clicking through files. "So, the girls' names are aliases. But Enzo will have the full names stored somewhere. Still, we have descriptions. And addresses. Here."

He pushes the laptop toward me and checks his phone, leaving me to scan the file.

And there it is. Hallie's address.

I blink. My stomach churns.

"I think I might throw up."

Drago inches his chair back.

"Conan, I know I'm the new guy around here. But I've been in this world a long time. Stay calm. Read the documents. Then we'll make a plan."

I click through until Contestant Ten's profile comes up.

The description is her.

The address is hers.

I knew it. I *knew*. But this…this is confirmation. This is worse than any fear I've ever had. One I never saw coming.

But it's one that is going to shatter my fucking life.

"Who entered her?" I demand, voice rising.

Drago stays composed. "Only way I'll find that out is by hacking Enzo. And I'm not sure that's the smartest move."

"No. But I can speak to the fucking asshole myself. Call him."

Behind me, my brother clears his throat. I spin around in the chair, now facing both of them—Declan and Finn—standing in the doorway.

"What's happened?" Finn asks, already striding in.

"Hallie. She's Contestant Ten. She's in the fucking games, and I need Enzo to explain himself. Now."

Finn and Declan trade a look. The tension is thick in the air.

"You're one hundred percent sure?" Declan asks, scratching at his stubble.

"Yes. I can fucking read." I shove the laptop in front of him.

"Is this really a coincidence, Dec?" Finn cuts in, anger tightening every word. "First Charlotte for you. Now Hallie for Conan? There's only one man who selects the contestants. The man himself. Our God. Enzo. So yeah, I agree with Conan. Get that asshole on the line."

Cracking my knuckles, a new fear rolls through me. One I've never felt before. One that settles in my bones.

Declan pulls out his phone and dials, putting it on speaker.

"We play this smart, Con," he warns.

"Declan?" Enzo answers.

My hands clench into fists. I want to rip his fucking head clean off—and I know Finn would help.

"Enzo," Declan says evenly. "We need to know who entered Contestant Ten into the games. It's important."

No more waiting around for weeks for Finn's elimination list. No more quiet compliance.

"I'm sort of in the middle of something—"

"I don't fucking care, Enzo. Send the damn list," I snap.

Finn smirks, eyes glinting with shared rage.

"Excuse me?"

"I know you're not deaf. My girlfriend's in the games, and I want to fucking know why. Now."

Declan clears his throat, glaring at me hard enough to pierce skin. Then it hits me like a ton of bricks.

Sex clubs.

Hallie.

There is only one man who is the common denominator here, and he's lying in Finn's hospital bed, with his death in our hands.

"It's a sensitive issue, Enzo. But we're going to need those names in the next ten minutes. Or we might have to reconsider this entire arrangement."

My jaw drops.

Did Declan just threaten to cut Enzo out of Decadence?

I'm proud of him.

Yeah, we needed Enzo to build this empire. But we don't need him anymore. He doesn't own us. And Dad would roll in his grave if he saw us bending over for that bastard.

The line goes silent.

"I'll have Romeo do it now," Enzo snaps, irritated.

I don't care. He can be as pissed as he wants. This isn't just business. Not anymore.

"Look, Conan," Enzo adds, "for what it's worth, I had no idea you even had a girlfriend. I'm not invested in your love life. Business is business. Clearly, she has some tie to it somewhere. Maybe if you'd looked over the applications when I sent them in—"

I chew my lip. I was busy. With Hallie. With rebuilding my MMA career. This chase wasn't my priority.

I never thought she'd end up in it. I didn't look over the applications because I didn't care who was entered. I didn't want to find a sub. It meant nothing to me.

And now my mistake has cost me everything.

"Noted. Thanks," Declan says, cutting the call.

He looks pissed as hell, sliding the phone back into his pocket with a sharp exhale.

"Conan. Don't ever fucking talk over me like that again." He steps in front of me.

I rise to my feet. We're nose to nose.

"What would you have done in my shoes, huh?"

"It was only a few weeks ago we ran to Russia to save your wife. We've always had your back. Now have mine," I growl.

Finn shoves between us, arms out.

"Enough. We don't turn on each other. Declan, give Conan a break. We're lucky he hasn't already hunted Enzo down and gutted him."

He turns to me.

"But have some respect. Declan's our brother, but he's also our leader. You'd never have spoken to Dad like that. Don't do it to him."

I nod once, tight.

"Friends?" I offer my hand to Declan.

He stares at it for a beat, then grins.

"Brothers." He clasps it hard.

His phone pings.

He glances at the screen, face going pale, then red with fury.

"What?" I ask, already dreading the answer.

"You won't fucking believe this, brother."

He turns the phone around.

My stomach caves in. My heart drops.

The name on the screen punches the air from my lungs.

I grab a glass from the desk and smash it against the wall, screaming until my voice breaks. I fucking knew that asshole was up to something. But me and my fists had to shut him up too quickly before he could give me the truth.

The games. It's too late. That's what he'd been warning Hallie about. The threat was real.

He meant this. The Decadence Chase.

That motherfucker.

"He owned a strip club," Finn mutters, rubbing the back of his neck. His face unreadable.

"You know what that means..." His voice trails off.

I'm trembling.

With rage.

With purpose.

"We get to bring a dead man back to life," I say flatly.

And this time, I'm going to find out why. There are no coincidences in this world. Not like this. What doesn't make sense is he got to Hallie first, before I even knew her name.

Was she always a pawn in this game?

Or did I walk right into a trap?

I know in my heart my girl has nothing to do with this. She's caught in the crossfire of a war she doesn't even know exists.

But I vow to make it right. I won't stop. No one, including myself, will hurt her again. And I will die protecting her if I have to.

CHAPTER 59

HALLIE

The base camp is weirdly cozy. So far, I'm the fifth woman to arrive. A couple of the others are already asleep on the hammocks.

"Hi," I greet the girl tending to the fire.

She has the same lingerie set on as me, just a different shade of green.

And the mask is the exact same as mine.

"Hey. You'll want to read this." She has a strong New York accent.

She holds out a sheet of paper to me, and I take it, perching on the log seat.

Congratulations. You've made it to base camp. This will be your home until the next nightfall. For now, you are safe. If you wish, you may remove your masks. Here, it's time for you to rest and recover before the final chase.

Once the dark settles, a siren will call. That will mark the start of the Decadence Chase.

All you must do is avoid capture from the Hunter of Inferno.

The last remaining woman shall win the two-million-dollar prize.

If you are caught, your time not only at Decadence shall end, but your life shall end too.

Sweet dreams.

"Great," I say sarcastically, handing it back to her.

The first thing I do is take off my mask; it feels so nice on my skin to let the air in.

"Why aren't you taking your mask off? It says we can," I question.

She doesn't look up from prodding at the fire.

"I don't trust them."

"Oh."

Yeah, maybe she is right.

She looks up, the fire reflecting in her eyes.

"But then, you didn't die or get eliminated for doing it. So, I guess I'll join."

That was clever. Waiting for someone else to take the fall. She's very calculated.

When she pulls off her mask, I smile. She's pretty. She shakes out her auburn hair and rubs her hands over her cheeks.

"My skin is so dry," she complains, and I laugh.

"Yeah. I didn't see any moisturizer in the rucksack."

Another girl creeps over and joins us, also revealing her face. This girl is blonde with bright blue eyes, almost similar to Lily. Tall and slim and a sweet smile.

"Hey," she greets us, sitting on the opposite end of this log bench from me.

"Can we just address the elephant in the room?" the auburn haired girl asks.

"Sure?" I shrug.

"What in the actual fuck is this? Like, how did we all land up here? There has to be some sort of link or reason."

I scratch at my scalp. She has a point.

"Should we maybe share details of our lives? See if we can find a common denominator?" I suggest.

"Yes. Good idea," the blonde chimes in.

"Okay. I guess I can go first." I pause. Should I be truthful? These girls aren't my teammates, they are my competition.

But they are all I have in here right now that could be a potential ally.

"I'm Hallie. I'm from Pennsylvania. Born and Raised. I'm a cardiac nurse at the hospital. My dad is dead. My mom is otherwise occupied far away from me. I have a dog."

I stop.

I also have potential links to the mafia.

"Any boyfriends or husbands?" The blonde asks.

"No," I reply quickly.

"I'm Chelsea. But my work name is Red. I work for Big Dave." I blink at her blankly.

"I work at a sex club, Hallie. That's my job. Dave is my boss. I service only wealthy individuals. I guess a lot of them have shady backgrounds. But they don't ever know my real name. I'm from New York."

Okay. So there are no similarities between our lives.

"I'm Abigail. But my work name is Angel. Same as you, Chelsea. I work for The Preacher in Ohio. It's kind of fucked up, I guess, but the money is good. Our clients are mainly within the church. It's a secret club I work in."

Well, there seems to be a similarity there.

"Are you sure you don't do sex work, Hallie? It's nothing to be embarrassed about. It's good money. Easy money most of the time," Chelsea tells me.

I shake my head.

"I promise you. I really am a nurse. Full-time." I hold up my hands.

No wonder they are both so stunning.

"This doesn't make any sense. We can ask the rest of the girls when they arrive and the other two wake up. There has to be something or someone. You don't just randomly get stolen from your night's sleep for this shit."

Abigail taps her long nail against her knee.

"I got taken from work. They just strolled in and took me straight to a Range Rover. They had to have known the owner to even step foot in my club."

This makes no sense.

How am I here? Was this a mistake? What could they possibly want from a nurse?

The only thing that springs to mind is my relationship with Conan.

Suddenly my chest starts to feel tight. Just thinking about him. Having to explain all of this. Would he still want me? Knowing what I've had to do.

What if he's in danger?

"W-we should probably get some rest," I whisper, and my stomach starts growling louder than my words.

"There is some food to cook up left in a freezer box. Eat first?" Chelsea suggests.

A warmth spreads over me.

None of us deserve to die here.

"Okay." I smile sweetly.

"So, a controversial opinion..." Abigail scoots closer to us.

"I think the Hunter of Inferno is hot as hell. I just get this feeling. Even though his voice is distorted. I just think, to come up with this, he has to have one hell of a kink. Don't you think?"

Chelsea shrugs.

"I don't know. Some old, ugly ass men have some kinks. But then, the challenge was interesting."

I swallow.

"What did you guys have to do?"

I don't even want to talk about mine, but strangely with these two girls, they're so open and honest, I don't feel embarrassed. We are all in the same shitty boat here.

And we end up chatting about everything and anything for hours, until my eyes can't physically stay open anymore.

I guess, as last nights on the planet go, this wasn't as awful as it could have been.

But I'd rather be drifting off with Conan's strong arms wrapped around me.

CHAPTER 60
CONAN

"**A**nything keeping him alive, rip them out," I order Finn the second I step through the doors.

Ben's face is still swollen, but he's awake and looking at me like the devil just walked in.

I drag a chair to the side of his hospital bed and straddle it.

"Ben. Does it feel good to still be breathing?"

He tries to smirk. But his busted mouth won't let him.

"Struggling there, pal?" I smack the side of his head.

Finn removes all the cables from his arms. The monitor screams for a second before cutting to silence.

"Scalpel." I hold out my hand.

"It's like I'm a kid playing doctors and nurses. Except, this time, it's real." I lean in closer, whispering. "And I don't have a fucking clue what I'm doing."

I chuckle as Finn drops the scalpel into my palm.

"Hmmm. Where to start? Shall we test how good it cuts first?"

I rip off the bloodied gown clinging to his skin,

revealing a mottled mess of bruises. Just the lightest touch draws blood.

"Nice."

I drag the blade down, slicing straight through to his stomach.

"W-what do you want?" Ben stutters.

"Now isn't the time to play dumb."

"Doctor, would this cut through bone? Or do I need something more substantial?"

Finn's mouth twitches, but he keeps his cool. He heads to the cabinet and returns with something far less surgical. A saw.

"Damn. You got everything here."

"Would you like some pain relief, sir?" I ask Ben.

"I want you to stop."

I shake my head slowly.

"Okay. I'll take that as a no. Now take a deep breath for me and relax, Ben. This will probably sting."

I grab his hand, crushing the bones until he whimpers, and flatten it to the side table.

Then I saw two fingers clean off.

His screams rip through the room, but I barely hear them. I'm focused on the flesh. The way it peels. The way it splits.

"Oh. There's the bone," I murmur, hitting resistance. I press harder. They snap off.

"Fuck!"

He thrashes.

I grip his forearm and plant the saw against it.

"I'd say it's good enough to go through this. I reckon I'm strong enough."

I pause, looking at him. He's drenched in sweat. Eyes wide, barely holding back tears.

"You can stop this, Ben. Just tell me why you entered Hallie into the games and who you work for. Simple as that."

He clamps his mouth shut.

So I start cutting again.

"I will make this as painful as I possibly can, Ben. I'm sawing your limp dick off next. Then I'll feed you your balls. Maybe I'll mix a little drug cocktail from that cabinet and shoot it straight into your eyeballs. If that doesn't kill you, I'll just keep cutting. Tongue. Toes. Hell, maybe I'll rip out your intestines too."

A sick smile curves my lips.

"And I've got one of the best doctors in America right here, keeping you alive just long enough to feel every ounce of it."

I pull the saw away and tap it against his cheek.

"Or…you tell me those two little things, and I won't do any of that."

I sit back, crossing one ankle over my knee.

"I'll give you a minute while I think about it."

Finn tosses me a smoke. I light it and blow the smoke right in Ben's face.

"Lovely weather today," I say, watching the sun crawl up over the tree line.

"Isn't it just?" Finn murmurs, hands clasped behind his back, staring out the window.

I picture Hallie out there. Cold. Alone. Waiting for The Chase. My stomach knots with rage.

When the cigarette's burned down, I snub it out on Ben's forehead. He howls like a wounded animal.

"Right. Decision time, Ben. To speak or not to speak? Hmm?"

"Want to start with an easier question, a warm-up?"

He nods.

"Okay. Where are your phone and keys? They weren't anywhere obvious in the club or your car."

He swallows hard.

"In the safe. Manager's office."

Finn nods and pulls out his phone.

Our guys will be on it. Drago'll have that phone cracked in an hour.

"Wasn't so hard, was it?"

I slap his face and sit back.

"Want to try another one?"

"Okay."

He looks like a rat. Acts like one too.

None of our men would fold this fast.

"Why did you enter Hallie into The Chase?"

His eyes flick to his mangled hand. His face goes pale.

"Revenge. I was going to use someone from the club. But then Hallie decided to be a fucking whore with you. Thought it'd be funny. She doesn't deserve to be happy."

I shut my eyes, breathe deep.

The monster claws at my skin.

"Why do you always try to belittle her?" I tilt my head. "It's the small dick, isn't it? Men like you always lash out when they get rejected."

He grits his teeth. I can't help but laugh.

"Can't even deny it."

"She is a slut. She deserves everything she gets for leaving me for the likes of you," he spits back.

I clutch my chest dramatically.

"Oh, how tragic. A man who cares for her. Makes her come violently. Would kill her prick of an ex without blinking." I lean in, venom dripping.

"Yeah. I'm still alive. You could've killed me twice now."

I roll my eyes.

"Only because I want you alive, silly."

He frowns.

"It's painfully clear you're not the brains of this operation. But I did find out you're working for your cousin. That British accent...I'd bet my last bullet your handler is Arthur."

Color drains from his face.

Bin-fucking-go.

"Save your life, Ben. He'd kill you in a heartbeat to save himself. That's who the Bowens are. Unloyal. Greedy. Cowardly cunts."

Ben's jaw ticks. Finn glances at me, impressed.

"We are not," Ben groans.

Oh, the slip.

"We?" I ask, knowing full well he's just admitted what I needed to know.

His eyes go wide, and I tut.

"Ben Bowen. Arthur really must be scraping the bottom of the barrel for men to send you after me. You're an embarrassment."

"Fuck you." He spits at me and I duck it easily.

"No, thanks. Even if I did swing that way, I'd want someone who performs better. You looked like a rabbit on crack fucking that girl on the couch. She looked bored. Probably how Hallie felt too."

God, I hate picturing her with him. With anyone.

I scratch my jaw, picking up the scalpel. Arthur's gonna get Ben's body as a present—with a little message attached.

I start carving.

"Oh, the 's' is kinda tricky."

Finn chuckles beside me.

"Takes some practice, Con."

When I finish, I step back.

The Bowens Suck Ass.

Block capitals.

"Missing something."

I grab Ben's arm.

"Anything vital I should avoid?"

"Front of the arm. Less chance he bleeds out too fast."

I nod and get to work adding the signature.

Love, Conan.

"I went for elegance. Wanted it to feel personal."

Finn tilts his head.

"I think it'll look beautiful in a gallery. Especially if the rest is...decorative."

God, I love his twisted brain.

"Any suggestions?"

His eyes light up.

"Look! Wait!" Ben panics.

"Hallie wasn't part of the plan. I fell for her. I loved her."

I laugh. Love? Please. I watched him fuck someone else on her couch.

"I just got scared. I fucked it up. At first I wanted her in the games to scare her back to me. I was never going to let her actually go. But then, you just couldn't leave her alone. It's such a twist of fate. You were so hard to find, Conan. But once Hallie got to you, you made it easy."

He spills.

"Arthur knew about Enzo's underground world. We opened up a club to secure an invite. Then Hallie brought you to me. I knew the second you walked through that door together, I'd lost her. And she had to pay."

My fists clench. Finn grips my bicep.

"So let me get this straight. You came to spy. Got jealous. Entered Hallie in The Chase to scare her. Fed Arthur intel. All because your dick couldn't handle rejection?"

I lean in close.

"What's the plan, Ben?"

"Arthur wants you dead. I want Hallie back."

That grin again. Ugly. Bloody.

"She'll never forgive you. You're sick. All of you. The Quinns need putting down."

A growl erupts from deep in my chest.

"So aggressive. You need locking in a cage."

Finn leans in.

"Reggie has the phone. We've got everything. Do as you wish, Con."

He steps back, slipping out the door.

It clicks shut.

Ben grins.

"None of you will kill me. Hallie's mine. Always will be."

That's the last thing he ever says.

I tear him apart. Smash his skull until there's nothing left but blood and pulp and bone.

Just like James Bowen. Just like Arthur and his father will be.

They wanted a war. They fucking got one. And I'll send this Bowen back to Arthur in a far worse state than his brother was.

CHAPTER 61

HALLIE

The eight of us huddle together, watching the sun begin to set.

We're cold. Exhausted. Dread sitting heavy in our bones.

None of us deserve to die here. But that's not how this works.

Only one of us walks out alive.

And it has to be me.

My heart's pounding. My eyes locked on the sun as it dips behind the trees.

The anticipation builds, tightening in my chest, waiting—just waiting—for that goddamn siren to wail.

I didn't sleep. I tossed and turned for hours, mind spiraling, obsessing over one thing:

How the fuck do I win?

Be the last woman standing. That's all. That's the rule.

And I think I've figured out a way.

This is *his* hunting ground.

But I'm going to make it mine.

The moment the siren blares, the girls take off, feet

pounding against dirt. All of them scatter forward, vanishing into the dense forest.

But I wait. Watching. Calculating.

I swing my gaze left, then right—

And I trust my gut.

I go left.

And I run.

As fast as I can. For as long as I can.

My legs scream. My lungs burn. Branches whip across my face and arms, the cold air slashing through the lace of my bodysuit.

The earth crunches beneath my boots like bones.

I keep going until I find it. My spot.

I don't know how long I've been running. Minutes. Hours. Time doesn't exist here.

But then I see it.

A massive oak tree, towering and thick with age.

We used to climb trees on hikes when I was a kid.

Dad would hoist me up and tell me to trust my grip. To hold on tight.

And I did.

So that's what I do now.

The branches look strong enough. They have to be.

I dig my boot into the bark, gripping smaller stumps and knots, hauling myself upward.

Don't look down.

I'm not a kid anymore.

And heights scare the shit out of me.

But so does death.

And that's what I'm hiding from.

He's not the Hunter of Inferno.

He's the Master of Hell.

I climb until my arms scream and my legs shake. Then I

find a branch wide enough to hold me. One that gives me cover—thick leaves, twisted limbs. Something to disappear into.

I wedge my back against the trunk, stretch my legs along the branch, and reach for every leafy twig I can, snapping them off and draping them around me like armor.

They've got drones. Cameras. I know that.

But maybe this will help. Maybe they won't see me.

Up here, I have the advantage.

But once the sun is gone, I'll be blind.

So I wait.

I let the silence stretch around me like a shroud.

And I think.

Of memories. Of home. Of the few happy moments I've had lately.

Especially Conan.

God, I wish we had more time.

I liked who I was becoming with him.

Braver. Softer.

Still me, but somehow freer.

It's the first time a relationship hasn't felt like a prison.

It felt like flight. Like fire. Like fucking freedom.

A silent tear slips down my cheek.

I don't wipe it away.

I just close my eyes and let it fall.

CHAPTER 62

CONAN

This is the first year I have entered my Decadence Chase with no fire in my veins.

I caught the first girl easily. I know just from how my body reacts that this isn't Hallie.

"Please! No!" she screams as I grip her shoulders.

We've got drones going and the twins out on foot to track her down.

I pull off this girl's mask, and her blonde hair bounces, her green eyes pleading with me.

"Shh." I hold my finger up to my lip. "Don't fight me."

She pales, her body going limp like she's about to pass out.

Jesus Christ.

Holding her up with one hand, I let the flare go off in the other, the loud bang hopefully enough to scare the other contestants.

Although I do have some blanks with me in my pistol.

"Be quiet," I whisper and lead her through the hedgerow back to the holding cabin, armed by Declan.

I walk her in and close the door, locking it too.

413

"One down, seven more to go."

"Yeah, I can count," I snap back to Dec.

"Movement near checkpoint three. Two of them confirmed in this area," Rowan says through my earpiece.

"On my way."

"Still searching for Hallie. It's going to be a task. The masks aren't helping." Drago's serious voice cuts in through my ear.

"I hunt for sport. I'll find her."

And I've got a taste for her, which works even better in my favor.

Making my way over to the checkpoint, I keep my footsteps light and listen out for movement.

I'm still having an internal debate between my head and my heart.

When I catch Hallie, do I reveal the truth and pray she forgives me? Or do I just set her free, no words exchanged?

I shake away the anxiety this gives me.

I know what she deserves—the damn truth. I can't let her live her life in fear, thinking whoever took her and brought her here is coming back for her.

I can't lie there with her in my arms at night, knowing what I've done.

I'm going to have to find my balls and tell her everything and deal with the consequences.

It's shit. It's going to hurt.

I'm just praying that she at least hears me out. I don't want to lose her. *I can't lose her.*

CHAPTER 63

HALLIE

I've counted six flares go off so far. Well…a couple of them I'm not sure weren't gunshots.

I haven't moved a muscle. I have no clue how long I've been up here.

There's rustling beneath me. I peer down, quiet as I can, and my heart hammers against my ribs.

It's one of the contestants.

And I think…it's just between me and her now. If I'm right about the flares meaning a woman's been eliminated, then we're the last two.

I rest my head back against the tree trunk and hold my breath.

When I win…how do I know they won't just kill me? How do they know that I won't go straight to the cops? Am I going to forever be looking over my shoulder, waiting to be taken again?

That isn't a life I want.

I don't trust them. I don't trust any of this.

Am I supposed to still run?

Fuck.

I just want Conan. If I'm running to anyone, it's to him. I know he will keep me safe. He will look after me.

With him by my side, I might get over the mental turmoil of this whole thing. I need him.

Part of me thinks I should just let myself die up in this tree instead. But I haven't gotten this far for nothing. If there is just even a chance that I get my freedom, I have to take it.

My stomach rumbles. I squeeze my arms tight around it, trying to quiet the noise.

Then I hear it.

Heavy boots.

Crunching through the leaves like thunder.

And I go completely numb. All the hairs on my arms rise like they know. That has to be him.

The Hunter of Inferno.

Okay, Hallie—think.

Maybe when I hear the final flare go off...I make a run for base camp. At least it's out in the open. I'm not staying up here if I've won this damn game.

I have to take the risk. Two million dollars is life changing, but right now? I'd exchange that just to survive.

Screams rip through the woods.

My whole body erupts in goosebumps.

Should I be elated? I've just won. Or so I think. If my guesses are correct.

But I'm not. I can't be. Not until I'm out of this hellhole.

I swear to God, I can hear him dragging her through the leaves.

A sob escapes my throat before I can stop it. I slam both hands over my mouth.

The screams cut off. Just silence now.

Horrifying.

Suffocating.

Like living inside a fucking horror film.

I wipe my tears with the back of my hand. Wait for the stillness to settle again.

And when it does, I'll make my move.

CHAPTER 64

CONAN

Disappointment crashes over me like a wave when I rip the mask off.

Still not Hallie.

She's unconscious—this one actually passed out, which, for once, works in my favor. I haul her up, her body limp and useless in my arms, and pass her off to Reggie.

"Maybe have Finn check her over. I think she just needs to come round," I mutter.

"Fine," he grunts, hoisting her over his shoulder like it's just another job. Another body. Another failed face.

He glances back at me. "Any sign of your girl?"

My pulse stutters.

No matter how many lies I feed myself, the guilt is crawling up my throat like it wants to choke me.

"No."

He shrugs, like it doesn't matter. "Well, she's won. She won't be far away."

And then he's gone, disappearing into the trees with the last not-Hallie, headed for the elimination cabin.

It's just me and her now.

I feel it in the marrow of my bones.

Hallie is smart. Strategic. She's not sprinting blindly through the woods like the rest of them. No. My girl is hiding. She's conserving her energy. Letting the fear do the work.

She's out here. Watching. Waiting.

And I can feel her. Not in some poetic, distant way. I mean, I *feel* her. The static in the air. The sweat slicking my palms. The sick twist in my gut.

She's close.

I head back to where I caught the last contestant. There was something there. A flicker. The air shifted, just for a second.

Now I move quietly. Like a predator stalking its prey, only this time, I don't want the kill. I want the impossible.

I want her to tell me it's okay.

But I also want her to surrender. To see me. To choose me.

My steps are slow. Then I stop entirely.

And I wait.

Every breath is a stone in my chest. Every second ticks louder than the one before.

Because this is the edge of the cliff.

The place where everything ends. Or begins. I'm not sure anymore.

And I know, the moment I lay eyes on her, it's over for me.

My rules. My games. My carefully constructed empire of retribution and justice and survival—it all crumbles at her feet.

There's a crack. Twigs snapping at my three o'clock.

I don't move. Don't breathe.

Then another sound. Light footsteps, like she's trying not to exist.

She's not running.

She's hunting for her moment.

I slide behind a tree, my back pressed to the bark, heart slamming against my ribs like it's trying to warn me.

This is it.

She's coming down from whatever perch she's been hiding in.

And I know—without a single doubt—that when I see her, everything I've fought to keep buried will come roaring back to life.

I'm not ready.

But I have no choice.

Because Hallie is about to step into my line of sight.

And once she does, nothing will ever be the same again.

CHAPTER 65

HALLIE

As soon as my boots hit the ground, I clutch the nearest tree like it's the only solid thing left in the world.

I have no idea if I'm the last contestant. I don't know where The Hunter is. And right now, it doesn't matter.

Because I'm the prey.

And he's coming for me.

I suck in a deep breath, adrenaline boiling in my veins, my chest heaving like my lungs forgot how to function. I shove off the tree and move silently. Every twig crack and every shift in the wind hits like a gunshot to my senses.

I don't run. Not yet.

The second I do, it's over.

I wait. Assess.

Nothing moves.

So I run.

I bolt for the camp, the trees slicing past me like shadows. I barely get a few feet before I hear him.

Heavy, deliberate steps.

He's behind me. And he's way too close.

I force my legs to move faster, the air burning in my throat. I weave through the trees, cutting right, making sharp turns, anything to shake him. But he's there. Right there.

So close I can feel his breath against my neck.

So close I can smell him.

And suddenly—I'm back in that chase with Conan. My body remembers.

The panic. The heat. The ache that burned under the terror.

I spot an opening, a sliver of moonlight spilling into the clearing by the tents. I'm weak, but I push forward. I can't let him catch me.

His breath hits my skin again, and I cry out, flinging myself forward.

But his arms wrap around my waist and we slam into the ground.

And the moment we hit the dirt, the second his hands touch my skin, I know.

Familiar.

Safe.

No fear.

Just heartbreak.

My eyes squeeze shut. My mouth can't form a scream.

He rolls on top of me, and I'm frozen, breathless.

Silent.

I fight him, clawing and kicking, but he doesn't move. Doesn't speak. Doesn't hurt me.

He just holds still like he's waiting for me to understand. And when I finally give in, my body heaving with breathless sobs, I open my eyes.

And there they are. *His eyes*. Behind the black mask. And my world ends.

I don't need to see more to know what's coming.

But I do.

I shake my head, eyes slamming shut, praying this is a nightmare I'll wake up from.

"No. Please."

He peels my mask off slowly and freezes. His finger brushes my cheek, so soft it almost breaks me. My eyes fling open.

He pulls at the bottom of his mask. Every second is dragging like it's trying to kill me.

Then he tosses the fabric to the ground. And I sob, it's raw and broken, as I stare at the man who made me feel safe. The man who looked after me. The man who I thought was falling for me.

The man who promised he'd never hurt me.

"You piece of fucking shit," I whisper, choking on the words.

My sob is violent. I cover my mouth, shoulders shaking.

No.

Not him.

Not my Conan.

He wouldn't do this to me.

He showed me the darkest parts of him, not this.

This—this isn't him.

If I close my eyes, maybe he'll disappear. Maybe this version of him will vanish, and I'll wake up to the man who made me feel alive.

"Hallie."

His voice shatters me. A blade wrapped in velvet.

"Get off me!" I scream, slamming my fists into his chest. "Get off!"

He finally moves, sitting back on his heels, and I suck in a desperate breath.

"Hallie. Look at me. Please, baby."

I scramble backwards, stumbling to my feet. He rises too, and I step further away.

"Stay away from me." My hand flies out to stop him, trembling violently.

His face—God, his face—is all anguish. And it almost ruins me.

Good.

"This is the real you?" My voice cuts like venom.

"Unfortunately. Yeah."

His breath stutters. Mine breaks.

"I'm so sorry, trouble. Please, let me explain."

I hide my shaking hands behind my back. I won't let him see me fall apart.

"Nothing to explain. I've just lived it."

"It's not what you think."

"Conan. I want to go home. Or am I now eliminated?"

My voice is cold. Detached. But inside, I'm dying.

Would he kill me? I know too much. I know everything. I'm a liability.

"I'd never hurt you, Hallie."

I laugh. Hollow. Shattered.

"You wouldn't? Well, what the fuck do you think you've just done to me? You've not just hurt me, Conan. You've fucking broken me."

This isn't pain.

This is annihilation.

"I—I didn't know it was you. Before it was too late."

"Now you're just fucking lying to my face. How is New York, by the way? Training hard?" I seethe.

He lets out a ragged breath. His eyes, they're full of sorrow. Like, he really is telling the truth. But how can he be?

He is just trying to save himself. He's been caught. And now, I'm doubting if anything is real. I need to leave.

My chest starts to close in on me and I rub along my collarbone, trying to relieve the pressure building.

"I just want to get as far away from you as possible."

His bloodshot eyes lock on mine. I can't breathe.

"I'm sorry. I'm so fucking sorry. How can I make this right?"

He wipes his tears away like they're not cutting him apart.

"You can't. Just let me go. Not just from these woods. Pretend you never met me."

He grips his hair, pulling at the roots.

"I can't pretend I never met you, Hallie. Because the weeks I've known you have been the best time of my life. I can never let that go. I can never let *you* go."

I press my hand into my chest like I can stop the pain.

But it's everywhere.

He didn't just break me. He burned me.

"You need to forget me. For both of our sakes."

He shakes his head, desperate.

"I know I won, but I don't want your money. I want nothing from you. Give it to the girl who came second. I just want to leave now."

His eyes beg me to stay.

"Tell me how I can make this right…"

"Unless you have a way to turn back time, beastie, that's just not possible. Don't waste your time trying."

It hurts. Every word. Every step away from him feels like ripping my soul apart.

Heavy footsteps approach.

I glance past Conan to find Declan and Finn moving toward us. Grim. Silent.

Declan places a hand on Conan's shoulder and pulls him aside.

"Dr. Quinn, please just take me home. I won't tell anyone, you have my word. I'll hand in my notice, I'll move away. I don't want any money. I just want my dog and a new start away from this…" I glance at Conan. "Away from *him*."

"Hallie, I'm really fucking sorry," Finn says.

My eyes widen and I step back.

Is he going to shoot me?

They all promised to protect me. But maybe I needed protection from them.

"I meant I'm sorry for what's happened. I'm not going to hurt you."

Relief nearly takes me to my knees.

Finn stays cold, unreadable. But then he shrugs off his jacket and places it over my shoulders. I wrap it around myself like armor.

"I—I can go home?"

He nods, hand shoved deep into his pocket.

Finn steps closer.

"Just turn around and walk away, don't look back. Just let him go. We will look after him, don't worry," he murmurs.

I glance back once.

Conan's wrecked. Declan tries to reason with him, but it's like he can't even hear.

My heart splits down the center. But I do what I have to.

I turn.

Finn leads me away.

"Hallie! Hallie! Please!"

I stop. My eyes close, a sob dragging through me.

"Enough, Conan. Let her go," Declan orders.

I don't want to look. I can't. I'm not strong enough to watch him fall apart.

It doesn't matter how much pain he's caused me, I can't watch the man I once loved break in front of my eyes.

"Don't leave me. I'm begging you. Hallie!!"

His screams echo through the trees like a dying animal.

I glance up at Finn. His jaw tightens, pain flickering in his usually calm expression.

"Finn, please don't let him near me," I whisper.

He nods once.

He gets it.

"Just keep walking. Reggie and Rowan are on their way. They'll drag him back and sort him out."

I nod, but my body is giving out. My heart's in pieces.

When we reach the mansion, Finn unlocks his Mercedes.

"I'll drive you home."

Images of my dad's death flood me. Again, Finn is there to hold me together.

I'm broken again, and Finn, he's calm.

I climb in, and he hands me a blanket. I rest my head against the cold glass, trembling.

"You okay, Hallie? Like, seriously? That challenge, it's a lot. Do you want me to check you over?"

I glance at my arms—cut, bleeding. Doesn't matter. Nothing matters anymore. I'm numb.

"No. I just want to go home. I'm fine."

We drive in silence.

When we reach my street, I don't wait.

I bolt from the car.

My front door bursts open, and Lily stands there, barefoot and frantic.

She catches me before I fall. We drop to the ground and I sob like I'm dying.

Years of grief.

All of it.

Ripping from me like a scream I've held in too long.

"Hallie, what happened? I've been worried sick," Lily whispers, her fingers running through my hair.

I shake my head.

"I—I can't talk about it."

She leads me inside.

I'm still covered in dirt.

Still in this fucking lace lingerie.

Still shattered. With my heart left in those woods.

CHAPTER 66
CONAN

"**G**et the fuck off me!" I shout, shaking the three men from me.

They tighten their restraint, my arms locked behind my back.

"Hallie!" It's a desperate cry.

The disappointment on her face.

Not hurt or upset.

I fucking gutted her. I let her down.

And now? She's gone. It's all my fault.

I sink to the dirt and they let go, and my chest heaves.

"Fuuuuuck!" I scream at the top of my lungs.

Balling my fists, I smash them into the ground. Over and over again, hoping I'll be able to feel something. Just anything.

Physical pain mutes the emotional turmoil.

But it doesn't work. It never comes. I'm completely numb.

There was life before Hallie. It was dark, but it was bearable.

Then there was life with Hallie, where for the first time I

started to picture my future with a goddamn smile on my face.

Life after losing Hallie? I don't know how to do it.

Is this just how I will live now? Empty? Like I'm missing the other half of my soul?

I will never love again. There is only one woman who owns my heart. I had my chance at happiness, and I fucked it up.

"Conan!"

It's like I can hear my brother shouting, but I can't switch out of this state.

Pure fucking devastation.

The product of my own actions.

I might as well have cut my heart out of my chest and stomped on it. Repeatedly.

I hate myself.

I hate everything that I am.

I hate that I was never good enough for her.

And I hate what I've done to her.

A man like me doesn't deserve to be happy.

All I do is break people I love.

I probably gave my mom that heart attack with all the stress I caused her.

My father died because of me and my stupid fucking rage.

No matter what I do, I always make myself the goddamn villain.

Hallie is safer far, far away from me, before I ruin her too. More than I just did.

She never asked for this lifestyle. Neither did I.

It was never a privilege. It's a fucking curse.

But it's one I have to deal with.

I just don't know how the hell I'm ever going to live without her.

She was the highlight of my day, every day.

"Conan. Come on, we've got you," Declan whispers, and they drag me up onto my feet.

Tears burn in my eyes. I can't look at any of them. I can't let them see me like this.

I rip my arm away from Declan's grip, and I run, letting the tears fall down my cheeks as I head back to my cabin.

Grabbing the keys to my McLaren, I need to get away from Decadence. From everyone. All I can see is that hatred as she looked at me.

I promised I'd never hurt her and gave her permission to kill me if I ever did.

As I jump in the car, all I want to do is drive to hers. To explain everything. Unravel the final missing pieces of myself and let her have them.

Let her choose me.

I'm not sure she will ever forgive me for this, and it fucking stings.

So, instead, I head to my garage. And do what I do best…punch the shit out of things to stop myself from falling to pieces.

Because as much as there are many other people to blame for this, I can't run from the fact that I am the problem.

These were my games, under my rule.

I was meant to protect her, and instead, I ruined her.

CHAPTER 67

HALLIE

You'd think after a week of having a door slammed in your face, you'd get the message and stop coming back. Especially after the fifth day.

But no, not Conan.

I've blocked his number and refused to see him.

It's almost like he enjoys being told to fuck off at this point.

Bertie's tail starts to wag, and I snuggle up closer to him.

"What is it, boy?"

He jumps off the sofa and lifts his paws to look out the window.

I glance at the time on my phone and sigh.

Now is about the time even my dog gets excited. Traitor.

Pulling myself off the couch, I hear the deep rumble of a car.

Normally it stops down the road, but this time it gets louder and louder, like it's parking right outside my damn door.

I rush over to the window and open the blinds a bit more.

Hmm. That's not his McLaren. I mean, it is—except for the chrome silver finish.

Wow. It's beautiful.

I hold my breath as Conan emerges from the car. Closing my eyes, I brace myself for the knock.

But it doesn't come.

Instead, something drops to my floor.

What the hell?

I keep watching him as he strolls away without looking back and hops into a Range Rover that speeds off.

Letting out a breath of pure relief, I press my palm to my chest. Lily has been here all the other days to get rid of him, so I didn't have to come face-to-face with him, but she had to go to the gallery today.

I wrap my arms around myself. I just feel so lost.

I creep toward the front door and stare at the set of keys with a silver heart dangling and a note attached.

Gritting my teeth, I pick them up and stomp into the kitchen, ripping the letter out of the envelope.

Trouble,

I know you don't want to see me, and I don't blame you.
I'll give you space if that's what you need.
But I can't give up on you.
I miss you so much, Hallie.
I didn't know it was possible to feel like this about someone until you.
I don't know how to earn your forgiveness, so I'm going to try everything, starting with the car.
She's the exact same as mine down to every single spec, well, except the paintwork.

*So maybe, one day, when you feel like seeing me, we can
have that race?*
I hope we can one day.

Love always,
Conan

I don't know how many times I re-read this note. His
messy, scribbled writing—it's just so him.

Glancing down at the keys, nausea washes over me. A
few days ago, I'd have loved nothing more than racing him.

I don't need the car. Or money.

I need someone I can trust. Someone who doesn't kidnap
me in my damn sleep and make me play a sick game in the
woods.

I pull out the chair and slump over the table.

Thinking of how I had everything to losing it all within a
single day.

The door opens, and I don't move. I don't have to hide
how upset I am from Lily.

"Hey, Hallie…what's going on?"

I sit up and wipe my eyes.

"Nothing. Pity party for one," I sniffle.

She frowns.

"Is asshole not here? The car?" She points back toward
my driveway.

"Yeah. Read this," I say, holding out the note to her.

Her face reddens as she reads it, then she sets it on the table.

"He bought you a car? And thinks that's going to fix it?"
She scratches her head.

"The car is worth half a million."

Why am I defending him?

"Yet you're still here in tears again. The car doesn't fix anything, Hallie. But he isn't going to stop. Is he?" She glances at the note.

"No."

He's a hunter.

"So, what's your plan?"

"I need to go to the hospital, hand in my resignation, and speak to Dr. Quinn."

It's a risky move. But there are more races coming up. Maybe taking the two million from the games would have been smart. But I want nothing to do with any Quinn brother.

They can screw their dirty money.

And their cars.

There will be other jobs.

"So you don't want the car?"

I shake my head.

"We could get some anger out on it?"

My eyes go wide.

"The car didn't hurt me. It doesn't deserve that."

"Are you sure you really want to quit? I know how much you love that job." She steps closer, resting her hand on my shoulder.

"Yeah. It's best for everyone involved if I just go. There will be other jobs. Other states."

"You know wherever you go, I'm going too?"

I rest my hand on top of hers.

"I'd never make you leave with me."

She smiles.

"I like adventure. Might be fun. Fresh start, you know?"

I swallow the lump in my throat.

Leaving Conan for good. It's meant to be what I want, but it still really hurts.

CHAPTER 68
CONAN

The door slams behind Finn as he walks into the bar of Inferno. He completely ignores me and Declan and heads straight for the counter.

"What's up his ass?" Declan asks.

"No clue."

We both keep quiet as Finn pulls out a chair at our table and sits, proceeding to down his whiskey in one long gulp.

"Hallie quit," he tells me matter-of-factly.

"W-what?"

"You gone deaf, Conan?"

"No. But…what?"

I'm trying to process this. She loves her job. It's her calling. For her to quit means I fucked up worse than I thought.

He glares at me and pulls out his cigarettes.

"My best nurse, who I've been mentoring for two years, just handed in her resignation and couldn't even look me in the eye. There. Explained better for you?"

I recline back in my chair, tipping my head toward the ceiling.

Fuck.

She's refusing the prize money. Quit her job. I can't let her throw her life away because of me.

"Oh. I've got these for you too." He rifles around in his pocket and tosses keys at me.

"It's been left in the parking lot at the hospital. Come collect it."

I stare down at the silver heart in my palm, and sadness washes over me.

"I don't know what to do," I mutter.

"Have you tried a heartfelt apology?" Declan suggests calmly.

"She won't see me."

Declan tuts and pours me a whiskey.

"Don't wait for her to see you. You fucking show her," he tells me.

He has a point. I've let Lily bat me away for days. I do believe Hallie was right, and that little blonde woman is definitely a mafia princess. She's downright scary.

I'm glad Hallie has her.

"I can't call or text because I'm blocked. I can't get through her front door because of Lily. So the next option is…" I trail off to think.

"I barge my way into the house and make her listen?"

That doesn't even sound right out loud.

Declan nearly spits out his drink. "Fuck. No, little brother."

"Just go home and think. She wants space? How can you give that to her yet also show her you really care? Make her soften her hatred enough to at least allow you close enough to speak to her."

I blink at him.

"Thanks for the riddle. I'll see what I can come up with."

Declan smiles.

"You have the facilities to pull off anything you can imagine. Remember that."

I stand up and finish the rest of my drink.

"That's my night sorted. I'll be up bright and early for our meeting tomorrow."

Finn just stares off into space, and I leave him to it. I know better than to wind him up when he's pissed off.

"Or you could leave her alone and just stick to fucking the women in Inferno?" Finn says casually.

"Fuck no. Thanks."

Yes, Inferno may be the most sought-after and elite sex club, right inside our chocolate factory, but there isn't a single woman in this club who would catch my eye now.

Fuck, if I can't have Hallie, I don't want anyone. I might never get my dick wet again.

The first thing I do on my walk back to my cabin is search for local florists, dialing the first one.

"Hi. Floral Delight. How can I help?" A very chirpy woman greets me.

"Uh. Hi. I was wondering if you could help me with an ongoing mission of mine."

There's a slight pause.

"Sure. What do you need?"

A smile creeps up my lips.

"A delivery of flowers, I don't care how much they cost, every single day to the same address until I tell you to stop."

Now there's a long pause.

"Every day? Are you sure?"

"Positive. I'll send over a color scheme for each day."

"Okay. When would you like to start?"

"Tomorrow," I reply quickly.

I will find a way to show her that I'll fight for her. That I'm not the man she thinks I am.

Especially not when she's with me.

I need to remind her of the Conan she brings out. The man I want to be.

Because Hallie is my future, and I can't let this go without fighting to my last breath for her.

CHAPTER 69

HALLIE

"Hey, what about LA? Or Las Vegas?" I call out to Lily, who is busy making dinner in the kitchen.

"Vegas could be fun. But I'd have to speak to my dad. I'm not sure I can go there."

I frown.

"Why?"

"Oh, just business things with him and the men who run Vegas." She says it so casually.

I wonder how much she actually knows about Conan's world.

Ugh. Why did I have to think about him?

"Okay. So, I still need to put this place up for sale."

She stirs the pasta, her face deep in thought.

"I can get us money. I don't think selling this place will be good for you."

I swallow. Maybe it is what I need. A fresh start. Not living in a place that just reminds me of my loss. But thinking of selling my dad's house makes me want to throw up.

"Lils, I just don't think I have another option. I don't know if I can be this close to him."

"I understand, Hallie. I get it."

The pasta boils over, and she starts panicking and flapping her hands. At least that gives me a laugh.

"What about Washington?" I call out.

Nowhere I look feels right, because Pennsylvania is my home.

"How about we start with a girls' trip?" Lily shouts.

Hmm. Now that sounds nice.

"Let's kinda take baby steps up the impulsive scale first? Rather than flee our homes, let's take a vacation."

She has a valid point. I look around the room at the pictures on the wall of me, Bertie, and Dad.

Can I really let this go?

Should I have quit my job?

Fuck. I do need a break.

The doorbell rings, and I spin my head. Nerves rattle through me. I can't face him. Not yet. But this is my problem to fix, not Lily's.

I drag myself off the sofa and brush my fingers through my hair. But as I open the door, a rush of disappointment fills me when no one is there.

Except a massive bunch of pink and yellow roses left on the doorstep.

Tears burn in my eyes as I pick them up and pluck out the card. It says two words.

I'm sorry.

Shaking my head, I put them back where I found them and slam the door.

I don't know what I want from him, and it's pissing me off.

It's like I can't breathe without him. But it hurts too much to be near him.

And the gifts? They're like adding salt to my wounds.

A reminder every day of what we've lost.

Because he is my person. I know that.

And soul mates aren't supposed to treat you like this. But soul mates don't hide who they truly are from each other—monster or not.

CHAPTER 70
CONAN

Drago turns his laptop to face us with a stern look.
"I've pinpointed some potential members of the Bowens who may be in this state. Hacking Ben's phone turned out to be a goldmine of information."

I nod.

"I don't really give a fuck about them. I want Arthur," I grit out.

Drago chews his lip.

"I don't believe Arthur has entered the U.S. at all."

Finn clears his throat.

"I called my sources in London. I have eyes on the cunt. He's still there," Finn confirms.

I turn to Declan.

"So are we going to London?"

He shakes his head.

"We don't have clearance from the King brothers yet," Finn tells me.

My mouth drops open.

"Finn. Are the Kings your sources? They talk to you?"

Holy shit.

The King brothers—and their sister—are the most feared mafia in the United Kingdom. We always had a distant truce with them. A mutual enemy, the Bowens.

"Yes. I used you murdering James to my advantage to get a footing with them. Theo King is prepared to assist us, but only when the time is right. And if he can get it passed through the Elders."

Declan smirks, and I can tell he's impressed with Finn. Our crazy mastermind.

"And the time is right once we eliminate any footing the Bowens have here," Declan tells us.

I tap my rings against the table. All I can think about is the disappointment on Hallie's face.

The hatred.

I want Arthur dead. Now. This whole long process of having to prove ourselves to get to him pisses me off.

My time and effort needs to be on getting my girl back.

"Conan? Any thoughts?" Declan presses.

I snap my head to his.

"No. Not really. Not my priority right now. I gotta get to Hallie."

Finn kicks me under the table. I don't even flinch.

"Conan," Declan warns.

"What?"

"The Bowens' men are here with one purpose—to kill you."

I nod.

"Yep. I know. I can take care of myself."

"And you don't care if they come after our empire? You know they're greedy cunts, always wanting what they can't have," Finn adds.

I shrug. "We all know we won't let them take anything."

Declan tuts.

"This isn't you. You're normally the first one itching for a fight. You don't want revenge against Arthur?"

I stare into Declan's blue eyes, keeping my expression cool.

"I killed his baby brother. What did we expect?"

This is all my fault. Me killing James in the cage five years ago started a war in Ireland we didn't need. A war that lost us our father. And has followed me for years since. I just need to speak to Hallie. I need her to hear me out. I need to apologize on my damn knees and beg for forgiveness.

"Cool. Okay. Great, Conan. But see, there is a slight issue with this shitty attitude you've got," Finn tells me.

"Yeah? What's that?"

He's trying to press my buttons to get a reaction out of me.

"Hallie. They probably know about her. Ben entered her here, remember? They fucking know. Therefore, she's now at risk. Now, I'd say you might want to kick yourself up the ass and fucking help us remove them before they become a threat to her."

I swallow past the lump in my throat.

"I. Um. Fuck."

I slam my fist into the wood, and my drink spills.

"Maybe she does need to stay the fuck away from me," I mutter, shaking my head.

"It might be a good idea to get her out of the state for a while," Finn replies coolly.

Ouch.

That hurts. Fine. They want me to become a monster. I can do that. I guess that is who I am really.

"Just tell me what you need me to do. I'm angry enough to burn them to the ground."

Finn rubs his hands together.

"Nice suggestion. A good starting place. Let's burn their club down first and leave Ben there with the message."

That burning rages through me.

"Yeah. I like that plan. Let's burn these motherfuckers."

Declan smirks.

"That's the spirit, brother. Hallie will come 'round."

I'm not so sure. But I'm not giving up.

No fucking way.

"She won't even take the flowers inside," I mutter under my breath.

"What?" Finn asks.

"Nothing."

"I'll send you locations for the rest of the men I believe to be involved," Drago tells us.

I snap my eyes to him. He's someone we want with us.

An absolute tank of a unit with violence flooding his veins, all hidden behind a professional exterior.

"You not coming with us, Drago?" I ask with a smirk.

He glances to Declan.

"Up to you, boss."

Declan shrugs.

"Why the hell not. Just don't get injured. Charlotte and Isabella will kill me."

Drago laughs, and we all fall quiet.

It's taken weeks for Drago to be back to full health after the torture Vlad—Charlotte's ex-husband—inflicted on him.

I saw his battered body, and I honestly thought he was dead. But of course, Dr. Quinn got him back.

And made him our weapon.

"I'm good, Declan. I can fight."

I rub my hands together. I've been itching for him to join us out on jobs.

"I have somewhere I need to go first. I'll meet you guys back here in a couple of hours."

All eyes are on me.

They know exactly where I'm going. And they all say nothing.

CHAPTER 71
HALLIE

Song- Man or a Monster, Sam Tinnesz, Zayde Wolf.

Sitting in silence with only my thoughts to keep me company is driving me crazy. Even Bertie has had enough of my wallowing and is deciding to nap.

I have so many questions burning in my brain. Questions only letting Conan in will provide answers to.

Only he can explain why he broke my heart like that.

Perhaps I need some closure before I go on vacation. Or maybe I just want to see him. Part of me hopes he has a perfect excuse lined up and I can forgive him.

But there are no chances of that ever being a reality. I know what I went through. I know what that game was.

I know he's a fucking monster.

But the why is driving me stir-crazy.

I peer out of my blinds. He's still sitting in his McLaren across the street. He's been there for an hour now. I don't know what he's waiting for.

Either for me to come out or for him to get the balls to knock again.

Lily isn't here this time to scream in his face.

My heart races when the door opens and he appears, that grief-stricken expression I can see even from here.

He jogs over, and I back away from the door, my hands trembling. It's like I'm running off pure instinct when I grab the handgun Lily hid in the hallway and tuck it behind my back.

I open the door before he can even knock.

His bloodshot eyes widen, and he just blinks at me.

Neither of us says a word. We just stand there, staring at each other's pain.

When he goes to take a step toward me, I aim the gun at him.

"Take another step closer, and I'll shoot you in the dick, Conan." My voice shakes, but I lift my chin defiantly.

His gaze fixes on the gun in my trembling right hand.

"Leave me alone," I shout.

He shakes his head but stays where he is.

"I can't do that, trouble," he tells me quietly.

"Why the hell not?"

"Because…" He closes his eyes and takes a deep breath.

My heart almost stops. Not now. He can't do this to me now.

"Because I love—"

"Don't you fucking dare say it," I scream, even though deep down, a part of me needs to hear him say those words.

When he flinches, a little part of me dies inside.

Loving Conan is going to kill me.

But I can't let him say the words. I can't stand to even hear them right now.

Because he doesn't love me. How the hell could he?

The man I fell for—he wasn't a monster. But the man I now know him to be is just that.

"I never want to see you again, Conan." My voice nearly breaks as I say the words.

There's no cheeky grin or soft-spoken whisper from him that can make this better.

I rub the ache in my chest, staring into his sad green eyes.

"You don't mean that. Not really. Please, Hallie. Don't leave me. I fucked up. I know that. I'm sorry. I'm so fucking sorry. Just let me explain."

"What the hell is there to explain, Conan? You had me kidnapped, then thrown in the fucking woods for a sick game of survival. One that you, you sick son of a bitch, run. You created a game for your fantasies—fine. But that doesn't include me, does it? You think I want a man who hunts women in the woods to fuck them? How many of the girls did you stick your dick in while I was competing?"

I feel physically sick.

"None. I wouldn't do that. I only want you, Hallie."

I let out a laugh, tipping my head back.

"Yeah. For now. Until you get that urge. Or what? Until you host your next games. Get out. I can't even look at you."

He takes a step forward, and I take one back. He's in my house now. Fuck.

"The games are my past. They're not what you think. Not entirely anyway."

He clears his throat.

"I don't believe you. I'm sure there are plenty of willing women out there to go running with you."

That hurts to say.

"Hallie. I'm sorry, okay? I had no idea you were a contestant. That you'd be mixed up in this fucked-up lifestyle. We host the games to hunt the real evil men in this world. Like the man who entered you."

"Right. Of course. Evil hunting evil. How perfect. You can all just kill each other, yeah?"

"It's our way of life."

I nod. Wait. Who the hell entered me if it wasn't Conan?

"Who?" I spit.

"Who, what?"

I take another step back until I crash into the wall.

"Entered me into your fucking games, Conan."

He rubs his hands over his face.

"Ben. I've taken care of him. This time, properly. I shouldn't have left that asshole breathing the first time."

All the air is knocked out of my lungs.

"Why? And y-you killed him?" My hands shake.

Even now, I'm still not scared of this man.

"He did it to get back at me, Hallie. It wasn't your fault. It was mine. I had no idea of his real family, his real last name. If I'd have known…"

"You'd have killed him quicker?" I fire back. This seems to be his solution to most things.

Violence. Hunting.

"Yes. And I'd kill him all over again for you. I'd kill anyone who hurts you, trouble."

"You hurt me too," I whisper, holding back my tears.

He slowly lifts his hand to me, wrapping his fingers around the gun, and I let go. His touch feels like fire.

"Then you have permission to do whatever you need to do. I told you before, I'm included in that list." He lays the gun flat on his palm in front of me.

"No."

I shake my head and let the tears fall. Losing him like

this is hard enough. Losing him entirely—by my own hands? Never.

"Don't make me ask you to leave again, Conan. We're done."

"I'm not giving up on us, trouble."

He cages me in, his hands braced on the wall above me.

"I'll make this right. I won't lose you. I can't."

I press my palms against his chest, but I don't push him away. His heart pounds against my hands.

"This is one fight you can't win, Conan."

I swear to God, he sniffles like he's about to cry. Why is this so damn hard?

He deserves this. He's evil. But the longer I'm in his presence, the less I'm sure I truly believe that.

"Even as friends?" he whispers.

I try to push him away, but he doesn't budge.

"Nothing. You are nothing to me."

He nods and steps back. The further away he gets from me, the more it feels like my chest is closing in.

"You'll always be everything to me, Hallie. Even if you hate me for the rest of your life. I'll love you until I die. You are my first and only love, trouble."

He takes in a shaky breath.

"Is this what you came here for? Or is it more flowers? Cars? Gifts won't make this right." I stare at the three bouquets of flowers still dying on my doorstep.

"I know, Hallie. I know that. I—I'm just lost. I'm trying. I want to give you space, but I don't want you to think I'm giving up. But then I come here just because I'm desperate to see your face. I don't know. In my fucked-up brain, I'm thinking eventually you'll see I'm not the man you think I am. That I am the Conan you fell for. And that you'll hear me out, properly. You'll let me back in. That's all I want. A chance to make this right, Hallie. To prove to you that I can be the man you need. Because I don't know if I can live the rest of my life without you, so I at least need to try every damn thing I can think of, just in case you do, one day, decide you don't hate me anymore."

His voice breaks, and he rubs his hands over his eyes. I want to go to him. I hate seeing him like this. And his words —they hurt me deep in my core.

And maybe one day, he will be right. I'll see him for the man I fell in love with.

But today is not that day.

CHAPTER 72
CONAN

The silence consumes me. She doesn't know how to respond. That sparkle in her eyes has gone out. I fucking did that.

I look into her living room and see two red suitcases. She follows my line of vision.

"Me and Lily are taking a girls' trip for a few days." She says it flatly.

I look down at my feet. Fuck, I want to bawl my eyes out.

She has nothing to say to my declaration. But I won't give up.

"Take my private jet. Anywhere you want. Please."

With the Bowens' threat still alive, I need her to be safe.

"Did you not hear me? I don't want anything from you." She blinks at me, and her jaw twitches.

"For safety reasons. Nothing else. We own a resort in Barbados. It's really cool. Right by the beach, a pool bar. And a safe location. The penthouse is always available for us. Just give them my name at check-in."

She shakes her head as I place the gun that's been burning a hole in my palm down on the side table.

"Please, Hallie. Trust me. I am listening to you, and I wouldn't ask if it wasn't important. You know my lifestyle. That's all you need to know."

"This is fucking crazy," she mutters under her breath.

That sassy spitfire side of her makes my heart flip.

"As crazy as you holding me at gunpoint?" I quip.

Her eyes light up, and I am on fire.

I've missed her. I need this woman like air to breathe. No. I need her more than that. I'm fucking dead inside without her.

"You're stalking me. My dad always told me it's okay to shoot in extreme circumstances."

"Your dad was a clever man."

Maybe she should have shot me to put me out of my damn misery.

"He was."

I know this hurts her to talk about. I get it.

"So, is that a yes to using my jet?"

She rolls her eyes.

"I suppose so. I don't particularly fancy being caught up in your manic life."

Ouch.

"I told you. No matter what, you will always be protected."

I clench my fist at my side to stop myself from reaching for her and tucking her hair behind her ear.

"How do I know where to go? And when? We were planning on heading to the airport tomorrow morning."

I frown.

"You haven't booked anything?"

"No. This is an impulsive decision for the goal of fun."

That is not safe. Jesus.

"Finn will send you the details."

She straightens her spine, a sadness creeping over her pretty face.

"What's up?" I ask softly.

"Does Dr. Quinn not hate me for quitting on him?"

"No, Hallie. His anger is at me, not you."

She blows out a shaky breath. I just want to hold her close and never let go.

"Okay. I'll take you up on your offer. I'm sure Lily will enjoy the jet."

I nod.

"And you won't? It's amazing. You'll love it."

She shrugs and looks away.

"I'm not sure what I even enjoy anymore."

She pins me with a stare that's filled with sadness. That same emptiness I feel.

"You will find it again."

I hope it's with me.

Giving her a smile is the best I can force myself to do when inside I am wrecked. I back away, trying not to look at the flowers now decorating the step.

"Have a good trip."

She hugs herself and stays firmly in place.

I turn to walk away, but before I head to my car, I look back at her, still standing there, watching me go.

I don't know what I expect her to do. Tell me not to go? That she'll hear me out?

I know that's not happening.

My life has never been a fairy tale. But I really fucking wish it was.

CHAPTER 73

HALLIE

"Okay. I know we hate Conan right now, but you deserve this vacation from him." Lily slides down her sunglasses and lays back on her lounger.

Hate is a strong word.

I grab my cocktail and stare at the waves crashing against the shore. The ocean is so clear it looks almost unreal, streaks of turquoise blending into pale gold sand that stretches for miles in either direction. A warm breeze dances over my skin, carrying the scent of salt and hibiscus.

"Yeah. It's nice."

"Better than nice. This is fucking beautiful. Shall we go get matching tattoos later? Drinks? Food? All of the above?"

I smile and take a sip from my straw. The cocktail tastes like coconut and lime, cold and sweet on my tongue.

"What tattoo shall we get?"

"We can figure that out when we get there."

Impulsive. That is the motto of this trip. I guess getting my first tattoo is up on that list.

I let my gaze drift across the terrace. White linen

cabanas sway lazily, casting deep shadows over plush loungers piled with oversized pillows. The resort rises behind us in tiers of whitewashed stone and glass, all clean lines and palm trees lit up by strings of tiny golden lights.

As I lie back down, I unlock my phone, pulling up Conan's contact number. Should I unblock him to say thank you?

I feel like I should, because this is the trip of a lifetime. We're getting the five-star treatment every minute of the day.

The penthouse suite feels bigger than my entire house. Floor-to-ceiling windows look out over the sea, and there's a private plunge pool on the balcony. Everything smells faintly of expensive spa oils and fresh flowers.

I could stay here for weeks.

"Have you spoken to Conan since?" Lily asks.

"Nope."

"Do you want to?"

I suck in a breath.

"I honestly don't know."

She sits up and faces me. Sunlight catches the gold flecks in her hair.

"Look, I know how much he meant to you. I'd never be upset with you for speaking to him. It's your life, you're only here once. Listen to your gut."

I take another gulp of my cocktail.

"I'll rethink after this trip. I just need to regather myself first. It was a lot. And it really fucking hurts, Lily."

I told her everything. She didn't judge. She didn't tell me what to do. She just listened.

"I know it does. So no more Conan talk for the remainder of this trip?"

I pout.

"Well, unless I wanna vent about him being an asshole."
She grins.

"Shit talking men is exactly what I wanna be doing," she chuckles.

"Shall we get another drink?" I grin.

Her face lights up.

"Shots too?"

"Yes."

This is exactly what I needed—a few days away in paradise.

Although I miss Bertie. Lily's assistant has him while we're gone.

I'll have to call her later to make sure he's being a good boy.

Even that is now a punch in the gut. Good boy now has a whole new meaning that I'll never be able to forget.

Goddamn it, Conan.

CHAPTER 74

CONAN

"So, order is just to kill? No torture required?" I ask Finn as he drives.

"Yes, Conan. We know Arthur is hiding in London still. He's untouchable there." He keeps his eyes on the road.

"Only for now."

My phone pings and my stomach flips. I live in hope that one day it will be Hallie's name flashing across the screen.

I pull it out of my pocket and sigh when I see a message from Reggie.

I open the attachment and smile.

Ben's club engulfed in flames.

I turn it to Finn, who also grins.

I type back a quick response as Finn pulls up to the location.

ME

Don't forget to leave the present.

That being Ben's mangled corpse. I know Arthur's spies will send the message back to him. I can't fucking wait.

He can hide in London for only so long.

Once we get the green light to enter the UK again, I'll be on that private jet.

"How many are in here?" I turn back and ask Drago.

"Three. Could be more."

I nod. Three of us against three of them. They don't have a chance.

Their 'safe house' isn't even remotely safe. No one is safe in Pennsylvania. It's under the Quinn brothers' rule.

Why did Arthur even think he could step foot in our territory?

We all exit Finn's Mercedes and pop open the trunk. Finn slides on some knuckle dusters and grabs a gun. I opt for a blade. My pistol is already safely in its holster.

"Let's fuckin' go." Finn hurries us along to the front door of this tiny shack of a house.

Finn calmly knocks twice on the door.

"We're asking permission to kill them?"

Finn doesn't flinch.

"No. Our father taught us to always have manners, Conan."

The door slowly creeps open and a sliver of a man's face emerges.

"Oh, fuck."

He goes to slam the door, but I hold out my hand and shove it wide open. I charge in, grabbing him by the throat and pounding him into the wall. As he gasps for air, I shove the blade into his stomach and drop him to the ground.

"We got two more incoming," Drago says behind me.

As one guy launches at him, Drago pulls back a fist and lands it straight into the guy's jaw, sending his head rocketing back.

Once he's on the ground, Drago steps over him, gun pointed between his eyes, and lodges a single bullet into his skull.

My guy is bleeding painfully to death by my feet. Finn is grappling with the third man, and he looks like he's having fun.

And then he gives us his favorite move—the blade across the throat. His guy drops to a limp pile on the ground, and Finn simply steps away, dusts off his jacket, and fixes his flat cap.

He turns to us and motions for us to be quiet.

Hmm. Footsteps upstairs.

I point up, and he nods. We follow behind Finn, who leads us up the stairs. He aims for the only closed door and slowly creaks it open, revealing a man struggling to open the window.

Without a word, I point my gun at his head and pull the trigger.

"Nice shot," Drago tells me.

"Thanks. I prefer my targets to be moving, though."

That hunting part of me doesn't just mean with sex. It's ingrained in every part of my life, even down to killing my victims.

"Now what?" I turn to Finn.

He shrugs nonchalantly.

"Burn it."

"How many men do we think Arthur has planted over here?" I ask Drago.

"It's tough to say. At the moment it's like whack-a-mole. When they pop up, we hunt them down."

I grin.

"Cool. I can deal with that. Then we're heading to Arthur, right?"

Finn nods slowly.

"Once we have the all-clear from Theo, yes. I don't know when that will be. He has a few issues going on in London. If we declare war on their turf, we need the Kings ready."

This is, right now, the only thing making me feel any shred of life.

The thought of killing the man who murdered my father.

The man who has wrecked my world.

His time will come.

I GROAN as my phone lights up on the stand. I look at the clock. Three-fucking-a.m.

Rolling over, I pick it up and squint at how bright the screen is.

And that's when I see it.

Am I fucking dreaming?

Hallie's name.

I sit up like a bucket of ice water has been poured on me and answer.

"Trouble, are you okay?"

My heart races.

Loud music booms in the background.

"Hi. Hey." She sounds nervous.

Her voice. I needed to hear that. It's like a drug.

The music quiets down, and I hold my breath.

"What's up? Are you okay?"

She takes a breath.

"Yeah. Sorry, I shouldn't have called."

"Don't hang up," I plead.

Just having her on the phone is enough to quiet the mess inside my head.

"It's just, I'm drunk and I missed you. I know I shouldn't, but I do. I meant to text you, but I'm a bit tipsy and called you by accident," she rambles.

And I smile.

She misses me?

I let out a ragged breath.

"I miss you too, darlin'."

"I—I can't." Her voice breaks and the line goes dead.

Fuck.

I try to call her back, but she rejects it. And when I go to text her, it never sends.

I flop back on my bed and let out a breath.

She misses me.

That is something. She didn't call to say she hates me.

Fuck.

This hurts.

CHAPTER 75

HALLIE

The door to the penthouse opens and I crack open my eyes. The hangover headache is already setting in.

"Good night?" I croak to Lily.

She holds up a hand.

"This is the most shame I've ever felt on a walk of shame, Hallie."

When I laugh, it hurts my chest.

"That good?"

"I mean, his dick was good, yes. But then I sobered up and ran as fast as I fucking could before he woke up."

I can't help but laugh.

"He's staying here?"

She nods slowly and pours us both a glass of water.

"Yep. So, I can't leave this suite until we fly home."

I roll my eyes, taking my glass as she drops down on the bed next to me.

"Don't be dramatic. It's a one-night stand."

"I feel icky."

She actually shivers.

"Go take a shower and we can nap. It's fine. You used protection, right?" I pin her with a glare.

"Uh. I think so? I'm pretty sure."

I slap her arm.

"Come on!"

"What?! I know the first time we did. I don't know about the seventh!"

"Let's talk about it when the hangovers have gone away. Deal?" I tell her.

"Yeah. Did you crash here on your own?" she asks.

I nod.

"Yes."

"There is a but coming?" she questions.

"I called Conan when I was leaving the bar."

"Oh God. Did you rip him a new one?"

I shake my head.

"Worse."

"Fuck. You told him you love him and want his babies?" The shock in her voice makes me laugh.

"Okay. No. Better than that. I said I missed him."

"Oh. Well, your drunk brain was just telling the truth."

"It does get worse." I trail off.

"When he said he misses me too, I hung up and blocked him again."

She spits out her water.

"Damn. You really are out to make him suffer."

I swallow the lump in my throat. I don't want to see him hurt. I don't know what I want. Time to think.

But then when I do think, he is the only thing on my mind.

"Do you think you could forgive him?" Lily asks seriously.

"I honestly don't know the answer right now. Sometimes I think it might have been better if he cheated or something."

Lily shakes her head.

"He hasn't though, has he? He hasn't fucked anyone else since you two started your whole friends-but-in-love thing?"

"No. He hasn't. But he's lied to me. What's to say he isn't lying about everything?"

Lily takes a deep breath.

"I don't know the guy. Except I have told him to fuck off on multiple occasions. You don't fake that kind of heartbreak. That's all I can tell you. Yes, what he did is on a magnitude scale of fucked up. But—and I am not defending his game. If, like you said, he's in the Mafia, there are lots of reasons to explain why. People in that life, they don't do things because they want to. They also do it to survive. Just like the game he put you in. Maybe hear him out. And if you don't like his answer, tell him to fuck off again."

I let her words sink in and my head pounds even harder.

"That was a lot."

"Just think it over, Hallie. You don't need to do anything right now other than nap, sunbathe, and party again."

I smile at her.

"I'd be so lost without you, Lily."

She smiles back.

"I know. You think you'll say this in a week's time when you've had enough of me invading your space here?"

I roll my eyes.

"I'd never be sick of you."

"Good. But I'll remind you of this. We're on day two of our trip. We have five more to go."

With that, she jumps off the bed and heads into the shower to wash her sins away.

And I just lie there, thinking over what she's said.

Maybe when I'm home, I'll hear him out. But not any time soon.

I'm not ready to be hurt by him all over again.

CHAPTER 76

CONAN

"**I**rish prick." The sweaty guy throws his fist toward my face.

I duck and send him flying into the table. My phone vibrates in my pocket as I pummel his face.

Surely we've dug out most of the Bowens here by now. There's no way Arthur can afford to send any more guys over.

Just as the guy goes limp, my cell goes off again.

"Fuck," I hiss, stumbling backward and pulling it out.

I don't recognize this number.

I answer and stay silent.

"Conan?"

I'd recognize that voice anywhere. I've become accustomed to it recently.

"Don't tell me your next words are 'fuck off'," I say, casually making my exit from the latest Bowen victim's house.

"No." She sounds like she's whispering.

"How did you get my number?" I ask.

She chuckles.

"I have my sources."

Who is this woman really?

"Is Hallie okay, Lily?" I ask, a sudden panic forming.

Why would her best friend be calling me while they're on vacation, especially when she thinks I'm the enemy? And after Hallie's drunk call, I don't know what to think.

"Yeah. I've just sent her to the bar. Look, we have an issue, and I don't know who else to call."

I unlock my car and get in.

"Anything. What do you need me to do?"

"Okay. So, how are you with dogs? Golden retrievers, to be exact?"

Oh, fuck.

"I'm fine. I've met Bertie. I assume that's who you're talking about?"

"Yes. Georgia, my assistant, is dog-sitting. And, well, she thought she'd take him to the woods for a walk. She let him off his lead and was busy replying to emails, and…"

"Don't fucking tell me she's lost Hallie's dog, Lily."

"Watch your tone, Conan. But yes. She's looking for him now, but I thought, seeing as you… have good hunting instincts and know your way around the woods here, you could help."

Wow. She can manage to throw a jab at me in any conversation.

"I can't believe this," I mutter.

"Go easy on her. She's only nineteen. She doesn't even own a dog. She had no idea Bertie's recall is about as useful as trying to get a fish to swim back to you."

I bite back a laugh. But internally, I'm stressing. I need to find him before it gets dark.

"Which woods exactly?" I ask.

"Hawke Creek State Park."

"Tell her to meet me by the entrance in about twenty-five minutes."

"Okay."

There's a pause on the line.

"Is Hallie okay?"

She sighs.

"No, Conan. Not really. I hate seeing her like this. She was just getting her spark for life back again."

I wince at her words.

"I never meant to hurt her."

"But you did. Doesn't matter if it wasn't intentional. Give her a little time."

"You don't hate me? You think I've got a chance?" I ask, grabbing my keys.

She laughs.

"I do. And no, I don't hate you. I hate Ben. But you? I saw you bring my best friend back to life. I know you care. She's stubborn and afraid to lose people, so she's going to push you and keep pushing."

"I'm not giving up. I might be evil, as you probably know, but never to her."

"Trust me, I've met evil. You're far from it."

A chill runs through me. There's more to her than she lets on.

"Lily, when I find him, I'll keep him with me. I don't trust this woman with Hallie's baby. Just let me know when you're on your way back from the airport, and I'll drop him home."

"I'll send you the pin to the key safe. Thank you, Conan."

"Any time when it comes to Hallie. Okay?"

I mean it. Even if it's ten years from now and she's in trouble, I'll drop my life to help her. I owe it to her.

I'll never stop, even if it means being her protector from afar.

"Oh. While I have you. Are you doing anything next Saturday? I've got a show at my gallery, but I'm hosting an afterparty at Vibes. I've got VIP tickets if you want to come? Bring some friends?"

I know the owners well—or, well, they pay us for protection.

"Sure. Sounds good. It'll be me and four others."

"I'll text them now. Just send over their names."

"Will do. After I get Bertie home."

After I hang up, I turn out of the road and follow the GPS.

I've always wanted a dog but never had one. But seeing how much Hallie loves Bertie just sold me on the fact I need one.

CHAPTER 77

HALLIE

I return with the cocktails to a sheepish-looking Lily.

"What's up?" I ask, handing her the pink drink.

"Nothing."

I know she's lying.

"I'm arranging an afterparty next Saturday for the big showing…you in?"

She flashes me a grin that I can't say no to. Even if I'll probably just want to cuddle with Bertie all night.

"Yeah. Of course I'll be there."

"Oh. Have you heard from Georgia today? How's my baby doing? I miss him."

"Yeah, he's fine. All good."

"Shall we actually go get these tattoos now? I was thinking a four-leaf clover. Luck of the Irish?"

I smack her arm and she bursts out laughing.

"No? Too soon?"

"Yes. Way too soon. Poor taste, Lily." I try to keep a straight face.

"Right now I'd go for 'if you have a penis, stay away from me' on my forehead."

She rolls her eyes.

"Drama queen. You can't swear off all dick. Oh, what about becoming a nun? That could solve all your issues."

"Shut up. Fine. I'll go back to cock one day. Just not now."

"Good girl." She wiggles her eyebrows.

My cheeks heat, remembering Conan's deep voice and how that set me on fire.

"Conan loved me calling him a good boy," I blurt out.

Lily's jaw almost hits the floor.

"Conan? As in that tatted cage-fighting mafia badass? The fucking huge one?"

I nod, taking a sip of my drink.

She smacks her hand on the table.

"That is hot, Hallie. Ugh. Could you boss him around too? Like all mommy style? Get him on his knees?"

She pretends to fan herself, and I giggle.

"Yep. But not for long. He switches super fast on me."

Her eyes go wide.

"You were fucking a switch. My god, Hallie. You've done us proud."

I chew on my lip. It was so much more than that. He made me laugh every single time I spoke to him.

Those butterflies when he appeared? Will I ever have that again?

"Hey, Hallie. You've found it once. You'll find it again."

She places a hand over mine, and I look away.

"I guess."

"A switch. Filthy. I love that for you," she mutters.

"Yep. It was pretty incredible."

Nope. I need more drinks to drown this pain away.

I miss him. I can't deny that.

CHAPTER 78

CONAN

As I pull onto the gravel, Georgia's head flicks up, and there's fear in her eyes.

I'm absolutely livid, but I have to keep my cool. The last thing I need is Lily against me.

But I'm still pissed off. The one thing in the world Hallie needs right now is Bertie. And she lost him.

I slam the car door and approach her calmly.

"Hi," I greet her.

She runs her fingers through her purple hair.

"Hi. Umm. You're Conan?"

I give her a curt nod.

"Can you take me back to the exact place you last saw him? Do you know if Hallie ever takes him here?"

I glance down at her shaking fingers.

"Georgia. I'm not angry," I lie.

"We just need to find him before it gets dark. Okay?"

She nods.

"I can't believe he just ran."

I close my eyes and take a breath.

"That is what dogs do."

I can't help myself.

"I know, but most of the time he's so lazy. Just sleeping."

I shake my head.

"Come on. Let's just get in and start looking."

I stride toward the gate and yank it open.

"Right, show me."

I gesture for her to lead the way. We head off down a rough stone hill, water trickling beside me.

I scan the area. There are plenty of little animals he might have chased after.

Once we get to the flat ground, we weave through the trees until we end up next to a small pond.

"Here?" I ask.

"I was sitting here." She points to the rock.

"Which way did he run?"

She points west.

"Okay. You stay here. He might track his scent back to here, or yours even. I'll head that direction and see."

I can feel the fear coming from her.

"If you need me, scream."

Before she can reply, I set off in a jog through the tree line.

There's still six hours of daylight.

I keep tracking for paw prints, descending deeper into the trail. She's right—he does run fast.

The sun streams through a gap in the trees and I inhale the fresh forest scent. This is what I love most.

Being outdoors, turning off my brain, and just hunting.

I'm almost an hour in, following fresh prints, when the sound of water falling catches my attention to my left.

It's worth checking. Bertie is probably thirsty on his little adventure.

The water cascades down the rock face, landing in a small lake.

And there he is. On the right, just lying down on the leaves and relaxing.

My foot crunches on a twig and his head snaps up. He barks in warning.

"Bertie. Come on, boy. It's me." I make my voice excitable for him.

"Come on. Let me take you home to Mom." I tap my knees, and he jumps up.

Relief fills me when his tail wags and he bounds toward me.

"Hey, boy." I ruffle his head.

He keeps nudging my hand to carry on. I take that opportunity to loop the rope I brought from my car into his collar.

Crouching back down, a wave of emotion washes over me. His tail wags like crazy.

"You can't leave your momma, Bertie. She really needs you."

He lets out a little bark. I think he knows I'm talking about Hallie.

"You miss her too?" I whisper and tickle under his jaw.

As I sit on the ground, Bertie joins me and rests his head on my lap.

"At least you still like me, bud," I sigh.

I just let nature calm me.

Peace.

I've found Bertie, which means Hallie will be happy. That's all that matters.

"Right. Let's get you back. You've got a few nights with me," I tell him, jumping to my feet.

"I've seen you bed some dogs before, but this is fuckin' new," Finn teases.

I sit up and rub my eyes, finding him standing in my bedroom doorway.

"Do you ever knock?"

"No. We got shit to do. Which means you need to get your ass out of bed and come with me."

I groan, and Bertie rests his head on my chest.

"I can't. Bertie needs me."

Finn pins me with a glare.

"What if I told you it involves murder?" he says with a sadistic grin.

"I'd say you have my attention."

I carefully move Bertie off me and tuck him into bed like a human.

He's so cute. I'm going to miss him when he goes back to Hallie tomorrow.

"I'd love our enemies to see you tucking a dog into your bed. It's really a look, Con," Finn teases.

"I am not ashamed of my soft side, Finn."

"Are the twins coming?" I ask, shoving on a T-shirt.

"Of course."

It's always more fun when they join our adventures.

"When are we going to London?" I ask, giving Bertie one last head scratch.

"I'm working on it, Con. We just gotta keep focusing on making it safe here while we wait."

"Be a good boy. All your water and food is downstairs. I won't be long," I tell Bertie.

"Are you fucking talking to a dog like he's a person?" Finn asks.

I glare at him. Doesn't everyone do that?

"I did. And he basically is. He's Hallie's world, so now he's mine too."

Finn shoves his hands in his pockets.

"Keep this up, I'm sending you for psychiatric testing."

I chuckle and clasp his shoulder.

"I'll go if you go. And we both know you'll be the one ending up in a padded room and a straightjacket, you fucking psycho."

His jaw twitches and I wait for his reaction.

Nothing.

"A true psychopath can bullshit their way out of diagnosis, Conan. No one would lock me up anywhere. And if they tried, I'd slit their throats first."

Jesus Christ. I step back.

"What happened to you?" I ask.

He chuckles.

"You don't want to know. Now, let's go kill some men and have a beer after."

I sigh. I know something happened to him when we were kids. He was always the smart and quiet one compared to me and Declan. But I remember a day—I must have been about ten—when I heard my dad throwing glass in his office, ranting about something happening to Finn. But I was confused. Finn was just sitting in his room, doing a Rubik's cube over and over, staring at a wall. There wasn't an injury on him.

But he was never the same after that. Like something snapped inside him. He just turned off.

I love him the way he is. But I'll always wonder. And I don't dare ask again.

I sigh.

"Okay. Let's go."

CHAPTER 79

HALLIE

I think I'm losing my mind.

I swear my dog smells like Conan.

I've been home three days now, and that strong, masculine scent is still clinging to his fur.

Sliding my hands along my curves, this black dress looks cute. It hugs me in at the waist and shows just enough cleavage. I have to look professional for Lily's art gallery, but hot enough to go clubbing after.

"Right, Bertie. Be good for Lisa."

He comes and sits by my feet. For some reason, Georgia said she couldn't look after Bertie again. So I've found a new dog-sitter for the time being.

I have no idea what time I'll be home. Once me and Lily start, sometimes we don't venture in until four a.m. But I can't wait to see what she's pulled off, she's been so excited about this new artist.

I grab my bag and do one final sweep of lip gloss before I head out to wait for my cab.

I guess this is what I have to get used to again. A normal, single life.

How long will it take for me to stop thinking about Conan every free second I have?

CHAPTER 80

CONAN

I'm weirdly nervous stepping out of the car. The flashing sign of the club almost taunts me.

"Con. You know I love you, right?" Declan says from behind.

My brothers are both getting bored of babying me, waiting for me to explode and fuck my life up.

I spin to face him.

"Yeah. Why?"

My knuckles crack as I squeeze them, waiting for him to answer.

"You're a huge guy. Covered from head to toe in tats. There's a very small—no, fuck that—zero percent chance of you walking into this club unnoticed. By anyone."

Okay. He has a slight point.

I don't care about anyone else seeing me. Just not Hallie. She can't know I'm watching her.

That's the only reason I'm here. I just want to see with my own eyes that she's okay.

That, despite her warnings, I'm choosing to ignore them.

Because I can't go a fucking day without seeing her. Even if she refuses to see me.

Maybe I will have to watch her life unfold from the sidelines because I fucked it all up. A sick and twisted punishment.

But I'll always live in the hope that one day, she will come around. Fuck, I'll take a friendship at this point.

Anything that means she doesn't hate me anymore.

"Look, Declan. I know you're worried about me, or what I might do. But I'm simply here to enjoy myself with my family and have a fuckin' drink before I go back into heavy training."

I look to Reggie and Rowan for support. Rowan catches my drift as he steps beside me.

"We all promise to behave." He pouts at Declan.

I can feel Finn's glare beating into the side of my head.

He ain't happy with me. He lost his best nurse because of me. And deep down, she was his friend too.

"Just give her space, Con. Don't make a damn scene. If this is what you need to do to get over it, we've got your back." Declan clasps Finn on the shoulder. He just grunts.

"I won't. I swear." I hold up my hands.

Declan nods and heads to the bouncer, with Reggie and Rowan on his tail. Leaving me with Finn.

"Finn. I'm sorry this fucked your work up."

He stops walking and shakes his head.

"Yeah. I'm pissed off she quit. But I'm more fucking irritated that Enzo put her in The Chase. That he missed Ben and his links to Arthur. The fucking wizard that knows everything did nothing to protect you or her."

I scratch my head.

"It's quite the puzzle to put together, though, Finn."

He scoffs.

"I'm protective of one thing in this life, and that's my family. I'll do whatever I have to do to keep you all safe. I can't see you lose yourself like you did after Mom died."

A sadness creeps in and makes it hard to breathe. I try to bat it away, fucking bury it quick before it hurts. It's like Finn can read my damn mind.

"I've lost Hallie for good, haven't I?"

Finn shrugs.

"Honestly? You're asking the wrong guy. I wouldn't know love if it hit me in the side of the head with a sledge-hammer. But, psychologically speaking, I'm sure there are ways to win her over. For example, not being a dick in this club would be one."

I choke on a laugh. I was really expecting some technical, intelligent answer to come out of his mouth.

"Got it. Don't be a dick."

"You haven't gone a day without being one so far. So good luck."

He whacks me 'round the head and strolls off toward the entrance. The bouncer looks away and lifts the rope for him. I quicken my pace to join them.

We head straight to the VIP booth, nestled in the back corner, with the perfect view of every spot.

So I can see her wherever she may be.

The waitress rushes over with a tray of whiskey and, of course, a bottle of our dad's whiskey.

The music blares, the strobe lights flash, yet all I can do is scan the crowd.

I'll know when I spot her, because my stomach will flip and everything will feel lighter.

CHAPTER 81

HALLIE

"**I** fucking love this song!" Lily screams in my ear.

I giggle and join her on the dance floor.

I promised her a night of no sulking. I think this was her way of saying, *I'm sick to fucking death of watching you wallow in self-pity with tubs of ice cream. Get the fuck out of the house.*

We dance until our feet burn and our drinks are empty.

"Shall we get another?" I ask her.

The alcohol is starting to help me forget why I'm so sad.

"Damn right." She grabs my hand and all but drags me to the bar.

As soon as we approach, goosebumps erupt over my skin. I rub at my forearms, glancing around.

This is weird.

"What do you want?" Lily shouts.

Oh.

"Um. Rum and coke. Please."

I'm distracted, looking around the room like I'm hunting someone. I can feel eyes on me, and it's unsettling.

"That bartender is kinda cute. Want his number?"

My eyes go wide.

"Absolutely not. I'm done with men."

Lily rolls her eyes dramatically.

"Yeah, yeah. Whatever. We need to get you laid."

I shake my head.

"No. We really don't. That won't solve any of my issues."

Not when my heart can't forget about Conan.

She hands me my drink and I knock it back. Lily bites on her lip with a naughty grin.

"Oh, we've got this Hallie out to play. I can't wait."

"What?"

She pouts and sips her drink through the straw.

"The '*I don't give a shit, let's get blackout wasted*' is my favorite Hallie to drink with."

I let out a laugh.

"Just make sure I don't end up leaving with the bartender, please." I bat my lashes.

The last thing I need is that anxiety in the morning.

Not that I have a job to go to anymore.

"Shall we dance instead?" she asks.

"Yeah. I like that plan."

She finishes up her drink and we push our way through the crowd back onto the dance floor.

This time, a group of guys approaches us.

"Mind if we join?" the tall one at the front asks.

He's pretty stacked in his tight blue shirt and jeans. His hair is short, and he has a neat beard. Kinda cute.

"Carry on."

With each song, we laugh and shake our butts to the music.

"What's your name?" the big guy asks.

"Ha—" I swallow.

"Harlow."

He flashes his teeth as he smiles.

"Nice name. I'm Jason." He holds out his hand, and I shake it.

Instead of letting go, he spins me under his arm, and I crash into his chest, my hands landing on his pecs.

I quickly push away so I can get some air.

"Dance with me?" he asks, looking down at me.

What have I got to lose?

Nothing can ever hurt as bad as losing Conan. There's a gaping hole in my life.

CHAPTER 82

CONAN

"**C**onan," Finn warns.

I see red.

"He's got his fucking hands on her," I growl.

Rowan slides me a whiskey. I swallow it in one gulp. It does nothing to calm my rage.

"Don't be a dick. She's not fucking him on stage, is she? It's just a dance. Calm the fuck down or I'll tranquilize your ass."

Great.

Each song that goes by is like torture. This really must be my punishment.

This is hell on earth.

Seeing another man's hands on my girl. And I have no right to say anything. Because she isn't mine. Not anymore.

Pushing myself up, all eyes are on me.

"I'm going to the toilet. Do I need a babysitter?" I hiss.

"Yes. Rowan. Go with him," Declan orders.

Poor choice. Rowan will cause havoc with me, not stop me.

I clock the guy that was dancing with Hallie also heading to the same destination as me. Perfect.

I quicken my step, and he holds the door open for me. As it closes, I grab him by the scruff of the neck and lift him off the floor.

"What the hell, man!" he stutters.

"Keep your fucking hands off my girl," I spit.

He shakes his head. God, this is pathetic. She can do better.

I drop him and he backs away, straight into the wall.

"I—I didn't know she had a boyfriend!" He throws his hands up.

I feel Rowan's eyes on me, so I shoot him a look to shut the hell up.

I know I'm not her boyfriend. That ain't the point.

I step closer and shove my finger into his chest.

"If you so much as brush your hand on her one more time, I will cut it off. Got it?"

He nods frantically.

"I won't. I'll get my friends and go. Sorry."

I step out of his way as he scrambles to the door. Wiping my mouth, I turn to Rowan.

"So, umm. You know that asshole is gonna tell Hallie what you've just done, right? And you're going to look like the bad guy here."

I suck in a breath.

"Fuck. I hate it when you're right. Suggestions, young wise one?"

He shrugs. "Be the bad guy."

I arch a brow.

"She kinda fell for you before like that. Minus the whole chase shit, yeah. But she likes you as you. You know? So maybe try a new tactic? Girls like possessive."

"Jesus. You have a point."

Hallie did like me for the brute I am. Maybe it's time to show her just how much I want her.

"Worth a shot."

I head out of the bathroom and rest my back on the bar, my eyes locking onto her.

Now it's just her and Lily dancing.

And then she spots me.

Her laughter falls. Her eyes turn to slits. And she stomps over.

"Yeah. I'll wait back over with the guys for this," Rowan tells me and leaves.

Great.

Here we go.

Operation Possessive may not have gone to plan.

CHAPTER 83

HALLIE

I'm about to turn back to Lily when Jason storms across the dance floor toward me, rubbing his jaw.

"You know some psycho just attacked me in the bathroom? Grabbed me by the throat. Said he'd cut my fucking hands off if I touched you again."

My stomach drops.

I don't even have to ask who it was.

"Sorry," I mutter, though I'm not sure why I'm apologizing.

"Yeah. Whatever. I'm out of here." He shakes his head and pushes past me, disappearing into the crowd.

I swallow hard, feeling that familiar static in the air.

And then I see him.

Conan.

Leaning against the bar like he owns the place.

God, he looks smug with his arms crossed over his chest, leaning back on the bar.

Smug, but handsome as hell.

And that suit. Fuck. I could rip it off him with my teeth.

Okay. I need to calm down on the alcohol.

He flashes me a grin and I stomp towards him. I am so done with this bullshit.

"Did you tell that guy not to dance with me?" I jab my nail into his chest.

"Hmm."

"Did you?"

He leans in, and my breath hitches.

"I didn't exactly say those words. I just explained what would happen to him if he touched what's mine again."

I pull back and blink at him.

"Yours?"

I can't help but laugh. Maybe he's losing his mind too.

"I can't with you." I toss my hands in the air.

Shaking my head, I turn. I'm disappointed when he doesn't stop me. But I keep my head held high and strut back to the dance floor.

His?

I was.

Now I'm not.

"What the hell is Conan doing here?" I ask Lily.

She sheepishly looks past me.

"I may have invited him."

"What?!"

"I thought it would be a good and neutral place for you guys to talk it out."

"Lily," I hiss, tugging her to the standing table at the side of the floor.

"I don't want to talk. Because I'm weak for him. I'll just fall under his spell."

"You miss him, Hallie."

"I do. But he hurt me. I can't forget that."

"I'm sorry. I was just trying to help. I promise I'll stay out of it. I'm team Hallie. Always."

I roll my eyes. I can't be mad. I'd probably do the same thing for her.

"He told Jason not to dance with me."

"Roar," she purrs and pretends to claw me.

"Possessive men."

"Oh my god. You're so drunk," I laugh.

Whatever buzz I was feeling died a quick death when I saw Conan.

But he replaced it with a different kind of spark. And now, I can feel his eyes staring at me.

So I'm going to give him a show.

I'm not his property. He lost me. And now, he can pay the consequences.

He has no idea how horny two-drink Hallie is.

"Come on, let's dance." I grab Lily by the hand and drag her back onto the dance floor.

Straight into the middle of a group of guys.

"Hey, gorgeous." One slides up behind me, his hands running down my waist.

"Hey."

I discreetly move so we turn; now I'm facing Conan.

Who looks absolutely murderous.

He shakes his head.

I blow him a kiss, exaggerating my hip movements. I don't even know what this guy behind me looks like.

I don't care.

The look on Conan's face is a picture. My heart flutters.

But that pull between us? It's still there, stronger than ever.

He doesn't move. He's like a statue. A gorgeous one.

"You wanna maybe take this to the bathroom?" the guy whispers in my ear.

And I cringe.

"No. Thank you."

He spins me to face him, grabbing hold tight to my wrist.

"Fucking dick tease," he grits out, pressing his face against mine.

I yank my wrist away and push at his chest. He stumbles back.

And the next thing I know, a tattooed fist flies across and lands in his jaw, sending him flying.

The music carries on, but the crowd is silent. All eyes on me.

But it's not me they're looking at.

I turn to face the furious beast behind me. Fuck. He can't get in trouble.

"Come on."

I yank his hand and drag him through the VIP area. I swear that's Finn in the corner. But I don't have time. I lead us through the hallway and out to the parking lot.

The fresh air is a welcome distraction to the fire inside me.

He pulls me to a stop and spins me to face him.

The next thing I know, my back is slammed against the wall.

His lips a breath from mine.

"You're crazy, Conan."

"So I've been told."

"I had it covered."

He smirks and brushes my hair away from my shoulder.

"You did. But he deserved that. I heard what he said. I

saw him grab you. You're lucky we're in a public setting, Hallie." There's a threat to his tone.

Reminding me who he really is.

And why this can't happen.

But holy hell, the way he's eye-fucking me right now is so distracting.

"I wouldn't have been dancing with him if you didn't piss me off," I counter.

His jaw ticks.

"I'm sorry," he whispers.

I roll my eyes and he grips my jaw gently.

"So you keep saying."

His touch sets me alight.

As I stare into his eyes, there's a flicker of the man who stole my heart in there.

The one I can't let go of.

"I'll keep saying it until you believe me, trouble. I don't care if it takes weeks, months, or years. You best believe I'll keep saying those damn words in every possible variation until I prove myself to you."

I don't know what comes over me. I press my index finger against his lips.

"Shh. You're ruining it."

He arches an eyebrow.

"Ruining what exactly?"

I grin and tug him closer by his tie.

"Kiss me and find out."

His gaze flicks between my eyes and my lips. I hold my breath.

I want this.

One last time.

To remember what it's like to be completely consumed.

"Fuck it," he mutters.

He grabs me by the back of the head and slams his lips over mine.

And I slide my arms around his neck to pull him even closer.

As his tongue dances with mine, his fingers dig into my ass.

I lose myself in the moment.

In Conan.

CHAPTER 84
CONAN

Song – *Make Up Sex* by MGK

I'm breathless as I pull away. I cup her cheeks and can't resist stealing another kiss.

I've missed her. So fucking much.

That kiss just put a tiny piece of my heart back into place.

"Can we go back to yours?" she whispers.

I stroke her cheek with my thumb.

"If that's what you want, darlin'."

Fuck. My heart is racing.

She nods, but she's holding something back. I can tell in the way her eyes keep shifting.

"Tell me," I press.

"This isn't us getting back together. I want this to be a hate fuck. I've always wanted to do that."

I stutter with a cough. Her face is stern.

She's dead serious.

I silence her by brushing her curls over her shoulder and sinking my teeth into her throat.

Her back arches, pressing her tighter against me. My grip on her hip hardens.

"Does a hate fuck still work if we both hate the same person?" I whisper, running my tongue up her neck.

I could never hate Hallie. But I'll always hate myself—probably more than she despises me.

"Just shut up and take me home, beastie."

She. Said. My. Nickname.

My heart is about to explode. But I hold it together, keeping up with her little act.

I'm going to give her what she wants. I can't fuck this up. Not now.

Grabbing her face, I force her to look into my eyes.

"Don't call me that. We aren't friends, remember? We aren't anything. You're just my little whore for the night."

I release her, and she pants, holding herself up against the brick wall.

"Come on."

I turn on my heel and head to my Bugatti.

Her heels click on the pavement as she tries to keep up. I open her passenger door and smack her ass as she gets in.

I swear she let out a moan. This is torture.

I get the girl back, but not really.

I'll take it. Any time with Hallie, I'll accept.

I tease her the entire drive home, running my hand along her thigh and dipping under her dress every so often. My cock is throbbing.

It's a quick drive, yet it feels like hours.

When we finally pull up outside the garage, I cut the engine and grab her throat, pulling her toward me.

"You're going to listen to every damn order I give you tonight, Hallie."

She bites her lip and nods. I squeeze tighter.

"Such a good little slut," I whisper.

I lean in to kiss her but stop just close enough to feel her breath falter against me.

"Let's see just how much you hate me, shall we?"

I let her go, the red welts already forming on her neck. I'll leave her with marks all over so she can remember how I make her feel.

Leading her into the side door of my gym behind the garage, she barely makes it two steps inside before I slide my hand up the back of her head and yank it back.

"Strip," I command.

I let her go, and she steps forward, turning to face me. I'm mesmerized by her.

My breath hitches as she painfully slowly unzips the side of her dress. It falls to the floor and she steps out of it, kicking it away with her heel.

She goes to speak, but I hold up my hand to silence her.

"No talking. I only want to hear you scream my name or moan it. Nothing else."

Her eyes go wide, and she swallows.

I twirl my finger.

"I'd like a full show."

With her hands on her hips, she starts to turn.

"Slower."

I bite down on my fist when her bare ass is on display.

"Bend over. Hands to the floor."

She doesn't hesitate. She gets in position. I unbuckle my belt and free my cock.

It looked delectable during Pilates in those leggings. But naked? Fuck.

I step forward and rest both hands on her ass cheeks, pulling them apart. Gathering saliva in my mouth, I bend down and spit on her asshole.

She yelps and tries to shuffle away.

I tut as I grab her thigh firmly and pull her back to me. Circling my tip around her puckered hole, I bite down on my tongue to stop myself from groaning as she moans.

Fuck. I need my dick in there. But not tonight. I want to give her what she wants, but I don't want to completely ruin her.

I push my finger in, and she lets out a strangled moan. My other hand rubs the globes of her ass.

"Filthy little whore for me."

"C-Conan," she moans.

With my fingers pumping in and out of her ass, I slide my free hand along her soaking pussy.

"Oh, you must really, really hate me, Hallie," I tease, sliding along her wetness.

She drips down my hand as I thrust three fingers inside.

"Oh my god!" she screams.

"Rules, Hallie," I say sternly.

Dammit. I need a taste. And I bet her legs are fucking burning in this position.

I withdraw from her and step back.

"Up," I command.

She does. Her legs wobble as she turns to face me. A beautiful flush spreads up her throat.

I close the distance between us. My hand shoots out, grabbing her neck as I walk us back until her ass hits the full-length mirror.

Our chests rise and fall in rhythm. The air around us crackles. And we just stare into each other's eyes, her heart pounding against my palm.

"Fuck it," I mutter, slamming my lips over hers.

It's a desperate kiss. Her hands work on my shirt, ripping away the buttons and frantically pulling it off my shoulders. I help her finish the job. Her nails drag along my back as I hoist her up, letting her wrap her legs around my waist.

"You better come so fucking hard for me, Hallie. And I ain't stopping. I'm going to make sure you can feel me for the rest of your life."

She pants, her eyes flicking between mine and my lips.

"Do it," she whispers and leans in for a kiss.

My fingers tangle in her hair to deepen it. She moans into my mouth.

"You want my dick? Hmm?"

I thrust my hips, letting my cock slide against her pussy.

"Yes."

"Do you hate me?"

"Y-yes," she falters.

But it sparks something animalistic in me. I line myself up and violently thrust inside her, all the way to the base.

She screams so loud it makes my ears ring. As she arches her back, it exposes her neck, so I bite down on her throat.

Sucking and nipping at her skin as I don't hold back. I let her pussy strangle my cock. Over and over.

My back stings as her nails pierce the skin.

"Is this what you wanted?" I grit out.

I squeeze her throat tighter. She claws at my forearms, and I pull back, looking into her eyes as they go wide.

I can smell her arousal laced with fear.

That's what she gets for summoning this side of me.

I release her a touch and she gasps for air. Instead, I slam my lips against hers. My climax building by the second.

I've missed her. So fucking much.

"Give yourself to me," I hiss.

I glide my hand onto her ass and push my finger between her cheeks, teasing her asshole to tip her over the edge.

And it works.

She erupts around me. Her wetness soaks my dick, my thighs.

Her screams echo through the room and pierce into my heart. My name on her tongue.

My muscles burn as I violently come inside her, coating her, claiming her.

Mine.

"Good girl," I praise her.

"Fuck. The fact you're a squirter is the hottest damn thing in the world."

I don't pull out of her. Instead, I wrap my arms around her waist and carry her into the bedroom I have here.

Flipping on the lights, I toss her down on the double bed.

"We ain't done, trouble."

I tear off my pants and kick them across the room.

"I said a hate fuck. We did that," she fires back.

I nod and stride to the edge of the bed. She quickly sits upright as I lean over her and grip her pretty little face.

No tenderness. No love. Just a fuck. Just like she begged me to do.

"You're done when I say you're done. Not a second before. That back there wasn't a hate fuck. We keep going until you prove it's real. Until you show me that you actually hate me, trouble."

CHAPTER 85

HALLIE

O h, fuck. He's really called my bluff here.

I can't make it believable that I hate him.

Because I don't.

He crawls onto the bed and I scramble back until I hit the cold wall.

He chuckles.

"Nowhere to run, trouble."

He grabs my calves and drags me toward him until I'm flat on my back on the mattress. Nudging my thighs apart, he settles between them, hooking my legs onto his shoulders as he bends down.

His hot breath beats against my needy pussy.

"Conan!" I beg.

"Only good girls get eaten out. Can you be good for me?"

I shiver as he digs his fingers into my ass so hard my eyes water.

"I can!" I cry out.

His tongue flicks my clit, and my eyes slam shut, my back arching off the bed.

His palm presses down on my lower tummy.

"So fucking sweet it should be a sin."

He licks me out like a man starved, until my body is shaking around him. My hands claw at the covers, squeezing to relieve the pressure.

"Come for me," he demands.

My toes curl as he sucks my clit, and I lose it. I let my climax consume me until I'm a shaking, breathless mess. My ears ring and my body sags.

He maneuvers himself so he's leaning over me. I blink open my eyes and find him watching me, his nose brushing mine.

He gently trails his fingers over my breasts and back between my thighs. I can't close them because he's in the way.

I jolt when he pushes two fingers inside me.

"I don't think I can." My voice is barely a whisper.

"Give me one more, Hallie. You can do it."

He ups the tempo, that fuzzy heat sweeping through me again.

"That's it. Good girl. Give in to me."

I spread my legs wider and let him finger fuck me to oblivion.

"Hmm. So much hatred here," he mocks.

And then his hand clamps over my nose and mouth.

My eyes fly open. Panic surges. The harder I try to breathe, the more my lungs burn.

I claw at his arms, but he doesn't let up, only curling his fingers deeper inside me.

"Give me what I want, and I'll let you breathe."

That darkness flashes across his eyes.

Holy fuck.

This is hot.

This is hatred.

I swear to God, the second he lets me go, I'm going to show him what I mean by a hate fuck.

My hips roll as my head gets lighter, pleasure heightening to an impossible peak.

Just as it all gets too much, he removes his hand.

I gasp for air—and I feel myself lose control.

I climax so hard I see stars. I'm screaming, crying, and holding onto him for dear life as he coaxes me through it.

"That's it. Such a good girl," he whispers in my ear.

My body trembles as I come down. He doesn't let me go. He doesn't even remove his fingers.

When I open my eyes, he's just watching me.

"You asshole," I choke out.

He sits up and slides his hand out of me with a smirk.

With all the strength I can muster, I sit up and launch myself at him.

I shove at his chest, but he doesn't budge.

I keep hitting him. Letting it out. All of it.

The pain.

The heartbreak.

The devastation.

The loss.

The lies.

The fantasy I believed.

"I hate you!" I scream.

I pound my fists against his chest as tears stream down my cheeks.

"I hate you," I say again, my voice breaking.

He remains rigid. Taking it.

"Say it back, goddamn it!" I sob.

His hands clamp over my wrists. I look away, trying to steady my breathing.

"Let it all out, baby. I can take it."

I shake my head.

"You did this to me!"

"I know. And I'm so fucking sorry."

I blink through my tears and see the raw pain behind those green eyes I loved so much.

"Why can't I let you go?" I whisper.

He tugs me against him and wraps his arms around me, holding me tight. His heart beats wildly under my cheek.

"Because what we had was special. It was real," he sighs.

"And you fucked it all up."

"I'm sorry."

This is too raw. Too close.

This isn't what I signed up for.

I don't want his apologies.

He can't take back what he did. He can't change who he is.

"I don't want to hear it, Conan."

I wriggle out of his grip and he lets me go.

I wipe my tears with the back of my hand and force myself to breathe.

"Hold me down and fuck me from behind. With my hands behind my back. Tell me what a slut I am for you."

He frowns, confusion etching across his face. Isn't this who he really is?

"I'm not here to talk. Or listen to your apologies. I'm here to be thoroughly fucked. And if you can't stick to your end of the deal, I'll go back to the club and find someone else to finish the job."

I hate myself the second the words leave my mouth.

I knew how much that would hurt him.

Maybe I want to push him away so far that he'll stop chasing me.

That he'll finally give up on me.

A growl rumbles from his chest. His nostrils flare.

And I know exactly what I want from him.

As fast as I can, I clamber off the bed and make a run for the door, flinging it open and heading into the gym.

My heart thunders as I dart toward the octagon cage.

Just as I reach for the knob on the door, my hair is yanked back. A scream tears out of me.

My back slams into the metal.

"You want to be fucked like an animal? Hmm? Ass in the air while I ruin you?"

I let out a ragged breath.

"Yes."

"You want to be used and at my mercy?"

I nod.

"Words," he presses.

"Yes, Conan. You want me? That's how you get me."

He runs a hand through his hair.

"Fuck," he hisses.

When his lips crash into mine, I melt into the kiss.

Just like that first time.

The world fades away.

It's like he's trying to show me he's still here. That even though this isn't love…it still is.

We keep kissing as he guides us onto the padded mat.

When he pulls away, he spins me around and pushes me down onto all fours.

He kicks my legs apart, and a shiver runs up my thighs.

"Hands."

I lean down, resting my cheek against the mat, and put my hands behind my back. My shoulders burn.

He grips my wrists in one hand.

Without warning, he thrusts inside me. My face smashes into the floor.

I close my eyes and let him use me.

Pulling out slow so he can slam back in deep. Over and over.

His grunts fill the room.

I scream when he slaps my ass so hard my eyes sting.

This is what I wanted.

And fuck, it's setting a fire inside me.

"So tight, Hallie."

"Such a good little slut."

Smack.

"I'm going to fill you up with my cum, Hallie. Is that what you want? To be my dirty whore, dripping with me?"

"Yes!"

"Good," he growls.

As another climax rips through me, he doesn't stop. He keeps going, taking everything until he finally joins me on the edge.

My name falls from his lips like a chant as he fills me.

When he pulls out, my body gives up and I collapse onto the mat.

He scoops me up like I weigh nothing, cradling me against his chest.

"You don't have to be nice to me," I whisper.

"Shh. I got you. I've given you what you wanted. Now let me look after you properly. Please."

I'm exhausted.

And I don't want him to let go.

We've already crossed so many lines tonight.

What's one more?

He opens the shower door and carries me inside, still holding me close as he steps under the warm spray.

"Ugh. That's so nice," I moan.

"Hallie," he warns.

His cock twitches against me, and my eyes go wide.

He sets me down on my feet, facing him.

I look up as the water drips over his face, those green eyes burning into mine.

I can't help myself.

I forget everything.

I push up onto my toes, wrap my arms around his neck, and kiss him.

Not full of hate.

Not full of pain.

But passion.

Just like we had.

CHAPTER 86

CONAN

Song- The Night We Met, Nath Brooks.

The way she's kissing me is putting another part of my heart back together.

As hot as that was back there, it wasn't us.

That was the old Conan—the one who didn't give a fuck. Not the man obsessively in love.

The side of me she brought out, the part I didn't even know existed. But it's there, and it's only for her.

I let her control the kiss, my hands sliding down her tight waist.

Maybe for the rest of the night, we can just be us again.

Maybe I should show her the softer side of me. Make love to her rather than fuck her.

"Can we change the rules, darlin'?" I cup her face.

"To what?" she whispers.

"Let me worship you now. Let me show you the other side to me. Let me take care of you."

547

I can see she's holding back tears.

I hold my breath, waiting for her answer.

"Okay. Deal." She smiles softly.

And my heart nearly beats out of my chest.

I've got the rest of the night to try to show her how much I care.

How much I fucking need her more than I need air to breathe.

This is the real us.

And I will worship every inch of her until she realizes just how much she means to me. Until she knows how sorry I am for ever hurting her.

That Conan is gone.

I need to prove to her the man I can be.

I ROLL OVER, expecting to find Hallie to pull against my chest. But I'm met with empty sheets.

Panic claws through me.

I sit up and switch on the side light.

And there she is—tugging on one of my sweaters, looking like she just got caught sneaking out of class.

"Are you really slipping out in the middle of the night like I don't mean anything to you?"

I can't hide my irritation now.

She won't give me a chance to explain, but she'll let me fuck her senseless.

She let me make love to her, for hours, until our bodies gave out.

She let me believe there was a small chance of

redemption.

"You don't," she fires back.

I flinch but try to hide how much that hurts.

I know what she's doing.

She knows last night felt too real, and she's scared.

Scared to let me back in.

And I don't blame her.

But it doesn't make this any less agonizing.

"Turn around and look me in the face and tell me that, trouble. Tell me how much you hate me. Because last night, you couldn't get enough of me. So say it again, and I'll believe you. I'll leave you alone."

I regret the words the second they leave my mouth.

I can't leave her alone.

Even if it was just the hate fuck she'd always wanted, I'm just glad it was with me. That even for one night, she chose me—in the most fucked up way possible.

She slowly turns to face me, her bloodshot eyes swimming in pain.

"Conan, I—" She pauses, taking a shaky breath.

Every muscle in my body tenses.

"We can't do this again."

"This?"

She gestures between us.

"We can't sleep together. It's best if we just leave each other alone. Okay?" She stumbles over her words.

"That isn't what I asked you to say." My voice comes out flat.

"It doesn't even sound like you're convinced by your own words. If you want me to stop, say it with your chest."

I throw the covers off and stand—completely fucking naked—and stride toward her.

Her eyes flick down to my cock.

I tut.

"My eyes are up here, Hallie."

She scowls, dragging her gaze back to my face.

God, she's so beautiful when she's worked up.

"I'm here. I'm ready. Say it," I press her.

It takes everything not to grab her face and kiss her senseless. To somehow make her feel what I feel. To see how fucking sorry I am.

"Say what? Why are you trying to hurt yourself?" she whispers.

I grin.

"I told you once I like pain. Remember? If you want me out of your life for good, you know what to do."

Maybe this is the closure I need. The final fuck off.

I can't move on.

I'll always be stuck in the life-after-Hallie phase.

Because, like my mom said, there's one person on this earth for everyone.

Hallie is my person.

I've lost her.

So I'm destined to spend the rest of my life miserable and alone.

I deserve it.

Maybe this is a fight I can't win.

"Last night was a mistake, Conan. We are over. For good. Done. I don't want to be with you. I don't want you to chase me. I want you to stay the hell away from me. There is nothing you can explain to make this better. Unless you can change what happened? You had me kidnapped and entered into a game where women die to survive your fucking sick game. I'm not a contestant."

I shake my head. As she grabs for the door, I press it shut with my hand above her head.

"No one died in The Chase, Hallie. It's all fake. All the women are fine—they're given new identities and a new life away from the fucking scum who entered them. There's a bigger picture here. I'm just a goddamn pawn in this game. We maintain order for someone much higher than us. I'm sorry. I'm so fucking sorry that you got caught up in this. If I'd known Ben had entered you, this wouldn't be happening."

Her breath hitches. I can almost feel the relief radiate off her.

"I'm glad no one died for me to win. But do you also see how I can't be with a man who is capable of doing this? Who gets a thrill from hunting? Do you know how fucking petrified I was? And that cabin? Conan, you had me tied up in a sauna and coaxed an orgasm out of me. Did you do that to other girls? How many girls did you make come that day?"

"None. Because I stepped back this year. I only took control of yours because I was drawn to you."

A fire blazes in her eyes.

"So you didn't know it was me. I could have been anyone, and you wanted to make them come. What if it wasn't me? What if I made another guy come? Hmm?"

The anger in her voice is palpable. The air between us dead and cold.

"Well? Come on. Explain yourself."

She shoves at my chest, but I hold her steady.

"Tell me how you want me to forgive that, Conan." Her voice rises.

"But it was you." I don't know what else to say.

I've seriously fucked up.

"You chased me for weeks. You made me believe it could be more. You made me feel again. And then I'm thrown into the fucking woods, and my whole life explodes."

She erupts into sobs. I pull her into my arms.

"I really, really liked you, Conan. And now I've lost you as a friend—and that hurts too. You can't have wanted me, not really, if this was what you were doing behind my back."

Everything crashes down around me.

She's right.

She deserves so much better than me.

I'm a monster.

"I'm so sorry, Hallie."

I close my eyes and rest my head on top of hers, taking in her sweet rose scent for the last time.

"I'll stop. I'll leave you alone. I promise," I whisper and pull back.

She wipes her tears and tries to smile.

"You are a good man, deep down. You'll make someone very happy one day," she says before turning to leave and almost sprinting out of my garage.

I stumble back and sit on the edge of the bed, covering my face with my hands.

In my thirty years on this earth, I've never felt so devastated.

Like my heart has cracked clean open.

CHAPTER 87
HALLIE

I sprint around the corner and see Lily sitting in her car, waiting for me.

Sliding into the passenger seat, she doesn't say a word. She just drives.

"Want to talk about it?" she asks quietly.

"We fucked."

"I gathered that, seeing as I'm picking you up at five in the goddamn morning. I haven't even had a coffee yet. My eyes are burning."

"Sorry." I slump in my seat.

My bottom lip quivers as I try to hold back the tears.

"Let it out, Hallie. You'll feel better."

"I told him I never want to see him again. That he was just a fuck. And…I think this is it, Lily. I think he's going to stop."

My voice shakes, and the cries turn into sobs.

"That's what you wanted though, right? You can't be half in. Not with a guy like Conan. It's probably for the best. Otherwise you'll just hurt each other over and over."

"I thought it was what I wanted. Now, I'm not so sure."

It feels final.

Yet I'm still so drawn to him. Like a moth to a flame.

I believe what he told me. And if anything, it eases some of the guilt pressing on my conscience.

But when he wrapped his arms around me, for those few minutes…the hurt stopped.

I was safe again.

"Oh, Hallie. I'm so sorry. It will get better. I promise—you'll stop hurting."

I nod, but deep down I know this will stay with me for a long time.

Conan isn't a man you just let go of.

He's made a mark on my soul.

"I think I might ask Dr. Quinn for my job back," I blurt out.

Work gave me a purpose. And it's not like I spent hours a day with Finn anyway.

"That's a good start."

"I don't want to sell Dad's house either."

Lily nods.

"I know."

"Okay. Let's see if I can put my life back together tomorrow."

"Hallie, you never broke it in the first place. Okay?"

It feels like I did.

What if I've fucked up?

I hurt him. I know I did. I felt him flinch. I felt his heart crack.

How far can I push him away before he really doesn't come back?

"I think I've made a mistake, Lily. He wasn't just a hate fuck."

I run my hands through my hair.

"Let's get you home, cleaned up, and fed. Then we'll make some coffee and talk it out. All of it."

"I don't know what I'd do without you, Lily."

She smiles.

"Well, for starters, you'd be walking home."

CHAPTER 88

CONAN

"**G**o away!" I shout at whoever is behind my cabin door.

The knocks get louder.

I toss back my whiskey and turn up the music, trying to drown it out.

It's not just the knocking I want to drown.

It's the ache in my chest. That burning feeling. The sadness hollowing out my heart.

I'm miserable.

The door slams open, and in stride Finn and Declan.

"What part of 'fuck off' don't you understand?" I spit.

They share a worried look before approaching me.

Like I'm some rabid animal in a cage they're about to tranquilize.

Shit.

Maybe Finn really might put my useless ass down.

"Conan. You okay, bud?" Declan asks calmly.

"Fine. Whatever gave you the impression of anything otherwise?"

I throw my arms wide to gesture at the state of my cabin.

Three days' worth of boozing. Not leaving the place. The occasional break to throw axes in the shed.

This is my life now.

Pointless.

Lonely.

Fuck. I miss her.

"Conan. You showered today?" Finn asks.

I shrug.

"Fuck knows. What day is it?"

I'm drunk.

Again.

"You worried about me?" I make a cute, pouty face at them.

I can see Finn getting more irritated by the second.

Good. Maybe they'll leave me the hell alone to wallow in my pity.

"Yes. Actually. Very. You've missed training. You haven't been out of these four walls in days. You're losing the battle here," Finn says.

He picks up the bottle of Dad's whiskey and starts pouring it down the sink.

I launch myself over the counter to stop him.

"What the hell are you doing?" I shout.

As I go to grab the bottle, Finn snatches it out of reach.

"Conan! Stop!" Declan's voice cracks like a whip.

I freeze, turning to face him, my nostrils flaring.

"Both of you. Out."

Declan squares up to me.

"No. Sit down, little brother."

My jaw twitches.

"Fuck. Off." I spit.

"We're not going anywhere, Con. Like it or not, we're

your brothers, and we ain't letting you drink yourself into the grave. You're better than this," Finn chimes in.

"I'm an adult. I'll do damn well as I please."

As I turn, I stumble, catching myself on the counter.

I let out a breath.

Fuck. I'm a mess.

The room goes silent. No one moves.

"I've really fucked it all up," I admit, voice low.

"You're really giving up now? That's it? Chase over?" Declan asks.

I shrug and head for the couch, slumping down and kicking my feet up on the coffee table.

My brothers follow and sit on the chairs opposite me. Like a damn intervention.

"Look. I'm in mourning. Let me have one more day."

Declan chuckles.

"Not happening. Now, why are you giving up? Conan, we've seen you cave in men's skulls in a cage. Fighting is in your blood. This ain't you."

I swallow the lump in my throat.

"This is different. Everything was with her. I'm just fucking empty." I run a hand over my face.

"So don't give up," Finn says, his voice low.

"I promised her I'd stop. That I'd leave her alone."

Finn screws up his face.

"She clearly still feels something for you if she came back with you after the club. Women don't do that otherwise."

"She wanted a hate fuck," I say, deadpan.

Declan's face twists.

"If you love her, you gotta fight, Conan. Dig fucking deep. Sort your shit out. Get back in the cage. Let off some steam. Then focus. We can help you make a plan. You can win her back. You always go after what you want," Declan tells me.

"She's not a prize, Dec. She's the love of my life. The one I hate fucked and made love to in the same night—and still got rejected. I've got a whole ass future planned with her that I'm still working on, one that might just haunt me for the rest of my life. I don't know what to do. I can't take back what happened. And all she can see is a monster. Which I am."

Declan shakes his head.

"She doesn't think that. She wouldn't even speak to you if that were true. But if you keep going down this road, she won't ever come back. Show her you're serious. Don't give up."

I sigh and close my eyes.

"Why does love have to hurt so damn bad?" I mutter, rubbing at my eyes.

I'm exhausted.

"That's how you know it's the real deal, brother. Remember how much I hated Charlotte? For years? And now look. It's worth the risk. Take it."

That does give me a flicker of hope.

I've seen hatred turn to something real with Declan and Charlotte.

"You've got your grand plan in motion, right? Get to work on it. That future you wanted—take her to it."

"You think?"

They both nod.

Just having my brothers here makes the load feel ten times lighter.

"Thank you," I say quietly.

"That's what we're for. We couldn't sit back and watch

you beat yourself up anymore. We want you back, little bro," Declan tells me.

"I really am a mess, aren't I?" I laugh, though it sounds hollow.

"Yes. But you always have been. Ain't nothing new," Finn smirks.

"Just because I'm drunk doesn't mean I can't throw a punch."

"Yeah, yeah. Go sober up. Shower, you stinky beast, and then meet us at the gym," Finn orders as he stands.

"Alright. Yeah."

I don't know what I'd do without them.

CHAPTER 89

HALLIE

My fingers hover over Conan's number. I'm so close to hitting dial.

After taking a couple of days to process the hate-fuck-turned-love-making session a few nights ago, I've come to one conclusion—I have to know the truth.

Because I can't let this man go. Even despite the games. The more my brain replays what happened and who he really is, the more I can't help but think there really is more to it.

That if he was truly that awful of a person, he wouldn't be so wrecked by losing me.

He wouldn't have let me fall in love with him in the first place.

That's the one official conclusion I've made in the nights eating only ice cream for dinner—*I love Conan.*

And I don't think there's anyone else out there for me.

He asked me to hear him out. I'll give him that before I make my final decision.

I toss my phone down as the door opens.

"We're playing a game," Lily announces, holding up a bag and rushing over to the table.

I close my laptop. My search for nursing jobs is still going nowhere. I'm just being a baby, scared to ask Dr. Quinn for my job back.

"What game?"

She tips out the contents of the bag—boxes and boxes of pregnancy tests.

"Pregnancy roulette," she says dryly.

"You think you're pregnant?" I ask warily.

"I'm a day late."

"A day? I love the drama with you," I chuckle, picking up a test.

"Better to be safe than sorry."

"And I'm involved in this how? I didn't have a one-night stand in Barbados."

She glares at me.

"No. You didn't. But you've been hooking up with Conan still."

Oh. Yeah.

"True."

My heart flutters. Holy shit.

"Hallie. What?"

"I don't know when my last period even was."

I rub my scalp.

"Think, Hallie. You had one just after Ben cheated, right?"

I nod slowly.

"Did you have one after that?"

"Fuck. I don't know."

My life has been a whirlwind lately.

"Okay. So maybe what, six or seven weeks? You're normally regular, though."

I swallow the lump in my throat and look down at the test in my hand.

"I really don't think I've had one."

I know it now.

And I've just told Conan that we're done, done. Because I panicked. Because he makes me feel too much.

The night after the club, when he held me while I slept —it was everything.

I felt whole again.

But he really fucking hurt me.

"Come on, Hallie. Let's just do this," Lily says gently, holding out her hand and helping me stand.

"What if it's positive, Lily? What do I do?"

She rubs my back as the panic starts to rise.

"Your body, your choice, Hallie."

I rest my head on her shoulder.

It would be a little part of me—and the only man I've ever loved.

That's the only answer.

"I'll go upstairs. You can use the downstairs," I tell her, and I dash up to the bathroom.

I let out a shaky breath as the door clicks shut.

After I pee on the stick, I wash my hands and find myself sitting on the hard floor, hugging my knees with the test lying face-up on the tiles.

And I just stare.

Waiting.

As two lines appear, I pick it up with trembling fingers.

"Shit," I sob.

In all this chaos, it turns out there's something more important than anything.

Our baby.

"Hallie..." Lily calls up.

I open my mouth, but no words come out. Just sobs.

I rest my head on my knees and cry.

For the love I've lost.

All I can think about is the way he pleaded with me to hear him out.

And I shut him out.

Am I a monster too, for doing this to him?

The door crashes open, and Lily is on the floor next to me, wrapping her arms around me tight.

"Hallie. It's going to be okay. I promise you."

I shake my head.

"I can't do this alone, Lily."

"Shh. You'll never be on your own. You know Conan is going to be by your side every damn step of the way, whether you like it or not. And so will I."

I wipe my tears and sniffle.

"That's what I'm afraid of. I don't want this to be the reason I forgive him. I need to know the truth."

She nods and gives me a soft smile.

"Hallie, you've been running from the truth for weeks now. I think it's time you hear him out. If you don't like it, we can think of a plan. Maybe we never tell him. Or, if you do believe him…you tell him, and you let him back into your life."

"W-what if he doesn't want the baby?"

"Then that will also be your answer. Close the door on this chapter, for you and for the baby."

I close my eyes.

"I need to book a scan. Fuck. I need to get a job. And decorate. Oh my god, Lily. I need a job. I can't even race now, I'm pregnant!"

My brain spirals, and I descend into panic. I quit my job with no backup.

"One thing at a time, maybe? You've got months to figure it out."

She picks my phone up from the floor and holds it out to me.

"But you need to start by speaking to Conan. You know it in your heart."

CHAPTER 90

CONAN

Slamming the wrench down on the side, I wipe the sweat from my forehead.

I'm doing anything to distract myself while I figure out a plan to win Hallie back. Or at least get her to talk to me.

"Fuck!" I slam my hand down on the bench.

And then I just keep tearing it apart. Swiping the contents from the shelves. Smashing glass. Anything to numb this agony.

I've ditched the drink and stopped locking myself away, but I still can't stop it all from hurting.

If I'd known that love would feel like this, I might never have let myself fall so hard.

Nope. That's not true. I'd fall in love with Hallie a hundred times over and never regret it.

I can't give up on her.

She says she can't be my friend. That I'm nothing to her.

But I felt her pain when she said those words.

The only way I'll ever give up is if she kills me. And even then, I'd chase her through eternity.

Mine.

I just have to try harder. Starting with working on my anger.

I never want to scare her again. She needs to know I'd never hurt her.

Getting my championship win.

Burning the Decadence Chase to the ground.

None of that really matters. Nothing does.

The only fight that matters is winning back my girl.

My phone vibrates on the side.

I'm expecting it to be Declan demanding I get my ass back to Decadence.

I needed a break from that fucking place.

My garage is my solace. That's where I'm staying until I figure out my head again.

As I flip it over, all the air is knocked out of my lungs.

I answer and freeze.

"Conan?"

Her voice is quiet.

She sniffles, and my heart starts to pound.

"Hallie, are you okay?"

"Yeah. Kind of. I need to see you."

Fuck.

This doesn't sound good.

"I'm at the garage. Want to meet me here?"

"Is anyone with you?"

"No."

She's holding something back.

"Hallie…what is it?"

"I want to hear you out, Conan. I need the truth."

I blow out a breath. Am I dreaming? Why does she sound so upset?

Fuck.

I'm not even sure the truth will save my ass.

But I'll get down on my knees and beg for her forgiveness.

"I can give you that. Why the change of heart?"

There's a pause, and my palms start to sweat.

"I—I didn't mean everything I said the other night, Con. I'll never hate you."

That's something, I suppose.

"I'll see you soon, trouble. Want me to order some food in?"

"No. Not hungry. Feel a bit sick today."

That panic spikes in me again.

"Are you sure you're okay? You sound…sad."

She lets out a soft, humorless laugh.

"Because I am sad, Con."

Fuck. That hurts.

"I'm sorry." It's all I can say right now.

"I know you are. I'll be with you soon."

She hangs up, leaving me staring at the wall.

Resting my ass on the bench, I look around at all my cars. Tears burn in my eyes as I stare at the car I bought for Hallie, sparkling under the lights.

Oil seeps across the floor around it. Crushed glass is scattered by my feet.

I need to clean up my fucking mess.

Story of my life.

CHAPTER 91

HALLIE

After four more tests, I can officially say I'm pregnant.

And now I need to rip the band-aid off and actually speak to Conan.

After everything, I deserve this—at least to close the door on that part of my life for good.

My Shelby roars to life as I back out of the driveway.

I need a drive first to clear my head. Then I'll head to his garage.

I'm nervous. But I'm also still angry. And pissed off at myself for being cruel to him.

The one thing Conan has proved in these weeks is that he is remorseful. And he cares. Probably more than he should.

As I merge onto the highway, I put my foot down and open the windows, letting the breeze whip through my hair.

It's quiet out here for this time of night.

A little glimmer of light is starting to appear in my life.

A baby is a huge deal. I've always wanted to be a mom. A real one. Not like mine.

I want to give my baby everything.

As I switch lanes, I glance in the rearview mirror. The black BMW behind me follows.

I keep going, slowing down near the next exit. I don't indicate—I just shoot off.

But when I check the mirror again, the BMW is still right behind me.

Something gnaws at me. Or maybe I'm just anxious and overthinking—today's been a lot.

I pull up the GPS on the screen. Fifteen minutes until Conan.

I ease onto the brakes to slow myself down, but instead of overtaking, the car slows too.

I don't like this.

It's probably nothing. But I need to hear his voice before I have a meltdown.

I hit his number on the screen. As always, he answers fast.

"Hallie."

His voice is low, steady. My safe place.

"Conan. Umm…"

I take a left when the GPS tells me to. No blinker. My heart sinks when the BMW sticks to my tail.

"Hallie, what is it? Talk to me."

"I think someone's following me, Con."

I push my foot to the floor, my car rocketing ahead.

"Where are you?" His voice doesn't waver.

"I'm eleven minutes from your garage. Just turning right onto…"

I glance down, reciting the street name.

"I'm on my way to you. Just stay calm and keep driving towards me. You got that, baby?"

I suck in a ragged breath.

"Y-yes."

"Wait. Please stay on the phone. I need to hear your voice."

"I'm never leaving you, trouble."

A calmness washes over me.

He's got me.

He always did.

"I'm just starting my engine. I won't be long."

I swallow the bile rising in my throat.

"They still behind you, darlin'?"

I check. Grit my teeth.

"Yep."

"Keep driving calmly. Don't let them think you know."

"Got it."

"I've texted my men. They're coming from Decadence as backup."

A shiver rakes down my spine at the mention of that place.

"Do you own the chocolate?" I ask, needing anything to distract myself.

"Yes. We do. You like it?"

"I did. Loved it even." My voice is flat.

"You never know…one day you might love it again."

This isn't about chocolate.

"You really didn't know it was me?"

He doesn't even pause.

"No. There's no way in hell I'd have put you through that. I swear on my life—on everything and everyone I've ever loved—I didn't check the applications. I didn't care. Because all I cared about was you."

Tears sting behind my eyes.

"S-sorry. This is probably a bad time."

"A little. But I promise, I'm done with that now. I'd already told my brothers it was my last year before The Chase even started. That is my past, Hallie. I swear."

I turn right. The BMW doesn't follow.

"Conan, they didn't take my turn."

"Good. But keep driving, okay? If they were tracking you, this could be to throw you off."

My pulse hammers.

"What's going on? How are you so calm?"

I'm right on the verge of a panic attack.

"Ben was part of a much bigger organization. One I made enemies with in Ireland years ago. And let's just say I've been burning the city down to make a point."

"Because he entered me?"

"Yes."

This mafia world is insane.

"Will you ever be completely safe?" I ask. My hand slides to my stomach, like instinct.

"No one on this planet is ever completely safe. But at least we're prepared. That's how I look at it. And trust me, I'd fucking die to protect you, trouble. Without even a second thought."

My breathing gets heavy. I shake my head.

"I don't want you to die. I don't want—"

"Shh. It's okay. What's your GPS saying?"

"Four minutes."

"You coming up to the junction?"

I nod, slowing as the red lights appear.

"I'm just ahead. Keep driving forward. Go straight to the garage. I'll deal with whoever was tailing you."

"You'll be safe?"

"Always. We gotta talk, right? And I gotta get my girl back."

My heart skips.

His girl.

CHAPTER 92
CONAN

I see her headlights and exhale in relief.

She's here. She's okay.

On the screen, the red dot shows Finn closing in fast from the east.

But just as my light—and hers—turn green, headlights emerge from my right.

The BMW.

Motherfuckers.

She crawls forward, oblivious, and the car barrels through the red light straight for her.

I slam my foot on the gas.

"HALLIE. FOOT DOWN. GO!" I roar, the engine snarling as I hurtle toward the blacked-out BMW.

"Conan!" Her voice cracks with panic.

Everything slows—the way it always does when I'm about to do something reckless. My hood connects with their doors in a deafening impact. Metal warps, glass explodes. My head jerks forward so hard I see stars, the seatbelt digging into my ribs.

But I keep my foot buried on the accelerator.

The BMW lurches sideways, flips over itself once—twice—and comes down in a shuddering heap. Dark smoke pours from under the crumpled hood, billowing into the night air.

I grab my gun from my lap.

"Conan! Can you hear me?" Hallie's voice is a broken plea in my earpiece.

"Baby, lock your car and pull over. I'm coming to you."

We've got backup on the way. She's safer with me than on her own.

I kick my door open and jump down onto the asphalt, adrenaline buzzing like electricity in my veins.

Gun raised, I stalk over to the wrecked BMW. The smoke stings my eyes as I peer through the shattered window.

Two men slump motionless inside, but they're still breathing—shallow, ragged.

Good. They can live long enough to answer my questions.

They wanted to try me?

They picked the wrong fucking day. And clearly they have a death wish.

CHAPTER 93

HALLIE

Hearing the impact through my phone nearly gives me a heart attack.

I clutch the steering wheel, trying to force a steady breath into my lungs. Don't freak out. God.

What the hell is happening?

I keep the engine running and slam my thumb on the lock button. In my side mirror, I see Conan stalking toward the smoking BMW, his gun drawn, his entire body radiating lethal intent.

My hands won't stop shaking. My whole body is trembling with fear.

Then more headlights appear around the corner, tires screeching against asphalt.

Panic claws up my throat.

Whoever was in that car following me—they tried to kill me.

Tears spill over, blurring my vision as I glance into the rearview mirror, praying this nightmare will end.

CHAPTER 94

CONAN

Just as Finn barrels around the corner, I yank open the driver's door, gun aimed straight ahead.

The bastard is slumped over the steering wheel, blood pouring from a cut on his forehead.

I take a step closer—and that's when I see it. The glint of metal resting in his lap, barrel lifted, pointing right at me.

Fuck.

I don't think. I just fire.

Our shots explode at the same time.

I don't feel it at first. I just stagger back, staring in shock as a hole blooms in the side of his skull.

Fuck. Fuck.

My hand comes up to my chest. Warmth soaks my fingers. My ears are ringing.

I need to get back to Hallie.

"Conan!" Finn's voice is shouting somewhere far away, ragged and panicked.

I keep walking. One step, then another, toward Hallie's Shelby. But with each step, the world gets fuzzier around the edges.

Pain ignites under my ribs, searing hot, stealing my breath.

I'm almost there—just a few more steps. Her taillights blur into a halo of red.

My foot catches on nothing. My knees buckle.

I hit the asphalt hard, the impact rattling through my bones.

"Conan. Stay with me."

Finn's hands are on me, but my gaze is locked on the car door opening and Hallie's silhouette rushing toward me.

Her face appears above me, blurred and beautiful, the only thing keeping me tethered to this place.

I'm moved onto my back. Someone—her—presses firm hands against my chest.

Finn is yelling into his phone. He never yells. He sounds…scared.

I can't look away from her.

"Conan. Can you hear me?" Her voice is so soft, so familiar, it feels like a lullaby.

I have so much to say—so many things she needs to know.

"I can hear you."

I just have to hold on a little longer. She has to know she meant more to me than anything in this fucked-up life.

CHAPTER 95
HALLIE

Song- Hold On, Chord Overstreet.

I fall down onto the ground beside him and pull his head onto my lap, taking over from Finn to put pressure on the wound.

Finn is as cold as ice as he gets off the phone to the emergency services.

"They'll be a couple of minutes," he says coolly.

I glance over at the twins, currently dragging the man who shot Conan into the back of Finn's Range Rover.

Conan coughs and I stroke his stubble.

"We're getting you help, beastie. Just hang on."

Fuck. I want to scream. Tell him not to leave me.

He shakes his head, and I rest my forehead against his. I can't let him see the panic in my eyes. I need him to fight one last time.

"Trouble, if I'm going to die, just please make sure you're holding my hand when I go. Maybe that way, we'll get another shot."

Tears stream down my face. I put more pressure on the wound, his warm blood coating my fingers.

"No. Don't say that. You're not going anywhere." My voice starts to break.

He lifts his hand to my face, his thumb chasing my tears away.

"Can you at least let me say those three words now? I need you to hear me say them, because I mean it. I want you to be the first and only person in my life to hear it. Please."

A sob catches in my throat, and I press my lips to his.

"Say it," I whisper.

"I love you, Hallie. I didn't realize you could feel a love like this before you. I love you. I love you."

This hurts. The ache in my chest nearly consumes me.

"I love you, Conan. I've never stopped—how could I? You're my soulmate. We will get you through this. And then you can tell me again. Every day."

He coughs, and my resolve starts to crumble.

"Forever?" He can hardly get the word out.

I pull back to assess him. His eyes are heavy. I discreetly slide my hand to his throat, but his pulse is getting hard to find. When I feel his chest, it's beating quick, ragged.

No. No. No. No.

"Yes. Forever, beastie."

A tear slips down his cheek.

"Hallie," Conan whispers.

I look down just as his eyes flutter closed and his body goes limp.

"No—no, no, no!"

I carefully lay him flat on the pavement, my hands shaking so violently I can barely lace my fingers together. I tilt his head back and start chest compressions.

"Come on, Conan. Breathe—breathe for me!"

My tears drip onto his chest as I count, pressing as hard as I can.

"One, two, three—Conan, please!—four, five—"

I can't get enough air into my lungs. I'm sobbing so hard I can't see straight.

"Finn! He's not—he's not—" I scream.

Finn drops to his knees beside me and wraps his hands around my wrists, gently pulling them away.

"Hallie. Let go—I've got it."

"No—"

"Hallie." His voice is flat but unyielding. "You need to let me do this."

I choke on a sob as he eases me back. My hands hover over Conan's face like if I just touch him, he'll open his eyes again.

"Come on, brother. Fucking fight," Finn shouts, pressing on Conan's chest with steady, practiced force.

The paramedics crowd around us, the bright lights blurring with my tears. My hand is ripped from Conan's, and my heart breaks watching him get lifted onto the stretcher.

"We need to get him into surgery," the lead paramedic tells us.

"Take him to St. George's. I'll have them prep an O.R. I'm Dr. Finn Quinn."

"Got it." They nod and slam the door shut.

"Come on. Let's go." Finn leads me back to my car. I hand him my keys with trembling hands, and he follows behind the ambulance as closely as he can.

CHAPTER 96
HALLIE

"**W**hat do you think, Finn?" My voice is tiny.

He doesn't look at me. His jaw is tight.

"It doesn't look promising, Hallie. We might have to prepare ourselves for the worst."

My throat closes. But I can't believe it. Conan is a fighter. He has to pull through.

When we reach the hospital, Finn jumps out and races inside, already on his phone. I follow, every step heavier than the last.

I watch them wheel Conan through the double doors toward surgery. My stomach lurches.

Finn paces, talking in low, angry tones. When he hangs up, his gray eyes find mine.

"Finn…I—I'm scared. Are you going to operate?"

He shakes his head.

"I've called in the best surgeon I know. The only woman I loathe as much as she loathes me."

I stare.

"No. Dr. Quinn. You hate her. She hates you. You can't let her operate on him."

His face doesn't change.

"She'll relish saving my brother. It'll give her a win over me. That's exactly why Conan is safer with her. I'm too… emotional to do it."

If I didn't already feel like I was dying, I'd punch him. Emotional? Finn?

"I'll be in there to oversee. I need to go."

"Wait—"

"Go to your office. I'll send Declan and the men to escort you to Conan's room once I have it."

He turns to leave, then hesitates. His eyes soften—just a flicker—and it rattles me more than anything.

"These men are here to protect you. Don't be scared, okay?"

I can only nod. He disappears through the doors.

I stand there, swallowing bile.

I pull out my phone to call Lily, but then I see the blood on my hands. Conan's blood.

"Hallie?"

I crumble. My knees give out and I slide down the wall.

"Can you come to my office at the hospital?" My voice breaks. "I need you."

"I'm coming. Right now."

My phone clatters to the floor. I bury my face in my hands, trying to quiet the sobs.

A hand touches my back. I jerk upright.

"Hallie. It's me, Charlotte."

I look up, eyes blurred with tears. Declan is behind her with the twins. More men filter in behind them.

Declan looks wrecked but is trying not to show it.

"Come on," Charlotte whispers. "We need to get you safe in your office. Can you walk?"

I nod. She links arms with me and guides me down the hall.

At the sink, she gently washes my hands.

"All gone."

I let out a shuddering breath. My tears don't stop.

She wraps her arms around me, and I break.

"He's going to be okay, Hallie. I promise."

But Declan's eyes say something different.

"Conan would want us to protect you," he says quietly. "But more than that, he'd want you to know how much he loved you. You were his person. That makes you part of our family. No matter what happens."

I can't hold it in.

"I—I'm pregnant." I blurt it out. I have to tell someone. I feel like I'm spiraling. I need them.

His eyes widen.

"I can't lose him. He needs to know."

My voice shakes. My hands won't stop trembling.

"You're having my brother's baby?" Declan's voice goes soft.

I nod, wrapping my arms around my stomach.

Charlotte sets a hand on my shoulder.

"You're not alone in this. How far along?"

"I don't know. Six weeks? I only just tested."

She takes a slow breath.

"We should check on the baby. This was a lot of stress. Do you know someone here who can help?"

I nod. My chest feels like it's splitting in two.

"Yes. But I don't want to leave. We need to be here when they move him."

"I'll wait," Declan says. "Charlotte will stay with you. I'll send word when I know anything."

As Charlotte and I start down the hall, she leans close.

"I'm pregnant too," she murmurs.

My tears fall harder.

"How far?"

"Thirteen weeks. We were going to announce it this weekend."

I manage a weak smile.

"Our kids…they'll be cousins."

"They will."

And I try to cling to that tiny flicker of hope, but it hurts more than anything. Conan might not get to see this. I bet he'd love that, seeing his and Declan's kids growing up together. Causing havoc like they probably did as kids.

Fuck.

I can't do this.

CHAPTER 97

HALLIE

Song- Memories, Dean Lewis

Clutching the printed picture against my chest, I hold my breath as I walk into Conan's room.

He's still in surgery.

He will be for a few more hours.

Lily rushes over and pulls me into a bear hug. Her warmth should comfort me, but I feel nothing. Just numb.

I've run out of tears.

I'm running on fumes, and I don't know how much longer I can keep going.

"Can I see?" she asks gently, like she's afraid I'll shatter if she speaks too loudly.

I hold out the ultrasound picture with trembling hands. She takes it like it's the most precious thing in the world. Her eyes fill with tears she's trying desperately to hold back.

She's trying to be strong for me.

"Can I?" Declan's voice is rough as he steps closer.

I nod without looking up.

I can't.

He draws in a ragged breath, pressing the hands over his eyes. Charlotte winds her arms around his waist, resting her cheek against his chest as if she's trying to hold him together, too.

"Conan…a dad." His voice cracks. "I never thought I'd see the day."

"You still might not."

The words spill out of me, bitter and raw.

I'm angry. So goddamn angry.

At the world.

At him.

At myself.

Because if I'd just listened—just let him explain—maybe none of this would be happening.

Maybe I wouldn't have to stand here wondering if the father of my baby is about to die.

Life can rip away everything you love in an instant.

I saw it happen to my dad.

And now, I'm watching it happen all over again. He tried so hard to reach me.

He tried to prove he loved me.

And I pushed him away because I was too afraid to let myself hope. I was too afraid to believe that maybe—just maybe—someone could love me the way he did.

"I need some air," I choke out, my throat burning as I turn away.

I don't wait for anyone to follow.

I just run.

I don't stop until the doors burst open and the cold night air hits me like a slap.

It steals my breath, but I don't care.

I want to feel something.

Anything.

"Hallie!"

Lily's voice cuts through the chaos in my head.

I stop, but I can't turn around.

If I look at her, I'll fall apart.

She wraps her arms around me from behind and holds on so tight it hurts.

"I can't tell you it's going to be okay, because I don't honestly know," she whispers, her voice thick with tears. "But I can tell you that you have an army around you to help you. You aren't alone in this. You never were."

"He told me he loved me," I gasp, my chest heaving. "He said goodbye to me, Lily. He looked me in the eye and told me he loved me, like he already knew it was the end."

My voice cracks on the last word, and a sob breaks free.

I press my fist to my mouth to stop the sound, but it's useless.

"Did you tell him you loved him back?"

I nod.

God, I nod so hard my neck hurts.

"I did. I told him. But what if it wasn't enough?"

She presses her forehead to mine.

"It was enough. It's always been enough."

"Shall we go back inside?" she asks softly. "We don't want to miss any updates."

"Okay."

My voice is so small, it doesn't even sound like me.

CHAPTER 98

HALLIE

The armed men outside Conan's room nod silently as Lily guides me past them.

The moment we step inside, the stillness hits me like a brick.

It's too quiet.

Too clean.

It doesn't feel real that he might not be here to fill it with that deep, rumbling voice ever again.

I sink into the nearest chair, my body too heavy to hold itself up anymore.

Lily moves behind me, wrapping her arms around my shoulders.

I close my eyes, letting her hold me together because I don't think I can do it on my own.

The clock on the wall ticks, every second loud and deliberate, counting out my punishment.

I feel like I'm trapped in a loop—waiting for someone to come and tell me the last shred of hope is gone.

When the door finally creaks open, I jerk upright so fast I see stars.

Finn steps in, still in his blue scrubs.

My stomach lurches when I see the blood splattered across his chest.

Conan's blood.

His red-rimmed eyes scan the room and land on mine.

Something in them flickers—something so raw it makes my heart ache.

"Finn." My voice comes out hoarse. "Say something, goddamn it."

I shoot to my feet, swaying where I stand.

If he doesn't speak, I think I might collapse.

He scrubs a hand down his tired face.

"We've stabilized him," he says finally, voice low. "We got the bullet out and repaired the internal damage. His heart is functioning as expected."

I grip the back of the chair so hard my knuckles burn.

Every word feels like it's being pulled from him, like he doesn't trust that saying it out loud won't make it disappear.

"We're monitoring him in intensive care," he goes on, his eyes pinned to mine. "He's still out of it, and he will be for a while. We'll keep running tests, and once we're satisfied, we'll bring him back here."

Declan moves in beside me.

Without a word, he wraps his arm around my shoulders.

It's the only thing keeping me standing.

"He's in the clear?" Declan asks, his voice breaking. "He's going to pull through?"

Finn's jaw ticks.

"So long as there are no complications, yes. I don't anticipate any. The team did an outstanding job."

A strangled sound leaves me.

It takes me a second to realize it's a sob.

I turn and bury my face against Declan's chest.

His arms close around me, and I let myself shake.

Relief. Grief. Hope. All crashing over me in a wave I can't outrun.

I pull back, wiping my eyes with the back of my hand.

It doesn't matter if I look like hell.

I don't care about anything except that he's alive.

I step toward Finn.

He straightens, like he's bracing himself for impact.

I can see it now—the exhaustion he's hiding, the brittle edge of fear he refuses to let slip.

"Thank you," I whisper, my voice cracking. "Thank you for saving him."

He swallows hard.

His mouth opens, but nothing comes out.

Instead, he just gives me the smallest nod, like if he tries to speak, he'll break too.

"Get some rest, Hallie," he says at last, voice rough. "I'll come and get you when you can see him. Okay?"

I nod because it's all I can manage.

But inside, my heart is already running to him.

I want to bury my face in his neck and never let go.

I want to tell him that our baby is safe. That he's safe.

And that this time, I'm not going anywhere.

CHAPTER 99

CONAN

Song, Ordinary Love- Alex Warren.

I blink, trying to adjust to the bright lights.

Where the fuck?

I try to sit up and groan. No chance.

The blur starts to clear, and two figures are beside my bed.

"Finn?"

I'd recognize that flat cap anywhere.

"Conan. How you feeling?" he asks.

"Umm. Like I've jumped off a cliff onto a load of rocks, then got shot?"

He chuckles and steps closer.

"Not far from the truth. Car crash, then a shooting. Oh, and I may have broken some ribs doing the CPR."

My mouth falls open.

"Where is Hallie?"

I vaguely remember the moment before I lost consciousness. She was holding me.

It was warm and safe. Like I was finally home.

The monitor beside me starts to beep. My heart rate picks up.

"She's fine, Conan. Right outside that door."

He gestures to the chair beside me.

"And that's where she's been sat pretty much the entire time."

I let out a shaky breath in relief. She's okay. Even if I'm in agony, it was worth it, because she's alive.

"Can I see her?"

The doctor beside him flips through my notes. He keeps glancing over, probably wondering if I'll pass out again.

"Yes. Then we're going to get you out of here as soon as we can get the sign-off. You can recover at mine. I've got everything we need."

I frown.

"I don't wanna be hauled up in your little medical dungeon, thanks though. I'll go home. I feel fine." I lie. I just want to get out of here.

Finn arches a brow.

"Okay. I feel fine so long as I don't move. And fuck, I need a glass of water, doc."

He chuckles and hands me a cup.

"Always the diva, Conan."

He sits beside ime as the older doctor clears his throat.

"Because it's you, Dr. Quinn, I'll write up the discharge papers."

Finn nods, and the guy slips out. I pull back the covers and open the side of my gown, cringing at the freshly stitched scars along my abdomen.

"Did you do this?"

It doesn't look as neat as Finn's handiwork.

"No. Dr. Miller."

"You let your arch-nemesis save me? Wow. I'm not sure if I should be concerned or impressed."

Finn stands and straightens his jacket.

"I don't have an arch-nemesis, she's more of a workplace rival. But, you should be grateful."

Hmm.

"I am, brother. Thank you."

He squeezes my shoulder lightly.

"Good luck with Hallie."

And then he leaves.

"Once I've recovered, please tell me we're going after Arthur."

He stops by the door.

"Their move was a declaration of war. Theo King and his brothers will be here soon. But for now, there are no more Bowens left in Pennsylvania. We just have to wait for the green light to go to London."

"Good."

Hallie isn't safe until Arthur is dead. But for now, she's here.

I just need to convince her to let me back in her life.

"You have bigger things to focus on now, Con. Just let me take this one."

For once, I actually agree.

Because I can't let myself get killed. Not now. I won't leave Hallie behind.

"Okay."

As he slips out the door, I hold my breath when Hallie walks in.

Her hair's in a messy bun, glasses perched on her nose, but they don't disguise the puffiness around her eyes.

Her bottom lip quivers as she closes the door.

"Hi, darlin'."

"C-Conan." Her voice breaks, and she rushes to the side of my bed.

I lift my arm and wrap it around her. I just want her close.

I need her near me. My lifeline.

Closing my eyes, I hold back the tears as she sobs against my chest.

"Are you okay, trouble?" I ask.

She sniffles and straightens up, glaring down at me.

"Conan. You've just been in a car crash, been shot, nearly died—and you're asking me if I'm okay?"

Jesus. It's all a blur.

"You saw everything, Hallie. I need to know you're okay. That must've been terrifying."

My throat burns when I swallow. Every time I cough, it feels like my lung might come out of my mouth.

"Having the love of your life lose consciousness in your arms was slightly traumatizing, I'm not going to lie. But it doesn't matter. You're here, and you're going to be okay."

Fuck, every muscle in my body is screaming. But I'm also kind of fuzzy from the painkillers.

"Love of your life?" I ask.

My stomach flips.

"Yes. You remember, don't you?" She frowns.

I catch hold of her hand.

"Yes. I remember. And I still mean it, Hallie. I love you."

I hold my breath. What if she only said it because she thought I was dying?

"I love you so much, Conan."

"Thank God."

"Come on. Let's snuggle." I scoot over, ignoring the pain so she can climb in next to me.

Her head rests on my chest, and I drape my arm over her shoulder.

"What happens next, trouble?"

"Umm. I think you're getting discharged early on the premise that—"

I chuckle.

"No. Not medically. I mean, what's next for us?"

"Oh."

She sits up, twirling her thumbs in her lap.

"Hallie?" I prompt.

"Close your eyes and hold out your hand, beastie." Her tone leaves no room for argument.

I do as she says.

I hear her rifling through her pocket, and something smooth, almost like paper, settles in my palm.

"Okay. Open."

I look at her before I look down. She's nervous as hell.

When I glance at what she's given me, I swear to fucking god my heart stops.

Five weeks, two days. A little grainy blob.

"Surprise."

My eyes fill with tears. I just stare at the picture, speechless.

"Hallie. Fuck. I don't know what to say."

I've never felt happiness like this.

This gives my life a whole new meaning. A purpose.

And to think a few hours ago, I was nearly a dead man.

Someone out there must be looking out for me.

Maybe I'm not all that bad.

CHAPTER 100
HALLIE

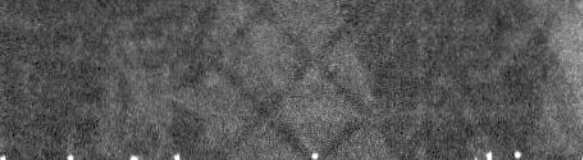

*W*hy isn't he saying anything?

Shit.

"Conan, I'm going to need something from you."

Then I see a tear fall down his cheek.

"Oh, beastie."

I carefully wrap my arms around him.

"Please tell me these are happy tears. Not 'I've never wanted a kid and I want to run away' tears."

I pull back and cup his face.

"They're 'my life is finally falling into place and I've never been more in love in my life' tears."

Oh.

My heart melts.

"You're going to be an amazing dad, Conan."

Our baby is going to be the most protected kid in the state. This man nearly got himself killed saving us.

"T-this is really happening. And you're happy, right? You want to do this?" he asks.

"Yes, Conan. I want it all with you."

I rest my forehead against his and close my eyes.

"Hallie, I still need to explain everything to you. I need you to understand and forgive me. If that's even possible."

I shake my head and press my lips against his.

The kiss ignites my soul.

And that's all the answer I need.

Me and Conan were destined for each other.

"I'll listen, and I'll understand. But I forgive you, beastie. That's in the past. Now we have a future to focus on."

"I love you, trouble. And get used to me telling you at every opportunity I can."

"I love you. Now, I was thinking…rather than live at Finn's to recover, what if you moved into mine? I can take care of you. Seeing as I'm jobless, I've got the time."

He bites his lip.

"You mean, I get to be nursed back to health by my sexy girlfriend?"

I hold up my finger.

"I've been upgraded to baby momma."

He chuckles.

"There's a couple more upgrades you'll have too."

My stomach flutters.

"Yeah?"

He nods.

"I'd love to move in, Hallie. And then, what if we buy somewhere together? A proper family home."

A sadness shadows his face, and I stroke his cheek.

"Mom would have been so excited that I'm having a baby with you."

I sigh.

"My dad would have too. But I bet they're both looking

down on us with a smile. Hey, our dads are probably best of friends up there, drinking whiskey."

He laughs and pulls me in for a kiss.

"I will never, ever, let you down again, Hallie."

"I know," I whisper.

"You need to get some rest, beastie."

He presses his lips against my temple and rests his hand on my belly.

"How am I supposed to sleep when I'm so fucking happy? I'm going to be a dad. We're having a baby. And I've got you back."

I don't think I've ever been more at peace than I am right now.

"You never lost me. Not in my heart. I think I was always going to find my way back to you."

"Or I was going to chase you until you did."

I shake my head and chuckle.

"Too soon?" he asks.

"No. Your dark humor is actually a major turn on for me."

"Good. I suppose I'd best sleep so I can get back to running after you."

CHAPTER 101

CONAN

One week later...

"Conan, wake up, baby," Hallie whispers.

I feel Bertie nudging my hand with his wet nose.

"Hi, trouble," I croak.

"You've got visitors coming today, is that okay? You feel up for it?"

Finn has been here every day, checking up on me.

Bertie hasn't left my side.

And Hallie has been an angel.

She thinks I don't know that she just lies next to me while I'm sleeping, stroking my face and whispering how much she loves me.

"Declan?" I ask.

"And Finn, of course. And the twins. I've made some lunch. Are you hungry?"

"Starving."

I groan as I sit myself up. She rushes to my side to help me.

The pain in my ribs—hell, everywhere from my neck down—is quite something.

I just need to get better.

"What would you like?" she asks, taking a seat on the edge of the bed.

I slide my arm around her waist.

"Your pussy."

She blushes, and I lick my lips.

"We have guests coming. And you're in recovery."

I pretend to pout. She giggles.

"Conan Quinn. You are being a very naughty patient trying to flirt with the nurse."

She leans over and presses a kiss to my lips.

As she goes to pull back, I grab the back of her head and kiss her harder.

She's been treating me like I'm fragile. When it comes to her, I'm not.

"A bullet hole ain't gonna stop me from tasting you."

My tongue slides against hers.

Her hand cups my face.

"If you behave, maybe later I'll let you indulge, sir."

I growl and grip her throat loosely.

"Promise?"

She nods. My cock already twitches.

"Can you be a good boy, Conan?"

"You know I can for you."

"I'll let your brothers up." She quickly pulls back and gets off the bed.

I'm empty without her.

When my brothers appear, followed by the twins, they all surround my bed.

"I assume you have news? You didn't just want to see me with no shirt on in bed?"

They chuckle, and Rowan raises a brow.

"Well, I mean, you caught me," he says, holding up his hands.

"We do have news. It seems like Theo King has made progress in London, and he'll be flying out for a meeting with us next Friday," Declan explains.

"Nice. Finally."

"Drago believes we've captured and killed all the men associated with Arthur. But we still need to remain on guard. He might send more."

Great.

"We do what we have to do to keep our families safe."

Finn steps forward.

"We'll be stationing someone outside Hallie's house, monitoring twenty-four-seven. But it may be best if you move back to Decadence."

I shake my head.

"Not happening. I can't take her back to the place that broke us. There's another option. Once I'm better and can actually fucking move without being out of breath."

My brothers know what that option is.

Something I've had in place for a while.

"How breathless are you?" Finn asks.

I panic.

"Just a bit, if I try to do too much. Probably because my ribs are broken and I've got a load of ruptured shit inside my chest?"

"Yeah. Something like that. I'll book you in for a scan so I can check everything's healing as it should."

I salute him.

"Got it, boss. Am I clear to have sex?"

Declan coughs, and Reggie chuckles.

"I suppose, if she rides you? You need to not move too much. It's been a week, Conan."

Hmm. Okay. I can work with that.

"Hallie's made you all lunch downstairs."

"We know. Charlotte is down there now."

That makes me smile.

And they're pregnant at the same time, which is so fucking awesome.

We get to see our kids grow up together. And Charlotte and Hallie have each other.

"It's all worked out well," I say, looking to Declan.

"God. You're making me feel all mushy. Maybe I should find a girlfriend," Rowan pipes up.

"You should. Could lose your virginity then."

"Reggie. Tell Conan I ain't a virgin!" Rowan demands.

"How would I know?" Reggie's face remains stern.

"Well, seeing as you watched me stick my dick in Angel's ass last night while you face-fucked her, I'd say you're a pretty reliable source to confirm I ain't a damn virgin."

He slaps Reggie's bicep.

I laugh so hard I have to grab my chest. Pain shoots through me like lightning.

"Tag-teaming strippers?" Finn asks.

"No comment," Reggie mutters, biting back a grin.

"Well, you guys are the ones getting in the way of me getting laid right now. Go eat your food. And I'll eat mine. Tell Hallie to get up here."

They all mutter under their breath as I shoo them out.

"Thanks for coming. I'll see you all next week." I blow them a kiss as they file out.

Finn stops by the door and turns back to me.

"Scan. Tomorrow, Conan."

His face might not show it, but I know he's worried about me.

I know he was in surgery with me. He oversaw it. He fucking broke my ribs trying to save my life on that road.

"Love you, brother," I tell him.

He blinks a few times, then a small smile breaks through.

"Love you too, bud. Don't ever fucking scare me like that again."

"I'll try. Can't promise it. I've got a family to protect."

He nods in understanding.

"Talk to Hallie. I think she misses you."

He frowns. As much as he hates to admit it, people care about him.

And Hallie was his friend before I entered the scene. Since my fuck-up, she quit her job, and they lost that friendship.

And then I traumatized them both.

"Misses me? I doubt it. I was just her boss."

I roll my eyes.

"I know about the night her dad died. You don't ever comfort anyone. She cares about you. We all do. Just talk to her. For me?"

"Ok."

CHAPTER 102

HALLIE

Song- Provider, Sleep Token.

I slowly creak the door open. Conan has been so miserable on bed rest. Though his scan last Friday was positive. He's healing well. He's getting more and more active. But it's only been two weeks. He isn't the normal statistic, though. His fitness levels are insane. His build alone probably saved his life.

And nothing can tame that cheeky side to him. He tries to hide how frustrated he is that he can't do everything right now. But soon, he'll be back in fighting shape. Grayson already lined up a trainer to rehabilitate him.

He's not letting his Championship dream go lightly. And I hope one day, I can watch him win that.

But today, I thought I'd cheer him up.

When I see he's asleep, I tiptoe to the end of the bed.

Pushing my glasses back up, I start to unbutton my white coat.

He groans as he wakes. His mouth drops open.

"Fuck. Trouble. Fuck."

He sounds breathless.

"It's Nurse Hallie to you right now, sir."

He runs his tongue along his lip and nods, eyes scanning my outfit. Or lack of it under the lab coat.

"I thought I wasn't allowed to do any strenuous activities, Nurse Trouble?"

I shake my head and open the jacket further so he can see the lacy set I put on for him.

"Oh, Mr. Quinn, you won't be doing anything. You're going to lie there like a good boy and let me see to you."

He spreads his legs open, hands behind his head, showing off his huge biceps. But it's that mischievous smirk that turns me on.

"Oh, baby. Service me however you please. I remember you told me once I needed my balls checked? Now might be a good time. Tongue works best, or so I've read online. But while you're there, my dick probably needs some attention."

I press my finger to my lips to hush him. I've got myself a yap king. Good thing I fucking love him.

"There's only one of us that's medically trained here, Mr. Quinn. I'd appreciate it if you just shut the fuck up and let me work."

I crawl onto the bed and settle between his thick thighs.

"And if I recall correctly, you still have to beg for my forgiveness, Conan. You think taking a bullet for me was really going to be enough?"

He chuckles and coughs.

"I'll do anything you want me to do, darlin'. Just tell me what."

I run my nails along his rock-hard abs, just above his boxers.

"I was joking. I don't need anything. I forgive you. I love you. This is just about letting me look after you."

His eyes search mine. He blows out a breath.

"I'm all yours, trouble. Uh—Nurse Hallie. Use me however you wish."

I grab his erect cock through his boxers and caress it gently.

"Lie still, then, Mr. Quinn. Let me get back to work."

I bend down and pepper kisses around his bandages below his ribs.

Freeing his dick, I slowly pull his boxers down and run my tongue along his shaft.

"No problems here, sir. Very nice," I praise, then twirl my tongue around the head before taking him deep in my throat.

My eyes lock onto his.

And that's when I see it—just as they darken—that spark of life.

The one he lost after I left him.

I moan around his cock. His jaw clenches, like he's trying his hardest to hold onto his self-restraint.

I suck around the tip and let it pop out of my mouth.

Using my fingers, I delicately run them over his balls, my other hand stroking his length.

I shuffle back and run my tongue along them, just as he asked.

When he whimpers, shuffling against the mattress, I glance up and see him grabbing the blanket for dear life.

"Hallie. Hallie. Hallie," he pants my name.

"Yes, baby?" I purr.

"You're making bed rest really fucking difficult right now, darlin'."

I tut.

"It's against the law to handcuff my patients to the bed. But I might have to break that for you."

I run my tongue up his stomach and climb over his body, straddling him.

He tips his head back, and I sink my teeth into his neck. He thrusts his hips up, nudging his dick against my pussy.

I lick along his stubble to his ear.

"Beg for it," I whisper.

"Be a really good boy, beastie. Beg for my pussy."

He sucks in a breath as I push my hips down to hold him in place.

"Beg," I order.

His head tilts, eyes burning into mine. A flash of pure fire.

That switch has flipped.

I bite back a grin.

His hand shoots out, grips my throat, and tosses me onto my back.

My hands claw at his bulging forearms.

I spread my legs as he settles between them. His fingers thrust inside me, the sound of my wetness filling the room.

"Oh, fuck," I moan.

"Not how this goes, trouble. You want this side of me, don't you? That's why you push me. Now you've got him. Now beg for it. Beg me to fuck you and make you mine again."

My body quivers as he slides out his fingers.

"Conan," I warn.

I feel him grin against my lips.

"You know what you have to do, trouble."

I wrap my legs around his waist and tug him tighter, feeling his cock pressing at my entrance.

"Do I?"

It's a battle of submission. It's hot. Dangerous. Raw.

It's us.

My hands glide into his hair, yanking his head back so he has to look at me.

As our eyes lock, we both grin.

I tip my chin defiantly.

"Roll on your back, sir, and let me ride your dick. Now."

He nips my lip, then crashes his mouth over mine. I moan as he rolls us over.

Once I'm on top, I pull myself up, hands on his throat, putting pressure there to lift my ass and line myself up.

My mouth falls open as I sink down slowly, taking every inch. Letting him stretch me, fill me in ways that make me feel alive again.

"Oh, Conan," I moan.

"So fuckin' gorgeous, Hallie. Look at you. Fuck."

His fingers dig into my ass as I start to bounce.

"Oh, shit."

I roll my hips all the way down to the base, the pressure rubbing against my clit.

"You're perfect, you know that?" he rasps.

I shake my head.

"You are. You're so perfect to me."

As I look at him, he's just watching my eyes. Studying me. Admiring me.

I've never felt more seen. More beautiful.

I quicken the pace, using more force as our skin slaps.

My breath comes in ragged moans.

"Come on, baby. Give it to me."

My moans turn to screams. He holds me by the throat, guiding my rhythm.

"Yes. That's it. Take it like a good girl."

He thrusts up to meet me.

"Hallie, I need to get deeper."

Before I can answer, he sits up, scoots back against the headboard, still buried inside me.

"Conan. Be careful, please," I whisper against his lips.

"You drive me wild, Hallie. I'll be fine."

He squeezes my throat, dragging me in for a kiss.

His hand on my hip holds me steady as he pounds into me. He swallows my cries.

"Come in me, beastie," I pant. "Let me feel you claim me. Make me yours again."

"Jesus, Hallie."

I kiss him harder.

"I fucking. Love. You," he says between thrusts. "Come for me, baby."

My whole body ignites, every nerve alight.

I squeeze around him as my climax wrecks me. I'm trembling so hard my head goes fuzzy.

He is all I can feel.

"I love you. I love you," I chant.

His orgasm rips through him. He roars out my name as he spills inside me.

I pull back, cup his face, my thumb trailing his lip.

"In my expert medical opinion, you're healing nicely."

He chuckles and slaps my ass.

"Yeah? So round two in the shower?"

"Don't push it," I scowl, but I can't stop smiling.

Running my hands over his bandages, he holds my hand over his heart.

"I don't regret a single thing. I'd do it again in a heartbeat for you."

My throat closes as his hand slides to my stomach.

"And for him or her."

I close my eyes, willing my tears to stay in. Everything is okay. He's here. Our baby is safe. But when I blink, all I see is his blood on my hands.

"Hallie. Talk to me."

My bottom lip quivers.

"I'm scared I'm going to lose you for good this time. And I can't. I keep seeing it—how it felt when I thought you were gone. And I—"

He pulls me in, wrapping his arms around me.

"I'm not going anywhere, Hallie. Not for a long time. Because now I've got you two to live for. I'm going to try my hardest to be the best partner and dad I can. I'll always come home to my family."

I nuzzle into his neck.

"Are you sure this is the life you want, Conan? Tied to one woman and a kid?"

"Hallie." He lowers his voice, tugging me back by my hair.

"All I want—now, tomorrow, next week, next month, fifty years from now—is you. You are it for me. You are the purpose I've been hunting for my entire life. You, trouble. And as many kids as you'll let me put in you. And maybe some more dogs to keep Bertie company."

He cups my face.

"Say you believe me," he whispers.

I don't hesitate.

"I believe you. And that's all I want too. I choose you, exactly as you are, beastie. It's always going to be you."

He closes his eyes and rests his head against mine.

"Let me take you back to Decadence. Let me explain everything. Show you what really hides behind the gates. I need you to see all my skeletons. And then, once you've seen it all, you get one chance to run, where I won't chase you."

I blink, panic rising in my chest.

"Does it get worse than what I've seen?"

He blows out a breath.

"Depends on your definition of worse. But what happened to you...probably is the worst, yes."

The pain in his voice is raw.

"You want to tell me it all? No hiding. No sugar-coating?"

"We have to. To move on, you have to see my demons."

I sigh and press a kiss to his temple.

"I see the man behind all of it, and I love him. It will be fine, beastie. But we're not going anywhere until the doctors sign you off. Got it?"

He salutes me.

"Whatever you say, boss."

I climb off and rush to the bathroom. I quickly clean up and run warm cloths under the tap before heading back into the bedroom.

"I'm meant to clean you up," he says.

I roll my eyes.

"We're equals. You're injured, and I'm looking after you. Now lay back."

He does as I say, and I gently clean him.

I toss the cloth aside and scan his naked body.

"You know, when you suggested kissing me in front of Ben, I was so convinced you were way out of my league."

He rests his hands behind his head, smiling.

"Sit on my face, baby. I'll show you how wrong that is."

I giggle.

"That doesn't even make sense."

"No. Probably not. But you're naked in front of me, and

I'm desperate to eat you out. There is no league. Just us. Now take a damn seat. Let me clean you up. Equals, remember?"

I can't argue with that.

"Grab the headboard and ride my face properly. No holding back."

I position myself over him and sit.

"Good girl." He swipes his tongue along my center.

"I like it when you flick my clit with the tip of your tongue," I tell him.

"Oh yeah? Keep telling me what you like."

When he does exactly that, I arch my back and moan his name.

"Just like that."

No matter what, this man will always take care of me.

I'm the luckiest girl in the world.

CHAPTER 103

CONAN

"Hey, beastie!!" Hallie calls up the stairs.

I sit myself up in bed. I think I might miss this day napping thing.

But I'm itching to get back in the gym. I'm just waiting for Finn's sign-off and then Grayson will be flying in my new trainer.

Bertie rolls onto his back beside me and whines for belly scratches.

"Hey, I'm the patient here. Not you." I chuckle, giving in easily.

If I'm like this with our dog, then lord help me trying to say no to my child.

The door opens and an excitable Hallie races in.

"Hi, beautiful," I greet her, holding out my arms.

And of course she runs straight over, sits on the side of the bed, and snuggles into my chest.

"You seem happy, what have you been up to?" I ask, stroking her hair.

"I got you something," she beams.

She sits up and pulls a small green box from behind her back.

"What's this?" I ask, eyebrow arched. "Are you getting down on one knee?"

Oh, fuck. If she does, then that really ruins my plans.

She shakes her head with a grin.

"No. I mean." She pauses, as if she's now toying with the idea.

I place my hand over the box.

"You know I'd still say yes. But please just be patient?" I tell her softly, stroking her cheek.

"Clearly I didn't think this whole thing through. But I just wanted you to have something, and you wear rings a lot, and I just saw it and had to."

I press my finger over her lips.

"This is totally a proposal now," I tease.

"Open it," she demands.

I take the small box and open it, finding a stunning, thick platinum band inside, with four green gems in a line."

"One for you. One for me. One for our baby. And I couldn't leave out Bertie."

My heart swells in my chest.

"Look inside," she whispers.

I hold my breath as I take it out, and, fuck me, my eyes start to burn as I hold back the tears.

In little italic letters it reads:

I choose you, always.

"Hallie," I say breathlessly.

She leans forward and presses a kiss on my cheek.

"I want you to have something on you all the time so you remember that no matter what, every day, for the rest of my life, I choose you. For exactly who you are. No matter your past. Even on the bad days. It's always going to be you for me, beastie."

I didn't realize how much I needed to hear her say those words out loud.

That she chooses me.

She wants me for exactly who I am.

And accepts who I was.

I don't believe people can completely change. I'll always have some of the ugly parts of my past that reappear.

But I can learn. I can make myself a better person for her.

And every day I'll try and be the man she deserves.

"I-I'm speechless. Fuck. Hallie."

I wrap my arm around her and pull her close, closing my eyes as I rest my head on top of hers.

"Conan. Speechless? That's a damn first," she giggles.

"Shh. I'm about to say something cute. Let me do that, then you can mock me."

I feel her body shake as she tries to stop her laughter.

"I promise, I'm going to make you the happiest woman alive. I want to be worthy of being the man you choose— and keep choosing. You have no idea how much that means to me, darlin'. I love you."

She pulls away and cups my cheek, plucking the ring out of my hand.

"You want me to get down on one knee, or?" She grins.

I shake my head.

"How about put it on my index finger for now? And then it can be my wedding ring when we actually do get married?" I suggest.

She smiles and nods.

"I like that plan."

"And before we do that, I want to show you my past? I

think I need to. Close that chapter for us? I need you to see my life and the truth behind it. I want you to see that side to me."

I don't want anything from my past to get in the way of my future, and that's why Hallie needs to come to Decadence with me.

She needs to see Inferno.

And meet the Quinn family for who they really are.

Yes, we do bad things to even more evil people.

But, we pride ourselves on family. In loyalty. In protecting the ones we love with our lives.

We aren't monsters. Not entirely.

Or perhaps we are.

But we have good hearts, and like my mom said…that's all that really matters.

And I want Hallie to see that.

To know, that no matter what, she has my heart and soul.

CHAPTER 104

CONAN

The pain from my injuries might be fading each day, but that ache in my chest never goes away. It always creeps back in when I think about what I did to Hallie. And about confronting my demons with her. Our final test.

Finn cleared me to leave the house. Just under three weeks since it all happened. I'm probably pushing myself too hard, but I have to. I want to.

I don't know if I'm more nervous than Hallie as I punch in the code to the gates.

The iron bars swing open, and there she is.

Decadence.

The sweetest hell on earth.

Us Quinn brothers might rule it here, but sometimes I wonder if we're the ones who are actually prisoners behind these gates.

It wasn't until a ray of light pulled me out of the darkness that I started to see the monster I'd become. Or maybe I became evil to survive.

I'll never really know.

But it gave me Hallie. It gave me a family. And a bullet hole in my chest.

I clamp my hand down on her bouncing thigh.

"Welcome to Decadence, trouble."

She looks up at the purple sign above the chocolate factory doors but doesn't say a word.

This place broke us. But it's also the heart of my family. My two worlds need to exist together. I just hope she can see the good in all of us. Enough to make her stay.

"Please tell me who came up with the honeycomb and cherry flavor. Was it you?"

I frown. That's my favorite one. The only batch I ever had an input in before I got bored.

"Yeah. I liked both flavors separately, but together they blended so well. The crunch against the soft cherry..."

I kiss my fingertips.

"Magical combination, Conan. Good job. That chocolate kept me company on my lunch breaks more times than I can count."

I trail my finger along her bare thighs.

"See? There's always been a bit of me in you."

She bursts out laughing, and my heart fucking flutters.

"Yeah. Ain't that right. And now I've got part of you growing inside me."

I press my palm over her stomach.

"Destiny."

I never believed in that. Not after losing my mother. And then my father.

In a fucked-up way, the tragedies that nearly ruined me led me here.

I know my mom's been guiding me this whole time. She knew.

"Does this mean I get a lifetime supply whenever I want?" she whispers as we drive the track toward my cabin.

"Whatever you want from me is yours. I keep telling ya."

She blushes and looks away. I hold my breath as we pass Inferno.

From the outside, it's a beautiful white estate, blooming flowers and fountains softening the edges.

"Who lives there?" she asks.

"That's stop two on our tour," is all I tell her.

She nods slowly.

"Skeletons?" she asks.

"Something like that," I mutter, pressing my foot harder on the accelerator.

When the cabin comes into view, my shoulders drop.

"Bertie would love it here, Conan."

I smile as she laces her fingers through mine.

"Yeah. Until he runs off again."

I snap my mouth shut when I feel her eyes burning into the side of my head.

"Again?" she squeals.

I pull up outside the cabin and cut the engine.

"Okay. Confession one. When you were in Barbados, Georgia took Bertie on a hiking trail and let him off his lead."

"I'm going to kill her."

I chuckle, ignoring the stab of pain in my chest as I turn to her.

"Lily called me. I found him. He was fine, chilling by the lake. Having the time of his life."

God, she looks hot when she's all agitated.

She yanks her phone out, probably ready to murder someone by text. I place my hand over the screen.

"I took Bertie back to mine for the rest of the week and snuck him back to you before you got home."

She gasps.

"I thought I was going mad," she mutters, shaking her head with a grin.

"What?"

"I kept smelling your aftershave on his fur. I thought it was because I missed you."

"Awww." I stroke her cheek.

"Thank you, Conan. You didn't have to. Especially not then."

"Bertie's your family too. I couldn't not. Plus, he and I had a great time. His recall should be way better now. We worked on that in the woods behind my garage."

"No way. That little traitor. I've been trying for years to train him."

"Be more dominant, baby." I wink, and that earns me a light smack.

Damn, I love that side of her. Something I never thought I'd want or need. Now, I crave it.

I'll do anything she demands, as long as she calls me a good boy.

"I'm trying," she protests, throwing her arms up.

"Yes. You're trying with me, but not your dog, Hallie. Trust me, you're doing a perfect job with me."

She slaps her hand against my bicep. I catch her wrist in my palm.

"Don't push it, though. You know I can turn," I lean in, my mouth at her ear.

"Just as quickly as I submit."

She shivers against me.

I release her and climb out of the car, jogging around before she can open her own door.

I help her out and link our hands as we walk into the cabin.

I once thought of this place as my peace.

But I was wrong.

Because I'm only at peace with her.

My peace isn't a place. It's a person.

She lets go of my hand and drifts into the kitchen, studying everything like she's trying to figure me out through the furniture.

It's grand for a cabin. All clean lines and minimalist style.

"So this is where the beast sleeps, huh?" she asks.

"Yep. My home, I suppose."

She shakes her head and saunters back to me, wrapping her arms around my waist.

"Was your home. Remember?"

I swallow hard.

"Let's hope."

I'm done with this place.

"So where next? That big white house—Finn's?"

"Nope. It's owned by all three of us."

That's all I give her.

I want her to make her own judgments. Ask her own questions.

Accept my past so we can move forward.

Because that's what Inferno is to me.

My future is right here in my arms, wherever she wants to drag me.

CHAPTER 105

HALLIE

"**R**emember, this was the man before I met you," Conan says quietly.

"Okay."

I'm kind of terrified as the doors swing open and two smiling, barely clothed women greet us.

"Welcome, Mr. Quinn," the blonde purrs.

I dig my nails into his hand, fighting the urge to bolt.

He nods once, like this is all normal, and nearly drags me through the grand reception area.

I yank him to a halt.

"Conan Quinn. Is this a strip club?" I hiss, my voice sharp with disbelief as I take in the glossy floors and all the polished doors.

It's so fancy. So deceptive.

"Worse."

"Jesus Christ."

I press my lips together and force myself to look around.

"Show me, then. Mr. Kinky."

He flashes me that dangerous grin. God. My heart is thumping all over the place.

Before I can think, his arm snakes around my waist and hauls me against him, backing me into the wall.

"Only kinky for one woman now," he growls, low and dark. "You get all my kink. Got it?"

A throat clears behind us, and I peer around him to see Declan and Finn standing there like they're bracing for an explosion.

"My kinky man. I hear ya," I mutter, shoving his chest.

Declan's brows lift. Finn looks bored. Probably wishing he were anywhere else.

"Hi," I manage.

"Hallie." Finn inclines his head, expression unreadable.

"Welcome to Inferno," Declan says.

"Hmm. Good to be back," I deadpan.

Declan actually flinches.

They're all trying so hard to help Conan. It's…weirdly sweet. Charlotte was right—they are sort of adorable, in a twisted way.

"Oh, Dr. Quinn," I say, meeting Finn's stare.

He smirks faintly.

"I never processed your resignation. You've been on paid leave this entire time, and you will remain so until you're ready to come back."

"You—you're sure?"

Conan slides his arm tighter around my waist and presses a kiss to the top of my head.

"We need you, Hallie."

My heart squeezes.

Coming from Finn, the most stoic man alive, it feels like something big. Like an acceptance I didn't know I needed.

"Thank you," I whisper.

A heavy silence settles.

"So why the sex games?" I blurt, looking straight at Declan.

I wince. "Wait, let me rephrase that. What exactly was Ben trying to achieve by entering me?"

That's the question that's haunted me since the day it happened.

Declan looks almost relieved to be answering something straightforward.

"Inferno…" He gestures around. "Behind these doors, we offer an elite experience. This place is the foundation for not just our business but for others around the world. Ben worked for our sworn enemies. They wanted a foothold here. But, it seems you were just caught in the crossfire by being with Conan."

My brain scrambles to connect the dots.

That night. Our revenge.

"That's what his threat was. He said something like he couldn't stop the games and tried to get me back," I gasp.

"I'm so sorry, Hallie," Conan whispers.

"We thought we had solved the problem. But he already put the plan in motion; we couldn't stop it because we didn't know. It didn't cross our minds that he would have any contacts with our games. Let alone enter you."

"He's a fucking asshole," I seethe.

He cheated on me, in my damn house, and then did this to me. I have a good heart, I know that, but I can say this one time, I'm glad he's dead.

"So they enter women…to get access?"

He nods once.

"Welcome to the world of illusions. Those men think they're gaining power. They don't care about the women they sacrifice. And those are the men we…remove."

A cold shiver creeps down my spine.

"But the world has to believe we're the villains, or it doesn't work," Conan murmurs against my ear.

I swallow hard.

"So that's why you made us believe we'd die here? The men…they think we're dead?"

Finn claps his hands together, impatience flickering across his face.

"The only ones who meet their end are them."

Declan's tone softens.

"We give the contestants new identities. New lives. We protect them."

I blow out a ragged breath.

"Sometimes you have to do bad things to stop worse," I say quietly.

"So they're all safe?"

"Yes, baby." Conan squeezes my hip.

"We're sorry you got wrapped up in this," Declan says, almost gentle.

"What made you start all this? It's…creative."

"There are higher powers pulling the strings. This was our spin on it. But it's one we're outgrowing."

Finn's jaw twitches, but he stays silent.

"Thank you," I say, meeting Declan's gaze. "For explaining. I don't think you're bad people. For what it's worth. I saw how hard you fought for him. How much you love him."

"Clean slate?" Declan offers his hand.

I look at it for a second, then step forward and shake it.

"I'd like that."

It feels a little like making a pact with the devil. But this devil would die for the people he loves.

So maybe it's worth it.

When I turn back, Conan is smiling at me in that way that makes my chest ache.

"No more, Hallie. I'll never host another Chase again. I swear. I'm done."

I rise on my toes and kiss him.

"Good boy," I murmur.

"But you can chase me any time."

His eyes darken. My cheeks flush.

"Now show me your sex dungeon," I say, nodding to the double doors.

His grin is wicked.

"As you wish, baby." He slaps my ass, making me yelp.

Inside, the bar is full of men in expensive suits and women draped over them like lingerie-clad ornaments.

"Explain," I demand, arms crossed.

"Do you come here often?"

He shrugs, annoyingly nonchalant.

"To drink, sometimes. I haven't used the facilities in a while. My tastes are more…outdoors."

"Show me one."

He leads me to a set of gilded doors. I pretend I don't notice all the women staring at him like he's the main course. He doesn't look at any of them.

Inside, I barely have time to take in the leather bench and the cross on the wall before he pins me against the door, mouth on mine.

I push at his chest.

"I want to see. Move."

He bites his lip but steps back.

Holy shit.

I drift over to the floggers and whips hanging neatly along the wall, touching the braided leather.

"Oooooh."

I spin to face him, heart pounding.

"Pants down. Bend over the bench. I need to punish you for being so bad."

He chokes on a laugh, his eyes glinting.

"Now," I say firmly.

"This is hot. But are you sure you're ready for the consequences?" He steps close, towering over me.

"Oh, I'm counting on them, beastie. Now bend over."

I drag the whip down the front of his shirt, pausing over his cock.

"Don't you dare," he warns.

I arch a brow, daring him.

Slowly, he unbuckles his belt and lets his pants fall.

I swallow hard as his cock springs free.

He walks to the bench, bending over, muscles taut.

"Good boy."

I strike him once. A red welt blooms across his skin. He doesn't even flinch.

I do it again, harder.

"Fuck, trouble," he groans, his hand curling around himself.

"One more," I say softly, "then you can come in my mouth."

When the third strike lands, he spins so fast it makes me gasp. His eyes are pure darkness.

"Knees," he rasps.

I drop immediately.

"Open. Tongue out."

I obey, my heart hammering.

"Good girl."

He taps his cock on my tongue, then slides deep, making me moan.

My hands squeeze his ass as he fucks my mouth, every inch of me burning.

"Fuck!" he groans, his hips jerking.

Warmth spills across my tongue, and I swallow every drop.

He pulls out, breathless, and I wipe my lip, looking up at him.

"My turn?" I ask sweetly.

He shakes his head, hauling me up.

"Your punishment starts now."

"Did it feel good? Me whipping you into submission?"

His grin is wicked.

"Yeah. But now I need you."

"Patience will be rewarded." He kisses me, slow and deep, until my knees go weak.

I pull back to catch my breath.

"Could we…come back here again?"

He studies me and then nods.

"I'll reserve a room for us. Any time you want to tie me up, you just say the word."

"Please."

"Anything for you." He hooks my chin. "Any other questions?"

I shake my head, then pause.

"Wait. One…"

He lifts a brow.

A cold smile curls his mouth.

"You only come here with me?"

His eyes widen.

"I would never even consider it otherwise."

I laugh, pressing my forehead to his chest.

"I know. You love me too much."

He drops to his knees, lifting my dress over the small swell of my belly.

"And you," he whispers, pressing his lips to my skin. "I love you more than life."

I slide my fingers into his hair, blinking back tears.

When I try to pull him up, he catches my wrist, gaze heating.

"While you're down there…"

I suck in a breath as he parts my thighs.

"You play dirty," he murmurs, kissing the inside of my knee.

"But I can't say no."

He licks me softly, just the way I like.

"Like that, Con. Slow…fuck."

I'm trembling when he finally pulls my panties back into place.

"Conan!"

He kisses me through the lace.

"Patience," he purrs. "Now let's go home."

CHAPTER 106
CONAN

This is my first day without Hallie.

Life is pretty much back to normal.

I'm still in pain, but it's nowhere near what it was. It's livable.

I'll be back in the cage in no time. But not yet.

Hallie would spank me so hard I'd pass out.

First, we just have to get rid of this thorn in my side, the one currently hiding out in London.

As we approach the slaughterhouse, Reggie plants his hand on my shoulder, and I stop.

"It's good to have you back, Con."

"Yeah. I'm back. But you'll be seeing a lot less of me."

"What? Why?" Rowan pipes up beside him.

Reggie rolls his eyes at him.

"Me and Hallie are buying a place outside Decadence. And—we're having a baby."

That even earns me an eyebrow raise from Reggie.

"Of course you don't use protection," he says flatly.

"Not with Hallie. No."

"When's the wedding?" Rowan asks.

That's the thing that's been chewing at the edges of my brain every damn day.

I want to be her husband.

I'm just waiting for the right moment to ask.

Or maybe I need my balls checked again.

"Soon. Hopefully."

My phone pings.

Dec: You're good. Come in.

I unlock the door to the slaughterhouse.

The twins follow close behind me.

Pushing the plastic flaps aside, I head for the back room, a smile stretching across my lips.

Chains hang from the ceiling, and dangling by their feet are Arthur Bowen's men.

Every last one of them.

Except Ben.

His body was burnt in his club, but we made sure Arthur got a glossy photo of my knife work.

Wouldn't want him to miss the craftsmanship.

Declan and Finn stand in the center of the room, their faces unreadable as they speak in low voices to Theo King.

And King of London he will be, if we have anything to say about it.

"Theo, meet Conan. Our youngest brother," Declan says.

I stride forward and hold out my hand. He shakes it firmly.

"You boys did a good job with this," Theo says, his thick British accent smooth enough to mask the menace underneath.

It gives me chills.

I remind myself he isn't Arthur.

He's the key to Arthur's final downfall.

"Our pleasure," I say, grinning.

"Now, when can I take out their leader?" I ask, rubbing my hands together.

Theo smirks, brushing a hand through his black hair.

Everything about him is too perfect—the clean shave, the polished loafers, the tailored black suit.

The only giveaway is the tattoos on his neck and the scars across his knuckles.

"Patience isn't Conan's strong suit. But this time I agree with him," Finn adds, voice low. "We need to act with haste to eliminate Arthur."

I glance at Finn, surprised.

He never backs me up on this shit.

I nod once in gratitude.

Theo tilts his head, studying us.

"We have one final card to play back in London. Once that's in place, I'd be more than happy for you to come and finish the job."

"How soon?" I press.

Declan shoots me a look.

I know what he's thinking.

You've got a baby on the way. Slow the fuck down.

"Within the year," Theo says calmly. "Declan and Finn have filled me in on the details. I understand. But if I negotiate this carelessly with the King elders, we risk everything. I'm going for a full London takeover. That starts with eliminating Arthur's father, Charles."

I blow out a slow breath. He makes sense.

"That'll cause war," I say.

Theo's grin is all teeth. The kind that makes a man's blood run cold.

"I know. And that's where you come in."

"You think the elders will go for your plan?" Declan asks.

"You give me the shipping routes and distribution lines here, then yes. It proves we can work with the Quinns instead of the Bowens."

Of course there's a deal. There's always a fucking deal.

"We've got the ports. We run the distribution across the States. We can offer you that," Declan says. "In return, we want a cut of the profit—and an alliance. One that ends the Bowens' reign."

Theo nods slowly.

"Those terms are agreeable to me. I'll call a meeting as soon as I'm home. My brothers are already on side. My sister will be too. I can be very persuasive."

Interesting.

Their sister gets a vote.

"We work old school, though," Theo adds. "There may be further terms to an alliance. Ones I'll try to avoid. But it may come down to that."

Finn pulls a pack of cigarettes from his pocket and offers them around. I pass.

The only drug I need is Hallie.

And the occasional painkiller.

"Old school. I like it," I say. "What kind of terms? A marriage?"

Theo's face stays perfectly blank.

My grin falters.

Oh.

I turn to the twins, smirking.

"Looks like one of you is up next."

Reggie sighs in disgust.

"I best head back," Theo says, straightening his cuffs. "I've got an important date. But it was good to finally meet the famous Quinn brothers. I look forward to our future endeavors. I'll be in touch once everything is set in stone."

We trade goodbyes, and Declan escorts him out.

I turn to Reggie and Rowan.

"You two doing anything for the rest of the day?"

There's a dull *thud* behind me.

I spin around to find Rowan using a hanging body as a punching bag.

"Go to my gym if you need to work out," I snap.

He shrugs.

"It just looked fun. Okay. I'm done now."

"I need your help, and I need you to concentrate," I say pointedly, looking at Rowan.

Hallie has a full shift today.

I want to surprise her after work.

"It involves some DIY."

Finn rubs a hand over his face.

"And some blackmail," I add.

Finn's eyes flicker with something that looks suspiciously like joy.

"I'll take that one," he says, voice low.

"I know."

CHAPTER 107

HALLIE

I let out a yawn as I leave the hospital.

As the doors open, I hear the engine revving.

I know that beautiful sound anywhere.

I glance up and smile as Conan waves from inside his McLaren.

Before I even hit the sidewalk, he's getting out of the car and striding toward me. I let out an excited yelp as he scoops me up and kisses me.

"Good shift?" he whispers, lips brushing my cheek.

"Yeah. So tired, though. This whole working-while-pregnant thing is tough. And I've not even hit the worst bit yet."

"Have you been feeling sick today?"

I kiss him again.

He's so damn cute when he's worried.

"Only a little bit after lunch. I'm fine."

His eyes search mine, and he sets me gently back on my feet.

"What can I do to help?"

"Nothing more than you already are." I sigh, leaning into him. "Can we watch a movie tonight? Get some popcorn?"

He shakes his head slowly, that mischief glinting behind his eyes.

"I have something else planned."

I narrow my eyes at him.

He grabs my hand, lacing our fingers together, and leads me to the car, opening the passenger door with a flourish.

We hit the road, and Conan taps his fingers against the wheel, humming under his breath.

"Where are we going?" I ask.

"To my lair."

I roll my eyes.

"I've already seen that."

He chuckles, and his hand settles warm and heavy on my thigh.

"Five minutes and you'll see. We have a pit stop first. Actually, it's two surprises."

I pout, trying to get something out of him.

He just grips my chin lightly.

"That pretty little face won't work on me, trouble. Behave."

I slump back in my seat and hide my grin.

We leave town and head into the outskirts. The fancy part of the city, as my dad used to call it.

But we pass all the huge houses and keep going.

Finally, Conan turns onto a gravel track and stops in front of a massive set of iron gates.

He enters a code, and I hold my breath as they swing open.

It's like something out of a fairy tale. A sprawling country estate, flower beds blooming in every color, hedges cut into perfect shapes.

But there's still no house.

He takes a sharp turn, and then—

"Jesus," I whisper. "This is a monster of a house. Who the hell lives here?"

It's gorgeous. Purple flowers arch over the door. White shutters frame every window.

Fit for a princess.

"We do."

My head snaps around so fast I nearly give myself whiplash.

He's holding up a set of keys, smiling like he's been dying to say it.

"No," I breathe, my hands flying to cover my mouth.

My eyes dart between Conan and the house and back again.

"Yes, trouble." He leans across the console and grips my chin, pulling me closer.

"The house isn't even the best bit." He brushes his lips over mine.

"Are we moving your whole family in here?" I tease, trying to keep it light because my heart feels like it might actually burst.

"No," he murmurs. "Just lots of babies and puppies, darlin'."

A warm, fizzy ache blooms in my chest.

"And we'll keep your dad's house. Because it means a lot to you. Okay?"

I burst into tears.

"Conan. This is…so much."

He wipes my tears with his thumbs, pressing kisses over my cheeks.

"Nothing is too much for my girl." He leans back, studying me. "Now, let's get that smile back on your face."

He starts the engine again and drives us around the back.

The yard is massive, with a long single-track road disappearing around the trees.

Another set of coded gates appears.

When they open, my jaw just drops.

A whole racetrack.

"I have so many questions," I blurt. "Like—so many. There is no way. What?"

Who has a private track in their backyard?

He parks next to my grey McLaren—the one I once returned to him in a fit of stubborn pride.

"Want to know a funny story?" he asks, turning to me.

"Always."

"Remember the first time? The real first time—at the garage?"

"Oh, how could I forget?" I say, cheeks going hot.

"So. A couple of days after that, I heard the owner of this estate was looking to sell. Something drew me here. When he showed me the extra land…the first thing I thought of was racing you here."

I swallow a lump in my throat.

Even then.

Even when I thought he was just a fling—he was planning a future.

"It was more of a dream. A fantasy. But I bought it and hired an army to make it happen."

"Even when we split up?"

"Yep." He gives me a slow, sheepish smile. "I had all the faith."

"And if all else failed…it was going to be another groveling attempt. I told you I wouldn't give up."

I look around us, speechless.

It's almost too perfect.

Our own little world, hidden behind the gates.

"Please tell me somewhere you've added a cage," I tease, "and a gym?"

He slides his thumb over my bottom lip, grinning.

"That'll be a future project. I've still got my garage gym. Next step is decorating—and the baby's room."

I rest my hands over my belly, feeling my heart swell.

I'm almost twelve weeks now.

"Do you want to find out if it's a boy or a girl?" I whisper. "Or keep it a surprise?"

He leans closer, forehead resting against mine.

"What would you like to do, trouble?"

I breathe out.

"I think…a surprise."

Even though I'm dying to know, this is the one thing that truly doesn't matter.

"Surprise it is." He kisses the tip of my nose. "And speaking of…we've got one more."

My mouth falls open.

"What else could you have possibly done?"

CHAPTER 108
CONAN

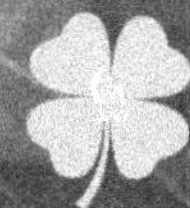

I lead her over to the driver's side and open the door.

She goes to get in, but when she looks down, she stops.

I'm already on one knee, a box open in my hand.

"Conan," she whispers, her voice catching.

"Turn around, please, trouble."

She does, her hands flying to cover her mouth, tears already brimming in her eyes.

"Hallie Morris," I begin, my heart thundering, "will you please—God, I'm down on my knee begging you—please be my wife? Marry me?"

She lets out a squeal that makes my chest ache in the best way, and I stand just in time for her to jump into my arms.

I'm so fucking happy I don't even care about the pain in my ribs. I spin us around, her laughter ringing in my ear.

"Yes!" she cries. "Beastie—one hundred times, yes!"

"Oh, thank God." I brush my lips over hers, breathing her in.

When I finally set her down, she's smiling so wide her cheeks flush pink.

"What happens now?" she asks quietly.

"We get married," I murmur against her temple, "we move in here, we have our baby…and we live happily ever after."

She grins, the kind that creases her eyes and makes me fall for her all over again.

"What about your work?" she whispers. "What if whoever it was comes back?"

I shake my head. There will always be threats in this life. But nothing we can't stop.

"Not happening," I promise. "We've sorted it. And there will come a time, soon, when we can end it all for good. But we're safe here."

"I trust you," she whispers.

"Hallie…" I tip her chin up. "It sounds like you're trying to guess what's going to go wrong."

Her brown eyes shine up at me.

"It's not going to," I tell her. "I won't let it."

She sighs, her lashes fluttering.

"Usually when things go so right…they tend to come crashing down."

"Not this time." I press my palm over her stomach.

"This is it now. A new start."

A new life.

"I love you," I tell her.

"I love you more." She peppers my face with kisses until I'm laughing.

"Can we get married, like…next week?" she asks, pouting and batting her lashes.

"Hell yeah." I can't help the grin that spreads across my

face. "Vegas? Just the two of us? Party in the new house once it's done?"

She squeals again, and God, I'd give her anything to hear that sound forever.

"Oh my God—yes! Yes! Yes! Can we spend a few days there? There's so many things I wanna see!"

I crash my mouth over hers, swallowing her excitement.

"I have a few friends in Vegas," I murmur against her lips. "I'll get everything arranged. It'll be perfect."

"I'm joking." She giggles, brushing her thumb over my jaw. "We aren't doing it next week. We can do it when you're fully recovered. Okay? I can wait a little while."

My chest goes tight.

"I'd wait forever for you," I whisper.

She leans back, studying my face, her smile soft.

"So…let's say…three weeks?" She winks. "You should be okay to fly."

"God, I am so obsessed with you," I growl, tugging her closer.

"Good." She nips my bottom lip. "Because I'm completely mad for you, beastie. You make me so happy. I'm glad you chased me."

My brows rise, and I glance out over the fields stretching in every direction.

"You see how much land we've got?" I smirk.

"I can chase you for the rest of our lives now."

Her body melts against mine, and that fire ignites in her eyes—just like it always does when she's with me.

She is my purpose. My peace. My fucking everything.

And she always will be.

CHAPTER 109

HALLIE

I turn to the side to assess my dress in the mirror. The bump is getting bigger, which means my dresses are getting tighter—and a lot shorter.

I've never seen a man look as happy as Conan did when we went to our twelve-week ultrasound. He was so nervous, practically vibrating with anxiety. But as soon as we heard that heartbeat and saw our little baby on the screen, all his nerves turned into pure elation.

And now…I'm nearly halfway through my pregnancy.

We've gone from me helping him recover to him fussing over me.

"You look beautiful," Conan murmurs as he steps behind me.

"You look handsome as hell, beastie."

Him in black jeans and a tight black tee? My favorite look on him.

His hands wrap around my waist, and he rests his chin on my shoulder.

"Are you excited?" I ask softly.

"For our pretend gender reveal to tell our friends and family we got married in Vegas without them last week— and actually don't know the gender of our baby?"

I giggle.

"Yes. And also revealing our new house. It's…quite something."

We've worked hard over the last few weeks decorating this place. Most of the main rooms are done. We've gone for neutrals, splashes of black, and a few plants here and there.

And the kitchen is to die for.

Actually…all of it is.

It's perfect.

I place my hand over his on my stomach, running my thumb along the platinum wedding ring on his finger.

"You can wear this every day now," I tell him.

"Yeah," he grins. "I can tell everyone I'm officially taken."

"You were taken a long time ago, beastie. You were mine after that first kiss."

"Hmm, mmm."

"I never believed in this kind of love, you know?" he says quietly. "I'm so fucking grateful I crashed my car that night."

I turn to face him, wrapping my arms around his neck.

"Fate," I whisper. "I think people call it that."

The doorbell rings, and I press one last kiss to his lips.

Butterflies erupt in my belly as he looks down at me, a little smirk tugging at the corner of his mouth.

"I hope you're ready to see how wild these Quinn parties get."

"If anyone starts swinging on our chandeliers," I warn, "I will get my new whips out on them."

His hand wraps around my throat, his thumb brushing along my jaw.

"No, you won't, darlin'," he growls, eyes darkening.

"They're for us only."

CHAPTER 110
CONAN

"Well, congratulations, brother," Finn says as he sits beside me on the couch and hands me a fresh beer.

"Thanks."

I don't take my eyes off Hallie, who's laughing with Charlotte in the kitchen. I have no doubt it'll get louder once Lily arrives.

"I'm not sure whose love story is more dramatic, yours or Declan's," he mutters.

"I don't know…Hallie never tried to kill me. I'd say he takes the crown with that one."

Finn chuckles.

"Yeah—except yours did nearly kill you."

"I didn't die though. I'm good. Better than good. My new trainer reckons next year I can pick back up for the championship fight."

He smiles.

"Good. You deserve your shot. You're a good fighter. Now you've got the key to your anger, you should smash it."

Hallie glances over and winks at me.

Fuck, she is stunning.

And pregnant? I have a constant hard-on when I look at her.

"She is the key, isn't she?" I say quietly.

He nods.

"Yep. Mom and Dad would have been happy. Especially Mom, seeing you like this. It suits you."

"Yeah. It does. It feels right."

We sit in silence, finishing our beers.

"What's next for you? You've got your trials coming up soon…"

"I'm focusing on getting us that ticket into London, Con. Declan's letting me take the lead and work with Theo. Enzo is even on board. But we have to find our replacements for yours and Declan's games in return."

I swallow, searching out Rowan and Reggie, who are standing with Drago and Declan.

"You thinking what I'm thinking?" I ask with a smirk.

"The twins can be trusted?" Finn counters.

"Yeah. They've proved they're capable. They've stepped up lately. I vote they get the next games."

"Declan!" Finn shouts.

The room goes quiet.

Declan strolls over with a quizzical expression.

"What do you think, boss? Reggie and Rowan get their own games?" I ask.

"My thoughts exactly," he replies.

"Shall we tell them?" Finn asks.

"A day of celebrations," Declan chuckles.

"Rowan, Reggie, Drago—get your asses over here," Declan calls out.

I hide my laughter as Rowan looks genuinely concerned.

"We have a proposition for you two," Declan says, addressing them.

"All ears, boss," Reggie grunts.

"The Decadence Games and Chase are no more. But we need two replacement games. What do you think about taking them over?"

The twins share a look, and Rowan grins.

"Separately?"

I glance at Drago, and Declan catches my train of thought.

"You wanna do it together?" Declan asks them.

They both nod.

"It'll be more fucked up if we both orchestrate it," Reggie confirms.

"Drago…" I say.

His blue eyes are wary.

"Fancy your own game too? You're part of the family now. The choice is yours."

He scratches his stubble.

"I get freedom to decide what it is I want? All the details?"

"Yep. Just not the contestants," Declan confirms.

"Count me in."

I push myself off the couch.

"Looks like we need a good bottle of Irish whiskey to celebrate—a wedding, two babies, and two more fucked-up Decadence games," I say.

I beeline straight over to Hallie and wrap my arms around her waist from behind.

"Wife," I growl in her ear.

She shivers against me.

"You having a nice time?" I whisper.

"I am."

"You wanna have an even better time?" I ask, brushing her caramel curls off her shoulder.

"What do you suggest, sir?"

"Meet me at the racetrack in half an hour."

I don't give her a chance to answer. I press a quick kiss to her neck and grab my whiskey.

The men have followed me over to the kitchen island. Declan starts dishing out the glasses.

"What's this? You all look like you're hiding something," Charlotte questions, narrowing her eyes.

Nothing gets past her.

"Just business," Declan replies.

She tuts and struts over, whispering something in his ear.

Finn takes the whiskey from me and begins to pour them out.

"The twins and Drago have been given their own games to host," I tell Hallie.

Honesty is the only way now.

Even if it's things she doesn't necessarily want to hear, I'll always tell the truth.

"Oh, cool. They seem pretty happy about it."

I glance over. She's right. Rowan looks like an excitable kid.

"Gets me out of it—that's all that matters," I say with a smile.

She grabs my hand.

"Thank you for telling me, Conan."

"Communication is key, right?" I smirk.

No more secrets.

No hiding who I am.

Because I don't need to.

My wife loves me—for me.

The front door flies open, and Lily rushes over to Hallie.

I step back.

"Congratulations, Mr. & Mrs. Quinn!" she shouts, throwing her arms up.

"I find out my best friend got married via a banner on her gate."

Oh god. She sounds mad.

All the men start backing away.

"I am shocked. Hurt. Devastated."

A smirk plays on my lips.

I fucking knew Hallie wouldn't keep this secret from her.

"Drama never was your strong suit," Hallie giggles, hugging her best friend tight.

Drago clears his throat behind me.

"Uh. Something's come up. I need to head out. I'll see if I can get it cleared up and come back later."

I don't even reply before he's jogging out the door.

That's fuckin' weird.

Lily turns to me.

"You think she could hide that? I watched it on live streaming from the chapel."

"I knew it."

Hallie sticks her tongue out at me.

"Is this a good time to admit you told your brothers too?" Declan pipes up.

"I did not!" I protest.

Hallie looks shocked and amused all at once.

"I didn't. I swear."

I flip Declan off, and the room erupts in laughter.

"Anyway. Cheers to the happy couple," Lily says, picking up my whiskey and knocking it back.

"Time to party!"

Isabella and Bertie come running in from the yard.

"Uncle Conan! Can I pick the music?"

She wraps her arms around my leg, and I scoop her up to my hip.

"Depends what genre."

She rolls her eyes dramatically.

"Heavy metal. Obviously. The ones we play in the gym?"

A smile tugs at Charlotte's lips.

"I've been teaching her well," I tell her.

"Conan," Lily shouts, narrowing her eyes at me.

"Yes, Lily?"

"Are you going to tell them what happened with the fake creepy priest, or am I?" She smirks.

Oh, fuck.

And this is why I'm giving Hallie a re-do. As funny as she found it, I'm slightly mortified.

"Conan, what the hell happened with a fake priest on your wedding day?" Rowan cackles.

I bite the inside of my cheek.

"Hallie…you wanna do the honors?"

She smiles so brightly I can't help but laugh.

"Absolutely."

CHAPTER III
HALLIE

Song- Supermassive Black Hole, Muse.

A shiver runs down my spine as I hear his heavy footsteps approaching.

The sun is just starting to set behind the trees lining our track.

I've already slipped off my heels. I know what's coming.

He stops behind me, grips the back of my neck, and leans close, his breath warm against my ear.

And he says one word.

"Run."

He releases me, and excitement floods my veins as I take off.

He doesn't follow. He's giving me a head start. Hopefully a decent one, considering I'm nearly four months pregnant.

As I reach the tree line, I veer toward the pond.

Jesus. I'm already out of breath.

I slow to a jog and slip behind the biggest tree I can find, pressing my back against the rough bark.

"You can't hide from me, trouble," Conan calls out.

I hold my breath as his footsteps draw closer, my heart hammering, my sex drive spiking to a level that should probably concern me.

Then silence.

I turn, peering around the trunk, searching for him.

Where the hell…

I let out a scream as he grabs me by the hair and yanks me back against his chest.

His hand clamps over my mouth.

"Be quiet," he growls, his voice a dark caress. "We don't want our family to hear what I do to you in the woods."

I tremble as he slides his hand under my panties.

"Soaked. As always, wife."

I nod, breathless.

He spins me, pinning me to the tree, his eyes black with hunger.

"Mine."

He thrusts two fingers inside me, making me moan behind his hand.

"All fucking mine."

He uncovers my mouth, and I gasp for air.

"Yours," I pant.

"You wanted me to catch you easily, didn't you?"

His tongue drags along my throat, and my head tips back on instinct.

"Y-yes."

"Why?"

"Because I need you inside me."

"Hmm. I need my cock inside your tight cunt."

"F-fuck!" I cry out.

"Hear how wet you are?"

He crushes his mouth over mine, stealing every ragged sound.

"I'm always wet around you, Conan," I whisper when he pulls back.

His gaze holds mine, and it's feral.

"Turn around."

I hesitate, my breathing ragged.

"Now."

I swallow and slowly turn, pressing my palms against the bark. The cold air skims my flushed skin.

He takes his time, sliding his hands down my sides, over the curve of my hips, pausing to tug my panties to my knees.

"Keep your hands where they are."

I hear the soft metallic jingle of rope unclipping from his belt.

My stomach flips.

"You knew exactly what this would turn into," he murmurs behind me. "Didn't you, trouble?"

"I knew," I whisper, cheek pressed to the tree. "I knew you'd make me yours out here."

His palm lands, a sharp smack that makes me gasp.

"And you love it."

Another strike.

"Yes. God, yes."

He binds my wrists gently, threading the rope around the trunk so my arms are stretched high above me.

"Can you feel how vulnerable you are?"

"Yes," I breathe.

"Good."

His palm smooths over my belly. His touch gentle. A reminder that even in these moments, he'd never hurt me. Not really. Only what I beg for.

I hear his zipper slide down.

"You're going to take every inch of me," he rasps, pressing the thick head of his cock between my thighs.

A whimper escapes me.

"Beg for it."

"Please," I pant. "Please, Conan, fuck me."

He groans, gripping my bound wrists with one hand, the other guiding himself to my entrance.

"Mine," he snarls, and drives into me in a single, claiming thrust.

I cry out, the sound echoing through the trees.

"Say it."

"Yours," I sob. "I'm yours."

"Every fucking part of you."

He starts to move, deep and unrelenting, and I arch back into him, craving more.

"Don't you dare come until I say," he growls, each thrust punishing and perfect.

"I—I can't."

"You can."

His hand slides to my clit, circling it just enough to make me shake.

"You will."

I'm trembling so hard my knees nearly buckle, but he wraps an arm across my chest, holding me steady.

"You're so fucking tight," he hisses. "So wet. You were made for me, wife."

I can't form words. My mouth is open, no sound but shattered gasps.

His pace slows, drawing out every delicious friction until I'm teetering on the edge.

His thumb teases my clit again—slow, patient torture.

"Come for me, trouble."

I shatter, the orgasm ripping through me so violently I scream, my knees giving way as he holds me up.

He thrusts deep, grinding against me, drawing out every trembling aftershock.

"Fuck, Hallie." His breath hitches, and I feel him spill inside me, warmth flooding deep as he growls my name against my neck.

For a long moment, all I hear is the wind in the trees and our ragged breaths.

He eases out, unties my wrists, and turns me in his arms.

He kisses my tear-slicked cheeks, then crashes his mouth over mine.

"You okay?" he whispers.

I nod, too exhausted to speak.

He smooths my hair back, resting his forehead on mine.

"Good. Because the night isn't over yet, trouble."

He grins as he slides my panties back up and adjusts my dress. I yelp when he scoops me into his arms.

"Conan—what are you up to?"

"Getting you cleaned up so you can marry me again. This time in front of our friends and family."

"What?" My eyes fill with tears.

"You deserve the best, darlin'. And as special as it was getting married by a priest who fancied me, we both know I can do better."

"You're incredible, beastie. You know that?"

He smiles, kissing me softly. And the moment our lips meet, those same sparks ignite inside me, like they always have.

This man would do anything for me.

He'd burn the world to keep me safe.

He'd chase me to the ends of it.

And no matter how dark or chaotic life becomes, all he cares about is making me smile.

That's how I know it's real—the kind of love people spend lifetimes searching for.

Because he isn't the villain in my story. He's the storm that washed all the pain away.

Conan Quinn didn't just spark something in me—he struck a match and set my soul on fire.

I started breathing again the moment our lips touched.

He set me free and claimed me in the same heartbeat.

I'm exactly where I'm meant to be—wrapped in this man's arms, ready to watch him become the kind of father every child deserves.

We both spent too many years hiding in the shadows, letting grief rot us from the inside out.

It's as if we were destined to drag each other into the light.

And for the first time, we don't just get to survive.

We get to live.

And I am so damn lucky I get to do it with my beastie by my side.

I get to call him mine.

Forever.

THE END.

EPILOGUE

CONAN

6 months later…

"**I**'m so proud of you, baby," I whisper against Hallie's sweaty forehead.

She just pushed out our little boy like a true queen.

She's stronger than any fighter I've ever come up against.

At one point, I thought I was going to pass the hell out.

When her blood pressure monitor started blaring, and I watched how hard she was pushing her body…

I panicked.

And the screams.

Jesus. I've never heard anything more full of agony in my life.

I'd rather be shot again than give birth.

Women are the real warriors.

"He's perfect, trouble. Just like his momma."

I stroke his tiny cheek as I pace the room, rocking him gently.

693

"He looks so little in your huge arms," she giggles.

He has the sweetest little button nose and big dark eyes. And judging by the thick, dark hair already covering his head, he's definitely got my genes.

He lets out a soft little moan in his sleep, and I swear to God I nearly cry.

My heart has never felt this full.

"Hallie."

"Yes, beastie." She smiles at us, her eyes glassy.

"Can we have more? Please."

She laughs, her shoulders shaking.

"Yes. But I need a year before I even think about doing that again."

"I can wait." I wink.

"Bertie's going to love chasing him around."

"Yeah. They're going to be a handful. I bet you were as a kid. You've got that cheeky look about you, Conan."

I chuckle.

"Yeah. My mom always said I was. But she used to find it hard to tell me off because she said I was too funny."

"I can see that," she murmurs, her voice soft.

A lump rises in my throat.

I wish my parents were here to see this.

My mom would've made the best grandma.

"You okay, beastie?" Hallie asks quietly.

I suck in a breath.

"I miss them," I admit. My voice feels raw. "I'm so unbelievably happy. For the first time I can remember, everything feels…perfect. I've got a family. I'm madly in love with my wife. The house, the dog, the legal MMA… and she didn't get to see any of it."

I look down at my beautiful little boy, tucked against my chest.

I hope I can give him everything he needs in life.

I hope he ends up as happy as I am right now.

"She would be proud of you, Conan," Hallie says softly. "And she's watching. I'd bet my life on that."

I swallow hard, blinking back tears.

"Liam?" I ask.

We never picked a name beforehand—we didn't even know the gender.

So we decided to wait. To see what name felt right when we met our baby.

"Shut up," she breathes, her smile breaking wide. "I was thinking that. Liam Quinn. Sounds pretty powerful."

I don't know how, but Hallie and I are always perfectly in sync with each other.

"Hi, Liam," I coo, brushing my knuckle over his soft cheek as he wriggles in my arms.

There's a soft tap on the door, and Declan pokes his head in, Isabella clutching his hand, Charlotte beside him with their two-month-old son, Noah.

Charlotte closes the door behind her as Isabella runs straight to me.

"Can I see him?" she pouts.

"Of course you can."

I crouch to her level, and she leans forward to peek into the blanket.

"Aww. Uncle Conan. He's so cute."

I press a kiss to her temple.

"So are you, whirlwind."

"Wanna hold your nephew?" I ask Declan, straightening.

"Yes. Give me."

I carefully pass Liam over. Charlotte is already sitting beside Hallie, chatting away. My girl looks exhausted but still somehow stunning.

I really need her to get some rest. I don't know how she's still awake.

"Conan."

Declan's tone is low, and something in my gut goes tight.

I know whatever comes next isn't good.

"I know now isn't the time to tell you. But I'm not going to lie to you."

I let out a slow breath, rubbing my palm over my face.

"Spit it out."

"Finn's been arrested. Drago's already at the station acting as his lawyer. They won't tell us what they've got on him yet."

I frown.

Finn is always careful. And the cops don't give a shit about mafia shit in our state—we've got them in our pocket.

This is something else.

"What's the Commissioner said?"

"He's going to get back to me. He doesn't even know yet."

"Fucking hell. I'm not leaving here, Dec."

Declan chuckles under his breath.

"I wouldn't even let you if you offered. I've got the twins with me. Don't worry. I'll have him out by nightfall."

I nod.

I know he will.

But Finn is going to be on a goddamn warpath to find out who put him there.

Liam starts to fuss in Declan's arms, so I scoop him back up and press a kiss to his soft hair.

Hallie's whole face lights up as I carry him back over to her.

"Being a dad looks ace on you," Charlotte says, grinning.

"Thanks, crazy." I wink.

"Momma want another snuggle before she gets some sleep?"

"Yes. Gimme my baby boy."

I lean down, laying Liam gently across her chest. She kisses the top of his head, tears sparkling in her eyes.

My heart swells so big it almost hurts.

I press a kiss to her cheek.

"I love you, Hallie."

She looks up at me, her voice a soft, tired whisper.

"I love you, beastie."

I run my finger along Liam's cheek. In this moment, everything has pieced together perfectly in my life.

And I can't wait to get my family home and start living.

"And I love you, little Liam."

These two own my heart.

Always.

BONUS SCENE
HALLIE

A little chapel with flickering neon hearts in the window. No guests. Just me, Conan, a lopsided flower arch, and the strangest priest I've ever met in my life.

I was already nervous, even though this was exactly what we wanted—just us, no fuss, no drama.

But the drama had apparently decided to come anyway, dressed in a white collar.

The priest, or fake one, drones through the introductory spiel, and Conan keeps his eyes locked on me, holding my hands tightly.

This is it. I'll walk out of here, Mrs. Hallie Quinn.

As I glance over, the priest, who must be in his late thirties, has long dark hair. He hasn't taken his eyes off Conan; it's almost like he wants to ask for his autograph…or his phone number.

"And do you, Hallie Morris," he begins, pointedly ignoring me to look Conan up and down, "take this…impressively built man…to be your lawfully wedded husband?"

My mouth falls open.

"Um. Yes," I stammer.

Conan is rigid. As if he is trying to control the beast inside. I know what he's thinking.

He nods thoughtfully, a little smile tugging at his mouth as he turns to Conan.

"And do you, Conan Quinn," he purred—*purred*—"take this woman to be your wife, forsaking all others?" His gaze flicked to me, his lip curling almost imperceptibly. "Even though she seems a bit…ordinary next to you?"

I blink. Did he really just say that?

Conan's jaw flexes, and he looks like he's one second from tearing the guy's head clean off.

"*Yes,*" Conan grinds out through clenched teeth.

"Very well," the priest says. He let out this little sigh, almost wistful. "You may kiss the bride."

Conan shakes his head and grabs my cheeks, pressing his lips over mine. His tongue exploring my mouth, my body pressed tight against his.

"Wife. You're my wife," he whispers against my lips.

That's all that matters. Even if this whole situation is kind of strange. We're married.

The priest clears his throat, and Conan growls under his breath.

"The fuck is going on with this guy?" he asks me quietly.

I shrug but nearly laugh at Conan's irritation. I wonder if he knows that the priest is flirting with him.

"Congratulations," he says.

Conan slowly turns to face him.

"You know," he says, "if you ever get tired of…her… you'd be welcome to give me a call. Or, you know, the two of you could always…expand your horizons."

For a heartbeat, the world falls completely silent.

Then Conan moves.

Faster than I can react, he grabs the priest by the collar and yanks him forward, his other hand already balled into a fist.

"Conan!" I gasp, catching his arm.

I bet Lily is having a laugh watching this on the live stream.

"Wait!" the priest wheezes, holding his hands up, though he still doesn't look particularly sorry.

"Why? So you can insult my wife again?" Conan spits.

"You're hot, Mr. Quinn," he says. "Any chance you'd consider an open marriage? We don't have to leave her out completely."

This guy must be high.

Conan doesn't even hesitate. His fist cracks into the priest's jaw with a sickening crunch.

The man stumbles backward, colliding with the flower arch. The whole thing groans and then collapses in a spectacular tangle over him, petals and fake ivy raining down on top of him.

I clamp a hand over my mouth, my shoulders shaking.

I was trying so hard not to laugh. But I can't hold it in any longer.

"So," I manage, voice strangled, "I need to be worried not just about women…but men, too?"

Conan's chest heaves as he glares at the priest. He turns to me, his dark eyes softening just enough to make my heart flip.

"This is your fault," I scold, poking his chest. "For being so damn hot."

"Shh," he murmurs.

He grabs my face in both hands and kisses me so hard my knees nearly give out.

When he finally pulls back, I'm breathless, dizzy, completely his.

"And priests, apparently," I whisper with a giggle.

"Come on," he growls, lacing our fingers together. "Let's get out of here before I put him through the wall."

I didn't even look back.

Vegas, apparently, was just as unhinged as we were.

We walk out, hand in hand; I can hardly see through my tears of hysterics.

"Conan. I can't."

I have to stop as soon as we get outside into the blazing sun.

"You just knocked out our fake priest for trying to fuck you on your wedding day. You can't even write this shit."

I double over. And now, Conan joins me.

"It's a new one, even for me."

I look up at him and burst out laughing again.

"We need to buy that recording," I tell him as I stand up straight.

"That's blackmail material," he teases.

"We can show our kids when they're older."

His eyes go wide.

"That wasn't my finest moment."

I blow out a breath.

"Imagine if the priest was trying to get in my panties, though. It could have been worse."

Conan blows out a breath.

"He'd be dead and buried by now."

He steps closer, tugging me close by my waist.

"Talking of getting inside you. I've booked us somewhere special. I can't wait another minute to take you as my wife."

My cheeks heat in anticipation.

"What are we waiting for, beastie? I want you."

I always will.

DR. QUINN WILL BE SEEING YOU SOON...

Two rival heart surgeons.

But they both have the same side project… killing.

A dark Irish mafia romance with a dark rom-com style twist. There is betrayal, blackmail, workplace romance and a love that burns.

Finn will be unleashed on September 30th (or earlier)

PRE-ORDER INTENSE HERE: https://my-book.to/jPMoBT

And don't forget… the series doesn't finish there.

The first Luna Mason MFM is coming, with the twins, Reggie and Rowan and their mafia princess in INDULGE.

PRE-ORDER THEM HERE: https://my-book.to/RPF3C

The series will finish with a grand finale, with Daddy Drago and an FMC that you've probably just fallen in love with in Ignite.

A grumpy mafia boss and his sassy ballerina… in a **DAD'S BEST FRIEND ROMANCE.**

Instinct is available to **pre-order now, releasing early 2026:** https://mybook.to/vK40

Want more Conan & Hallie?

Desperate to know what happened at their Vegas wedding that has them all laughing?

Well, here it is.

Conan at his finest.

Sign up to my newsletter to receive a **BONUS SCENE**.

Enjoy x

Read it here: https://dl.bookfunnel.com/on9i55wkch

To stay up to date with exciting news and releases, the best place to find me is in my FB Group: **Luna Masons Mafia Queens.**

And if you want **signed books,** store exclusives and all the *naughty art,* you can purchase directly from my store:

www.lunamasonbookstore.com

MORE FROM LUNA MASON IN THE BENEATH UNIVERSE

Beneath The Mask series has been picked up by Kensington and **TRADITIONALLY PUBLISHED!!!**

You met Keller and Grayson in Ignite…

You can read all four online (all platforms including KU) and they will be releasing in bookstores throughout 2025:

You can find all the details for Distance, Detonate, Devoted and Detained here!

https://www.kensingtonbooks.com/pages/beneaththemask/

Some of the characters from Beneath The Secrets made an appearance in Ignite. You can read their stories in Beneath The Secrets.

A Dark and spicy Russian mafia romance set in Vegas.

ALL ARE LIVE ON AMAZON and KU!

Chaos (Jax 'The King of Chaos' Carter and Sofia)

An ex-husband's brother romance, where the MMC is a boxer, biker and has a vibrating tongue piercing.

https://mybook.to/QaGijx

Caged (Nikolai and Mila)

An explosive enemies to lovers, with a sexy single dad and assassin FMC.

https://mybook.to/Fc18uiK

Crave (Alexei and Lara)

A childhood best friends to lovers, that is also a brother's best friend romance. (This is the one where he puts a lollipop in her ass, and owns a pet flamingo)

https://mybook.to/rTb4

Claim (Mikhail and Ana)

A masked mafia boss and his step sister. Full of kidnapping, a sassy mafia princess, and a Cane Corso that steals the show.

https://mybook.to/6Nyh"